On Best Behavior

Jennifer Lane

OMNIFIC PUBLISHING
LOS ANGELES

Omnific Publishing
1901 Avenue of the Stars, 2nd floor
Los Angeles, CA 90067
www.omnificpublishing.com

First Omnific eBook edition, September 2013
First Omnific trade paperback edition, September 2013

The characters and events in this book are fictitious.
Any similarity to real persons, living or dead,
is coincidental and not intended by the author.

Library of Congress Cataloguing-in-Publication Data

Lane, Jennifer.
   On Best Behavior / Jennifer Lane – 1st ed.
   ISBN: 978-1-623420-53-6
   1. Romantic Suspense — Fiction. 2. Russian Mafia — Fiction.
   3. Chicago — Fiction. 4. Psychology — Fiction. I. Title

10 9 8 7 6 5 4 3 2 1

Cover Design by Micha Stone and Amy Brokaw
Interior Book Design by Coreen Montagna

Printed in the United States of America

*To those who strive for healing and redemption…
may you find your way, with love.*

1. Conjugal

Grant was about to knock on the door when he turned to her. "You ready?"

Sophie felt a rush of anxiety at the prospect of seeing the man inside once again. It had been over a year, and the circumstances of their last encounter had been less than ideal. She mustered a shaky smile. "Yes."

"Are you sure?" Grant frowned. "I thought your face was flushed from the wind, but now you seem nervous. We don't have to rush this, you know."

She shivered, recalling the January wind that had blasted them as they walked to the church. Warmer weather couldn't come fast enough. "We do if we want it to happen this summer."

Grant's hand dropped. "That's no reason to take the plunge. We can come back later."

She looked into his worried eyes and reached for his hand. "Grant, I have absolutely no qualms about marrying you. I'd do it today if we could."

"Then let's just go to the courthouse now."

She rolled her eyes. "You know I'd love that, but my dad would kill me. No, we'll do it this summer, like we planned. We'll do the big church wedding." She turned back to the door.

He tugged at her hand, drawing her to face him again. "Sophie, talk to me."

"It's just…" She sighed. "It's been a while since I've seen Pastor Tom."

His thumb massaged her palm in soothing circles.

"The last time I saw him…I was in handcuffs."

Sadness filled his eyes as he put the pieces together. "For your mother's funeral."

"Two COs brought me from Downer's Grove." She despised the tremor in her voice. "They said I was lucky the warden let me attend."

"That sounds so humiliating." He gathered her in his arms. "I'm sorry you had to go through that."

She closed her eyes as she melted into his strong chest and breathed in his clean bergamot scent. His hand smoothed her hair while he spoke to her.

"You're different now, Bonnie. Wiser, tougher…*stronger*. And if anyone could forgive you for past mistakes, it'd be a man of God. Surely Pastor Tom understands what you've been through and knows who you really are."

Her shoulders relaxed. After a moment, she looked up at him. "Thank you. You're right—Pastor Tom has known me since I was a kid. He wouldn't judge me or just give up on me."

Grant kissed her forehead before letting her go.

She brushed her hand down her coat then tossed her hair back, chin up.

"There's that confidence," he said. "There's that strong backbone of yours."

She cocked an eyebrow. "Don't you forget it."

He laughed.

Turning back to the door, she sighed. "I guess it's good you realize in advance what kind of woman you're getting, you know, with this whole *till death do us part* thing." She felt the intensity of crystal blue eyes floating down her spine.

"I sure do. It's a beautiful backbone, by the way."

His silky voice unnerved her, as usual, and she rapped on the door to distract herself. If not, their inevitable making out would be inappropriate in the church hallway.

A man in his early fifties with thinning sandy hair and intelligent brown eyes opened the door. His eyes crinkled at the corners when he smiled. He stuck out his hand. "Sophie."

She returned his warm smile. "Pastor Tom. Thanks for meeting with us. This is Grant Madsen, my fiancé."

"Tom Kelley," he said as he shook Grant's hand, looking up a bit to meet the taller man's eyes. He led them inside his office and gestured to two chairs. Sitting across from them behind his desk, Pastor Tom continued smiling at her, and she glanced down at her long, camel-colored coat.

"You seem well, Sophie," he said.

"Thank you." She fidgeted as she offered a smile.

The pastor leaned forward. "How's life been treating you?"

"All right." She shrugged, adding an anxious chuckle as her hands splayed open, palms up. "No, uh, no handcuffs this time."

Pastor Tom frowned.

Grant grasped one of her hands in his.

She swallowed, looking up and putting on a brave face. "Anyway, I'm happy to report that Grant and I are no longer on parole. It's behind us now. We're here to talk about moving forward."

The pastor said, "Then I'm glad it's all in the past." His eyes shifted over to Grant. "Sophie's father told me you two met on your parole officer's doorstep?"

Grant winced. "Yes, sir—not your most typical hookup spot. Mr. Taylor isn't exactly my biggest fan."

"Aw, he's coming around," Sophie countered.

Pastor Tom hid a smile. "Well, if you can win over Will, you can win over anybody."

That's certainly true, Sophie thought.

"How *is* your father?" Pastor Tom asked her.

"He's doing well. The construction business is picking up."

"That's good, but I wasn't necessarily asking about his work life."

"Oh." She paused. "He said his talks with you have helped a lot, but it's still tough. We miss my mom. That's why this whole wedding thing's so important to him, I think."

"And that's why you're here," Pastor Tom said. "Wedding talk. Tell me what you're planning."

Grant nodded for her to field that question.

"We'd like to get married this summer, here in the church," she began.

❧

After what seemed like a four-hour wedding meeting, Grant hustled down Michigan Avenue, weaving around slow pedestrians, toward his job at Alex Remington's hotel. Even though it was a balmy nineteen degrees, shoppers teemed the Magnificent Mile, toting bags from American Girl Place and Niketown. He reviewed the details of the meeting as he walked, huddled inside his long, navy-blue wool coat—a Christmas gift from Uncle Joe. His White Sox jacket just wasn't cutting it in these temperatures. His main duty was to find a spot for their reception. He smiled. He knew the perfect place.

Some passengers disembarked a tour bus, and as he crossed in front of them, a voice called out, "Madsen!"

He stopped short. He'd know that voice anywhere. Was his mind playing tricks on him? Power of suggestion? He searched the area for his irascible former boss but failed to locate him.

"Madsen, I'm right here, dammit!"

He looked again at the man getting off the bus—a shorter man of average weight with carefully combed black hair and a crisp business suit—and did a triple take.

"*Rog?*"

Then came that familiar hearty laugh. "Of course! Who the hell else you know leads architectural bus tours, dumbshit?"

This was *definitely* Roger Eaton. Grant tried to shut his slacked jaw. "You look, uh, great, Rog. I barely recognized you, you look so good! I mean, uh, that didn't come out right…"

"Real nice, little fucker. Way to treat your elders."

"Sorry, I—you must be following your diet, huh? You're back on good terms with Ms. Broccoli?"

Roger gave a proud grin. "I got me a real life Ms. Broccoli now. A real sweetie."

"You—you have a girlfriend now?"

"Ana," he confirmed. "She lives in my building."

"That's great! Did you meet her on the elevator or something?"

"Nah." He shook his head. "She was at the gym on the sixth floor."

"*You* were in the gym?"

"Don't look so surprised! I used to be real fit, back in the Navy. I know my way around a gym."

"Yes, sir."

"I met her doing free weights. This hard-body señorita was putting me to shame on squats, and I asked her how she got such a tight ass—"

"And then she decked you."

"Nah, she loved it! She's real proud of that butt—she should be. She took me to one of her classes, and I got hooked. She's a Zumba instructor."

Grant absorbed that information for a moment. "You do…Zumba?"

"It's great! Much more fun than PT. You just get going…" He did a little two-step maneuver on the city street, dancing to an unknown Latin beat. "Cha cha cha. Heeuh? Ana does this a little better than me…"

Grant tried to hold it in. He really did. But his body quivered, his shoulders shook, and soon a whooping laugh erupted—which lasted quite a few seconds.

Roger abruptly stopped his dance. "You judge, Madsen. Not cool."

"You're right," he said, finding it difficult to compose a straight face. "That wasn't cool of me. Zumba's obviously working for you."

"Lost thirty-five pounds since September."

"Wow! And your hair…piece…looks real good too."

"Ana helped pick this one out."

Don't laugh, don't laugh. "So, uh, when do Sophie and I get to meet Ana?"

"I was thinking of bringing her by Capone's one night, make her suffer through your singing."

"I'd be honored," Grant said. "But actually, I was going to call you. Um, I'm going by an alias now—some things have changed…"

Roger looked at him with a newfound respect, and his voice lowered conspiratorially. "Last time I talked to Joe, he said you were in conversations with the FBI, thinking of working for them."

"I'm giving it a shot. Nothing's happened yet, though."

"What's it like working for those tight-ass feds?"

He smirked. "Probably the same as working for *your* tight-ass boss."

"True that. So what's your alias then?"

"Mick Saylor."

"What the fuck kind of name is that?"

"Sophie helped me come up with it. It's sort of a private joke."

"So it's Saylor and Taylor now." He shook his head. "The fucking Bobbsey twins."

"Huh—I never put our names together like that before."

"Way to think it through first, Mick Dick."

His head spun with the volume of insults hurled his way.

"How's Taylor doing, by the way?" Roger continued.

"She's great. She's teaching full time at DePaul now."

"You two still shacking up?"

Grant grinned. "Yep, but not for much longer. We're engaged."

His eyes widened. "Finally! About time you both realized nobody *else* would want you. You might as well stick together."

"I've missed this." His heart swelled with fondness for his former boss.

"Then come back and work on my ship this summer."

"I'd actually like to ask you something about that, sir."

Roger narrowed his eyes. "You sneaking behind my back again, trying to hire someone else for my cruise like you did with Taylor?"

"*Hey.* As I recall, that worked out pretty well for your business. You should be so lucky."

He grunted.

"I wanted to ask if Sophie and I could have our wedding reception on your ship. Saturday, June eighteenth."

He tilted his head, considering.

"We'll pay you, of course," Grant added.

"With what? My ship's expensive to rent, you know."

"Mr. Taylor has agreed to foot the bill."

His eyes bugged. "I thought he hated you!"

"I charmed him with my singing."

He shook his head. "Keep dreaming, Sinatra. Hey, I haven't met Ana's dad yet—maybe I should try singing for him too."

"Don't you want him to like you? If so, I'd advise against it."

"I've missed this too, you pecker." He grinned as he glanced at his watch. "Gotta get back to Willis Tower for the next bus tour or my boss will be all over me. So, June eighteenth? Sure, that should work. I'll cancel the two evening cruises and expect a fat paycheck from Taylor's dad to cover the losses."

"You got it, Rog. Thanks."

"And Madsen?"

"Yeah?"

"Be careful out there."

He nodded. "You too. Don't let those tourists hit on you. You've got a girlfriend now."

"A *hot* girlfriend!" Roger echoed, starting a little merengue dance. "She's one lucky woman!"

Grant grinned as he walked away. "Zumba," he marveled. He couldn't wait to tell Sophie.

❧

A few minutes later, and feeling quite efficient, Grant welcomed the warm blast of air greeting him in the hotel lobby. As he peeled off his gloves and slid off his hat, he noticed there weren't any guests at the reception desk, and he knew what that meant. As much as he tried to avoid eye contact with the redhead working behind the front desk, she still aimed a seductive wink his way. Grant gave her a tight smile and hurried past.

Picturing Sophie's engagement ring, he wished he wore a sign that he too was off the market. But then he realized she was so beautiful even an engagement ring wouldn't stop men from pursuing her. At times he still couldn't believe she'd agreed to marry him. Excitement coursed through him just thinking about it.

He waltzed into the executive suite, and Alex Remington's administrative assistant looked up from her desk. "Hi, Mick!"

"Hey, Sarah. Could you let Mr. Remington know I'd like to see him?"

"He said you could go on in when you arrived. He's expecting you."

Surprised, he knocked on his boss's door before entering the opulent office.

Involved in a phone conversation, Remington gestured for him to sit in the chair across from the desk.

Sinking into the leather, he listened for a moment.

"He's here, and I'll send him up in a few…You're welcome. I hope it works. Keep in touch." Mr. Remington hung up the phone and gave him a stern stare. "You're late."

"Sorry, sir." Grant shifted in his chair. "I, uh, I ran into a friend on Michigan." He felt a bit confused. He wouldn't start singing for hours and typically his boss was too busy with hotel business to care much when exactly he arrived. "Would you like me here at a particular time, Mr. Remington? I promise I won't be late again."

His expression softened. "It's not me keeping a timetable here—it's the other party. It seems I'll be the designated go-between."

"Sir?"

"An agent's waiting for you in room six thirty-one."

"Oh." Understanding dawned on him. He'd been waiting for the FBI to make contact, but hadn't expected it would happen at work.

"Apparently they'd like you to report in to me at the start of your shift, and I'll let you know if they're here to meet with you."

"Why don't they just call me?"

"They don't want to take any chances."

Grant took this in. "I didn't mean to get you involved, Mr. Remington."

"Too late." He smiled. "I *want* to be involved. I saw what happened to Will and Sophie, and I'll do whatever it takes to stop mobsters from taking down more innocent people."

"That's exactly how I feel."

Mr. Remington grinned. "I always knew you were a good hire. Now, do you have any new songs on tap for us?"

"Andy and I are working on a *Guys and Dolls* song, sir."

"Great! Which one?"

"'Luck Be a Lady Tonight.'"

"Indeed. We could all use a little luck. You better get going—the agent's waiting."

He stood. "Thank you, sir."

He zoomed past reception, where thankfully the redhead was engrossed in checking in a hotel guest, toward the bank of elevators. *So it's beginning.* A charge of energy bloomed up his spine, leaving him jumpy as he stepped into the open elevator.

After making sure he wasn't followed, he stole down the hallway of the sixth floor. An agent responded to his soft knock, but he stepped aside and let Grant in without showing himself in the open doorway. Once the door was shut, Agent Lucas Bounter gripped his hand in a firm handshake. "Welcome back."

"It's good to see you, sir. Uh, is the task force involved with this assignment? I thought I'd be working with another agent."

"I've been reassigned to the organized crime unit," said Bounter. "Less of a chance Jovanovich and his ilk can hunt me down."

"Has he been a problem?"

"Nah. He's still on 'extended leave' in Serbia as far as we know, probably feeling lucky we didn't prosecute him. Hopefully he'll stay there." He gave a weary smile. "Busting him felt like taking down a Mafia kingpin — more so than arresting a corrupt politician — so this new job's not much of a stretch."

Grant noticed faint purple smudges under Bounter's eyes, darkening the rich brown skin of his face, and then the mussed comforter on one of the full beds. "You're sleeping in the hotel?"

"This is a makeshift office. Not much sleep's happening here now that things are heating up." He yawned and gestured to the small round table in the corner of the room, covered by a laptop and messy papers. "Please, come in, have a seat."

"I hope Mr. Remington's giving the FBI a good rate." He joined him at the table. "Rooms here aren't cheap."

"*Free* sounds like a pretty good rate to me."

His boss was indeed getting involved. "Wow, that's generous of him."

"Remington is a good man," Bounter agreed. "Though his motives aren't completely altruistic. It seems the criminal element has wormed its way to this hotel, and he doesn't want it to find a home here."

Grant gave him a questioning look.

"Last night was your first back performing, singing at Capone's Spirits, correct?"

"Yes, sir. Got my sea legs back."

"I know they trained you on observational skills during your time at the Academy. What'd you notice about last night's audience?"

"I didn't…" His voice drifted off as he felt the heat of the agent's stare. He closed his eyes, pushing himself to remember the guests watching him sing Sinatra and Bennett. There was the usual smattering of women wearing low-cut blouses, smiling back at him, but surely those weren't the people Agent Bounter had in mind. Who else was there? He frantically searched his mind, feeling his throat go dry.

"Anyone catch your eye?" Bounter prompted.

Mr. Remington had been there, standing off to the side, making sure his vocal chords still did their thing after the two-month FBI training hiatus at Quantico. Sophie had been there too, and he'd felt at home singing to her, focusing only on her…

"Well?"

He sighed. "I'm sorry, sir—I don't recall anything out of the ordinary."

"You're going to have to do better than that."

He winced.

"Particularly if you want to survive. What interfered with your concentration?"

"I'm not sure—I remember looking at Sophie, and—"

"She distracted you. That won't happen again."

"It won't?"

"No, it's too risky for Sophie to be there now. Important targets came in during your first song."

"The Russians were there? Last night?" He paled. "What about Sophie? Did they see me go over to her when I was done?"

"No, they were only there for a few songs. They had a drink, then left."

Panic laced his voice. "Why didn't you tell me? I would've kept her far from this place if I'd known."

Bounter held his hands out, palms up. "We had no idea they'd show up. You never know what to expect with these thugs. We thought *you'd* have to go to *them*, but it'll actually work out much better this way. Less risk of entrapment."

He felt sick. Sophie had been in the same bar with members of the Russian Mafia. "Who was there, sir?"

"You tell me."

"Uh, probably not Federov…" He watched the agent raise an eyebrow. "The *don* was there? And I didn't see him?"

"He was there with a woman and another couple, in the back. You'd have to look carefully to find him."

"Which I obviously didn't do," he muttered, angry with himself. He sat up like the snap of a sail in the wind. "Wait a minute. The woman with him when they walked in—was she a blonde? Wearing a red dress?"

The agent smiled. "Are you scoping the crowd for dates, Mr. Saylor?"

"No, sir. I thought she might—" his voice dipped "—try to buy me a drink after. She looked the type."

Bounter seemed to stifle a laugh.

"But then she was hanging off the guy, so I knew I was safe."

"That woman was Kebin's date, not Federov's."

"Andrei Kebin?"

Bounter nodded—he seemed relieved Grant had at least learned the targets' names. "Federov's girl isn't quite as much a looker as Kebin's."

"They didn't show me photos of the girlfriends."

"That's because the girls are usually a revolving door with those two." Bounter pulled out a manila folder.

As Grant studied the photos of the Russians and their current girlfriends, he felt a tendril of disquiet settle in his gut. These men didn't look all that different from his father's family. Except that the Barberis were mostly in prison, whereas these men were free. He was determined to end their freedom too.

"What do you need me to do next, sir?"

"You wait."

Grant scowled.

"We think it's better for them to come to you. Makes them less suspicious."

"How do we know they'll return to Capone's?"

"Eh…" Bounter shrugged. "We don't know for sure, but it seemed like they were enjoying themselves until Federov got a text message. They left pretty quickly after that."

Grant nodded.

"We want you to sit at the bar after your set. No friends, just you. Flash around some money, ask where to find a good poker game. Make it subtle."

"So I'm not going to West Town to seek them out."

"Correct. Just have some patience. If you play your cards right, they'll find you."

Grant sighed. Sitting around waiting wasn't what he'd hoped for.

"Let's review your cover story for when you make contact," Bounter suggested. "Make sure we're on the same page."

"My name's Mick Saylor…" When he told Bounter how he got discharged from the Navy due to his gambling problem, his heart squeezed, thinking of Logan. They reviewed the reasons his knowledge of Naval Station Great Lakes and Navy submarines would be attractive to the Russians.

"Tell me more about yourself, Mick."

"I grew up north of Chicago, in Lake County. My mom died from cancer when I was twelve, and my dad took my brother and me to live near his family in Norfolk."

"What's your dad's name?"

"Jerry," he said after a pause.

"Hesitations like aren't going to fly."

He nodded and clenched his teeth. *Get it right.*

"Where do your dad and brother live now?"

"They still live in Virginia."

Bounter leaned in. "Why'd you return to Chicago? Don't you miss them?"

"I used to work at Great Lakes. I'm not close to my family anymore…They think I have a drug problem just because I smoked a little weed in high school."

"*Do* you have a drug problem?"

"Of course not." He gave his best disarming smile.

"What'd you do after high school?"

"I joined the Navy when I was eighteen."

"Did you work on any submarines?"

"Nope, I was on destroyers and bird-farms. But I know my way around subs."

"What'd you do when you got kicked out of the Navy?"

"I started working in the hotel as a bellman. I was joking around with the guys, singing in the lobby, and Mr. Remington heard me. He had me audition, and the rest is history."

"When did you start singing at Capone's?"

"Last September."

"You've been singing there the whole time?"

"Uh, I had to go home for a couple of months."

Bounter's head tilted. "Why?"

"My brother's sick." He swallowed. "Testicular cancer. He didn't really want me there, but I stayed until after his surgery."

Bounter smiled. "Just the right amount of emotion there, Mick. Very believable."

He took a deep breath. He didn't have to manufacture emotion when it came to his brother.

"And the testicular cancer's a nice touch. There's no way guys will ask follow-up questions on that one. Okay, I've got the hidden microphones with GPS here. Let's get one on you."

"Now, sir?"

"The Russians are on the radar. It's time."

As Bounter turned to pick up the tiny button-size microphone, Grant clenched his hands into fists, his anticipation building.

It's time.

2. Contact

From the driver's seat, Anita Green smiled at Sophie.

Sophie rubbed her hands together, glad the defroster was pumping out warm air for their trip. When her former advisor had asked for help with data collection, she'd volunteered. But now that they were en route to Downer's Grove Women's Penitentiary, she questioned that decision.

"How's it going, *Assistant Professor* Taylor?" Anita asked.

"Pretty good. Teaching two new classes is a lot of work."

She nodded. "I remember what my first year was like. Very busy. At least I had some reliable professors in the department to mentor me."

"It's great to have mentors." She mustered a smile. "I'm glad you're back from Spain."

"Me too. Except for this detestable weather." Snow swirled in the air but wasn't sticking to the roads yet. "I hope our drive back to the city won't be a skating rink."

Sophie couldn't wait for the trip home, no matter how much snow had accumulated. Her stomach was in knots as they drove closer and closer to the prison that had been her home for a year.

"Why didn't you use David's old syllabus for your history of psychology class?" Anita asked. "That might've saved you some time."

"Uh, you know, I wanted to make the class more current." Her stomach tightened even more as she remembered her run-in with David Alton back in October.

"A history class?" Anita paused. "I've noticed you seem rather tense around David in department meetings. Did something happen while I was away?"

"Something did happen, but I'm not sure if I should share it."

"I respect that. I was just curious because David seems different since I returned."

"Different how?"

Anita seemed to think for a moment. "Not quite as lecherous."

She laughed. "So he's come on to you too. You never said anything about it when I was your student. I thought it was just me."

"I didn't think it would be professional to discuss another professor with a student. Besides, it meant nothing to me since I'm married. I'm sorry it happened to you too—I had no idea."

"I think David got away with his little games because of the silence. But Tanya, Nora, and I decided that didn't work for us anymore."

Anita's jaw dropped as Sophie recounted how the three had secretly taped and then confronted David for sexually harassing women in the department.

"What a cad!" Anita's grip stiffened on the steering wheel. "Sounds like your confrontation worked, but why didn't you tell the department chair? Or the university ombudsman?"

"We thought about it," she said. "I was hesitant to make a formal ethics charge. I'm not exactly the queen of ethics myself."

Her eyes softened. "You've paid for your ethical breach, Sophie."

"I know." She sighed.

"Do you feel like you must *keep* paying?"

"Sometimes. Especially when we're headed to Downer's Grove."

Anita nodded. "Are you sure you want to do research with me?"

"Yes." After a moment she added, "Grant told me it was tough to return to Gurnee to confront his father, but it helped him move forward. And he was still on parole then. At least I don't have the threat of prison hanging over my head anymore."

"Being on parole must've been so stressful."

"It was. But Grant made it better. Hunter too. He also thinks it's a good idea to confront my fears."

"Spoken like a true therapist." Anita winked at her.

❧

Inside the prison, Sophie watched a female CO pat down Anita. *Great, I'm next.* She tensed as the CO approached. When the guard ran her hand along her inner thigh, she closed her eyes. Though it was not an unfamiliar experience, she'd never be comfortable with pat-downs.

The CO's male counterpart inspected their briefcases on the conveyer next to the metal detector. "What's this?" He held up a small tape recorder.

Her voice sounded small. "It's a mini-recorder, to tape the interviews."

"That's not approved." The CO placed the recorder in a box of forbidden items.

Unable to protest, she found her words stuck in her throat.

"Actually," Anita butted in, slipping on her heels, "Warden Sanchez did approve that. There's a letter in my briefcase. I could show you—" She halted when the guard held out his hand.

"Step back. I'll get it."

While Sophie zipped up her boots with trembling hands, Anita stood placidly. "It's in the side pocket."

The guard scanned the letter and seemed disappointed. "It's legit," he said, nodding at the female CO. "Put the recorders back in their bags." He glared at Sophie. "Those recorders better have all their working pieces when you leave, batteries included."

"Yes, sir."

"Follow me to the interview rooms."

They grabbed their briefcases and followed the officer, waiting to be buzzed through several locked doors. When they arrived at one door, the CO unlocked it and gestured for Sophie to enter. She gave Anita a jittery smile.

"See you in a few hours," Anita said as the door closed. She turned to accompany the officer to the next interview room.

Sophie shivered when she heard jangling keys lock the door behind her. She placed her briefcase on the table and collapsed into a chair bolted to the cement floor. *Keep it together*. She forced herself to take some deep breaths.

A few minutes later the CO unlocked the door and led in a large, imposing woman.

Noticing the inmate's handcuffs, she frowned. "I thought we were only interviewing minimum-security offenders?"

He guided the woman to another chair and shrugged. He pulled a piece of paper from his pocket and unfolded it. "This is the list Dr. Ashby gave me. Dominique volunteered for the study."

"Oh." She felt her face flush when the inmate shot her a challenging stare.

"You want me to take her away?" the CO asked.

She paused. "No, it must've been my misunderstanding. I'd be happy to meet with Dominique. Does she, um, does she need to stay in cuffs?"

"Yes. I'll be right outside." He departed, leaving the door ajar.

She tried to rein in her furious blush. "Sorry about that."

Dominique studied her. "Huh. When I go see Dr. Ashby I don't have to be cuffed."

"That's probably because Dr. Ashby's a psychologist for the DOC. They trust her."

Dominique continued staring.

She took out some papers and hoped her smile didn't convey her anxiety. "Please allow me to introduce myself. I'm Dr. Sophie Taylor, from DePaul University. We're conducting a study on the effectiveness of psychotherapy in prison. Today I'll interview you about your experiences in therapy here at Downer's Grove. Would you be willing to read about the potential benefits and risks of the study?"

The woman gave the slightest of nods.

Sophie was about to slide the informed consent document across the table. But instead, making every effort to be friendly, she took a deep breath, walked over to Dominique, and placed the paper on the table in front of her. "Please look this over and sign if you agree to participate."

Stepping back, she waited a moment before Dominique gave her an expectant look. "Is there a problem?" Sophie asked.

"I kind of need a pen?" the woman replied.

"Oh!" Sophie gasped. "Uh, they confiscated my pens…Let me see if I can get one."

She poked her head out the door, and the CO came in to supervise the inmate as she signed the document with his pen. He then collected it and stepped outside again.

"It looks difficult to sign with handcuffs on." She returned to her seat.

Dominique appeared unfazed. "I'm used to it."

"Are you okay with me recording this interview, as outlined in the informed consent document?" She pulled out the tape recorder.

"Whatever."

Pressing the record button, Sophie realized she would be recorded too. She said a silent prayer that she wouldn't sound like an idiot. She looked down at her paper. "This is a semi-structured interview, meaning I have some questions prepared but I might also ask follow-up questions to your responses, okay?"

Dominique nodded.

"How long have you been in therapy with Dr. Ashby?"

"Oh." She furrowed her brow. "I thought you'd start by asking me why I'm in here."

"Would you like to discuss that?"

"No." She looked down. "I started counseling 'bout a year ago."

"What led you to begin counseling?"

She shrugged. "To get out of my cell."

Sophie nodded. "To get away from your bunkie?"

The prisoner seemed surprised she knew the lingo. "Something like that."

"Do the police escort you to Dr. Ashby's office? That's what happens for maximum-security offenders, right?"

A suspicious crease tightened her forehead. "How you know that?"

"Well…" She blushed.

"Wait a minute…*you* were here! Across the street—I remember you. Didn't recognize you at first in your fancy duds."

She sighed, angry with herself for revealing too much. This was supposed to be Dominique's interview, not hers. But this setting full of locks and cages had rattled her.

"You're right, I was incarcerated here a while back, in another cellblock."

"You're…a doctor?"

She winced. "I was a psychologist. Now I teach and do research."

"How the world you go from here to there?"

"Well, I'm done with my parole…trying to put my life back together."

"So you were in prison here, and now you're some swanky shrink. You think you know all about me, then."

"I don't." She met her eyes. "Even though I'm a con too, I don't presume to know what it's like to be maximum security — to be cuffed anytime you get out of your cell, to be here for years, to suffer all the losses you have. Also I have no idea what it's like to be black, facing racism every day."

Her glare softened.

"That's why I'm here," Sophie said, attempting to keep her voice steady. "To try to understand your unique experience. To talk about what therapy has been like for you."

"Why you need to interview me? You probably saw a shrink too — you know what it's like."

"Not in here," she admitted. "I was too stubborn. But my PO made me see a psychologist when I got out, so I didn't escape therapy for long."

Dominique smirked. "They always get ya in the end."

"That's for sure." Sophie smiled.

A silence settled over them, but eventually Dominique said, "The reason I started counseling was my bunkie told me to do it."

"Okay." Sophie hesitated. "She's the one in charge?"

"Nah, ain't like that. My bunkie said she'd kill me if I kept waking her up at night hollerin'."

Pain pierced her heart as she thought of Grant. "Nightmares, huh?"

Dominique looked down. "Then I found out I got a better chance of getting back my kids, once I get out, if I go to counseling. That's why I keep going, even though it was stupid at first."

"What parts seemed stupid to you?"

They continued the interview for over an hour, and Sophie found herself completely absorbed, really connecting with the woman. She'd avoided most of the other inmates during her stay, but perhaps it hadn't needed to be such a lonely year.

"It sounds like therapy has been helpful for you, Dominique," she concluded near the end of their time. "Your nightmares have stopped — so at least your bunkie won't kill you now — and you have some ideas about how to discipline your kids effectively when you get out."

"Sounds 'bout right."

"What are your recommendations for improving therapy here? What could the DOC do to make it a more helpful experience?"

"The DOC wants to know what *I* think?"

"Yes! You're giving your valuable time for an interview, and we want to use your insights to make things better."

Dominique looked away. "Well, uh, they could hire you, I guess. I like you better than Dr. Ashby."

Stunned, she was speechless for a few seconds. "Um, wow, that's a really kind thing to say, Dominique. Thank you. I…I lost my license when I was arrested, though. No more therapy for me."

The prisoner shook her head. "Just like I said. They always get ya in the end."

Sophie could see sadness in the woman's drawn eyes — sadness that mirrored her own.

❧

Grant locked the door behind him and entered the darkened apartment. He found Sophie crashed on the sofa. The glow of the television framed her body in muted blue light. Her head tilted back, resting on the cushion, and her long strawberry-blond hair draped in soft waves around her face. She'd propped up her feet on the coffee table.

He sat next to her, studying her delicate features. She hadn't removed her makeup, and he noticed smudged eye shadow above her long eyelashes. She looked so serene. He reveled in the quiet after spending the night in a loud bar, stressed from hitting each note while scanning the crowd for any sign of the Russians.

Glancing at the TV, he saw the menu screen for *Titanic*. She must have fallen asleep watching the DVD, and she'd muted the sound before drifting off. The remote rested on her upturned palm.

As he reached for the remote, his hand paused midair.

"Ahhhhh…" she moaned.

He looked up to see her mouth twitch into a small grin. He wished he could be in the dream with her—it seemed like a fantastic time. As he slid the remote from her grasp, she stirred, much to his dismay.

She gave him a dreamy smile. "You're home."

"And you're adorable." Never taking his eyes off hers, he set the remote on the coffee table and leaned down for a kiss. There was an open box of Girl Scout cookies on the table, and she tasted like chocolate mint. Once their lips met, his time apart from her floated away. Each kiss was a reconnection…a homecoming.

He gave her some space, and she stretched, catlike, lifting her arms above her head and curling her toes. She yawned and frowned. "Aw, I missed the end."

He smirked. "I've got a secret for you." He planted soft kisses along the warmth of her jawline, then murmured in her ear, "The ship sinks."

She giggled and elbowed him. "Way to spoil it for me."

"Hardly. How many times have you seen *Titanic?*"

Her cheeks pinked as she sat up. "About ten."

"That's thirty-five hours of your life you're not getting back."

"Stop ragging on my favorite movie! You haven't even seen it."

"What's the point? There's no suspense there—we all know what'll happen."

"It's not about the suspense. It's about the romance." She sighed, her hand fluttering to her heart. "Jack Dawson's the most amazing character."

His eyes narrowed. "So this is about Leonardo DiCaprio."

"He certainly helps my enjoyment of the movie." A devious smile played on her lips.

He pulled away from her. "I bet you were dreaming about *him.*"

"What?"

"You were moaning in your sleep. Sexy dream with Mr. Dawson?"

"I…I can't remember?"

"Right." He lunged forward, his long fingers snaking under her shirt to tickle her as he adopted a German accent. "You *vill* tell me your dream!"

She squealed, shrinking away. "No!"

The tickling increased. When his roving hands made their way to her bottom, cascading giggles mixed in with her shrieks.

"Tell me, Bonnie."

She gasped for air. "I won't confess."

"Ve have vays of making you talk."

She shivered from his waltzing fingers, and when he gave her a respite, she broke free and darted into the bedroom.

He clicked off the TV and followed closely behind. "As if I vill let you get away so easy." He found her on the bed, lying on her back, panting and staring up at him with anticipation.

He snuggled in next to her, propping his head in his hand as his elbow rested near her ear. "Did you dream about Jack Dawson?" He tickled her soft neck, eliciting a sharp intake of air.

"I'll never tell."

His hand snaked up behind her ear, gently lifting her head to bring her closer.

"Mmm," she sighed, reaching up to cradle his face. "Put your hands on me, Jack."

He glowered.

"I mean, put your hands on me, Grant."

"That's better."

"Put your hands on me, McSailor."

She didn't need to tell him again. Clothes flew off, bedding was pulled down, and bodies melded together. Their legs tangled as she rolled on top of him, anchoring herself by clasping the sides of his head. He closed his eyes as she massaged his buzzed hair. His hands reached for her naked bottom, skimming circles with his fingertips. Instead of her characteristic moans, she squeaked.

"Ticklish, Taylor?"

"You know my bum's ticklish."

"That's why I'm putting my hands right there."

"Still torturing me for that dream, I see."

He lifted his hands from her bottom, and she gasped. "I didn't say you should *stop*."

His hands meandered back down, cupping her cheeks, and she rewarded him with a quiver through her body.

She peeked down at his hardness. "*This* ship's definitely not sinking."

"Not until it leaves port, at least."

"But it hasn't even docked yet, McSailor."

"Jeez you're impatient." He lifted his head to draw her into a deep kiss, guiding them together. They rocked slowly, sensuously. Her lips trailed down his neck, kissing his collarbone. He shifted slightly, touching her just right, and she let out a sated moan.

"That was the sound you made in your dream."

"All right, already, relax. It was *you* in my dream, not Jack Dawson."

"Why didn't you just say so?"

"I didn't want you to get a big head."

He chuckled, clutching her tighter.

"I love hearing your laugh rumble in your chest."

He loved the feel of her resting on top of him.

"In the dream, we were in that icy water together, and you hoisted me up on a floating piece of wood. When you tried to climb up too, it almost toppled. You just resigned yourself to freezing. You were only focused on saving me."

His chest swelled with pride. "So I was the hero?"

"Some hero, willing to die," she scoffed. "No way I'd let that happen. I eased myself back into the water with you—"

"*That* sounds stupid."

"Hush. I swam over to another piece of wood and dragged it back, so we both could get out of the water. We both survived."

Kissing the tip of her nose, he said, "I'm glad I'm dating a swimmer then."

"That always drove me crazy when Rose just gave up, letting Jack freeze—"

"Hey, don't spoil it for me!"

"I thought you said you weren't interested."

A steely thread of determination tightened in his chest. "I've got to see what this Jack Dawson character's all about."

"Jealous?" One eyebrow cocked up.

"Don't think so. Jack Dawson isn't holding you in his arms right now. *I* am." His hands kneaded the smooth skin of her back.

"Or maybe you want to watch Kate Winslet play Rose?"

He scrunched his nose. "Redheads aren't really my thing. So when did the moaning come into the dream?"

"That was later." She gave him a demure smile. "In a cabin on the Carpathia, after we were rescued. We had to warm each other up."

It may have been below freezing outside, but with her hot body on top of his, beads of sweat popped up on his forehead. "I bet we did a good job."

3. Control

As Grant finished updating Dr. Hunter Hayes on his work at the hotel, Sophie found their psychologist looking at her.

"What's happening in the land of academia?"

"Anita's keeping me busy on the prisoner counseling research project."

He nodded. "How was your return to Downer's Grove?"

"Wasn't as bad as I thought it'd be."

"Really? Why's that?"

"The interviews went smoothly—I had a lot of fun. I never thought I'd enjoy myself so much in that place. Here I was, interviewing a maximum-security offender—"

"What?" Grant butted in. "You told me they'd only be minimum security."

Sophie gave Hunter a look. "You can see he still does that protective caveman thing."

"Well *you* do the protective cavewoman thing, giving me a hard time about going undercover," Grant countered.

"That's different," she said.

"How?"

"The offender was cuffed, with a guard right outside. You're going to be on your own with armed criminals."

"And a wire," Grant added.

"Yeah, *that'll* save you."

"Okay, okay," Hunter said. "We've been over this territory before."

"That's for sure." Grant's voice sounded weary.

"Instead of sarcasm, how about one of you states your position on this issue, using 'I' statements? Then you can describe your partner's position, using validation."

Feeling fear and anger churn in her stomach, she crossed her arms and remained tight-lipped.

So Grant began. "I feel…strongly, uh, *compelled* to work with the FBI, to stop the abuse, and, and domination by ruthless thugs." Sky blue eyes bored into her. "You feel worried I'll get hurt. You don't understand why I'm taking the risk."

Her stomach relaxed just a bit. "Yes. I don't get it. We barely survived our first run-ins with your family, and now we're finally safe. We don't have parole hanging over us anymore. Why would you ruin that?"

He pulled back.

"Sophie, could you rephrase that last question? Make it less leading and more open-ended?" Hunter asked.

She nodded. "Grant, what makes you feel, um, compelled to stop them?"

He rubbed his jaw, looking unsure.

"Grant, I'm intrigued by the words you chose—*abuse* and *domination*," Hunter said. "Do you see this undercover assignment as a way to retaliate against your father?"

His eyebrows drew together. "Yes, but not completely. It's more about taking control back from those who've stolen it. Restoring power to the good guys."

"That was your motivation for joining the Navy, right?" Sophie asked. "Fighting for the good guys?"

"Yes."

Hunter tapped his chin. "Some believe it's not so black and white. The good guys versus the bad guys, I mean."

Grant leaned forward. "You don't think Americans are the good guys?"

She felt tension elevate between the men.

"Not always," Hunter said. "Our government's made lots of mistakes."

"Exactly." Grant nodded. "That's why government should be smaller."

"Or maybe government should try to help people."

"Creating dependency on a welfare state is hardly helping people!" Grant fumed.

"Ignoring the suffering of those in need certainly doesn't help."

"This is exactly what makes America so great, isn't it?" Sophie quickly offered. Both men paused, turning to her. "The opportunity to have your own opinion, to debate the best way to run the country."

Hunter took a deep breath. "I apologize. I don't know what got into me. Therapy's not the place for a political debate."

Grant sank back in his chair. "I'm sorry too, sir."

"No need to apologize, Grant. I'm the one who started it. Though I *am* impressed you didn't back down. You stood your ground, managed your anger well."

Grant gaped at him.

"You're surprised I'd compliment you right after arguing with you?"

Grant nodded.

"It's difficult for you to disagree and still maintain a relationship. Disagreements weren't allowed in your family. If anyone in your family disagreed with your father, he or she got hit."

Slowly nodding, Grant said, "Yeah."

"And, Sophie, I noticed you decided to enter the fray, trying to smooth things out. How'd you feel during the argument?"

"Nervous. My stomach was churning."

Hunter nodded. "Disagreeing with your father got you kicked out of the house."

She skimmed her fingertips down her long neck, thinking back to age nineteen.

"No wonder you both struggle with this disagreement about Grant going undercover. In your families, differences of opinion weren't allowed. Arguments led to aggression." Hunter paused. "But conflict's *healthy* in relationships. You're different people, with different beliefs, different backgrounds. Of course you see *your* side more easily. Being able to communicate those differences and understand each other's perspective is a way to resolve the conflict."

"It's hard for me to understand Grant's perspective on this," she said.

Hunter nodded. "I have to admit it's tough for me to understand as well. Grant, you already confronted your father—very successfully, I might add. You feel the need to keep fighting him and men like him?"

Grant tapped his thigh. "Maybe this is about my father *and* my mother." He glanced at Sophie. "I visited my mother's grave the other day."

"You did? I'd have gone with you, if you wanted."

"Thank you. Next time, that'd be great. And I'll go with you to visit your mother if you want."

She hesitated. She hadn't found the courage to visit her mother's grave yet.

"But this time I needed to go alone," Grant continued. "I needed to say some things to her. I told her about you, Sophie." His crystal eyes gleamed. "I know she'd be happy I found you in all this mess."

She felt her upper lip quivering.

"I told my mother how much you don't want me to do this FBI job. How worried you are about it." He scooped up her hand in his. "I feel like I have to do this. I'm not sure why…Maybe it's because my father *took* my mother. He stole her life away. I know she died of cancer, but he made her life miserable, short as it was. This is the only way I know how to make it up to her. She couldn't stand up for herself, but I can stand up for her. I have to fight back…for *her*. To honor her."

Tears splashed her cheek, and Grant smoothed his hand down her hair. "I also need to do this for Ben," he added. "Logan didn't show Ben the right path in life. And now Ben's on the *edge*. He can choose to follow his father's footsteps, or he can learn how to contribute to this world—to take responsibility for himself, to reach his potential. Somebody has to show him how to do that…and since I'm his uncle, it's gotta be me. Uncle Joe told me he regrets that he didn't fight back against the family. I don't want to have regrets. I *have* to fight."

"How can I argue with that?" she muttered.

"It'd be tough." Hunter sighed.

She turned to the psychologist, wiping the corner of her eye. "Hunter, please tell Grant he's not responsible for saving his mother or for saving Ben."

"Apparently she *can* argue with that."

Hunter chuckled. "Sophie, if one of your therapy clients asked you to tell her partner what to do, how would you respond?"

She made a sound of disgust in the back of her throat. "I wouldn't do it."

"And I won't either. I will say I agree that Grant isn't responsible for his mother or his nephew. But from what I hear, he's *choosing* to try to honor them. It's a powerful motivation for him. You may disagree, but this is the best way he knows to move forward. It's a way to take back the reins of his life."

"Yeah, what *he* said," Grant added.

She sighed. "I hate when you men double-team me."

"Grant's also been in the hot seat once or twice in here," Hunter said.

Grant scoffed.

"Grant, you're making tremendous progress," Hunter added. "You express yourself much better now than six months ago."

"Thank you, sir." He ducked his head, but Sophie could tell he was pleased. "I hope Ben starts making progress too."

"He's trying," Hunter said. "It's difficult for teenagers. They don't have a vocabulary for emotions, especially when they've gone through trauma. And Ben's been through more than most boys his age."

Sophie glanced at the clock. "Is it time for his session?"

"Just about." Hunter rose to pick up a chart on his desk. "You two want to stay for the first part of Ben's session, like we discussed earlier?"

"Yes, sir. I'll make sure Ben talks."

Hunter shook his head. "It's not like that, Grant. Ben doesn't know me all that well yet, and trust takes time to build. Just have some faith in the process. It's worked for you, and it can work for him too."

Grant stood and walked toward the door. "I'll see if he's in the waiting room?"

"Sounds good."

"Your praise meant a lot to Grant. Thank you," Sophie said once the door had closed.

Hunter sat back down. "I'm glad. Does this mean you forgive me for picking on you today?"

"Maybe." She smiled as she clasped her hands around her knees. "I just worry about him, you know."

He nodded. "It's hard when we can't change or control our partners. It's tough to accept them as is."

"Is that difficult for most couples? Like with you and Bradley?"

Hunter's eyes widened.

"Whoops, didn't mean to pry. Forget I asked."

He leaned in. "Control's a huge dynamic in any relationship. Don't even get me *started* about Bradley."

They shared a grin as Grant led Ben into the office.

Hunter and Sophie stood, and Hunter extended his hand. "Good to see you, Ben."

Ben mumbled something unintelligible as they shook.

"You shouldn't call him Hunter, Ben," Grant said. "He's Dr. Hayes."

He fidgeted as he looked down.

Hunter offered, "Sometimes my clients call me Dr. Hunter. Would that work for you, Ben?"

He shrugged. "I guess."

Sophie tentatively held out her arms. When Ben stepped into the hug, her shoulders sagged with relief. Since she'd embraced him in the police station last November, thanking him for saving her life, she'd made a habit of greeting him with a hug. Each time she worried he'd stop letting her. "You're getting taller every time I see you," she said.

Grant wore a proud smile as she looked at him over Ben's shoulder. Then she gestured for Grant to join her on the sofa while Ben slouched in the chair opposite Hunter.

"Ben, we discussed this last time, but I wanted to check in again," Hunter said. "How do you feel about your uncle and soon-to-be aunt being here for the first ten minutes or so?"

"It's cool," he said.

"But you're not okay with your mom being part of the session?" When Ben nodded, Hunter asked, "What's the difference?"

"Dunno…maybe it's 'cause Grant and Sophie have to do therapy too, so they know how sucky it is."

She felt Grant bristle, and she jumped in before he went off on his nephew. "We don't *have* to be here, Ben. We choose to keep coming."

He sprawled out on the chair, propping his feet up on the coffee table. "Why?"

"Get your shoes off the table. Show some respect."

Hearing Grant's sharp tone, Ben complied, sitting up a bit.

"We come here to make our relationship better," Grant said. "Get things out in the open, try to understand each other more, learn how to deal with the painful parts of life."

Ben peeked at Hunter, who sat quietly observing, then looked back at Grant. "So you get things out in the open…like secrets and stuff?"

Sophie glanced at Grant, wondering if he was also thinking about the Logan bombshell.

"Sometimes," Grant said.

Hunter asked, "Do you have some secrets you're thinking about?"

"Nah." Ben looked down.

Hunter studied him. "You had a swim meet on Tuesday, right? How'd it go?"

Grant smiled. "He did great."

"Not really," Ben said. "I died at the end of the one-hundred fly."

"You just have to pace yourself a little better next time," Sophie offered. "Breathe more the first lap."

Ben shuddered. "I hope there won't *be* a next time. Butterfly's the worst event—I don't know why Coach keeps sticking me in it. It's so unfair."

"He must think you're strong. You just have to train more, kick off the walls longer. You'll get it." She winked at him. "Butterfly's the *best* stroke, by the way."

"Then maybe you should swim it for me."

"Yeah, right."

"No, I'm serious." Ben leaned forward. "You're giving me all these stroke tips…Why don't you come practice with me one day? Show me how great your butterfly supposedly is."

"I haven't been in a pool in almost twenty years!"

Ben shrugged. "That's okay if you don't think you could cut it."

"What?" She folded her arms across her chest. "I could cut it. I would *dust* you in the hundred fly."

His eyes lit up. "Saturday. Let's test it out."

"I don't know about this," she said. "I don't want to embarrass you or anything."

Next to her, Grant smothered a laugh.

"Getting scared?" Ben taunted.

She uncrossed one arm and pointed her index finger at him. "You should be the scared one, little man."

Grant grasped her hand. "Okay, okay, you two. I had no idea you were so competitive, Bonnie."

"Sorry. Swimming kind of brings that out in me."

"Don't apologize." He leaned in, lowering his smooth voice. "I like it."

"Gross." Ben made a face. "Get a room."

"So *I've* totally lost control of this session," Hunter said. Sophie turned to find him smiling. "I'm very curious how this pool show-down will turn out."

Grant nodded. "Me too."

Hunter looked at Ben. "Before Grant and Sophie leave, is it okay if I share with them the recent conversation I had with your mother?"

Ben squirmed. "You don't have to."

"But it's good news," Hunter said.

"It's embarrassing."

"Hey, buddy." Grant rested his hand on Ben's knee, halting his fidgeting. "What's going on?"

Ben glanced at Hunter. "You can tell 'em, I guess."

"Ashley agreed to administer random drug tests to Ben," Hunter said. "And the results of the first test came back yesterday." He paused for dramatic effect. "Negative."

A smile flashed on Grant's face. "Way to go, Ben!"

"It's not that big a deal," he muttered.

"Yes it is." Grant patted Ben's knee, waiting until he looked up at him. "I'm so proud of you."

She watched Ben blush then avert his eyes. He didn't seem very proud of himself. "Ben? Is there anything else you want to share with us?"

He quickly shook his head.

After a few moments of silence, Hunter said, "Well, I guess Ben and I will continue on our own now."

"Okay." Grant reached out to shake his hand as he and Sophie stood. "Thanks, Dr. Hayes."

"Yes, thanks, Hunter," she added.

"See you both next week."

At the door, Grant turned to his nephew. "Keep up the good work, Ben."

❧

Once they left, Dr. Hunter was quiet for a moment. Ben stared at the floor.

"What do you think has helped you stay away from pot?" he asked.

Ben shrugged. Thirty seconds ticked by. "Nick's parents made him go to drug rehab."

"Nick's a friend of yours?"

"Yeah. But he didn't join the swim team with me and Dylan."

"Do you think swimming has helped you avoid smoking?"

"I guess." He felt a slight smile form. "I'll have a better chance against Sophie without that crap in my lungs."

"True. I think that's a great thing you did, by the way."

"Huh?"

"Inviting Sophie back to the pool," Dr. Hunter explained. "She's dealing with some stress, and exercise is a great way to cope with it."

"I didn't do it on purpose." He thought for a moment. "She's the one who got me thinking about joining the swim team, so I had to pay her back. That hundred fly is evil."

Dr. Hunter chuckled.

"Are you sure we have to do this drug test thing?" Ben asked.

"I *am* sure. Your mom's insurance doesn't cover drug treatment, but now that there's the technology to do home tests, we can at least include that part of treatment in our counseling. Drug tests are an effective deterrent."

Ben glared at him.

"I know you feel like it's a punishment, but we're trying to help you. You have a lot of risk factors for drug addiction."

"Like what?"

"There's evidence that addiction is biologically based, running in families. As I understand it, your grandfather's an alcoholic." Dr. Hunter's voice softened. "And your father was a gambling addict."

Ben tightened his fists and looked away, jaw clenched.

"You're feeling angry right now?"

Ben exhaled. "No."

"You kind of look angry."

"I shouldn't be mad at my dad. He's dead."

"How about focusing less on how you *should* feel, and more on how you *do* feel? Anger's a normal part of grief."

"It is?"

"Absolutely." Dr. Hunter waited a beat. "What makes you angriest?"

He skimmed his teeth across his lower lip. "He was such a hypocrite. Telling me how to live my life, when he's out there destroying people. What a joke."

"Destroying people? Like Grant and Sophie?"

Ben nodded.

"So maybe you're okay with Grant and Sophie attending the session because you feel indebted to them somehow, for what your father did?"

"Maybe. My dad messed up my mom's life too. She's never gone out on one date since they split when I was a baby."

"You feel indebted to your mom too?"

"She had to take care of me all by herself. And I've been a massive screw-up."

"I don't think you're a screw-up, Ben. You're smart, you're caring, and you're working very hard to improve your life."

Ben stared at him. *Does he know me at all?*

"And you're not responsible for your father's actions, or your mother's. They're both adults who make their own choices. You can't control them."

Ben tapped his fingers on his jeans, wondering if it would be okay to ask the next question. After a few moments, he decided to go for it. "You said addiction runs in families. Does, um, being a criminal—does that run in families too?"

Dr. Hunter sat back in his chair. "That's an excellent question. Some criminals have antisocial personality disorder, and I'm thinking their children have a higher risk for that because of the whole nature and nurture interaction. Kids might start with a genetic vulnerability then learn behaviors through watching their parents. You worry you've inherited the criminal gene?"

Ben chewed on the inside of his mouth. "Did my dad have that antisocial thing?"

"I can't diagnose him—I never met him. I do know that people with antisocial personalities can't really feel empathy. They don't tend to feel remorse for their actions. That doesn't sound like your father to me."

"It doesn't?"

"Grant and Sophie gave me permission to share some things we've discussed, just like you've done with them. Ben, do you know your father used to try to protect Grant from Enzo's beatings?"

Oh my God. Ben's eyes widened.

Hunter's tone was gentle. "You didn't know that."

"Grandpa b-b-beat them?"

"Sadly, yes. He was out of control when he drank. Grant's had a long road to recover from the abuse."

"I feel so bad for him."

"I do too."

"Did he beat up Grandma too?" Ben tensed, waiting for the answer.

"I believe so."

Ben thought he might barf.

"From what I understand, your grandfather was also abused by his father. That's another thing that can run in families: abuse. Ben, this is wild speculation, but sometimes I wonder if your father wasn't part of your life because he was scared he'd hurt you. He had no idea how to be a good parent to you. As much as you missed out on him being around, I wonder if he thought he was helping you."

Ben looked at the floor. "I wish he would've tried."

"You're hurt and angry he made that choice for you."

Ben nodded.

"You know, we're focusing on all the negative traits that can be passed down through families. But you've inherited some good stuff too. I never met your father, but I know your uncle. Grant's intelligent, kind, a hard worker—just the way I described you earlier. He's got a lot of integrity. He's honest, and he tries to do the right thing. You're headed in that direction yourself."

Ben dared to look up at him. "Really?"

Dr. Hunter smiled. "Really. Now let's talk strategy for beating Sophie in the hundred fly."

4. Consternation

New inmate Anthony "Tank" Tanketti strolled along the fence line of the prison yard, dirty snow crunching under his boots. He tugged his scratchy woolen hat over his ears.

After spending two months stuck indoors at the county jail while he waited for a transfer, Tank was grateful the Gurnee guards believed in putting the prison cattle out to pasture. He sighed. If only the cattle's unfettered access to each other out in the open didn't place him at risk for slaughter.

But maybe his connection to the Barberis would keep him safe. He caught a glimpse of two of Enzo's men across the yard, but saw no sign of the don. If Enzo was still in solitary, he'd be one enraged son of a bitch when he got out. He could only hope Enzo never found out about his role in Logan's murder. Grant said he'd kept his mouth shut, but something about the boy scout seemed less than trustworthy.

He recognized Jules "Jewels" Monroe, one of Enzo's men. He'd met Jewels five years ago at a poker game at Angelo's club. He'd just decided to approach the craggy-faced man, when a blond inmate stepped in his way.

He looked down at the boy's elfin features, figuring him for no more than nineteen. The boy grinned up at him, his green eyes slanting with menace.

"Outta my way, Pink Taco," he growled.

The boy stepped in closer, and Tank's hand balled into a fist.

"Don't you touch my boy."

The foreign voice came from his right, and he turned to see a muscled blond smirking. He tried to place the slight accent — German maybe? He certainly had a Nazi sneer.

Blond Hitler's icy blue gaze started at Tank's shoes, slid up his legs, languished below his belt, seemed to appreciate his sizeable pectorals, then arrived at his face with a challenging stare. "Tank's a good name for you, I think. Wouldn't mind you mowing me down one day." His eyes lingered suggestively.

Another young, blond, ponytailed inmate next to him snickered.

Tank felt the presence of Elf-Face at his left hip, and he contemplated his odds in three against one. Placidly he asked the leader, "Who the fuck are you?"

Blond Hitler gave Elf-Face a look of wonder, then looked back at him. "You have not *heard* of me? I'm insulted. Ricker Mullens, at your service."

"That's Mr. Mullens to you," Elf-Face contributed.

He fought the urge to backhand the little leprechaun and kept his eyes on Ricker. "How'd you know my name?"

"I make it a point to know Enzo's men." He sauntered closer, and Ponytail followed. "I especially like the tall ones."

As they neared, Tank reached out to squeeze Elf-Face's shoulder, and Ricker's face darkened. The boy squirmed as he dug his fingers into his collarbone. "If you like the tall ones, then why keep this gnome around? You takin' his picture for Travelocity or somethin'? Filling your prison scrapbook?"

Ricker's voice was a low growl. "Watch your mouth."

When he crowded Tank's personal space and diverted his attention, Elf-Face managed to shrug out of his hold.

"Barberi's still in the hole," said Ricker. "Been there two months already."

"Why the fuck should I care?"

"Because he's not here to protect your bubble butt. Not that he would have your back anyway. You're nowhere near as pretty as the last one of his goons he protected."

He realized Ricker was talking about Grant—of course Enzo had protected his son. It had nothing to do with Grant's looks. How could they not know Grant was Enzo's son? He wondered if these three wolves had given him the same treatment on his first day at Gurnee.

Ricker leaned in, and Tank smelled powdered eggs on his breath. "Why is Barberi in the hole?"

He bribed a corrupt politician to try to get a pardon. Tank glared at him, saying nothing.

Ricker inched closer. "Tell me why Enzo is in the hole, or bending over to pick up the bar of soap will be an entirely new cleansing experience."

He felt tension radiating in his shoulders as Ricker smiled.

"Speak now, or forever hole my piece," Ricker added.

"Just try it." Tank ignored the giggles of Ricker's minions.

In an instant, Ricker pinned one of his arms behind his back, and Elf-Face and Ponytail seized the other.

Tank strained against their hold, gaining some ground against the two boys but surprised by Ricker's strength. "Get the fuck off me," he panted, "or the family will kill you."

"The Barberis?" Laughter rumbled in Ricker's voice. "Do not think so. They are not saving you *now*, are they?"

To his consternation, he noticed Jewels and the other guy sticking to their spots, watching him and obviously aware of his predicament. Maybe they were testing him, seeing if he could keep his mouth shut about Enzo's private affairs?

Ricker laughed as Tank dipped his shoulder, trying to break free. "The family is real tight, huh? They don't give a fuck about you. Madsen either, at first. Barberi was letting me have that beautiful ass, just handing him over to me. Too bad the door slammed shut once the boy got out of solitary. No idea why."

Tank pondered that, careful to keep his face neutral.

"I repeat—why is Barberi in the hole?" Ricker wrenched his wrist. "You think you can fight us off with a shattered wrist?"

"I don't know why!"

"Bullshit." Ricker twisted harder.

Despite the frigid wind, Tank felt beads of sweat on his forehead.

"Out with it!"

"Why don't you ask Madsen?" Tank managed.

"Why the hell would I do that?"

"Grant…" Tank rasped. "He's Enzo's son."

The arm Ricker had been jerking back abruptly snapped free, and the others stepped away. The three con blonds circled around to stand before him. Ricker's eyes flashed with excitement. "Madsen is the son of Barberi? Why the different last names?"

Tank took a step back and pulled down his jacket, smoothing the crumples. "Grant's uncle adopted him when Enzo came here, twenty years ago."

Ricker rubbed his hand down his chin. "He is his son. Of course. Very interesting."

Ponytail pouted, speaking for the first time. "Madsen ain't here anymore—who cares about him?"

Tank watched Ricker's eyes cloud with hostility, and Elf stammered, "Shut up!"

Ponytail's mouth clamped closed.

A loud buzzing noise preceded an announcement that yard time was over. Tank wasted no time returning to the cellblock.

"You did not answer my question!" Ricker called after him. "I'll be back."

"I'm sure you will," he muttered, fighting the urge to rub his throbbing wrist. He could see Enzo's men shuffling into line far ahead of him. Why the fuck hadn't they come to his rescue? *Had* Madsen ratted him out to Enzo? That once-gnawing fear now exploded and chomped him in the ass. If Madsen sang, Tank would hang.

Grant held the last note extra long, looking into the eyes of a platinum blonde in the audience. She gave him an alluring smile. Then she turned to her boyfriend and spoke in his ear, likely yelling to be heard over the roar of applause as he and Andy finished the set.

"That's Andy Beecham on piano." He extended his arm, and Andy gave a little bow from the bench. "We'll take a short break now—the perfect opportunity to try our special drink for a cold night: Russian coffee!" He held up his mug and took a sip as the applause dissipated. Only the bartender knew there was no vodka in *his* drink.

"I'm gonna catch a smoke." Andy ducked out to the rear exit.

Grant barely heard the piano man, he was so keyed up. The blonde he'd sung to was Andrei Kebin's girlfriend—this time he'd made sure not to miss the Russians when they arrived.

At the bar, he met Larry the bartender's eyes and lifted his drink.

"Another Russian coffee coming your way," Larry said, taking his mug.

He slid onto the lone empty bar stool, wishing he could turn around to see what the Russians were doing. Then something touched him, and he looked down to find a manicured hand on his forearm. Next to him he found a brunette woman who applied makeup like Ben buttered bread: thickly and haphazardly.

"You've got an amazing voice," she said, removing her hand and cupping her mug. From her breath, he could tell she was a *big* fan of the Russian coffees.

"Thank you." Normally he would find an excuse to retreat to the broom-closet-slash-dressing-room at this point, but this was no normal evening. "What brought you out on such a cold night?"

"You, of course. Don't you recognize me? I've seen you perform dozens of times."

Gulp. "Really? How kind of you."

Her hand snaked back to his arm. "I missed you when you were gone in December. How could you leave us like that?"

"I, uh…"

"Excuse me."

He looked up to find Andrei Kebin nudging in between them, casting a shadow across the bar. The consigliore to the Russian don had slicked back his jet black hair and appeared tidy and confident in his maroon button-down shirt and black jacket. "Come sit with us, Mr. Saylor."

"Mick's fine. And you are?"

"Andrei. My girlfriend wishes meet you. And what Innochka wants, Innochka gets."

"Hey," Coffee Breath protested, pouting her thin lips. "*I* was talking to Mick. Buzz off."

Grant watched Andrei bristle. She obviously had no clue who she was dealing with.

"I was indeed talking to…um…" He looked at her for help.

"Sandra."

"Sandra," he said, looking at the Russian. "Perhaps I could meet your lady friend another time?"

Any lingering pleasantness vanished from Andrei's expression. "*Now* is best time. Bartender!"

Sandra jumped on her barstool.

"Another drink for *lady*," Andrei commanded, looking at her with disgust, when Larry came over. "And send round of *Stoli elit* shots to table. Come, Mick."

Grant hesitated, glancing at Sandra, then shrugged. "Sure. Pleased to meet you, Sandra." As he stood, ignoring her disappointment, he noticed he was a couple inches taller than Andrei.

They weaved through the crowd. Before reaching their table, Andrei confided, "Not sure I introduce you to Innochka. I believe she quite taken with you."

He nodded with a plastic smile. The last thing he needed was a mobster thinking he might steal his girlfriend.

"May I present Vladimir Federov?" Andrei nodded toward a well-built man with neat gray hair and piercing eyes. Vladimir stayed seated.

Grant held his breath as he reached over to shake the don's hand.

"Good entertainer," Vladimir said, elongating the vowel sounds. His roll on the "r" was more pronounced than Andrei's.

"Isn't he *so* good?" Innochka gushed, batting her thick eyelashes.

Vladimir's girlfriend, a waif-like brunette, was less enthusiastic. "Some modern songs you sing next, yes? No more old singing."

Vladimir laughed heartily, gesturing to the open chair. "Sit."

As Grant and Andrei took their seats, Vladimir tugged his girlfriend from her chair onto his lap, where she barely made a dent. "You must excuse my Katya. She quite rude." He snuggled his lips into the nape of her neck as she shied away. "Perhaps she need spank tonight."

There was a second of terror in her eyes, and probably nobody at the table caught it but Grant. Katya quickly recomposed her mask and wrapped her arm around Vladimir's neck. "Promise?" she purred.

Vladimir cocked an eyebrow, placing his hand possessively on the curve of her bottom. "She kinky too. Lucky me."

Innochka seemed to look to Andrei for permission before asking, "How long have you been singing, Mick?"

He peeled his eyes off Katya, forcing himself to focus. *Breathe.* "Not that long, actually."

"Really," Andrei said. "You seem like pro up there."

"I've got an excellent poker face." He drummed up his most charming smile.

Dumping Katya back in her chair, Vladimir studied him. "And you use poker face off stage also?"

He thought for a moment. "I call on my poker face all the time. Gotta keep your cards close to your chest."

"Such wisdom," Andrei said. "Ah, drinks are here."

Grant took one look at the waitress and realized she must be new. A strand of dark hair had loosened from her bun, and her hand trembled as she lowered a shot glass from the tray.

Vladimir waited until she'd distributed the five shot glasses and departed. He raised his glass, and his guests quickly followed suit. His eyes shined with mischief. "To poker faces."

Expecting to knock back a shot of water, Grant almost choked when the sting of vodka drenched the back of his throat. As the heat of the liquor warmed his chest, he flinched when Andrei slammed his shot glass on the table.

"Water!" he yelled. "What the fuck?" He shot out of his chair, scanning the bar for the waitress. Upon locating her, Andrei darted over and dragged her back to the table by the elbow. Several bar patrons stared, and Grant's heart thumped.

"What the fuck is this?" Andrei pointed to his shot glass. "You give me water, not Stoli!"

"I'm, I'm sorry," she stammered. Grant could see Andrei's grasp digging into her flesh. The waitress gave him a pleading look.

Andrei continued to fume. "You better damn well be. How the fuck you serve shot of *water?* You think I not notice? They fire you now."

Grant calmly looked over at the waitress, now close to tears. "Mr. Remington would want you to bring another round, on the house. Go get that for our guests."

She nodded shakily and disappeared.

"Sorry 'bout that," he said. "I think she's new."

"And useless," Andrei seethed.

"You know Alexander Remington?" Vladimir asked, eyeing him.

Grant nodded, feeling a delicious buzz from the vodka. "He's my boss."

"He like you?"

"I think he has a soft spot for me, yes."

"What this means—'soft spot'?" Katya butted in. The lines around Vladimir's eyes tightened at the interruption, but crinkled with amusement when she added, "He goes soft?"

Vladimir skimmed his thick fingers down her cheek. "My Katya not know word *soft*, of course. Means fond, darling. Mr. Remington *fond* of Mick."

"And why is that?" Andrei asked Grant.

"He's proud of himself for 'discovering' me. I started at this hotel as just a bellman, but he overheard me singing in the lobby one day, joking around with the guys. He asked me to try some Sinatra and Bennett. And here I am."

"What a story." Innochka let out a dreamy sigh. "What song were you singing in the lobby?"

He scrambled to think of a song. "Uh, 'OPP'?"

Andrei's forehead creased. "What?"

He swallowed. "One of the bellman's girls had cheated on him, and we were giving him a hard time about it. The song just popped out..."

"What this means 'OPP'?" Katya asked.

Grant blushed.

Innochka started giggling. "Oh, I know this song! It means other people's p—"

"I'm so sorry for my mistake." The waitress had returned, this time holding a tray of double vodka shots.

Grant was thankful for the interruption. For a moment he hoped he'd get vodka again since the first drink felt so good, then he quickly chastised himself. He was on assignment. *Keep it together, McSailor.*

"Please have this round on me," the waitress offered, carefully passing out the drinks. "This is our finest vodka: *Kauffman*."

Andrei chuckled. "Oof, that will cost you."

Grant vowed to repay the waitress.

Innochka gestured to the shot glass, looking at Grant. "Will this bother your singing?"

"Please," he replied. "I've already had three Russian coffees."

Andrei frowned. "They think Russians actually drink that shit?"

"You don't?"

Vladimir leaned forward. "*Never* dilute vodka. Is sin."

"I'll let Mr. Remington know," he promised.

"*Budem*," Vladimir said, raising his shot glass.

When Grant knocked back water this time, he was disappointed, but also relieved. Wiping his mouth, he noticed Andy returning to the stage. He met Andrei's eyes. "Thank you for inviting me to your table—I've enjoyed it. But it's time to get ready for the next set."

"Wait," Vladimir ordered. Grant froze. "You come my place tonight."

"Really?" He forced a smile, swallowing the nausea pressing at his throat. He hadn't expected the meet to happen so soon.

"Tonight. After sing."

"We show you *real* vodka," Andrei said.

"And test poker face," Vladimir added, winking.

"I—I'd like that," he replied. He was indeed about to be tested.

⟲

"Texas Hold 'Em," Andrei announced as he shuffled the cards. His eyes never left Grant's.

Grant hoped his slight smirk masked the panic he felt. He wished he'd paid better attention to the Navy guys' games back on the aircraft carrier, but he'd been so disgusted by Logan's gambling problem that he'd steered clear completely. Rules for all the games of poker swirled in his mind as he tried to remember the crash course he'd taken in Quantico.

Vladimir muttered, "Girls better get butts back in here."

It was just the three of them at a round table in a dimly lit room, waiting for the promised "real vodka" from the Russians' girl-friends. Red velvet curtains draped over the windows but otherwise the room was rather Spartan, the poker table stealing the spotlight.

One bodyguard had driven them from the club to this house in West Town, and he was now perched in the corner of the room, smoking a cigarette. Grant was sure several more bodyguards made their residence here. He hoped the tiny button recorder embedded in his shirt was working, transmitting to the FBI.

Andrei finished shuffling and looked up at his boss.

"No," Vladimir grumbled. "Need drink first." He glared at the bodyguard and spoke to him in Russian.

As the large man went to the kitchen, Innochka and Katya emerged carrying shot glasses of an amber liquid.

"Something different, you say," Katya told Vladimir, placing the glass in front of him.

"I wanted to make margaritas, but Katya said they weren't strong enough for you," Innochka added.

Grant paled, realizing the drink in front of him was the dreaded tequila. He hoped he wouldn't start singing after a few more shots.

"My girl know me well," Vladimir said, winking at Katya as he held his glass aloft. "*Na zdorovie.*"

As the three men downed the burning tequila, he remembered the feel of Sophie's skin during their unforgettable body shots. His smile faded when Vladimir tossed two blue chips into the kitty. He needed to focus on the task at hand.

"Bring bottle, then leave us," Vladimir ordered. The women complied.

For the small blind bet, Grant added his own two blue chips, and Andrei followed suit before scooping the six chips toward him and dealing two cards to each of them, face down. Grant peeked at his cards: a seven of hearts and an ace of spades.

Andrei dealt three cards to the middle of the table and with a flourish turned them over. A four of hearts, ten of diamonds, and ace of clubs.

A pair of aces! He tried to conceal his excitement, feeling Russian eyes on him, trying to read him.

Vladimir pushed two red chips to the middle. Grant had a sense the red ones were worth more than the blue ones, though he had no clue about their true value. He wasn't about to ask. Calling the bet, he added two red chips of his own.

Andrei paused, seeming to think for a moment, then slapped his cards on the table face-down. It was just him and Vladimir left.

Picking the top card from the deck, Andrei discarded it and turned over the next community board card in the middle of the table: a seven of clubs.

Vladimir shoved another red chip toward the pot.

Go big or go home, Grant told himself. He nudged two red chips to the pile.

One of Andrei's eyebrows lowered. He stared at Grant. Vladimir's face was like a still pond as he tossed one more red chip into the kitty. Andrei burned another card, then turned up the final card in the middle of the table. It was a six of diamonds.

Vladimir glared at the five cards on the table, and Grant hoped the don didn't have a five and an eight for a straight. But a three of a kind would also beat him. The Russian turned over his cards, first showing a five of spades. Grant held his breath. Vladimir's next card was a king of clubs, and Grant exhaled.

He turned over his cards and tried not to smile, showing his two pair. Maybe gambling wasn't all bad.

"Aces over sevens," Vladimir said, frowning.

Andrei shrugged, corralling the chips and pushing them to Grant. "Beginner's luck."

"Almost five thousand dollars of beginner's luck," Vladimir growled.

Grant's face froze. Counting the six blue chips and eight red ones added to his pile, he struggled to calculate. "The red chips…they're worth…five hundred?"

"*Da*," Andrei answered. "Blue chips one hundred each."

He nodded. The FBI had only given him five thousand, and he didn't even know how much the green chips were worth. He hoped his beginner's luck would continue.

Andrei poured another round from the bottle Innochka had left, and Grant knocked back the next shot. He was going to need it.

5. Con Tequila

"Thank heaven *that's* over," Kirsten Holland muttered, collapsing on the sofa.

"It's great to live in the same building again," Sophie said, handing her former roommate a glass of rosé. "But you're not allowed to move ever again."

"Cheers to that!" Kirsten grinned as she clinked Sophie's glass. "Moving is exhausting." They each took a sip. "I just couldn't stay in our old place by myself, you know? Even though the management company cleaned the stain…"

"I totally get it, Kir. You shouldn't have to live anywhere a man got killed. Talk about PTSD."

She nodded. "It was almost like Carlo was still there some nights, lurking around."

"Like a ghost?"

Kirsten tossed her thick brown hair over her shoulder. "Don't know if I believe in ghosts. But the living room did seem kind of creepy, a little colder than the rest of the apartment."

"Weird." Sophie met her eyes. "You *sure* you didn't see a little weasely guy with slicked-back hair sneaking around?"

Kirsten smiled. "Strutting around with his black cowboy boots, thinking he's God's gift to women?"

Sophie giggled. "Carlo the Cocky Ghost."

"What a narcissist. His gun was probably way bigger than his peen." When their laughter died down, Kirsten added, "Not that I should complain. He's the only man I've had back to my apartment in a year."

Sophie cackled then exhaled. "Ah. Glad we can laugh about it six months later."

"*I'm* glad you live just one floor down from me now."

"And you're much closer to DePaul here too. How're you liking your new position, Dr. Holland?"

"It's fun working with college students again." She smiled. "Thanks for helping me get the job."

Sophie shrugged. "Hey, all I did was tell you about the opening at the counseling center. *You* did the rest."

"It's a great place to get my supervised hours before the licensing exam." She groaned. "I don't know how I'll ever pass that sucker. Is the exam really as bad as they say?"

Sophie took a sip of wine. "Not really. You just have to study their materials and take all the pretests, which are much harder than the real thing. You only need a seventy to pass, by the way."

"Didn't you score like a ninety?"

Sophie blushed, taking another sip. She'd scored a ninety-one.

"Whatever—I know you did well. No wonder Anita's so proud of you."

Sophie looked down. *Not that it matters after losing my license.*

"How's teaching going?" Kirsten's voice had softened.

"Good. And the research project's coming along well."

"I thought you hated research!"

Sophie tilted her head. "Well, it's not as fun as counseling, but I'll take what I can get."

"Well, *I* keep sticking my foot in my mouth, reminding you about your lost career. Thanks for the wine." She stood. "I should hang some pictures before it gets too late to bang on the walls."

Sophie stood and took her glass.

"Speaking of banging, when's McSailor getting home?" Kirsten's smirk was the size of Texas.

Sophie had to smile. "Crude. You're crude, roomie."

"And you love me for it."

"I *guess*." Sophie set the glasses on the counter and hugged her friend. "Grant should be home in a few hours." A yawn came on. "This wine's made me sleepy. I hope I can stay up and wait for him."

"Tell him I said hi. I'll be down to annoy you both tomorrow."

"Let us know if you need any help with that banging."

Kirsten laughed. "Will do. Later, tater!"

Lurching awake on the sofa, Sophie scanned the darkened apartment. All was quiet except for the rasp of her breaths as she tried to orient herself. Then there was the noise that must have stirred her from sleep—a scratching at the door. She heard a slight clink of metal, the crunch of a key jamming into the lock, and harsh cursing from the hallway.

Was a Barberi thug trying to break into the apartment? She was fully awake now.

Soundlessly she crept toward the front door, halting at the clang of keys dropping on the hallway carpet. More swearing ensued, and her heart leaped to her throat. She was almost to the peephole when a soft chuckle floated through the door. Relief flooded her. She'd recognize that sound anywhere.

Yanking open the door, she had to look down to find Grant crouching at her feet, groping for the fallen keys.

"What's your problem?" she hissed, trying not to disturb the neighbors.

It took him five seconds to look up at her with glassy eyes and a goofy grin. Clutching his keys, he woozily stood, swaying on his feet.

Her mouth popped open. "You're *drunk!*"

"*Hóla*, Bonita." His smile broadened.

So much for not waking the neighbors.

He fumbled for her hand and pressed her flush to his chest. "The door—" she cried, hearing it click shut and locked behind her.

"I have keys!" he proudly announced.

She rolled her eyes. "A lot of good they did you before."

He nuzzled her nose, smiling dreamily, and she caught a whiff of Eau de Tequila. The low hallway light reflected in his dazzling eyes, which shone with mischief.

Her eyes narrowed. "Why were you drinking? I thought—"

He interrupted her with a scorching kiss, which made her bones wobble.

He followed his masterpiece by cupping her breasts in his hands. He skimmed his lips across her jaw, softly licking the skin near her ear. "You thought?" he prompted. He wasn't slurring quite as badly as his first tequila bender.

"Hmmm…I thought…I thought…*what* was I thinking?"

He grabbed both her hands, and she found herself moving in step with him, ballroom dancing in the hallway. Naturally he started singing Sinatra in his deep baritone, crooning about the kick of champagne.

Feeling déjà vu from the bridge of the cruise ship, she closed her eyes and swayed along with him. *Here we go again.* She let him twirl her, and, despite her consternation, a giggle escaped.

He tucked her close, his hand resting on the small of her back, humming a tune about liquor not affecting him at all.

I beg to differ. "So who were you drinking with, naughty McSailor?"

"No one as sexy as you," he cooed in her ear. The humming resumed, and his hand traveled south, caressing her bottom.

A zing of energy sparked from his touch, and she attempted to stay focused. "And what did she look like?"

Halting the two-step, he looked into her eyes, a smile floating across his flushed face. "Jealous, Bonnie?"

"You better not be doing body shots with anyone else."

He seemed to find this amusing, snorting loudly. "I doubt my drinking buddies would let me get that close."

"Drinking budd*ies?*"

They turned to their left when a neighbor's door swung open, revealing a glaring woman with bed-head and an intricate neck tattoo peeking out from under her robe. "Could you take it *inside?*"

He maintained his jovial grin, letting go of Sophie and approaching 7B. "Aw, don't be mad, ma'am." He kneeled and gently took the woman's hand, then planted a kiss. "I do apologize—jusss having a good time out here on the dance floor."

Sophie watched the woman teeter on the edge of fear and enthrallment, here in the hallway at two a.m.

"I'm sorry for all the noise," Sophie said, stepping closer. "He had a bit too much to drink, and it's time for me to put him to bed."

"I like the sound of *that*," Grant said, looking up at her but still holding the woman's hand. "But I was jusss about to offer our lovely neighbor here a dance."

The woman blushed. "Um, I have to go to work kind of early…"

"Mick," Sophie hissed, tugging at his arm. "Time for bed, honey."

Hearing his undercover name seemed to compel him to action. He stood, darted nervous glances down the hallway, then aimed a beseeching look at the woman. "I apologize, ma'am."

Relieved he'd returned to his senses, Sophie pulled him toward their door. "Sorry for waking you up!"

The woman watched her reach into Grant's pocket for the keys. "Quite a charmer you got there."

"Don't I know it," she said, smiling as she unlocked the door. She pushed the charmer into their apartment and watched him weave his way to the sofa. She supposed she should be angry at him for flirting with their neighbor, but she loved his completely carefree demeanor. It was so uncharacteristic.

He wiggled out of his long navy coat and tossed it toward a kitchen chair, missing his mark by a full coat-length. Very un-Grant-like. Not bothering to pick it up, he continued stumbling toward the sofa, humming Sinatra. Definitely not like Grant. When he began unbuttoning his shirt, she held her breath. Slowly his sculpted back came into view, his ropy muscles lean and taut. With a body like that, he had no business being so modest all the time, and she reveled in the show. He wadded up the shirt and tossed it to the corner.

"Whoa, sailor!" She waltzed into the room, picking up his coat and laying it neatly on the chair. "You taking off your pants too?"

He spun around and placed a finger on his lips with an exaggerated "Shh! They'll hear."

"*Who* will hear?"

"The po-po." He gestured to the discarded shirt. "They'll be listening for sssure tonight."

She frowned. The feds were okay with him turning off the mic when he was safe at home, but apparently manipulating the small recorder was beyond his skill set at the moment.

She reached up to trace the alcove of muscle above his collarbone. "Why are they definitely listening tonight?"

He shivered from her touch, then latched onto her hips and slid his cool hands beneath her fuzzy pajama shirt.

Squeaking, she jumped. "Your hands are *freezing!*"

"Bonnie, it's cold outside," he sang, abruptly sliding his hands up under her arms and lifting her like a pairs figure skater.

From above she watched his shoulder muscles flex and ripple, holding her weight. Her eyes locked on his as he slowly lowered her, and her legs snaked around his waist. She crossed her ankles behind his back, sat in his cupped hands, and ran her fingertips across his angular shoulder blades. "Let's warm up, then."

His mouth met hers, sucking and kissing, a contact buzz flowing from his mouth to her brain. He carried her into the bedroom, keeping his lips molded to hers, and gently set her on the bed. He frowned, eyeing her fleece pajamas. "I miss summer."

"You miss warm weather?"

He shook his head. "I miss easy-access silk nighties."

She giggled. "Here, I'll help you, drunk boy." Her pajama top was history in seconds, and she scowled at him just standing there. "Work on your pants, McSailor."

His eyes focused. "Yes, ma'am."

They didn't stay naked for long before they were both under the covers, pressing skin on skin to warm themselves.

His fingertips skimmed her back. "I wanted to do this the *first* time I got drunk on tequila."

"Me too." She smiled. "But I didn't want to take advantage of you in your inebriated state."

"You can ravage me any time, you vixen."

She giggled. "So you're not too drunk to give consent?"

"Lay your hands on me, Bonnie."

"Yes, sir."

❧

Lying on her back a little while later, Sophie searched for the right words. "Well, that was, um…unfortunate."

He groaned, rolling over and turning away from her.

"Grant, it happens sometimes."

He turned back to face her, indignant. "Not to *me!*"

She tried not to laugh. "I guess you've never done it drunk before."

His lips parted with wonder. "Ohhh." His head fell back on the pillow. "So that's the problem. *Phew.*"

She snuggled up to him, kissing his forehead. "Don't worry, your manhood's still intact. I won't tell anyone."

"Even your girlfriends? I know how you ladies talk."

"Not even Kirsten."

"Oh, Kirsten. Sorry I wasn't home tonight to help. Did she get moved in okay?"

"Yes. So are you going to tell me who you were drinking with?"

He bolted upright. "The Russians!"

"*What?*"

"Crap, I gotta call in. They're probably furious with me." He leaped out of bed and yanked open the bureau drawer, hunting for the hidden cell phone. When he located it, his face fell. "Five missed calls. It was on vibrate. Oh, no."

She watched him, infected by his contagious anxiety.

He dialed the number and closed his eyes, waiting for the call to connect. "It's me."

"*What was the first thing you were supposed to do when you made contact?*"

She heard Lucas Bounter's shouted words through the phone ten feet away, and she grabbed her robe to give Grant some privacy. She left him standing in the bedroom naked. "Call in, sir," he said as she closed the door.

A few minutes later she leaned on the kitchen counter, stirring sugar into two cups of herbal tea, when Grant emerged from the bedroom. A worried look had replaced his exuberance.

"Bounter didn't sound happy."

"He's not." Grant had pulled on some navy blue sweatpants. "I messed up big time."

She set the steaming cups on their small dining table. "What do you mean? Isn't it a good thing you made contact?"

He hunted for his discarded shirt, locating the crumpled ball near the corner. He set the button microphone to the off position and slid into the shirt, buttoning it as he joined her at the table. "They didn't expect it to happen like that…the Russians inviting me back to their place right after meeting me."

Her spoon paused mid-stir.

"I'm fine, Sophie."

"Is he mad you went with them?"

"No. Everything went like clockwork at first. I hinted around I was looking for a game, and they took me to West Town for poker. I somehow won the first hand but then got in over my head, just like we planned."

"How much did you lose?"

He shrugged. "Five grand…and then some."

"I thought you only carried five thousand."

"The plan was to get in debt to them from the start."

Her heart thumped, and she scampered off her chair. "But they could've killed you!"

"Relax, Soph. The mic has GPS, and the feds were right outside, listening in." He reached for her hand, but she began to pace.

"They were right outside…so they could collect your body after you were killed?"

"It's not like that. The Russians need me."

She paused, turning to him. "Why?"

"I shouldn't go into the specifics." He took a sip of tea, and she sensed he was stalling. "The less you know, the better."

"I don't like this." She resumed treading her carpet track.

His voice sounded nervous. "Come sit down. I'm getting dizzy watching you pace like that."

"The *tequila's* making you dizzy. I thought you weren't going to drink again."

"I didn't have a choice." She turned to look at him, wondering what he meant. "I can get away with water at Capone's, but there's no way I can refuse drinks from a host."

She eyed him. "You don't seem all that drunk right now."

"Getting chewed out by the FBI sobered me up right quick. Besides me not calling in right away, they're not too impressed with me."

Her hands rested on her hips. "What'd you do this time?"

"Well, for one, I shouldn't have woken up Tattoo. Shouldn't draw attention to myself like that."

She squinted. "Who's Tattoo?"

"The neighbor?"

"Oh! Seven-B." She snickered.

"At least you remembered to call me Mick. Agent Bounter said to tell you good job. You did much better than I did."

"What's that mean?"

Biting his lower lip, he admitted, "I let the Russians drive me home."

"Did they hurt you?" She approached the table and sank into her chair.

He shook his head.

"Why would he care about them driving you home then?"

He met her gaze. "Because now they know where I live." He winced. "I was supposed to relocate before that happened."

"Relocate? You were going to move *out?*"

"I had to. I can't risk them finding you. It's why I asked Kirsten to move in, to be close to you when I left. Agent Bounter has a place set up in Streeterville for me."

"You never told me that! No, Grant. You live with me—I won't let you go."

"Relax. He told me I'm not moving out now."

"Good."

He rubbed his cropped hair, looking down and sighing loudly. Eventually he looked back up at her, his eyes full of guilt. "I'm not moving now." There was a pregnant pause. "*You* are."

"*What?*" She shot up out of the chair.

This time Grant got up too, taking her hand. "I'm sorry, Sophie, but I can't have you anywhere near them."

She felt her face get hot, and she yanked her hand free. "There's no way I'm moving! You're going out there every night, risking your life, and I won't get to see you when you get home? Make sure you're okay? No. That's not happening."

"It's not like you have a say in this. The FBI will make you move."

"Like hell they will! They can't make me do anything…*I* don't work for them."

"Bonnie, please." He gently clasped her arms to stop her wild gesturing. "You know what happened when the Mafia got to you last time." His fingers grazed over the bullet wound above her left elbow. "I'll never forgive myself for that. Let me get you out of the next bullet's path. I'm begging you. I'd take a bullet for you, but please, don't take another for me. I can't deal with it."

She exhaled. "Did you know we'd have to live apart all along?"

"I had a pretty good idea. I asked them how we could keep you out of the action this time."

"Do you think it would've been a good idea to communicate this to me earlier?"

He looked down. "You're right. Dr. Hayes wouldn't be happy with my communication skills right now." He looked back up at her. "I'm sorry."

"So *I'm* supposed to live in this Streeterville hovel now?"

"Streeterville's hardly a slum, princess." Her glare ended his teasing. "Actually, they'll probably use it for another undercover agent since it's all set up with surveillance. I was thinking you could move in with your dad for a while?"

Her mouth dropped open, and her pacing resumed. After a few seconds, she said, "Okay, assuming I could deal with my dad better this time around, what am I supposed to tell him about me moving out? We already agreed he'd go ballistic if he knows you're around Mafia again."

"That's a tough one." He rubbed his jaw.

"I can't tell him we're fighting, or he might hate you again."

"Yeah. Don't tell him that." His fingers tapped on the back of a chair. "Hey, what if you told him we were trying to be chaste before our wedding? That you're saving yourself?"

She cocked one eyebrow. "That ship has sailed, McSailor."

"C'mon, he wouldn't believe you?"

"No way." She braced herself. "Not after…the sentencing. All the sordid details of my sex life came out then."

"Oh."

His grip on the chair appeared to tighten, and he held still for several moments. Finally, he approached her and wrapped her in a hug. "I'm so sorry you had to go through that."

She melted in his arms, grateful for how far they'd come since the summer. Grant hugging her instead of yelling made her trust him even more. It also made her feel guilty for referencing her past with Logan in the first place.

"*I* know!" She looked up at him. "I'll live with Kirsten!"

"No." He stepped out of their hug. "You can't be in this building."

She ignored him. "That way you can sneak upstairs when you get home at night."

"Sophie, no! It's not safe."

"Grant, you better figure out real quick that you're not telling me what to do in this marriage."

"Why are you being so stubborn? This is for your own good! I *won't* place you in that kind of danger again!"

"So it's safe for Kirsten to live in this building, but not me?"

He paused, and she knew she had him. "It's different. Besides, I thought Kirsten got a one-bedroom place like ours."

"She did. I'd have to use the sofa again."

"I feel guilty enough as it is, and now you won't even get a bed?"

She smiled coyly. "It'd be worth it, if you came up and slept with me."

"On a *sofa?*"

"It'd be cramped, but I doubt we'd be doing much sleeping." She glanced at his sweatpants. "That is if you can ever get it up again."

He gasped. "That was below the belt!"

She giggled, drawing closer. "Yes, it was." Reaching down, she slid her hand in his pants and grasped his length. "Is the tequila still bothering you?"

"No, but you are." His breath hitched.

"So you'll let me live with Kirsten then?"

He shivered. "I'll have to call…Agent Bounter…make sure it's okay."

She leaned in closer, her breasts pressing against his chest, grinning. "And I'll make sure Kirsten's okay with it too."

"Mmm." He gave her a measured stare. "I know what you're doing, Bonnie." One hand held her shoulder, the other brushed through her hair.

She nodded. "I shouldn't be manipulating you like this, but it's fun."

He chuckled.

"Sounds like we have a lot to discuss at our next session."

Grant tensed and pulled back. "Uh, I can't go to therapy anymore."

"You can't?"

"It's not safe. They're going to be on me now, checking me out. I can't be seen with you or Ben. I'm sorry. It will only be for a little while."

"Grant, if you get hurt…"

"I'll be careful."

Her mouth set into a determined line. "I'll help you next time they make you drink."

"How?"

"We'll build your tolerance. Tequila."

His smile was hopeful. "Body shots?"

6. Contempt

"Open on twenty!" the guard barked to the control booth. Enzo Barberi stood in the hallway and watched the bars of his cell slide open.

Squinting against the harsh fluorescent lighting, he forced his head up as the guard unlocked his handcuffs. Without a word, Enzo stepped inside the cell.

"Close on twenty!"

He heard the clang of the bars behind him. This cell was brighter than the one in solitary confinement, but it was still a cage. A human cage. A cage he could've escaped from if not for the FBI busting up his beautiful plan.

Setting aside his muscle magazine, Jewels Monroe looked up from the bottom bunk. "You don't look so good, boss."

"Fuck you." Enzo went to the filthy sink and splashed some water on his face, then peered up into the cloudy reflective surface passing as a mirror. Hard contours lined his ashen face, and his eyes had sunk into his skull. "You try staying in the hole for two months, see how you look." He patted his face with a stained gray towel.

Jewels slowly stood, waiting until he looked him in the eye. "Want me to start with old or new business?" he asked in a low voice.

"I've been holed away for ages, Jewels. What do *you* think?"

He cleared his throat. "There's a fresh fish now claiming Gurnee as his address. Just like you predicted after things got busted up."

"Only one, huh?" Enzo's jaw clenched. "A fat fish or a tall fish?"

"Tall. And scared shitless."

"You got it all set up?"

Jewels nodded.

He smiled. *Time to pay, Tank.* Then his smile vanished as he remembered the feel of the soft leather belt folded in his hands, watching Logan tuck a trembling Grant behind him, a defiant set to his mouth. Logan had been one brave boy.

His face hardened. *Time to pay for killing my son.*

❧

Pungent chlorine assaulted Sophie as she entered the windowless high school pool. She closed her eyes and inhaled a big whiff of the familiar smell. Memories of summer league swim meets tumbled through her mind: cheering parents, warm nacho cheese on crunchy tortilla chips, bouncing behind the starting block as she watched her teammate race the girl in the next lane. She smiled.

"Hey, Sophie!"

She opened her eyes to find Ben waving at her from one of the lanes. "'Bout time you got here! I was starting to think you chickened out."

Tucking her towel more tightly around her waist, she approached the pool edge. "Sorry, a student needed to talk to me after class."

"Where's Uncle Grant?"

She hesitated. "He couldn't make it. Um…I'll tell you more later."

Ben did not look happy.

"I know practice is over already because I saw the girls in the locker room, but where's your coach? He knows you're doing this, right?"

He gestured to an office off the pool deck. "He knows. He's in there."

"Good." *The fewer witnesses, the better.*

"He said he could only stay about twenty minutes for our race."

Her heart fluttered. "But I need to warm up!"

"Better get busy then." He grinned and swam down to the other end of the pool, where he hopped out and mounted the block to practice his starts.

After she tucked her long hair into a swim cap, she strapped on her goggles and curled her toes over the edge of the pool. She fiddled with the straps of her black racing suit, then took a deep breath and jumped in. She gasped at the cold water. This wasn't some overheated recreation pool with old ladies doing sidestroke. This was Illinois high school swimming, and she'd better get focused fast.

Five minutes later, her labored breathing after just one length of butterfly alarmed her. The soothing water welcomed her back to her childhood sport, but her endurance and form were no longer a twelve-year-old's. She wished she could back out of this harebrained duel. Why did she have to be so competitive?

Hoping to practice a start or two before their race, she dragged herself out of the pool and noticed Ben holding back laughter. "What?"

"You're so toast."

She perched a hand on her hip. "Nobody's ever won a race during warm-up."

He cackled as she stretched her arms in an attempt to shake the jelly feeling from her muscles. She joined her hands behind her back and leaned over, gracefully contorting herself into a deep stretch. When she came back up, he gaped.

"You're super flexible!"

She gave him a sly smile before diving in.

Just after she surfaced, the hallway door squeaked, and she turned to find her father, Will Taylor, looking anxiously around the pool.

His face fell. "Did I miss the race?"

"Dad! What're you doing here?"

"My daughter back in the pool? I had to see this for myself."

She groaned, and Ben gave her a puzzled look. "I told him about our little race when I went home to get my swimsuit." She turned to her father. "But I never expected you to show up! I'm nervous enough as it is."

He shrugged out of his thick coat. "Jeez, it's a sauna in here. Sophie, relax. I'm done being Psycho Swim Dad. I'll watch Ben swim. I've been hearing about his talent."

Ben tilted his head as he studied her father. He seemed a bit guarded—suddenly unsure and shy.

"So let's get going!" her father boomed, clapping his hands together. "I'll be Mr. Starter."

She rolled her eyes. As Ben took a few jumps on the pool deck, she felt her heart rate increase. Four lengths of butterfly stretched ahead of her like an endless dissertation. "Hey, Ben, how about we race the fifty 'fly instead?"

"Nice try, Sophie. We agreed on a hundred, and that's what we'll do."

"You tell her, Ben." Her father nodded.

"Great. *So* glad you made it, Dad."

He ignored her and adopted a stern stance. "Swimmers, step up."

Ben hopped on the lane-three block, and she climbed up the block for lane four. Pulling in a deep breath, she felt butterflies flitter in her stomach. Win or lose, this would be over in about a minute. She hoped.

"Take your mark…" They crouched in the starting position. "Hup!"

She streamlined off the start, kicking as hard as she could, and sensed she was about even with Ben at the first turn. But it got increasingly ugly after that, and he shot ahead. She barely finished the race.

Panting after she finally surfaced, she draped one arm along the gutter and waited for her double vision to clear. When she was able to speak, she murmured, "Good job, Ben."

The jerk wasn't breathing hard at all. "Thanks. You're just out of shape, you know."

"No shit, Sherlock."

Her father smirked. "Well, I guess you don't need me to tell you who won." When she looked up at him, his eyes danced. "A for effort, Soph."

"*What?* Dad, is that you? I totally died on the last lap!"

"But Ben's right," he said. "You're just a little out of shape. I think it's incredible you even tried this—it took a lot of gumption to get back in the pool after so many years."

She blinked up at him. One arm still hung off the gutter.

"And *you*," her father said, turning to Ben, who now stood waterlogged on deck. "You're really coming along! Sophie told me you've been working on your endurance, and look how strong you finished."

A blush crept up Ben's neck. He seemed to bask in the glow of paternal kind words.

Somehow able to pull herself out despite her shaky arms, she walked over and squeezed his shoulder. "I'm impressed, Ben. Even if I'd been in better shape, you still would've crushed me."

He shrugged. "That's a testable hypothesis."

She gawked at him. "I see you're listening well in science class." She noticed a scruffy blond man coming toward them.

"Who are your guests?" he asked, looking at Ben.

He blushed. "Uh, this is Sophie, and, um, her dad, uh, Mr. Taylor."

The coach shook her father's hand and smiled at Sophie. "Bob Brooks. You're Ben's aunt, right?"

"I will be, once I marry his uncle this summer."

"Coach, you're doing a great job with Ben," her dad said. "He's only been swimming a few months, and he just kicked my daughter's butt."

"Thanks again, Dad." She looked at Bob. "In my defense, I haven't been in a pool since I was twelve."

Bob's eyes swept down her body. "Which was what, six or seven years ago?"

Her father's eyebrows shot up.

"Hardly." Ben snorted. "She's, like, *old!*"

She glared at him. "I'm only thirty, Benjamin."

"Why don't you join us for practice now and then?" Bob asked.

"Yeah!" Ben nodded. "Then we could have a rematch."

She rubbed her collarbone. "I…I'll think about it." She glanced at her father, surprised he hadn't jumped in to egg her on.

He gave a noncommittal smile. "C'mon. I'll drive you two home."

Twenty minutes later, her father pulled his Mercedes to a stop in front of Ashley's apartment. "Here you go, Ben."

She gathered her bags at her feet. "Dad, I'm getting out here too. I need to talk to Ben."

He shook his head. "How will you get home?"

"The same way I got to the pool. A taxi."

"That sounds expensive."

She sighed. "Not as expensive as parking downtown." Before she knew it, he'd pressed two hundreds into her hand. "Dad! I'm working now, you know."

"Just take it, Sophie."

Ben's hand snaked over into the front seat. "Hey, if you're just handing out money, I'll take some."

"Nice try." She pocketed the cash. "Thanks for the ride, Dad." She kissed him on the cheek before exiting the car.

Relief washed over her as her father pulled away. She was glad not to risk him wanting to come up to her apartment when he dropped her off. She still hadn't figured out how to explain her new address at Casa Kirsten.

"Cool." Ben crunched the frayed ends of his wet hair. "My hair's frozen."

A shiver bloomed up her spine as the wind whipped down the sidewalk. "Let's get inside!"

When he let them in with his key, she noticed Ashley wasn't there. He cranked the thermostat and turned on a couple of lamps.

"That must be tough not to have your mom home at night." She followed him over to the sitting area.

"It gets her off my back."

"Oh. Are things still tense between you?"

He shrugged. "I guess they're a little better. She still gets on my case, though."

"What do you usually do for dinner?"

"There's a frozen pizza in there or something."

"How about I make you dinner?"

"Aren't you gonna eat with Uncle Grant?"

"He's at work too. C'mon, I'll make you something. Loser has to pay up."

He chuckled. "That's right, *loser*. Hope you cook faster than you swim."

"Ouch." She stood and went to the tiny kitchen. "Better watch out, or I'll spit in your food, sore winner."

He came over to sit at the bar as she rummaged through the cabinets. Her head peered around the cabinet door. "Pasta?"

"Sure."

She set a glass of water in front of him, along with some pretzels and peanut butter. "To tide you over until dinner's ready."

"Awesome. How'd you know I was starved?"

She smiled. "I used to be a swimmer, remember?" Grabbing a pretzel, she scooped some peanut butter and popped it in her mouth. Then she set a pot of water on the stove to boil and a skillet with olive oil heating up on another burner. "Grant wanted me to tell you he's sorry he couldn't make it today."

"Is he okay?"

"Yes." *I hope.* "He'll call you when he can, but I'm supposed to give you the heads up he won't be around for a while."

"Why not?" He spoke with his mouth full.

She paused her rummaging in the fridge. "How much do you know about his job?"

"The singing? He sings at Capone's."

"Anything else?"

He munched on a pretzel. "Oh, yeah! The FBI thing. That black dude wanted him to work for them."

"That's right," she said. "Grant's still singing, but he's also work-ing undercover now."

"That shit sounds serious."

She grinned as a few crumbs spewed from his mouth. "It is. So for now you can't come over and visit. Grant shouldn't be seen with you, just in case they're tailing him."

"Whoa. Who *are* they?"

"I'm not supposed to say." She halted her tomato chopping. "It could be dangerous for you."

"C'mon. Why would it matter if I knew? I won't be near Uncle Grant."

"Grant said I shouldn't tell anyone."

"But I'm not just *anyone!* Now you're stressing me out. It's not people my dad associated with, is it?"

She looked up into his worried eyes. "Uh-uh. I'm not going down this road again."

"What do you mean?"

"Last time we had a little chat while I cooked, it turned out to be a disaster."

His gaze lowered. "I won't run away again, I promise. Dr. Hunter says you can't just run away from your problems."

He looked so cute. She wanted to give him a hug.

"I was really upset," he admitted. "But now, to tell you the truth, I'm kind of glad I know about you and my dad."

She studied him. "Why is that?"

"It's good he had someone to talk to, before he died. I bet you were…nice to him."

She felt tears prick the back of her eyes. "I'm really grateful I met your father, Ben. He was a good man." Tomato chopping resumed. "Did you get to see him, um, before…before he died?"

"Yeah. We got in an argument."

"That's rough. Do you want to talk about it?"

A quick headshake. "So, me knowing about you and my dad didn't turn out so bad. You sure you can't tell me about who Uncle Grant's working with?"

"The truth shall set you free, huh?" She turned to the stove. "They're all the way over in West Town, so it shouldn't affect us much." Garlic sizzled in olive oil. "Don't worry about it. Grant assured me he'd be okay."

"Why does he have to do this?" His voice trembled.

She sighed. "I asked him the same thing. He said he's got to make up for what his family has done, for the hurt they've caused. I don't really get it, but Hunter told me to get on board because I can't change Grant."

"That sucks."

She nodded.

He was quiet for a moment as she sautéed some fresh spinach in the oil. "Too bad Grant didn't get to see our race. You better tell him the truth about your epic fail."

"Of course I'll tell the truth."

"And I'll have to let Dr. Hunter know his strategy worked."

She spun around from the stove. "What do you mean?"

He smirked. "Hunter told me you were nervous, and he said to act super-confident to try to psych you out."

A rosy blush heated her face.

"It worked, didn't it?"

"That's it. We're *definitely* having a rematch."

Ricker Mullens watched Tank from across the changing room adjoining the showers. Despite the other cons milling about in various states of undress, his gaze zeroed in on Tank's massive chest as he toweled off, then moved to his crotch as the tall hunk of meat pulled on his worn, navy blue prison pants. Tank seemed on edge—his eyes darted around the changing room—and his vulnerability made Ricker want him even more. The only block to taking Tank right there was the stern CO leaning against the wall.

One of his blond minions, Steven, sidled up and followed his gaze to Tank's chiseled body.

"Whatcha waiting for, sir?"

"For the fucking CO to leave," he growled. "Don't want to screw up anything with my exit from this hellhole."

Steven grinned. "How many more days you got in here?"

He glared at him, stepping closer. "None of your business."

Steven dropped his head, turned, and crept away.

Ricker's eyes tapered into slits. He'd punish the boy for his insolence later. For now, he had to figure out how to tap Tank's bulbous, muscular ass in the next two weeks, before the DOC gave him his sweet release.

The CO stared at a part of the room blocked from Ricker's view and gave a curt nod, seeming to communicate with somebody hidden behind the wall. "*Move* it, girls!" he bellowed.

Ricker cocked his head as Tank's frantic fingers laced up his work boots. The thrill of violence electrified the steamy air. *Something is off.* When the CO barked at Ricker to get moving, he stepped into the flow of inmates following the CO toward the cellblock. And when the CO looked away, he left the procession of cons and crouched in a dark corner, hidden from Tank by a table holding towels.

Hustling to join the cattle call, Tank grabbed his thermal shirt and drew it over his head just as Enzo Barberi rounded the corner holding a homemade shank. Ricker's mouth dropped open as Barberi plunged the knife into Tank's chest while he was still blinded by his shirt. A smothered cry leaked out from beneath the material.

One of Barberi's goons—he didn't know his name—pulled Tank's arm behind his back while Jewels Monroe yanked the shirt off Tank's head and brought him face-to-face with Barberi. He felt the heat of fury tighten in his chest as he watched the breach of his territory. Tank was *his*, damn it! But he'd never openly challenge Enzo Barberi. And he couldn't leave the scene now…The smell of fresh blood pleased him too much.

Tank looked down and must have seen the shank under his collarbone, its handle clutched by Barberi. Now both goons gripped Tank's shoulders, twisting his wrists behind his back. Tank gasped and fell to his knees, and Ricker guessed Barberi had shoved him with the shank, forcing the behemoth down. He watched Tank struggle, but every thrashing move seemed to get him another inch of blade in his shoulder. He finally stilled.

"Don't bother to yell," Barberi hissed, leaning in. "CO's gone. No one to hear me *cut* you."

Oooh. Ricker grinned and wished he had some popcorn for the "Shank Tank" show.

Serene coldness settled across Barberi's face. "You think you could get away with killing my son?"

Tank's eyes widened. "I didn't kill Logan!"

Who's Logan? That's not a nickname for Grant, right? Wait, Grant wasn't killed, was he? His heart hammered.

"Sure you didn't." Jewels grinned as he held Tank down. "And I'll be innocent of your murder too."

Tank's voice shook. "I'm no different from Jewels in this scenario. I was just holding him down. Carlo had the knife. I was just following orders!"

Barberi breathed out of his nose, sounding disgusted. "The only orders you follow are mine. And I order you to go to hell." He thrust the knife in deeper.

Tank groaned. "*Grant* told you I held down Logan, didn't he?"

His ears perked up, and he felt a stirring below his belt. Baby boy Grant was still alive.

"Why the fuck would you say that?" Barberi demanded. "Grant's got nothing to do with this. He botched that exchange just as bad as you and Meat did."

Ricker wondered who this "Meat" person was. He liked his name. But hearing Madsen's name was what really got his cock talking.

Tank panted.

"Now," Barberi said. "You tell me where the feds put Meat."

"Don't know," Tank gasped. "I think he sang. Witness protection?"

Tank cried out. Barberi must have twisted the knife. Ricker wondered if the blade had nicked Tank's heart.

"Meat wouldn't say a word. Grant's the one who sang—I know it." Barberi leaned in closer. "Fucking tell me now where they put Meat. No way the feds put Grant *and* Mario under protection. And my contacts can't find either in the system."

"Don't think Grant ever went down for this. Only me and Meat. Never saw Grant after the bust."

Barberi seemed to loosen his pressure on the knife, and Tank slumped.

"Grant wasn't arrested?" Barberi looked up at Jewels, ignoring Tank's squirms. "Why wouldn't he be arrested?"

Ricker strained to hear the exchange. He didn't exactly follow what was going on, but there was a thrumming tension in the air.

"He was *in* on it!" Tank suddenly blurted. He nodded with the excitement of discovery. "Grant was working with the feds."

Barberi jammed the knife in further, and Tank's complexion went the color of the peeling white paint on the wall behind him. "You're accusing my *son* of double crossing me?"

"The numbers," Tank panted. "Grant called out the apartment numbers we passed in Marina City." His voice faded. "I wondered why he said the numbers out loud. I bet he was wired."

Barberi froze for a moment, then began nodding. "Son of a bitch. *Grant's* the one who led the feds to Jovanovich."

He yanked the blade out, unleashing a torrent of blood. The shank clattered to the concrete floor. "Take care of this," Barberi spat as he looked around the room.

Time to go. As Ricker stole away, his mind whirred with images of Madsen walking around as a free man—his graceful, loping stride and crystal blue, vulnerable eyes…Barberi's son…Barberi's betrayer? This information *had* to be of some use when he got to the outside.

He hustled to catch up to the other cons marching back to their cells and looked down to see his cock straining against his pants. A smile spread across his lips. "Release is coming," he whispered. "Soon."

7. Pro/Con

"So, for her practice start, Sophie dives waaay down, like, scraping the bottom." Ben snickered, remembering her amateur form.

Dr. Hunter smiled. "Hey, cut her some slack. She's out of shape, right?"

"Whatever." He held up his hand. "Her dad started the race for us. I was a little nervous when she kept up with me at first, but then the piano dropped."

"The piano?" Dr. Hunter asked.

"It's a piano swim when it feels like you're carrying a baby grand on your back. Believe me, I've had a few of those, especially my first meet. She barely finished the race."

"Sounds like you managed your anxiety well."

"Yeah. I kept telling myself 'She's old and out of shape,' like you said I should."

Dr. Hunter laughed. "Please don't tell her I said that. I'll be in a lot of trouble."

"Why do girls care about getting older?" Ben wondered. "I can't *wait* till I'm older."

"It's not only women who worry about aging." Dr. Hunter crossed his legs.

"Really? You care about getting old?"

Dr. Hunter shrugged. "There's a lot of pressure to look young in our society. A lot of ageism out there. My partner's a plastic surgeon, I should know."

"That's cool. Your…partner? He's a dude, right?"

"Yes, he is." Dr. Hunter's smirk faded. "How do you feel about that?"

"Hey, man, it's cool. There're some guys at school who are gay. Some chicks too. No biggie. Uh, the dude—your partner—he must be pretty rich, huh?"

"He does pull in a nice salary, yes. But he went to school for a long time to get it."

Ben tapped his fingers on the worn knee of his jeans. "You must make a lot of cashish too. Sophie said she went to grad school for forever."

"Well, psychologists certainly make less money than surgeons."

"Oh."

"You sound disappointed?"

"I don't know. I thought it'd be kind of a cool job." He looked around the office, stopping at the large aquarium. "But I couldn't listen to people bitch about their problems all day long. How do you do it?"

"When you know venting helps people feel better, it's not so bad. There's a lot more to it than that too. It can be very rewarding."

"Maybe. Or I could go into construction, like Sophie's dad. He's loaded."

"The sky's the limit, Ben. Your future career is out there, just waiting for you to seize it. You're smart, and you're responsible."

Ben felt his cheeks warm, and he focused even more intently on the clownfish darting around the anemone.

"Do you believe that about yourself, Ben? That you're smart and capable?"

Yeah, right. "How can I be smart? My dad was just a dumb criminal. And my mom's not so bright either. There was way too much chlorine in her gene pool."

"Swimmer humor." Dr. Hunter shook his head. "I don't know your mom well, but your dad's side of the family seems quite intelligent. Look at the plan Enzo cooked up to get out of prison, and look how Grant figured it all out. He kept one step ahead of your grandfather. That definitely took some smarts."

"I guess. All I know is I sure don't want to work in some stupid restaurant, like my mom does."

Dr. Hunter nodded. "You said she has to work a lot of evenings?"

"Yeah. I keep asking her to get a dog to keep me company, but she won't. She says *she'll* end up taking care of the dog, even though I promise I'll do it."

"It would probably be hard to keep a dog in your apartment too."

He sighed. "It'd have to be some lame-ass small dog, but at least it'd be a dog."

"Hmm." Dr. Hunter paused. "What if you tried to negotiate with your mom? Maybe the dog could be a reward for a job well done. Say you keep up the negative drug screens for the next three months, and then she gets you a dog."

"*Three* months? How 'bout one month?"

"You're the one negotiating this deal, kid."

"Sweet."

Dr. Hunter smiled. "But you'll have to get your mom to go for it. And I bet you'll find she's smarter than you think."

"She's not a few fries short of a Happy Meal?"

"Correct. And I bet she wouldn't lose a debate with a doorknob either."

Ben shook his head. "You're bad!"

"*You* started it." After a moment Dr. Hunter offered, "The way I see it, your marijuana pro/con list just got a bit longer."

"Huh?"

Dr. Hunter leaned forward. "Remember when I had you write down the pros and cons of smoking pot? We just talked about a few more cons today. One, pot can slow you down in the pool. I bet you swam faster and beat Sophie partly because you haven't been smoking."

He shook his head. "Pot doesn't affect swimming."

"Really?" Dr. Hunter cocked his eyebrow. "Show me some research attesting to that, and I'll consider it. Otherwise I'll assume your stoner friends tried to convince you to believe that."

Ben smirked.

"Two, pot can interfere with your career plans. If you smoke, you have to worry about testing positive at work. And you won't do as well in school, which will limit your career opportunities."

Ben laced his arms across his chest.

"And three, smoking prevents you from negotiating a deal with your mom to get that dog you want." Dr. Hunter paused. "Now, tell me what pros you'd add to the list. Are you craving marijuana?"

Unfolding his arms, he stared at Dr. Hunter. *Could he be trusted?* Finally, he admitted, "Sometimes."

"Where would you get the money to buy pot?"

"Sophie gave me a hundred bucks the other night."

"I'll have to tell her to stop doing that." When Ben's mouth dropped open in protest, Dr. Hunter laughed. "Relax, I'm just kidding. So, when do you get cravings?"

"Dunno. Just sometimes."

"You can do better than that."

Ben glared, tapping his knee again. "There's…there's this girl."

"Ah." Dr. Hunter sat back in his chair. "Go on."

"Why? It's, like, embarrassing."

"If she's involved in making you want to use again, I want to hear about her. She sounds important."

"She's not so important." He looked down.

"How'd you meet her?"

"She's on the girls' team."

"A swimmer. Makes sense. You spend a lot of time together. What's she like?"

"She's got long, brown hair—it's really pretty." He grinned at Dr. Hunter. "And she's got a nice rack."

Dr. Hunter rolled his eyes. "What's her *personality* like?"

"Nice. She's really nice. She's fast, but she doesn't make fun of people who just started swimming, like me. Her times are way faster than mine, but she still talks to me."

"She sounds kind-hearted. And you're attracted to her too. So what's the problem?"

He squirmed. "My boy Dylan got me to admit I was into her, then he went behind my back and kind of asked her if she liked me. He said she got all nervous, and she told him she liked me as a friend. Then he asked her if she liked me as more than a friend. Like, if we could start talking. But she said she wasn't interested."

"How disappointing. Did she say why?"

He stared at the floor. "She said she didn't want to date a pothead."

"That sounds very hurtful." Dr. Hunter's voice was gentle. "Especially since it's not true."

He looked up.

"Just because you smoked pot doesn't make you a pothead. That's like calling myself a failure just because I've failed a time or two. Slapping a negative label on yourself based on isolated behaviors doesn't make it true."

"You've failed?"

"Of course. Many times."

"How?"

Dr. Hunter hesitated. "I made some choices I regret, when I first came out. It was a wild time in my life…I did some dumb things. Even now, when I argue with Bradley—uh, the 'dude' as you call him—I have trouble keeping my cool. Sometimes I say mean things."

"But that's nothing. Everybody does that." He fidgeted. "I've done much worse."

"You're saying your failures are bigger than mine? I don't believe that."

"Believe it." He hated the way his voice shook.

"Ben, I think you have something on your mind…something you want to share, but you're nervous to tell me. Am I right?"

He squirmed. "I guess."

"What's making it hard to tell me?"

He looked at his feet. "You'll tell my mom."

"Hmm. Not necessarily."

"Then you'll turn me in."

When Dr. Hunter didn't respond, Ben peeked up at him.

"This is about a crime?"

"Yeah." Ben's head dropped again. "I'm a criminal."

"I can't call the police unless you or someone else is in imminent danger." Dr. Hunter paused. "Sometimes you remind me so much of Grant, the way you get down on yourself. It's okay, Ben. It's all right to tell me. I know how frightening it is to talk about some things, but I sense you need to let it out. The truth shall set you free."

He breathed out through his teeth. "That's the same thing Sophie said."

"She's a smart woman, quoting me." Dr. Hunter grinned.

He fiddled with the shoelaces on his black sneakers. "You know… you know how you asked me about the last time I saw my dad?"

"At the video game place. Logan showed up unexpectedly."

"Yeah." He played with the frayed end of one shoelace, twisting it in his hand. "You asked me what we talked about."

Dr. Hunter nodded. "I remember you were angry with him because he didn't bring you a birthday gift."

"That's not the real reason I was mad." He let out a slow breath. "My dad caught me at Aaron Caldwell's house. He'd seen me there. He must've been following me or something."

"Uh, who's Aaron?"

His head dipped lower. "A drug dealer."

"I see. Your dad caught you buying drugs?"

"No." A frustrated edge cut through his voice. "I was *selling* drugs. Aaron was giving us our cut."

"Oh." Dr. Hunter hesitated. "That must have been a…tough time in your life."

He grunted.

"Your dad saw you selling drugs?"

"Well, no. We got some X from Aaron and sold it to losers at school. But my dad saw me at Aaron's and put two and two together."

"Ecstasy pills, huh?" When he nodded, Dr. Hunter said, "More evidence that your dad was smart. He figured out what was happening. But why…why did you get angry with him?"

Ben felt his lip tremble and cursed, silently. "Dad was telling me to stop. To watch out for getting busted. I yelled something like 'That's rich, Dad, coming from *you.*'"

"You were angry he was being a hypocrite."

"Exactly."

"So…Are you still selling drugs?"

"No! I only did it once, okay?"

"Okay. What made you stop?"

"Dunno…Gruncle Joe got up in my grill, I guess."

"*Grun...*? Oh, Grant's Uncle Joe?"

"Yeah, Great Uncle Joe. He caught me smoking pot at Angelo's, and he took it from me."

Dr. Hunter nodded. "But he doesn't know about you selling X."

"Nobody knows." He looked down. "Except for my dad. And he's just bones in the ground now."

Dr. Hunter waited a beat. "I think he's more than that."

Ben felt dread tighten his throat.

"Are you sure your dad's not the reason you stopped selling drugs? Seems to me he came to see you at just the right time. He was worried about you. He risked getting arrested to talk to you." When Ben's hand curled into a fist, Dr. Hunter added, "I know you're angry he got himself in that situation — running from the police. I'd be angry too. But he tried to do right by you that day. He didn't want you going down the same road he did. He tried to protect you, like a good father should, before he died. *That* was his birthday gift to you."

Ben couldn't help it; an angry tear slipped down his face.

"You really miss him."

"I—I—I never g-g-got to know h-h-him." He focused on controlling his breathing for a moment.

Dr. Hunter exhaled. "That was his tremendous loss, and I bet his biggest regret. He wasn't there for you."

He tried to collect himself. He blew out a breath.

"Do you ever feel like your dad might be with you now? Looking over you somehow?"

"Maybe."

"I wonder if your dad confronting you about going to Aaron's house is somehow related to you telling me about selling drugs. He was worried about you, and deep down you knew it wasn't right. You're trying to make it right by telling me now."

"Are you mad at me?" Ben asked.

"Not mad…more concerned. I'm glad you told me. This has been weighing on you for some time. How does it feel to confess?"

"Um, pretty okay. I don't feel so, uh, sick about it, I guess."

"Yes, confession can make you feel a lot better. That's why I think you should tell your mom, and maybe Grant too."

"*What?*" He felt his eyes go wide. "No way. You said you wouldn't tell my mom!"

"I'm talking about *you* telling her, not me. I want you to do it, as a means of moving forward and making repairs."

"You're crazy. She'll be so, so pissed! And Uncle Grant—he already doesn't care about me. This'll make him never talk to me again!"

"You believe Grant doesn't care about you? Where's that coming from?"

He looked away. "Sophie said he can't see me for a while, because of his undercover thing."

"She told me that too." Dr. Hunter nodded. "How does that mean he doesn't care?"

"It's stupid. I'm being selfish."

"I want to hear what you're thinking, Ben."

He took a deep breath. "Grant said he didn't want me turning out like my dad. He said he'd be there for me. But…he lied. I can't even call him now! He doesn't really care about me—he just cares about getting back at Grandpa. He only cares about the stupid FBI."

Dr. Hunter listened with a slight frown. "I can see how you'd feel that way. All you know is men abandoning you." Ben looked up at him. "You feel abandoned by your father, of course, and by Enzo and Angelo too. Joe's out to sea, and now Grant's not around."

He shrugged.

"But I *know* how much Grant cares about you, Ben. You're all he talks about in here. Grant loves Sophie too, and he's also leaving her to do this assignment. I know it's hard to understand, but he feels like he has to fight back. His family's hurt him a lot, and he can't rest until he tries to take down men like his father. It's his way of getting power back from his father. Father-son relationships are complicated."

Ben exhaled.

"I think you need to tell your mom and Grant about selling drugs," Dr. Hunter said again. "When Grant finds out, naturally he'll be upset, but his love for you won't end there. He'll do what he can to help you."

"What, like making me do pushups forever?"

Dr. Hunter seemed to swallow a smile. "Well, I guess pushups are better than going to juvie."

"Doubtful." He sighed. "But I suppose he can't make me do pushups if he's not around. At least there's that." They sat in silence for a few moments. "Dr. Hunter?"

"Yes?"

"What if…what if they kill Uncle Grant? What if he dies?" His eyes filled with tears. "I can't take it."

Dr. Hunter let him cry for a while. "You've been through so much, Ben. It really makes me sad. It's frightening to think about something happening to Grant. I just have to trust that he knows what he's doing…that he'll be okay."

He took a shuddering breath.

"This has been an intense session," Dr. Hunter said. "We have a few minutes left. I'm wondering, what are you up to the rest of today?"

"I'm meeting Dylan to play video games."

"I see. Breaking out of your routine, then? Trying something different."

He offered a small smile. "Better than selling X, I guess."

"But less lucrative."

"Yeah, those games cost a ton!"

Dr. Hunter nodded. "A lot of cashish. See you next Saturday at eleven?"

"Sure." Ben rose from the sofa, and Dr. Hunter followed suit. Before going to the door, Ben hesitated. *Would it be okay?* He felt like an idiot asking Dr. Hunter. His neediness was disgusting.

"Um, Ben, it's okay to say no, but I wondered…would you like a hug?" Dr. Hunter asked.

How'd he know? "Uh, sure." He shrugged. "If you want." He stepped into his arms, and after a moment Dr. Hunter patted his back.

"I'll do everything I can to be here for you, Ben. I don't want to abandon you, okay?"

"Okay." He squeezed his eyes shut and held on tight.

8. Conscience

ocus. Grant narrowed his vision to the cards in his hand.

"What'll it be, singer boy?" Andrei asked.

He took in a slow pull of air, trying to remember Dr. Hayes's tips for managing anxiety. One of the bodyguards had joined them for the poker game in the West Town house, turning their little group into a foursome, and the big dude's sizable heft distracted him.

Vladimir shifted in his chair. "You already lose tonight—why not fold this time?"

Grant looked at Vladimir, who held his hand close to his chest. *Is he trying to psych me out?* He finally tossed a chip into the kitty.

This earned a disdainful headshake from Vladimir's second in command. "Your funeral." Andrei flipped over his cards to reveal a diamond straight, easily besting Grant's pair of tens and Vladimir's pair of jacks. The bodyguard had wisely bowed out the previous round.

"You cheat," Vladimir grumbled.

Andrei grinned as he scooped the chips toward his pile. "Some have more luck than others." He eyed Grant's dwindling stash. "What song you did tonight? 'Luck Be a Lady'?" His eyes darted over to his girlfriend, perched on a loveseat by the wall. "I will sing 'Luck Be Innochka.' She *my* good luck."

Grant looked over and noticed Innochka absorbed in something on her phone. She giggled as she and Katya huddled over the device. She hadn't seemed to hear Andrei's compliment.

"*Idi syuda!*" Andrei barked.

Grant flinched at the sudden fury in his tone.

Innochka flitted over to the table. "*Da?*"

"Give me phone."

"Why?" Her hand retreated behind her back, hiding her phone. "It's nothing."

"Give to me!" He spun her around and yanked it from her hand, then grabbed her wrist and wrenched her arm tighter around her back. She gasped as he maneuvered her onto his lap with his hand still latched to her wrist.

Grant pressed on the balls of his feet, ready to intervene. He realized he'd stopped breathing, and he let out a silent exhale.

"What the fuck?" Andrei grunted, peering at the phone. "You girls watch *porn?*"

Innochka struggled in his hold. "I was looking for something for you. For a girl you'd like."

"Then why is *dick* on there? You don't need that. *I* satisfy you." A flush colored his cheeks.

Katya tiptoed toward the table, her eyes honed in on Andrei.

A pained squeak escaped as he twisted Innochka's arm more cruelly. "I'm sorry, Andrei." Her sharp inhale as she wiggled pierced Grant's heart.

With a shove, Andrei pushed her off his lap. She let out a cry as she landed on all fours. Before she could get up, Andrei planted the heel of his boot on the curve of her bottom and thrust her flat to the ground.

Grant's hands curled into fists.

"This phone mine now," Andrei hissed. "I already tell you what happens I catch you again. Up." He gestured to the stairs. "The room. Wait for me."

"Sorry, sorry," she moaned as she gathered herself. "I won't do it again."

"Go!" he barked. "And stay out of coke. You will feel every second of punishment."

Grant didn't know which he wanted to do more: follow Innochka or smash Andrei.

Katya chose the former. When she stepped up behind Innochka, Vladimir's hand darted to his belt. "Katya. You want same as her? No? You stay."

"*Da*." Katya's staccato nods matched the fear in her eyes, and she scrambled back to the loveseat. Innochka disappeared upstairs.

Revulsion bubbled in the back of his throat. *So Vladimir and Andrei beat their women.* He'd had inklings before, but now he knew for sure. These Russians were just like his father.

He looked up to find Andrei glaring at him. "You still owe us from last night." He looked at Grant's meager pile of chips. "And more for tonight. Where is money?"

Grant moved back an inch in his chair. "I already told you I get paid tomorrow night." His throat felt dry, and he reached for his vodka.

A low chuckle erupted from Vladimir. "This not bank."

The bodyguard smiled.

"You pay now," Vladimir warned.

"I'll have it to you tomorrow, I promise," he said, hoping the FBI was ready to intervene. He managed a smile. "I can still win it back tonight, you know."

Andrei snorted. "Think you have problem, Mr. Sinatra."

Vladimir studied him as Andrei shuffled the cards. "Tomorrow night," Vladimir said. "You pay, then show us around hotel. Your boss give you combination to safe?"

His heart thumped. "I—"

The shrill ring of Vladimir's cell phone cut him off. The don frowned as he answered, then spoke in rapid-fire Russian. Andrei folded his arms over his chest, and his knuckles whitened as he leaned in to listen to the exchange. Despite the crackle of electricity in the air, the bodyguard seemed bored.

Grant looked over to the loveseat and found Katya staring at the far wall, motionless. A Chicago wind would easily flatten her threadlike profile. He wondered if she'd consumed anything besides cocaine and vodka recently. His shoulders tensed when he thought he heard a faint sob from upstairs.

"Fuck." Vladimir pounced to his feet, ending his call.

Andrei popped up too and went to the front closet for their coats. "*Ublyudok*," he muttered.

Grant stood uneasily, watching the bodyguard head out the door with the other two close behind him.

"You stay," Andrei hollered over his shoulder. "We got business."

The door slammed, and Grant stared at the closed slab of wood. He glanced at Katya, who'd curled up into a ball on the small sofa. He took a step toward her but stopped when she pleaded, "Stay away for me. I not want trouble."

"I…" He sighed and shoved his hands into his pockets, scanning the room. *I don't want trouble either.* He decided to find some water to dilute the alcohol swishing around his stomach. Sophie had helped build his tolerance with some sexy body shots, but he'd been relaxed then. She couldn't help him tolerate the current combination of alcohol and anxiety.

As he headed toward the kitchen, he had the distinct sensation of someone watching him. He looked up the stairs and found Innochka peeking around the corner.

"They left?" she asked.

"Yeah."

"Good. I'll come down."

That drew Katya's ire. "Innochka!" She launched into Russian.

"They're *already* mad at me," Innochka retorted from upstairs. "I don't like the room. It's cold. I want to come down."

"Then keep me out of it," Katya said, turning back to stare into the distance.

"Would you, um, like a glass of water?" he asked, still gazing up the stairwell.

Innochka swallowed, considering. "Okay."

A sound at the door made her squeal and dash out of sight. He swiveled to face the entrance, but all was quiet. *It must've been the wind.* He stared up the stairs for a few moments, but Innochka didn't reappear.

He filled a glass with cloudy water from the tap and took a few gulps. He tried to steady himself, feeling shaken by Vladimir's demands for money and the FBI's reluctance to give him more. *You want to be indebted to them*, Agent Bounter had told him. *Draw them in just enough.*

Any more indebted, and he'd end up dead.

Maybe he should seize this opportunity to go home? *No.* Sophie lived in the same building. He didn't want to bring criminals near her ever again.

"No idea where they went," he whispered into the mic.

The sobbing upstairs had started again. He searched for another glass and filled it, making a beeline for the stairs.

"You should not go," Katya warned.

He paused. "There're many things I shouldn't do." He crept up into the darkness.

It wasn't hard to follow the loud trail of tears, and he found Innochka's room to the right. He knocked on the slightly open door. "I have some water for you?"

Silence.

"It might help you rehydrate after all that crying?"

After a few seconds she said, "What is re-high-rate?"

"Replace water in your body."

"Oh. Okay. Bring it, please."

He nudged the door open and a blast of frigid air greeted him. "Why is it so col—?" He froze when he saw her lying naked on a stained mattress, the only furniture in the room.

She made no effort to cover herself. "Vladimir said no heat."

"He turned off the vents?" He turned his back to her, squatting to set the glass of water by her feet before examining the heating vent on the worn wood floor.

"No!" she cried. "Can't touch it. Please."

"What?" Still turned away from her, he frowned at the wall. "I'll get a blanket then."

"No blankets. Not okay."

"That's ridiculous!"

Her voice was small. "You need to leave. Go. He'll be mad if he sees us talk."

The conversation would be much easier if he could face her when they spoke. "You're naked, it's freezing…I'm getting a blanket."

"No!"

But he was out the door before she could stop him. He searched an adjacent bedroom and yanked a tattered quilt off the double bed. He stepped back into the room and crouched down, wrapping her up despite her protests.

When she sniffed, he instinctively reached up to wipe a tear from her cheek. Her look of admiration was so intense that he quickly rose and shuffled back to lean against the wall, his head down. Moments of silence passed.

"He's going to beat you," he finally said. "And he wants you naked for it."

When he looked at her, she turned her head away, not meeting his eyes.

"Why do you stay?"

"Because sometimes he's very good to me," she answered.

Tattered maroon wallpaper peeled off the wall in strips, and the smell of cigar smoke hung heavy in the air.

"And Katya is my friend." She sighed. "But the real reason I can't leave is…he'd find me." She drew the blanket tighter around her shoulders. "He'd kill me."

He felt black fury. "Don't you have family to protect you?"

"My mother." She smiled faintly. "Back home. In Russia."

"You have no one in the States?"

"Just you." She tucked a strand of platinum-blond hair behind her ear as she swiveled on the mattress and blinked up at him. "Mick."

He noticed her grip on the blanket had loosened a bit, exposing the soft curve of one breast. His eyes darted away. He could almost see his breath as he exhaled.

"You're a nice man, Mick. You would never beat your girl. You would never hurt your girl."

Cringing, he remembered that awful night with Sophie, after he'd found out about her and Logan. "You don't know me."

"But I do." She gazed into his eyes. "When I watch you sing, I *see* you. Who you really are. You act all tough, all big around them, but that's not you."

Goose bumps prickled up his spine. Had he blown his cover? He tried to redirect the conversation. "Why is your English better than the others?"

"I studied hard." She pressed her lips together. "I did good in English…at school. My father told me I could be an international businessman one day."

"You could still get into international business."

"No. Too late." She looked down. "I came here instead."

"Why?"

Her sigh was heavy. "My uncle…he works for Vladimir. In Russia. They told him Andrei liked me. They wanted me to come here."

"Surely you could've said no?"

"Does not work that way." She grimaced.

His stomach clenched. "How *does* it work?"

She paused and sat up, seeming to listen for something. But there was only silence. "It was the only way to keep my uncle safe—if I came here. Or else they killed him."

His eyes tapered into slits.

"But it's fine. Like I said, Andrei is nice to me. He only beats me when I'm stupid."

"You're not stupid—it's not your fault. You deserve better."

She blinked up at him. "I know the real you, Mick. You're kind. You're good. You're not like them." She shivered, clutching the blanket.

He kneeled by the mattress, frowning. "I'm *not* good." Grant looked down. "I've done bad things. I've killed a man."

"Then he must have been a bad man."

He swallowed. "He was part of my family. My cousin."

Her recoil confirmed the disgust he felt inside. Who was he kidding, trying to put Vladimir and Andrei behind bars? *He* was no different from his father. Then he remembered Sophie's words. *"You're not like them. You're my McSailor."*

A soft touch made him smile, thinking of Bonnie, before he realized it was Innochka's hand stroking his face. The touch of a mobster's girlfriend. He leaped back, still crouched on his feet.

Her eyes got bigger. "What's wrong? It's okay. I don't judge you for killing this man. I know you had to do it." She reached out again to touch his face, and he leaned back some more.

"No, Innochka. You're with Andrei."

"He doesn't have to know." Her lips curled into a sexy smile.

His heart pounded. "No. It's not right."

Her smile widened. "You are even more cute when you're scared." She rose to her knees, letting the blanket slide off her shoulders.

His jaw dropped when she lunged for his collar and drew his mouth to hers.

"Stop!" He pushed back from her, rising and stepping away until his back was flush with the wall. Her face crumpled. "I'm sorry, Innochka, but that can't happen between us."

"You think I'm filthy," she cried, gathering the blanket around her again. "I'm stupid."

"No." He took a small step forward. "You're so pretty. You're very sweet. But you're Andrei's girl."

"He does not even like me," she moaned. "He just likes to order me around. He treats me like a dog."

"*You tell him I take care of your mother?*" Andrei roared, bursting into the room. "I take care of you too! You want for nothing."

Both Grant and Innochka jumped. *How long had he been listening?*

"*This* how you thank me? You whore!" He whirled back and slapped her face. "I leave for short time, and you *kiss* him?"

Holy Jesus. Thank God he'd pushed her away. He was now coiled like a spring, ready to restrain Andrei if he tried another assault. The sound of his hand smacking her face resonated in his mind.

She crawled to the back of the mattress, huddling in the far corner and cradling her cheek in her hand. "Sorry! I was so cold, and he gave me a blanket…"

"Give to me, now." His voice was icier than the air in the room.

Innochka peeled off the quilt with shaking hands and shoved it off the mattress onto the floor. This time she folded her arms across her chest, covering her breasts.

The Russian's eyes shone like an oil spill as he unbuckled his belt.

"Please," Innochka whimpered.

He whipped the belt out of its loops. "On your stomach," he growled. "I teach who you kiss. Who you *fuck*."

Grant stopped breathing. He was barely aware of Innochka's moans as she slid down the mattress to obey her boyfriend.

Andrei glared at him. "Leave us."

But he stayed put. He couldn't let this happen.

"I say, *leave!*"

"Don't hit her." Grant swallowed as he locked eyes with Andrei. "She did nothing wrong."

Andrei's face reddened, and his eyes bulged. He bounded right up to him, and Grant did his best not to step back. "You *not* tell me what to do, Saylor! You want bullet in head? Swim with the *ublyudok* in river?"

He held fast. He'd recognized the Russian word and wondered who the *bastard* in the river was. Had they just killed a man and thrown him in the river? Would *he* be next? *Think*, he ordered himself. "You kill me, you lose your money."

"Fuck the money!" Andrei's chest heaved.

"Please," Innochka begged. "Don't hurt him."

Andrei whipped his head around to stare at her. "*Suka.*" He launched into Russian too fast to understand, but Grant assumed it was an elaboration on the insult Andrei had started with: bitch.

"Please," she said again, tears tracking mascara down her blotchy cheeks. "He was just being n-n-nice to me."

Andrei drew his right arm back, the belt flying behind him.

Innochka moaned. "Please don't beat me." Grant was about to lunge for the belt when Andrei halted. His arm slowly lowered, leaving the belt hanging limp at his side.

"Not worry, 'Nochka," he said, looking at Grant. "I will not beat you."

Her sobs turned into shaky whimpers of relief.

Andrei moved toward Grant and offered him the belt. "*He* will."

"*What?*"

"I see you look at her," Andrei accused. "You know I outside door so you not let her kiss you."

"No!" *How do I reason with a mobster?* "I know she's yours. I *don't* want her."

"Prove it." Andrei forced the belt into Grant's hand.

As his palm curled around the cold metal of the buckle, Grant realized his mouth was still hanging open. Staring at Andrei, he pressed his lips together. Here was the test of loyalty he'd known would come.

Andrei grunted and gestured toward Innochka.

"No," Grant said, swallowing bile. "I can't."

Andrei's eyes clouded. "Beat her now. Prove you will not fuck like rabbits the second I turn my back."

"I *won't* become involved in this sick game."

Andrei glided toward him. Vladimir exuded pure strength, but Andrei was smooth and slick. He was like Carlo, only more lethal. His hand snaked to the back of his waist beneath his suit jacket, where Grant knew he'd concealed a gun.

"Do it or die."

All he could hear was the thud of his heartbeat. He felt cold sweat trickle down his back. He dared take his eyes off Andrei to look down at Innochka, who huddled in a trembling heap on the mattress. There was an angry red mark on her left cheek where Andrei had hit her, and there would be more marks on her if he carried through with this task.

With a sniff, she rolled over and tucked her body into the mattress, lying belly-down. She rested her forehead on the cloth and threaded her hands together on the back of her neck. Soft sobs escaped.

What would happen if he refused? They'd likely beat *him* instead. He could deal with that, but not with the evaporation of their trust. The FBI would be furious. If the Russians let him live—and that was a big if—they'd never let him inside again. And what if they killed him? Without the chance to say goodbye to Sophie? To Joe? To Ben? His heart seized up, making it hard to breathe.

Innochka trembling on the mattress reminded him of his mother cringing before his father hit her. He knew what he had to do.

He threw the belt on the floor. Shoulders back, he met Andrei's glare. "My father beat my mother. I promised myself I'd never hit a woman after that. And I *won't* start now." Andrei's eyes widened as he straightened from his attack pose. The man looked almost sad for a moment. What was *that* about? "I won't become a coward like my father."

There was a quick shift in Andrei's demeanor, and his eyes narrowed. "You call me coward?" He shook his head. "Your funeral."

He remembered Andrei had mentioned a funeral at the poker game. Only this was no game. Would Andrei pull out his gun now?

Andrei charged him and smashed a hard fist into his cheek, but Grant retaliated with a sharp blow to his gut. When Andrei bent over and groaned, Grant shoved him into a wall. The house shook from the impact, and Innochka screamed.

Undeterred, Andrei seemed to bounce off the hideous maroon wallpaper and attacked him again, this time going for his kidneys. Grunting, Grant unleashed a backhand across Andrei's head, sending him reeling to the side. Grant thought he'd gained an advantage until a moving mass zoomed from the doorway into his left side, slamming him across the room. He landed on the floor, dazed from the blow. It felt like a slab of rock had just plowed into him, and he looked up at the looming shadow to realize the bodyguard had joined the fight.

Wonderful.

Once the ringing in his ears faded, he heard gruff voices jawing in Russian. Through the gap in the bodyguard's tree-trunk legs hovering over him, he could see that Vladimir had arrived. The don gestured to Innochka as he scowled.

"Get up," Vladimir ordered, and Grant realized he was talking to him. He ignored the bodyguard's menacing sneer and peeled himself off the floor.

Vladimir glowered at him. "Why you attack my man?"

His eyebrows shot up. *Interesting revisionist history.*

"He not to be trusted," Andrei spat.

As Grant's cheek throbbed, he was glad to see a bruise forming on Andrei's temple.

Suddenly Vladimir had Grant pinned against the wall, a meaty paw pressed into his throat. So the don was strong *and* fast. "Informant?" Vladimir hissed. "Work for police?"

He struggled for air through his compressed windpipe. "No," he choked out.

"You try take us down?" Vladimir said. His black eyes glistened.

Where the hell was the FBI to break up this little party? Was his mic still working? Black spots crowded his vision, and he wondered how many seconds of consciousness he had left. He gasped, "No, sir."

Vladimir tilted his head, stared at him for a few long moments, then let him go.

It was a long way down to the floor, and he stayed crumpled there for several seconds, gasping for air. He saw muddy leather shoes step up to him. "You in American military?" Vladimir asked.

After he coughed, he looked up at him. He finally nodded, feigning reluctance to answer. "Navy. I got kicked out."

A small smile bled across Vladimir's face.

Andrei sidled up to his boss. "Why you get kicked out?"

He looked down again. "Too much gambling."

Andrei laughed. "This I believe, singer boy. You worst card player I see."

"Come." Vladimir grabbed Grant's collar and yanked him to his feet. "We talk business."

As Vladimir headed out the door, Andrei asked, "What about 'Nochka?"

Vladimir turned. "Not now." He barked to the bodyguard in Russian, something about getting Innochka some clothes. "We have business. Important. Mr. Navy Saylor help us with business."

Grant didn't even glance at Innochka as he followed Vladimir out of the room with Andrei close on his six. But relief flooded him. Apparently they'd found another way to test his loyalty. To hide the tremor in his hands, he shoved them in his pockets.

❧

Sophie jarred awake. With one ear still pressed into the pillow, she listened to the darkness of Kirsten's bedroom for a few seconds, but heard nothing. Just as she closed her eyes, the bedroom door hinges creaked.

Shooting up in bed, her heart raced. Then she made out a tall silhouette in the doorway.

"Why aren't you on the sofa?" Grant whispered.

She clutched her collarbone, letting out her panicked breath. "Kir's at her parents this weekend. She said I could sleep here."

"Oh." He also let out a slow breath. "When I didn't see you out there, I thought…"

"*What* did you think?"

He came to her, and she could see the fear in his shining eyes. "I…" He hesitated for a moment, then scooped her into a fierce hug. She melted into him, and it felt so good to be cradled in his strong arms. But tension radiated from his body.

"What's wrong, honey?" When he didn't answer, she offered, "Carlo's dead. Your father's locked up. I'm safe now—you don't need to worry."

"I know."

His grip didn't loosen at all.

"Did you make a mistake tonight? Is Agent Bounter mad?"

"No." He sighed. "He said I played it just right. We meet tomorrow to plan the next move."

"Good." She smoothed circles on his back, feeling the muscles beneath his dress shirt. "What happened, then?"

He was silent for almost a minute, then finally relaxed into her. She closed her eyes and felt the weight of his troubles pressing into her body.

He leaned back and skated his fingertips from her temple to chin with the softest of touches. Then she noticed the shadow of a bruise on his cheek.

"Where—?"

"I love you," he said.

Before she could respond, his mouth found hers. The kiss started as a gentle brush of lips, a warm feather of air settling over her skin. She inhaled his light scent of sandalwood. He hovered over her lips, and she felt the slight tug of his long fingers sliding through her hair. When she could wait no longer and leaned in to kiss him back, his pressure deepened, his touch more urgent. Desperation now pressed into these kisses, hard and burning. She clutched him to her chest as his mouth melded to hers.

She didn't know why he needed her right then, but she was there. She'd always be there—listening to his anguish, taking his pain. *He's been through so much.*

She prayed he'd make it out of this assignment alive.

9. Confide

The next day, Sophie smiled from the doorway as Tanya Mitchell scowled at her laptop.

"This makes no freaking sense!" the assistant professor muttered. Her headshake swayed her gargantuan gold hoop earrings.

"You need help," Sophie said.

Tanya swiveled to look at her. "I hate statistics," she whined.

"Me too." Sophie pulled a chair around behind the desk to sit next to her friend.

"But *you're* good at it," Tanya noted.

"Hardly. I mean, Anita's taught me a lot, but I'd much rather do therapy than research."

Tanya's face clouded, and Sophie feared she'd made the woman uncomfortable by bringing up her lost psychologist's license. She'd disclosed her sordid past to Tanya over a month ago, and not surprisingly she'd been horrified about Logan's role in the mess. Less predictably, Tanya had been completely forgiving of her ethical breach. She'd said she admired Sophie for bouncing back from prison. Tanya said she could understand how she'd fallen for Logan if he was half as cute as Grant.

"So what's stumping you?" Sophie asked, gesturing to the computer. "You said the regression analyses don't make sense?"

"Nice try changing the subject. Have you thought about petitioning the board to get your license back?"

"The Illinois Psychology Board won't reinstate a convicted felon, Dr. Mitchell."

"But the governor pardoned you."

She looked down. "I don't think that matters. I'm sure the board won't reissue my license because they think I'll exploit a client again."

"So they'll order you to get supervision or something. If you love counseling so much, you have to at least *try*. What do you have to lose?"

Heaving a loud sigh, she continued staring at her lap. "All sense of dignity. Can you imagine what it'd be like to go up in front of the board?" She looked at Tanya. "To face a bunch of old men who've been psychologists forever? What am I supposed to tell them? 'Oh, I'm *so* sorry I slept with my client. Sorry for my out-of-control libido. I'll never let it happen again.' It would be intensely mortifying for them to judge my sexual behavior…to judge *me*."

Tanya said nothing, but just as Sophie grabbed a printout of statistical analyses she added, "The judgment of board members isn't what's bothering you. It's *your* judgment that's the problem. You're way too harsh. You still haven't forgiven yourself."

"Ugh. Why do you have to be so damn intuitive?" Sophie asked after a moment.

Tanya grinned.

"*You're* the one who should be doing therapy," Sophie added.

"Honestly?" Tanya sat back in her chair. "Therapy is way too stressful. I couldn't wait for my internship to end so I could get back to teaching and research. How do you sleep at night after hearing clients tell you horrifying stories?" She shuddered. "It's not for me."

"It *was* stressful at times, I admit. And my own therapist has helped me understand that I took on too much responsibility for my clients, and that made me anxious. But now I see I don't have to *make* change happen—I just have to let it happen. The few times I was able to trust my clients to figure out their own answers, therapy was really fun."

"Even more reason to pursue your license."

She shrugged.

"Well, I still think you should try. But if you don't, you're in a good place. Research is a blast!"

"Except for statistics?" Sophie asked.

Tanya's smile vanished. "Yeah. The damn statistics."

Sophie handed her the printout.

"Okay, here's the deal. You know how I split the sample into the top third and the lowest third in terms of how much they'd adapted to American culture?"

Sophie nodded.

"Well, my hypothesis was that the most Americanized students would seek counseling more frequently than the group that held to their culture of origin."

"Makes sense," Sophie said.

"Exactly. But I only find a significant difference in help-seeking behavior when I compare the top and bottom thirds—and David told me it was ridiculous to throw out the middle third of my sample."

She frowned. "David?"

"David Alton," Tanya confessed with a wince.

"Why are you taking advice from him?" she asked. "How did he even find out about your study?"

"Oh, Nora let it slip in class when they were arguing about the performance of minorities on intelligence tests. She's apologized to me about twenty times now."

She laughed. "Poor Nora. I'm so glad she knows what David's really like."

"Yes, and she's keeping tabs on him. So far he hasn't hit on any of the ladies in this year's class."

"I'm glad he no longer thinks he's God's gift to female psychology students."

Tanya leaned in. "Speaking of God's gift, have you met Nora's boyfriend?"

She shook her head.

"*Ay yi yi.* That man is hot. Smokin' hot."

She nudged her shoulder. "We need to get *you* a man."

"Is it so terrible I want my own McSailor?"

"No, not at all. He's pretty nice to have around. That's what I'm saying!" She suppressed a yawn.

"Did McSailor keep you up late with kinky sex?"

"Jeez, you need to get laid. He got home late from his gig, that's all."

"And *then* you had sex."

"Our relationship is more than just sex, Tanya."

"I don't know why," she said. "If I had a man like that I'd sex him up one side and down the other."

"Knock, knock."

They looked up to see Kirsten standing in the office doorway, looking like she'd swallowed a canary. "I see you two are engaged in quite the academic discussion. You *do* know I can hear your porno talk all the way in the hallway, right?"

Sophie's cheeks flushed as Tanya stood and shooed Kirsten inside before shutting the door.

"Please tell me David wasn't in the hallway," Tanya said.

Kirsten took a seat. "Luckily, no." She turned to Sophie. "Hey, roomie."

"*Roomie?*" Tanya asked. "Still living in the past, Kirsten?"

"Oh, uh, yeah," Kirsten stammered. "Life hasn't been complete since Sophie moved out. At least I get to be in the same building as her, though."

"So what brings you over to the psych building, Dr. Holland?" Sophie asked quickly.

Kirsten rolled her eyes. "Had a no-show at the counseling center. Stupid students."

"But now you get paid whether or not the clients show, right?" Sophie asked.

A dazzling smile from Kirsten. "One benefit of working for a university counseling center. Though the salary is crap."

"Maybe you need a sugar daddy to pay the bills," Tanya suggested.

Sophie laughed. "*Aaaand* we're back to sex."

"I don't know, guys," Kirsten said. "I just read this article in *Psychology Today* about being single at heart. I think that's me." She shrugged. "I've always been this weird, nonlinear thinker…"

Tanya nodded. "I *saw* that article. I can't believe forty-five percent of American adults are unmarried. Where are all the single men? And more importantly, what do these people do for *sex?*"

"I got it!" Sophie shot out of her chair.

"You got what?" Tanya eyed her. "The way for single people to gain unfettered access to sex?"

"No. The answer to your stats question." Sophie yanked the paper out of Tanya's hand. "The reason the significant difference isn't showing up with the whole sample? Your data are *nonlinear*. Only by looking at the top and bottom thirds are you finding the truth."

Tanya absorbed that for a few seconds. "Holy Oprah Winfrey—you're right! So if I follow David's advice, I'll have non-significant results. My study will be loserville."

"Suck it, David," Sophie crowed.

"He wishes." Tanya smirked.

"I'm brilliant," Sophie said, with a toss of her hair.

"No," Kirsten countered. "You're a *nerd*."

Tank winced at the lingering sting of the knife wound in his shoulder. The prison doc had removed his stitches yesterday, but the gash still felt tender. He arranged his face in a mask of stone before approaching the wiry blond men hovering over the bench press.

"We got company, boss," the elfin one hissed as Tank neared.

There was a loud clang of metal as Ricker dropped the weighted bar on the clips and popped off the bench in one fluid motion. He pushed aside his ponytailed minion and stepped right up to Tank, who gave him a perplexed look as he barked a few words in guttural German.

"I don't speak Nazi," Tank said.

Ricker inched closer. "This bench is taken."

Tank nodded. "Not interested in the bench."

"*You* can't lift the weight," Elf sneered. "And it's only sir's warm-up."

Peering around the boy's shoulder at the fifty-pound plates on the bar, Tank chuckled. "One forty-five?" He stared at Elf. "That's about what you weigh, isn't it?" He stooped down and clutched the boy's knee with one hand while the other seized his neck. He scooped Elf off his feet and hoisted him above his head.

Elf flailed wildly. "Mr. Mullens!" His free leg bicycled as he tried to liberate himself.

Tank felt burning in his biceps and a searing pain in his shoulder as he heaved Elf up and down in a human bench press. He'd expected Ricker would intervene, but instead the blond sported a fat grin, and Ponytail giggled like a girl.

"Put me down!" Elf wailed.

He felt the boy slap his wrist like a bothersome gnat. His grip on Elf's neck tightened as he completed his tenth rep.

"Sirrr!" Elf cried. "Why don't you make him…put me down?"

Ricker shook his head. "Enjoying the show too much, powder puff."

Finding human weight far more unwieldy than metal plates on a bar, Tank finished his fifteenth rep hoping he hadn't busted open the knife wound. He heaved Elf back to the gym floor, not so gently. The minion scurried away, at first looking as if he'd hide behind Ricker but instead heading to the door.

"Steven!" Ricker boomed, halting the boy in his tracks. Evidently Elf had a name. "Get back here."

The boy swiveled and gingerly stepped back to his master, his eyes growing wider with each step. As soon as he was within striking distance, Ricker backhanded him across the face. Steven sprawled on the rubber floor.

Tank looked over to the two guards by the wall. They continued chatting, apparently uninterested in intervening.

"You *never* leave without permission," Ricker fumed.

Little Stevie cradled his injured cheek as he sat up. "But…but I was *mad* at you. You didn't protect me. You said you'd always protect me."

Ricker leaned down, glanced up at Tank, then looked back at Steven as he offered the boy a hand and pulled him to his feet. "He didn't drop you. I knew you were safe, sweetie." He pressed a soft kiss to the boy's crimson cheek.

What's the deal with this guy? Tank wondered.

"Rack up the weights for my main set," Ricker ordered, slapping Steven's butt.

Steven sashayed to the rack, and he and Ponytail struggled together to hoist a fifty-pound plate from its place.

"Nice little show," Ricker said, honing his icy gaze back on Tank. "You will not do so well with two forty-five." His eyes flitted down to Tank's crotch. "But I will cooperate much better when you lift *me.*" A grin spread as he extended an arm and leg, offering himself as a human barbell.

Tank shook his head. "Like I said, I'm not here to lift." He lowered his voice. "Mr. Barberi's got a job for you when you get out."

Ricker straightened. "Then he needs to talk to me himself."

"Don't work that way."

When Ricker sidled closer, Tank caught a whiff of his rank odor. "He only sends his *bitches* to deliver the message, eh?"

Tank glared.

"So why were you in the infirmary?" Ricker asked, his eyes dancing.

"Speaking of bitches…" Tank looked over to the two butterflies standing by the bar. "Mr. Barberi wants this conversation to be private."

The German considered this request, then turned to his boys. "You two, give me ten laps."

Ponytail opened his mouth to protest, but when Ricker took a menacing step toward him, he grabbed Steven's hand and sprinted to the corner of the gym.

"What will they do without you?" Tank mused.

"Already sold them. They will be good." Ricker's face darkened. "But if you *touch* them, you'll pay." He spat on the ground, centimeters from Tank's scuffed black prison boot. "I don't care if Enzo protects you."

"You should," he countered. "He still has a lot of money. Money you could get if you help us."

"I only listen to your offer if you tell me why you were in the infirmary."

"Forget it, you manipulative prick." He shook his head and turned to leave.

"Enzo will not be happy you failed with the offer."

"I'll tell Mr. Barberi you weren't interested," he tossed over his shoulder. "Too bad, too. Money could've set you up good on the outside. Lots of boys for your pleasure." He hid his grin when he felt Ricker move up behind him.

"I never pay for boys," Ricker said.

Tank turned around.

"But I need to hear this from Enzo. Not from you."

"You don't listen too well, do you?" Tank stepped closer, happy to have the slight height advantage. "I told you this goes through me."

Ricker's arms folded across his barrel chest. "You are the one who cannot listen. Tell me why you were down for the count."

"Listen, shithead—" His words wilted into a hiss as Ricker's thumb gouged into his knife wound through his shirt. How the hell did he know Enzo had stabbed him there? His eyes shot up to meet the guards' sharp gazes.

Feeling like he might vomit or pass out, he struggled to swallow. He blinked until the black spots faded from his vision and raised his shaking hands to push Ricker off him. But the man's vice grip was too strong.

"Oh," Tank managed. "I did tell you this was…about Grant, right?" A glint of interest lit up Ricker's eyes, and the thumb lifted.

"You did not." Ricker's voice sounded strained, like he was fighting for control. "All right, I will listen. But Enzo cannot afford my services."

"Oh, I think he can," Tank said. He stood up straighter. "Here's what he needs you to do…"

❧

"Mom?" Ben pocketed his keys and stepped into the warm apartment. He was surprised to find his mother shivering on the sofa, despite two heavy blankets piled on top of her. "Aren't you supposed to be at work?"

"I'm sick." Her voice scratched, and sweat plastered her blond bangs to her forehead.

He set down his swim bag. "That sucks."

She sniffed. "How was practice?"

"Good. We're starting taper."

"What's that?"

"It's when the coaches stop killing us every day, to rest us for the big meet." He smiled. "Sophie said taper's the best part of swimming."

His mother nodded. They stared at each other for a moment before she looked down. "I don't think I can pay your meet entry fees. I'm missing out on tips tonight, and I'll probably have to call in sick tomorrow too. Sorry."

She looked miserable, and he wished he could help her feel better. "It's okay. Sophie gave me some money."

"Oh." She reached for a tissue. "Good, that's a relief."

She didn't *sound* relieved. "Want, um, do you want some hot chocolate or something…tea, I guess?"

"That's sweet. How 'bout you dry your hair first, so you don't get sick like me?"

"It's okay, Mom." He shrugged off his coat as he headed into the kitchen. "Sophie said that's a myth. Germs cause sickness, not wet hair. Besides, it's like ninety degrees in here." He thought he heard her say something in reply, but the drone of the microwave drowned out her voice.

The cup rattled on the plate as he set the hot water on the coffee table. "I could only find this old black tea in the cupboard. It looks kinda ancient—we need to go shopping."

She mumbled, and all he caught was Sophie's name.

"What'd you say?"

His mother sat up a bit and stirred some honey into the steaming water. Greasy hair framed her face as she stared at her spoon. "Sounds like Sophie takes good care of you."

"Well, yeah, I mean, I only see her once or twice a week…" As he sat down in a side chair, it dawned on him what was bothering her. "But, you know, she's not my mom or anything."

When she glanced over at him, he noticed a glassy look in her eyes—caused by her sickness, he hoped, and not because she was about to cry. He couldn't handle that. After she took a sip, she closed her eyes. "Ah, this feels so good on my throat. Thank you, Benji."

"*Mom…*" He felt his cheeks warm.

"Sorry. It just seems like yesterday when you were…three or four, I think…and you were all snuggled on the sofa with the flu—God, you had the worst diarrhea—"

"Gross."

"Anyway, I brought some soda over to you. After you drank some, you looked up at me with those big blue eyes, and said, 'You're the best, babe.'"

His forehead creased as his mother laughed. "Why did I say *that?*"

"Well…" Her smile faded. "I bet you heard your father say it once or twice."

"He used to call you babe?"

Her mouth tightened. "When he wanted something from me."

He chewed his lip.

"I'm so proud of you."

"Why?"

"Your grades are excellent, and Dr. Hayes told me you're doing really well."

"Did he tell you anything else?" He heard his voice rise like a girl's.

"No." Her head cocked to the side. "Like what?"

"Nothing." He swallowed.

"Ben, honey?" Her stare was intense. "What is it?"

"It's nothing." He looked over to the kitchen. "I'm hungry. Want some dinner?"

She continued looking at him. "C'mon, you can tell me." The corner of her mouth quirked up. "Tell me, babe."

Forcing a swallow, he slowly met her eyes. He felt his fingertips tapping a rapid beat on his knee, and he compelled his hand to lie flat on his jeans. "Mom?"

She nodded.

"Dr. Hayes…he said I should tell you something."

"Okay?"

"You, uh…you *shouldn't* be proud of me."

She sniffed. "Well, I am. No matter what you've done, you're my pride and joy."

He winced. She was making this harder. Dr. Hunter's words swam through his mind as he scrubbed his hand through his hair. *Confession can make you feel better—it's a means of moving forward and making repairs.* "Mom?"

She nodded.

"I used to, well, one time I, um…I sold drugs."

Her face fell, and her eyes welled up in tears.

So much for Dr. Hunter's promise. "I'm sorry—I only did it once! And it was just ecstasy pills."

"Is that supposed to make me feel *better?*" Red blotches marred her face.

He squirmed as his mother began to sob. "Sorry! I shouldn't have told you." He leaned forward to get up, but she grasped his wrist.

"Stay." She sniffed as she wiped her cheek. "We *need* to talk about this."

He closed his eyes, motionless for a moment, then scooted back on the cushion. His hands curled over the arms of the chair as he braced himself for the onslaught.

"I'm sorry I'm crying," she rasped, snatching a tissue from the box. "I know you don't like it when I cry." Her eyes found his after she blew her nose. "But, Ben, I'm terrified of you becoming like your father."

He shot out of his chair. "I'm *not* like him!"

"All right." She blinked up at him, and more tears leaked down her cheeks. "Sit down, okay?"

Looking away, he blew out a breath. Finally his butt found the cushion again.

"What did Dr. Hayes say when you told him?"

"He said I needed to tell you, for some stupid reason. Wonderful idea that turned out to be."

"Did he call the police?"

"No! He can't do that." Ben felt a shot of panic rifle up his spine. "*You* won't do that, will you? You're not gonna turn in your own son!"

She was quiet for a moment then said, "No. I wouldn't do that. But there should be some consequence for this. Dr. Hayes told me I'm supposed to give you consequences."

"Awesome," he huffed. "I'm never talking to him again."

"Ben, calm down. You're just mad right now."

"*Shouldn't* I be?"

Her tears stopped. "No, *I* should be the mad one, with you breaking the law. It was bad enough when I found out you were using drugs, but *selling* them? Do you know how serious that is?"

"Of course! That's why I didn't want to tell you. I'm not stupid, you know."

"That's why I can't believe this. You're getting straight As — I never got grades that good — yet you go and do something incredibly risky and dangerous like that? Why? Why did you sell drugs?"

That last question threw him off guard. Why *had* he been such a dumbass? He unclenched his fists as he slumped in the chair. "Dunno," he finally mumbled, looking down.

He heard his mother stir her tea then take a sip. She set the cup down. "Were you mad at your dad?"

When he looked up, the anger had drained from her face. She just looked tired now. "Maybe."

"I know the feeling. He could drive me crazy sometimes."

He smirked. "Yeah."

"You're not like him, Benji. You know that? You're stronger than him. You don't need drugs…or gambling. Okay?"

His lip quivered. *What if I do need drugs? Weed sounds really good right now.*

"Okay?" she repeated.

The faces of Dr. Hunter, Sophie, and Uncle Grant swam through his mind. "Okay." His voice warbled like a baby's.

"So…" She rubbed the back of her neck. "You're, um, you're grounded for two weeks."

"*What?*"

"Come home after practice and do your homework. No going out with your friends."

"That's so unfair! I didn't have to tell you any of this."

"You're right, but I'm glad you did." She studied him. "And I want you to tell Grant."

A jolt of fear rushed through him. "No! He'll hate me! Please don't make me tell him. Please, Mom. You and Dr. Hayes don't know how mad he'll be."

"Dr. Hayes wanted you to tell Grant too?"

"We're not talking about that jerk." Ben laced his arms in front of his chest.

"If Dr. Hayes thinks it's a good idea, then I do too."

"Mom, please. I'll be good. I'll be home when I'm supposed to be. Just please don't make me tell Grant."

"I think you need a man in your life knowing what's going on." She hesitated. "You know, when I was your age, my dad wasn't around either. He'd split long ago. Mom worked two jobs to support us…" She looked toward the window. "When Mom found out I was dating your father, and he had a criminal record…" Her eyes turned back on him. "Do you know what she said?"

He shook his head.

"She said, 'Don't you dare get pregnant 'cause I can't pay for a baby too.' Great advice, huh? I wish she would've forbidden me to see him. I wish she would've grounded me, but she didn't. She didn't care."

"Okay, I get it. You care about me. But don't make me tell Uncle Grant!"

His mother studied him for a few long moments while he muttered silent prayers. "I'll think about whether or not to tell Grant. But you are grounded for two weeks. And that's because I *do* care."

His cheeks felt hot again, and he wanted to yell at her, but he couldn't find the words. She'd never talked to him like that before—it was usually ignoring him or screaming at him. He squirmed when she wouldn't stop looking at him.

"Your mom warned you not to get pregnant…How long did it take for you to get knocked up with me?" he asked.

"A few months." Her head dipped. "Like I said, I wasn't very smart."

"What'd your mom do?"

"Of course I didn't tell her," his mother said. "I moved in with your dad, and I finally told her about you after you were born."

"What'd she say?"

"She said I screwed up my life."

Ben looked down, uncomfortable with the conversation.

"But I don't see it that way."

He glanced up.

"I'm so glad I had you, Ben. I know it's been hard, but we're making it, right? We'll make it." She coughed.

It was hard to believe her. Maybe she would've been much better off if she'd actually listened to her mom…or if she hadn't met his dad, if she hadn't gotten pregnant with him.

"Now go dry your hair," she said, sitting up, "and I'm going to make you dinner."

"That's okay, Mom, I'll do it—"

"No, I'm home, and I'm making you dinner." When she stood, she swayed a bit on her feet, and he jumped up to help her.

"Scoot," she said, waving him away.

He gave her a sideways glance, wondering why she was ordering him around all the sudden.

"Don't worry, I promise I won't cough on your food."

He took tentative steps toward his bedroom and looked over his shoulder at his mother, who now peered blankly into the cupboard. *Had* he screwed up her life? Or was she screwing up his? He rolled his eyes as he went into the bathroom. He now had two whole weeks of boring nothingness to sit and figure that one out.

10. Conceal

Grant squinted at the shore patrol officer manning the naval base gate two cars ahead of them and blew out a breath. "Good, he's new. He won't recognize me."

"It's been a long time since you worked here, right?" Agent Bounter asked from the driver's seat.

"Almost ten years."

Bounter tugged his collar away from his bulging neck. "Damn, this collar's tight. What're they trying to do? Choke me?"

Grant grinned. "Hey, don't blame me. *Your* guys got these uniforms. When's the last time you even wore a tie?"

"Every Sunday for church," Bounter answered. "But my dress shirts aren't as tight or scratchy as this uniform. This has got to be the most uncomfortable thing I've ever worn."

Grant glanced down at his khaki jacket. He couldn't disagree more. Since he'd slipped on the US Navy uniform in Agent Bounter's office, he'd felt a confident swagger possess him. His spine lengthened, and his shoulders retracted. He should've been wearing this every day, not the stupid dress shirt and slacks of a lounge singer. "If you think *this* is scratchy, try a prison jumpsuit."

"Hmph."

Bounter didn't look at him, and silence filled the car as they inched forward, next in line. Grant wondered why he'd brought up his time in prison. He scanned the expanse of the Naval Station Great Lakes. *Oh.* He was about to reunite with the man who'd turned him in. Of course he was thinking about Gurnee State Penitentiary.

"Just play it cool," he said as Bounter eased the government sedan toward the security checkpoint. "Show him your ID and stare straight ahead."

Bounter's right hand began to lift.

"No," Grant hissed. "Don't salute! He's an NCO like you."

"Afternoon, gentlemen." The SP saluted once he noticed Grant's uniform. "Lieutenant," he added after Grant returned his salute.

Grant gave him a curt nod.

As the SP took Bounter's fake military ID, he said, "State your business."

"We have a meeting with Lt. Davis," Bounter replied.

The SP stepped into the small guard station. Grant watched him type on the computer. He peered at the monitor for a full minute, and Grant held his breath. Captain Lockhart could've easily put the kibosh on this sting operation, and that was *before* Agent Bounter had suggested they wear uniforms to blend in.

"Oh, here ya are," the SP said, returning the ID to Bounter. "Proceed east…" He karate-chopped his arm to point straight ahead. "Then take your third left. Visitor parking's one hundred meters down on your right." The SP lowered his head to look in the vehicle. "Y'all know where the lieutenant's office is?"

"We'll find it," Grant said. "Thank you."

"Yes, sir." The SP reached into the booth, and the fence slid to the right.

As they entered the base, memories of his childhood here flooded him…

His backpack had shifted from side to side as he raced inside the military family housing unit. He heard the screen door slam behind him.

"Shh," Uncle Joe whispered as he dashed through the kitchen. "Your mother's asleep!"

Grant froze. What was his uncle doing home in the middle of the afternoon? And why hadn't he learned to stop slamming the front door after three years of living with Uncle Joe? "Sorry." He peered up at his uncle. "Why's she sleeping?"

"She's not feeling well. She asked me if I could come home early and watch you."

"I'm eleven. I don't need a baby-sitter."

Joe seemed to suppress a grin. "You're right. But your mom worries about you, you know."

"She shouldn't. I can take care of myself." He dragged his backpack over to the kitchen table.

"Do you have homework?"

"Yes, sir." He took a seat.

Joe joined him at the table. "Does your mother usually make you do homework right after school?"

"Sometimes." He retrieved his Language Arts folder. "But today she said we could make a Mother's Day present. I guess that's not gonna happen now. She sure sleeps a lot."

"I know." Joe shook his head. "I keep telling her to see the doctor, but she won't go."

Grant dropped his head to hide his blush. His eyes drifted down the page of vocabulary words. He wondered how he'd use *concealment* in a sentence if he didn't know what the heck it meant.

"Grant?"

He looked up.

"Seems like you're hiding something. Do you know why your mom won't go to the doctor?"

He paused, chewing his lip. "No?"

"It's okay, you can tell me."

"But Mom'll be mad."

"Then we'll say I ordered you to tell me." Joe leaned forward. "Talk, Grant."

Joe wore his uniform, and the sharp fold of his khaki collar matched the tone of his voice.

"She…she said we can't afford it. Not until she gets a full-time job."

Joe sighed. "How'll she get a full-time teaching position when she's been too tired to substitute one day the past three weeks?" He shook his head. "I'll pay for the doctor. That's ridiculous."

"No. She said we take too much already."

"Nonsense. I *like* taking care of you." He smiled. "I like taking you to Sox games."

"The new park's sure awesome!" But when his uncle smiled back at him, Grant felt his excitement fade. "Mom said I shouldn't go next time. The tickets are too expensive."

"What? I *need* you with me. I need your moral support when our team loses to Detroit sixteen-zip on opening day."

He groaned. "That *did* stink."

His uncle reached into his back pocket and extracted a couple one hundred dollar bills from his money clip. "Give this to your mother," he said, pushing the money into Grant's hand. "And tell her to go to the doctor tomorrow. She'll accept this easier from you than from me."

"We can't take this!" he gasped.

But Joe had already headed into the kitchen. "I'm making you a snack," he called quietly.

Grant stared down at the bills in his hand. His father had carried around wads of hundreds, but he'd never let him touch them, and now the money seemed frightening to hold. He wondered how he'd get his mom to accept it.

"Here you are," Joe said a couple of minutes later as he set down a plate with two pieces of buttered toast. Grant's eyes lit up at the hefty dose of cinnamon sugar sprinkled on top—much more than his mom typically allowed. "So tell me about this Mother's Day present you were going to make…"

"Here we are," Agent Bounter said, easing the sedan into a parking space.

Grant started, then focused on the base ahead of them. Was it the cloudy day or the passing years that had dulled the finish of the concrete structures? He climbed out of the car to join Bounter near the hood.

A seaman approached them. Once the boy noticed the stripes on Grant's jacket, he executed a quick salute, which Grant promptly returned. The seaman scuttled past them in seconds.

"Why don't *I* get to be the commissioned officer?" Bounter pouted.

Grant chuckled. "Because *you* don't know how to carry it off." He nodded toward the three-story building. "C'mon, I'll introduce you to the captain." Though he felt jittery, his feet took off on their own, trekking to the office where his uncle's best friend worked. He knew the way quite well.

He'd been there many times when he'd worked on the base, and before that as a child…

The screen door slamming behind him had made his Uncle Joe jump in his chair. Grant winced and mumbled an apology as he shrugged out of his backpack. He hadn't expected anyone to be home.

Joe quickly shuffled some envelopes on the table, and something made him suspicious.

"What's that?" He came to the table.

His uncle swiped at his cheek and kept his head down. "Nothing."

Oh God, was he *crying?* His knees almost buckled. "Is…is Mom okay?"

"She's fine." Uncle Joe cleared his throat and looked up. "I mean, her doctor said she's stable. No change."

"Oh." He grasped the back of the chair and drew it to his chest, lifting the chair's front two legs. Then he leaned forward, bringing the back of the chair toward the table. He rocked the chair back and forth on its legs for several moments. "Does that mean she can come home soon?" he finally asked.

"I don't know," Joe said.

"Can we visit her tonight?"

"Sure, buddy." He pushed his chair back and stood. "How 'bout I get you a snack first?"

"Um…I'm not hungry."

Joe sighed. "Me neither." He looked back at the mail on the table. "I'll put those away later. Captain Lockhart gave me the rest of the day off. I'll clean up for a sec, then we'll go to the hospital, okay?"

"Okay."

His uncle disappeared into the back of the apartment, and he heard the rush of the bathroom faucet. He looked over at the TV, which held no interest for him. His mom didn't like him to watch it anyway. He tightened his grip on the chair. He wished he'd never made her take that money and go to the doctor a year ago. Things hadn't been the same since he'd overheard her and Joe use that word—that awful C word. His mom had been in the hospital for weeks now. Grant bet his dad didn't even know she was sick.

A glossy store circular sat atop the mail on the table, and Grant reached for it. Thumbing through the pages, he paused at the toy section. *Bummer*—the Creepy Crawlers set he wanted was still too expensive. He wondered if he could somehow make his own molds to create realistic insects. That'd really freak out the girls at school.

He didn't want Joe to know he coveted the toy—he'd already spent way too much on him—so he jettisoned the advertisement to the table. It came to rest near an opened letter, and he noticed the hospital's logo on the envelope. He slid the paper from the stack and found himself looking at a bill. His eyes scanned the number listed next to *You Owe*.

Fifteen thousand dollars? How would they ever pay that? Though Uncle Joe had tried to hide it, he knew money was already tight. His mother's tests and doctor visits had to be the reason Uncle Joe hadn't let him play any sports this year—not his claim that he wanted Grant to become more well-rounded by reading the military history books that lined the bookshelves in the apartment.

"I told you not to look at that!" his uncle boomed from behind him.

Grant spun around and pressed into the edge of the table as Joe charged forward. His heart galloped as he saw the fury in his uncle's eyes. "Sorry, sir!" He tried to get away, but the table held fast. He reached out to catch himself on the corner before he fell back. "I'm sorry, I'm sorry!"

His uncle instantly stepped back, splaying his hands out and offering his palms. A look of sadness and anger filled his eyes: the look he always gave when Grant messed up. The anger Grant understood, but the sadness confused him. Joe reached for his hand and led him away from the table.

When he spoke again, his voice was lower, calmer. "I didn't want you to see that bill."

"I'm sorry, sir." He looked down. "How…how many pushups should I do?"

Joe made a strangled noise, and Grant looked up just as his uncle lunged for him—he'd finally made him mad enough to hit him, he realized — but instead Joe grabbed him in a fierce hug. His mind raced as his cheek pressed into his uncle's uniform. Why was he hugging him?

"You're not in trouble, Grant," he said, his deep voice echoing in his chest. "I just didn't want you to worry about this. You worry about too much already."

"But how can you pay that bill?" He tried to breathe — tried not to let his voice shake so much. "What'll they do if we can't pay? Will they make Mom leave the hospital?"

Joe pulled back and stared down at him. "You see? This is what I wanted to avoid. This isn't your problem, Grant… You're twelve years old. I'll take care of this. I'll figure it out."

He nodded.

"Don't tell your mother about the bill, either."

"Yes, sir."

"You ready? Let's go, son. Let's go see your mother…"

"You ready for this?" Agent Bounter asked.

Grant glanced at the nameplate next to the door: *Captain Archibald Lockhart.* It hadn't been until after his mother's funeral that Joe admitted Captain Lockhart had loaned him the money to pay the medical bills.

He closed his eyes and exhaled. "Ready."

Bounter entered first and approached the lieutenant seated at the desk in the outer office. Captain Lockhart's door was closed.

"We're here to see Captain Lockhart, sir," Bounter told him.

The lieutenant looked up in surprise, then frowned as he examined his computer screen. "The captain told me to expect two civilians."

Grant glared at Bounter. "Petty Officer Hunter, you didn't inform the captain of our arrival?"

"I…" For a second the FBI agent's mouth hung open. "I must've made a mistake…sir." He turned back to the real lieutenant. "Please notify the captain that Lt. Saylor and Petty Officer Hunter are here to see him, sir."

The lieutenant shrugged. "All right. You gentlemen can hang your coats there and take a seat."

Grant found a hook for his jacket and cover as Archie's assistant announced their arrival over the phone. When he sat down next to his fake subordinate, he felt a sharp elbow stab his rib. Bounter mouthed, *Next time* I'm *the officer.* Grant grinned.

His grin vanished when the captain's door flew open, revealing eyes that sliced into him with their wrath. He'd known the captain would never forgive him for holding him at gunpoint, but Lockhart *had* agreed to this meeting with the FBI, hadn't he? Grant popped off his chair and braced to attention, feeling Bounter follow suit next to him.

Captain Lockhart stood at six-four, his brown hair now completely gray, the slight protrusion of his belly the only soft part of his physique. He studied them for what felt like almost a minute. "Inside, *now.*"

Grant made a precise turn and marched through the doorway with Bounter close on his six. Holding the door open, the captain seemed to emit heat as he passed. He stood at attention facing the desk, even though the ruse was unnecessary now that the captain had closed his door.

"How *dare* you wear that uniform!" he spat. Then he was right in front of Grant. "You were discharged for a reason. It's a slap in the Navy's face for you to show up like that."

Grant remained silent. He felt as small as he had three years ago when he'd faced Captain Lockhart in a standoff. He could almost feel the cold metal of Logan's gun in his unsteady right hand. He couldn't come up with the words he needed to diffuse the situation, and his lack of response seemed to incite the captain more.

"I'd never have agreed to this meeting if I'd known you'd pull this stunt."

"Captain, it was our idea," Agent Bounter offered.

"And who the fuck are you?" he stormed. "You're certainly no sailor with a stance like that."

Bounter gave up his attempt at standing at attention and reached into his back pocket. "FBI Agent Lucas Bounter, sir." He handed over his badge.

"Organized Crime Task Force," the captain read before flinging his badge back to him. "All I know is the FBI called this meeting. I didn't think I could refuse, so I agreed. *Then* they inform me Grant

Madsen's coming in." He slid back in front of him. "Joe told me you got out of the state pen. Have you committed a federal crime now?"

"No, sir." This was going a *lot* worse than Bounter had said it would.

Bounter cleared his throat. "Captain, Mr. Madsen's been pardoned for his crimes. Will you calm down, sir?"

"You come in here in fake uniforms, and you expect me to *calm down?*"

"We did it to protect you!" Bounter exclaimed.

He finally paused. "What do you mean?"

"Will you let us explain before you give yourself a goddamn stroke?"

Grant's eyes widened. He'd never heard anyone speak to the captain that way.

Captain Lockhart laced his arms across his chest. "Fine," he conceded. "Sit. This better be good."

Grant relaxed and followed Bounter to the conference table. A deep line creased the captain's forehead—probably a sign of disgust. He pursed his lips and nodded toward the table, where Grant took a seat. As he joined them, Grant noticed that he and the captain sat ramrod straight on their chairs, making Bounter look like a slouch.

"Captain Lockhart, you have a drug problem on this base," Bounter began.

He blanched. "I most certainly do not."

Bounter opened the folder he'd brought and removed several enlarged photos, which he fanned out on the table. He waited for the captain to inspect them. "I believe these are your men here, smoking weed?" He pointed to another photo. "Buying meth?"

"How do you know that's methamphetamine?" Captain Lockhart demanded.

Bounter arched his eyebrow. "We know, sir. It's what we do."

The captain sat motionless for several moments. "Okay." He scooped up the photos. "I'll have these men arrested today."

"No, you won't." Bounter snatched the photos back. "Arresting these men won't put a dent in your problem."

"And why is that?"

"There are officers involved."

"That can't be true. I trust my officers." He gave Grant a sideways glance. "Well, most of them, anyway. Why should I believe you?"

Grant finally spoke. "Because I'm setting up a sale to them as we speak, sir."

His lips parted.

"Captain, allow me to explain," Bounter said. "Grant's working undercover for us, infiltrating the Russian Mafia down in the city. When the don and his guys discovered Grant was former Navy, they wanted him to be the go-between. They'd already established contact with men on this base, but thought the officers would more likely trust one of their own. This drug problem runs deep. That's why my bosses had us dress in uniform to protect you."

"Why do *I* need protection?"

"Because after this deal goes down and you arrest the ringleaders, we can't let the Russians or the officers connect the dots between you and Grant. We have to keep this on the down-low."

The captain sat back in his chair, his hands folded in a tent. "That's why you had me pretend this meeting was with Lt. Davis. The uniform's for Grant's protection too, then? So nobody recognizes him later?"

Bounter nodded.

The captain took this in. "You're going undercover with the mob?" he demanded after a moment.

"Yes, sir," Grant replied.

"Why?"

"I…" He swallowed. "I just have to."

"What does Joe think about this?" he asked.

"He's not happy about it, sir, but he said it's my decision." He sighed. "I apologize for the uniform, sir. I tried to tell Agent Bounter it wasn't a good idea, but he insisted."

Captain Lockhart nodded. "I still don't like it." He paused. "But I have to admit you look good in khaki again."

"Thank you, sir." He decided to take a risk. "And I assure you I don't have a gun on me this time."

The captain's mouth twitched as he shook his head. "You better not. How's Joe?"

"Good, sir. His ship should return to Norfolk in a few weeks."

"I'm sorry about your brother."

Grant flinched. The captain always had been direct. "Thank you, sir." When he swallowed, his throat was tight. "And I'm sorry…for what happened between us. For threatening you, sir. It wasn't right, especially after all you've done for me."

"It *wasn't* right," he agreed. "But Joe's told me why you attempted that inane robbery: Logan promised to kill him if you didn't. You should've gone to the authorities. But still, I understand what you thought you had to do."

"Look," Bounter butted in, "it's nice you two are catching up and all, but we need to set up this drug deal."

The captain turned to him. "There *is* no deal unless I trust the players involved."

Bounter's smirk faded. "Right. Makes sense, sir."

"And speaking of trust, is there any evidence Commander Laurent is wrapped up in this mess?"

"No," Bounter said. "He hasn't been involved to our knowledge."

"Thank God. He knows his officers, and I want to bring him on board to arrange the sting, if the FBI's okay with that."

"That would be fine, sir. We're hoping it will go down within the next week."

Captain Lockhart rose and went to his desk to call the commander.

Once the call connected and the captain's booming voice filled the office, Bounter leaned in. "Wow, he was pissed. I take back what I said. You can still be the officer next time."

"There'll never *be* a next time," Grant replied. "I knew I should've refused to wear the uniform. You just don't do that. I've made a complete mockery of the Navy."

"I don't think so. I agree with the captain. You look like you were born to wear it."

Grant looked down at his tunic, fitted neatly over his chest. He wished he'd never have to take it off again.

But that wasn't his biggest regret. Being on base again, sitting in this familiar office, interacting with the captain…he wished he'd never taken that gun from Logan.

11. Convene

The next day, Grant flipped up the collar of his long winter coat and cupped his gloved hand over his face, hoping to thaw out the frozen tip of his nose. It was almost March, yet it felt like January. He scanned the street one more time but saw just the typical after-school traffic: dilapidated school buses and soccer moms in minivans picking up their high-schoolers. No Russian mobsters in sight.

As he bounced on his numbing feet, he wondered if the trembling in his torso was due to the cold or his stress. Although there'd been a blessed reprieve from the nightmares, he still wasn't sleeping well. Tomorrow night, the deal with the naval officers would go down—sooner than he'd expected. And the moment he thought about Sophie only one floor away from his apartment—the place Andrei knew he lived—his heart would thunder and not slow down for hours. He hadn't even visited her lately, too worried he might be followed.

All of this combined to make him incredibly foolish right now: hiding in the shadows of an alley, hoping to catch a glimpse of his fiancée. Before arriving, he'd traveled all over the city in an attempt to ditch any potential tail. He seemed to be in the clear now, but he never felt entirely sure. All he knew was he had to see her, and she'd told him she'd started joining Ben for his swim practices on Tuesdays and Thursdays. So he'd planted himself on the path from the school to the pool.

Suddenly he heard Ben's voice drifting his way. "Fuck, it's cold!"

The click of Sophie's heels on the sidewalk provided background music. "It *is* cold," she agreed, "but Grant probably wouldn't want you using that word."

"Not like he cares," Ben grumbled.

"*What?*" When Sophie stopped right next to the open alley, Grant plastered himself against the dirty brick wall. "Your uncle cares deeply about you!"

"Then why doesn't he come see me anymore?"

"Ben, we've talked about this. It's temporary. He'll be back."

"Right." Sarcasm dripped from his voice. "That's what Mom always said about Dad."

From the shadows, Grant watched Sophie, her face a mix of sadness and frustration. "My mom used to say that about my dad too…when he'd go out of town for business all the time."

"Hmph." Ben shuddered in the wind. "Please tell me Daddy Warbucks is giving us a ride home after practice today."

"Sorry. He's out of town —"

"For business," they finished together, and she giggled.

Grant closed his eyes as the sound of her laugh washed over him.

The wind howled, and Ben said, "Screw this, I'm running the rest of the way."

"But I'm wearing heels!"

"Not my problem!" he taunted over his shoulder, widening the distance between them.

Sophie shook her head then took off with her handbag and briefcase swaying at her side.

Before he realized it, Grant found himself jogging after them. When Ben turned around, probably to taunt Sophie some more, Grant ducked into a store to avoid blowing his cover.

"Can I help you, sir? Something for the lady in your life?"

As he peeled off his hat, he looked at the store employee — a plump woman in her fifties with a saucy smile. A quick perusal of the store displays told him he'd ventured into a lingerie shop.

"Uhh…"

An hour later he pushed through the revolving hotel door and hustled toward Mr. Remington's office.

"Oh goody, you bought me a present!" came a voice from behind the front desk.

Shit. He turned to find the redheaded receptionist's eyes widen as her tongue swept across her lower lip. Ignoring the guest approaching the counter, she eyed the hot-pink bag in his hand. "Did you get me some lingerie?"

He hid the bag behind his back. "Well…" He practically jumped when the tall hotel guest swiveled around. The man's high forehead looked familiar…Where had he seen him before?

The man evidently recognized him too. He smirked.

Hunter! That was Hunter's partner, a surgeon. What the heck was his name?

His knowing eyes met Grant's. "Good to see you again, Gr—"

"Mick Saylor," Grant butted in, offering him an outstretched gloved hand. "How are you, Doctor?"

The man was clearly confused.

Curiosity coated the redhead's voice. "You know Mick, Dr. Washington?"

In the moment it took for Dr. Washington to regain his composure, his first name—*Bradley*—suddenly came to Grant.

"Well, yes…yes I do."

"Are you staying at the hotel?" Grant asked.

"No, I'm picking up a colleague."

He squirmed as he felt the surgeon's gaze float down his body.

Still staring, Bradley explained, "We're headed back to a plastic surgery conference at McCormick Place."

"Isn't that awesome he does plastic surgery?" the redhead asked Grant. When he said nothing, her face lit up. "Oh! I bet *that's* how you two know each other. You must've been Dr. Washington's patient, right?"

He stared at her, speechless.

She turned back to Bradley. "You did a wonderful job on him. He's so handsome, I can't believe it."

Bradley chuckled. "Now, now…" He glanced at her nametag. "Miranda, you know I can't divulge the identity of my patients. That's a secret."

And Grant hoped he was good at keeping secrets.

"Patient-doctor confidentiality," Bradley added, winking at him. "You know all about that, right, uh, Mick?"

"Yes, sir." He wished he could get the hell out of there, stat.

Miranda sighed. "Isn't Mick so polite?"

Bradley sighed as well before his grin widened. "Unfailingly so. Miranda, it appears you have a bit of a crush on Mick."

"You think?" she said. Her fair complexion didn't redden at all upon the admission.

"Is he single, do you think?" Bradley asked.

Grant's eyes narrowed. Bradley damn well knew about Sophie—he'd met her at that Brazilian steakhouse!

"That's what *I* want to know," Miranda cooed, leaning forward on the counter so her cleavage formed a perfect crease.

"Dr. Washington," Grant finally said, "was Miranda about to call your colleague on the house phone? I wouldn't want to delay you getting to the conference."

Bradley glanced down at his watch. "You're right—it's getting late. Miranda, could you ring Dr. Peterson?"

"Of course, Doctor." Miranda's face was disappointed as she turned to the phone.

Once she was busy, he mouthed a silent thank you.

"Does Hunt know about all of this, *Mick?*" Bradley whispered.

He nodded and gestured behind him. "I sing most nights in the hotel bar, Capone's Spirits."

"Ah. Should we stop by one night?"

Feeling Miranda's stare on him again, he gave a slight shake of his head. "Maybe you should ask Dr. Hayes. Great to run into you, sir."

Bradley reached out to pump his hand. "Always good to see you, Mick. Go out there tonight and…break a leg. But don't let anything happen to that perfect face."

He chuckled nervously. "Will do." Only when Bradley turned the corner did Grant feel relief. This undercover thing was getting old fast. So was unwanted attention.

Opening the outer door, he popped his head into the office. "Just wanted Mr. Remington to know I'm here."

"He'd like to see you," said Sarah.

He pulled the rest of his body inside. Was Agent Bounter here to discuss tomorrow night's plans? Had the drug deal gone south?

"You can go on in," she told him.

He knocked on Mr. Remington's door and heard, "Come in." He quietly took a seat when he saw that he was on the phone.

"I have to run, now," he told the caller. "Make sure you stay focused on your job. I want the governor to receive top-notch service."

"Is Governor Grogan staying at the hotel, sir?" he asked after Mr. Remington hung up.

"He's coming in later tonight. Hopefully Miranda won't be the one to check him in."

Grant paled. "That was Miranda on the phone?"

"Yes." He grinned. "She called to ask a question about you."

He tensed.

"She wanted to know if you were single."

"Ughhhh." He drew his hand to his forehead.

Mr. Remington laughed. "I know Grant Madsen's engaged, but I wasn't sure what to tell her about Mick Saylor. Is he on the market?"

"With Miranda, I somehow think it wouldn't matter."

"Hopefully she's not as aggressive with our male guests as with our male staff," he replied. "So, I had dinner with Will the other night, and he was nervous that the wedding plans are behind schedule. How're things coming along?"

Grant winced. Planning the wedding was one conversation of many he and Sophie needed to have. But every time he picked up the secure cell phone or contemplated spending the night with her, he worried about bringing her into his world of crime.

"Don't tell me you're one of those grooms who leaves it all up to the bride." Mr. Remington's voice was stern. "My sales manager tells me our wedding receptions go much better if the man gets his say. Last Saturday the groom's buddies were complaining that we only served two varieties of beer."

"The horror," he said, earning a smile from his boss. "To be honest, I haven't seen Sophie much lately. We've got a deal going down with the Russians tomorrow—"

"Bounter told me you need tomorrow night off."

"Yes, sir." He felt his heart gallop. "Will that be a problem?"

When Mr. Remington smoothed his hand down his dark blue tie, Grant wondered how much his suit cost. "Of course not. The FBI is your first priority…though Miranda might be upset she won't get to watch you perform on her breaks."

He closed his eyes, leaned his head back, and groaned.

"How've you been sleeping, Mick?"

His eyes flew open, and he tried to sit up straighter. Then he sighed. "Not great."

"Bounter said you're under a lot of stress."

"I'm fine." Grant thought about Innochka cowering on that dirty mattress. "I'll be okay."

"I'll make sure of that." Mr. Remington gave him a mysterious smile. "Let's go talk to Tomacz, my driver."

From behind the tinted window, Grant watched Sophie and Ben leave the natatorium, chatting animatedly in their winter coats and hats. "Target acquired," he told the driver.

Tomacz nodded from the front seat of the limo. "Want me to cut them off at the corner?" he asked in his heavy Polish accent.

"Let's pick them up, but approach slowly. I don't want to alarm Sophie." He noticed her glancing over her shoulder, probably looking for a taxi. They'd likely have to walk a couple of blocks to find one.

As the limo inched forward, closing in on the two pedestrians, Grant saw a cloud of Sophie's breath crystallize in the icy air when she laughed at something Ben said. She gave Ben a playful shove, then wrapped her arm around his shoulders when he boomeranged back to her. She seemed so relaxed and confident, sauntering along in her high-heel boots. *God, I've missed her.*

He lowered the window and frosty air rushed in the limo. "Got some fries with that shake?"

She spun toward the vehicle with her mouth hanging open, and Ben almost shouted his name. Grant drew his finger to his lips, silencing the boy, then beckoned them both into the long, sleek black car.

He scooted over as Ben clambered onto the smooth leather seats, his growing teenage body all elbows and knees. Then Sophie stepped in behind him with her usual grace, smoothing her camel coat under her legs. Her cheeks glowed with a rosy blush beneath her stylish leopard-print hat. "Where in the *world* did you get this limo?"

He smirked. "Perks of the job." Calling up to the driver, he said, "Tommy, can you drop off Ben first?"

"Sure thing, Mr. Saylor." The divider between the front seat and the rear of the vehicle quickly slid into place.

"Sweet wheels," Ben marveled. "Smells good in here too."

Grant smiled and pulled his nephew into a sideways hug. "You bet, buddy."

Ben pulled away, dusting off his shoulder. "Dude, I don't hug."

"Since when?" he looked at Sophie, who shrugged.

"So this is Alex's car?" she asked.

"Yep. He's letting me borrow it to drive you guys home from practice."

Ben butted in. "Because it's so fucking cold outside?"

Grant stared at him, sensing a challenge. "That, and because I missed you two. I'm really sorry I haven't been around. Hopefully this thing I'm doing for the FBI will wrap up soon."

"Right," Ben scoffed.

"How's swimming going?" he asked.

Sophie's calming voice entered the conversation. "He just dropped two seconds in the hundred 'fly."

"That's great!" he said.

Ben looked away and fiddled with the built-in cup holders on the armrest. "It's not that big a deal." Something across the vehicle caught his eye, and he crawled toward the mini-fridge. Yanking it open, he asked, "Can I have some champagne?"

"How do you think I'll answer that?" he asked.

Ben smirked. "Some Coke?"

"Sure."

Ben cracked open the soda and sat back. After a long gulp, he asked, "Can you come to my dual meet tomorrow?"

Grant looked at Sophie then back at Ben. "Are you asking me?" "Yeah."

"Um…sorry, buddy. I have to work."

"But *I'll* be there," Sophie promised.

Ben's silence stabbed his heart. He felt the limo roll to a stop, and looked up to find Ben's apartment building to their right.

"Looks like we're here." Grant smiled at his nephew. "Say hi to Ashley for me."

Ben looked down. "She's at work."

"I thought you'd say that." He leaned forward and rapped on the divider, which rolled down a second later. "Can I grab one of those pies, Tomacz?"

"Sure thing. The smell is driving me crazy up here."

He reached out to accept the pizza box, which he then bestowed on Ben's lap.

The boy's eyes bulged. "You got me a *pizza?*"

"I knew your mom would be at work, and you'd be starved after practice. You'll probably have to heat it up, though."

Ben beamed—it appeared all was forgiven.

"Thanks, Uncle Grant. This is perfect."

Grant was surprised when Ben maneuvered the pizza box to the side to give him a quick hug before scrambling out of the car. "Bye, Sophie!"

"See you, Ben."

"Oh." He turned back to the limo. "Sophie? Could you call my mom and tell her I went right home after practice?"

Sophie paused. "Okay? Is there a reason why?"

"N-N-No reason," he stammered. "She just worries about me, ya know?"

"Sure."

As Grant watched his nephew juggle the pizza box and his backpack to take out his keys, he said, "I thought he didn't like hugs?"

Sophie's gaze lingered on Ben until he got into the building safely. "Maybe not, but *I* do."

"Me too." He gave her a lascivious look. "Uh, Tommy?"

The divider slid up. "Hold it," Grant said. "How 'bout you take a couple pieces for yourself and pass back that other pie?"

"Ah, I couldn't, Mr. Saylor."

"Please," he said. "A token of my appreciation."

Tomacz shrugged. "If you insist." He'd already taken a big bite from one of the slices by the time the divider closed.

"He's seen where Ben lives," Sophie whispered once the divider slid into place. "And now he'll know where *we* live when he drops me off."

"After a small detour first."

"A detour?" She studied him. "Where?"

"Patience, Bonnie." He reached into the fridge and withdrew a bottle of Riesling.

"But is Tommy safe?"

He poured them both a glass. "Mr. Remington said he trusts him with his life. He's picking up the governor and his entourage later tonight."

"Oh."

He handed her a glass then raised his for a toast. "To detours."

Her eyes still held a hint of suspicion, but she clinked her glass with his.

The cool wine slid down his throat, mixing with the heat in the limo to warm his belly. "How about some pizza?"

"How'd you know I was starving?"

"I saw that lustful look you gave Ben's pizza."

Her eyelids lowered a half-inch. "Maybe it wasn't the pizza I was lusting over."

He felt a thrill of action below the belt. He picked up a slice with pepperoni and mushroom then scooted closer, offering her the first bite. A moan escaped her lips as she bit off a small triangle, and she didn't take her eyes off him as she chewed. Her tongue swept out to lick a dab of red sauce off the corner of her mouth, stirring up more heat inside of him. It didn't seem so cold anymore.

The vehicle stopped, and she craned her neck to look out the window. "Navy Pier, huh? I love the lights on the Ferris wheel." Her gaze returned on him. "So you think you're getting some tonight?"

"I see you've figured out the purpose of our detour."

She ate a couple more bites of pizza. "I'm mad at you, McSailor. I promised myself I wouldn't have sex with you until we got to talk."

He feigned offense. "That's a *horrible* thing to say!"

Her eyebrow cocked up, and she crossed her arms.

He looked down. "I'm sorry I haven't been around. That's the real purpose of this detour, actually…" He looked back up at her. "Let's talk. What do we need to discuss?"

"Well, for one thing, our wedding's in three months, and I've gotten bupkis from you about what you want. My dad's totally breathing down my back about all the stupid details."

"I'm sorry I've dumped this on you. But I thought your dad hired a wedding planner." He took a bite of pizza.

"He did, but I don't want some *stranger* planning our day."

He reached for her hand. "I thought this big wedding thing was for your dad, not for us."

"It is!"

"Then why not let his person plan it?"

"But...Huh." Her slow nod increased speed. "Maybe you're right. *I* don't care what the wedding's like, and you certainly don't, so why get all stressed out about it?"

Could it really be that easy? "Aren't you going to argue with me about this?"

"Why would I argue? You just pointed out the obvious. Thank you." She grinned as she took a sip of wine. "I'm going to dump the whole thing on Cheri. My dad will be thrilled."

He polished off his piece. "And like Ben says, maybe your dad will stop getting all up in your grill."

"Let's hope. My grill's gonna burn him if he gets any closer."

He chuckled. "So what else do we need to discuss?" He wiped his hand on a napkin. Then he tucked a strand of wet hair behind her ear and tugged at her furry hat. "How 'bout we take this off?"

Her hand darted to her hair. "But I've got hat head."

"Impossible," he said, lifting the hat away. "Your hair's always beautiful."

"Don't try to distract me, McSailor." She shook her hair out and finger-combed a few strands. "I wanted to ask you how it's going with the Russians."

He pulled back. "The less you know, the better."

Her lips pressed into a tight line, and he expected her to berate him for *his* tight lips. But instead, she took a swig of wine and tossed her hair back before crawling toward him. Her hands snaked up his chest, and her fingers went to work on the buttons of his coat.

"Do you know what we discussed today in my class?" she asked.

He felt the third button come undone and shook his head, unable to form words.

"Gender differences in intimacy." She loosened the bottom button and pulled open his coat. "You see, men seem to need physical intimacy—sexual attraction—before they can establish emotional intimacy."

As she helped him shrug out of his coat, he told himself he needed to attend her class more often.

She went in for the top button of his shirt. She paused. "Is the FBI listening to our conversation?"

He shook his head. "They let me turn off the mic until I get back to the hotel."

"How generous of them."

When he reached up to unbutton her coat, she swatted his hand away. "Back to our class discussion. Women are different from men, of course. Women…well, we need emotional intimacy first, before we want physical intimacy. We need to feel close and safe—we need to *trust*—before we agree to have sex."

She then sat back and scooped another piece of pizza out of the box.

Watching her eat, he realized his mouth had fallen open. His eyes narrowed. "You're blackmailing me for sex!" Her eyes danced. "If I don't tell you what's cookin' with the Russians, you won't trust me, and you won't take your clothes off."

"You're sharp, McSailor," she cooed. "But I prefer the term *positive reinforcement* to blackmail."

"Positive reinforcement?"

"You tell me how you're risking your life, and I reward you by making your life a little better."

"Blackmail," he grunted, tapping his fingers on his knee. Maybe throwing a few crumbs her way would satisfy her? "Okay." He blew out a breath, wondering where to begin. "The Russians…they discovered I'm former Navy."

She sat up with wide eyes.

"It's okay—we wanted them to."

"Why?"

"I can't get into the details, but it's a way to build trust with them."

She scooted closer after discarding the crust in the box.

"The Russians are selling drugs to sailors at Great Lakes."

"That's horrible!"

"I know. We thought it was just enlisted men at first, but it appears there're officers involved too." He shook his head. "So stupid. They have no idea who they're getting involved with."

"Hmm…" She glared at him. "Who does *that* sound like?"

"The FBI's covering me, Sophie. I'm taking every precaution."

"So how does your Navy connection come into play?"

"We're working with Captain Lockhart to arrange—"

"Wait a minute," she interrupted. "Isn't he the captain who got you arrested?"

He sighed. "Yep. He wasn't too happy to see me."

"You *saw* him? What'd he say?"

"After the captain chewed out Bounter and me, he finally came around—once he found out some of his officers were involved. I sure wouldn't want to be in their shoes after the sting goes down."

Her eyes got big. "It hasn't happened yet? Are you involved?"

His stomach sank at her fear. He was doing this to her—making her worry about him again. *I'm a total jerk.* "You see?" He leaned in to cradle her face with his hands. "I don't want to make you worry about this stuff. I'll be fine. I will."

She closed her eyes and nodded. "I'm sorry." When she opened them again, the lights of the Ferris wheel reflected in them, revealing flecks of gold. "You finally get a night off from those thugs, and I make you talk about them. I shouldn't have blackmailed you."

"I thought you said it was positive reinforcement."

She grinned. "And now it's time for your reward." Her coat was off in seconds, and she lunged for his shirt buttons.

"Why are you in such a great mood?" he asked.

She paused her unbuttoning, then shrugged. "I guess it's the swimming. It's tough diving in that cold water, but I feel amazing after practice. All those feel-good chemicals swimming in my bloodstream."

"Then I'll have some of what you're having, please."

She grinned. "Coming right up."

She'd almost pulled his shirt off when he held up his finger. "Wait." Grant reached for the pink shopping bag near the front of the limo. "I bought this for you." He dangled the red teddy from his finger, its price tag still on.

Her mouth popped open. "In *this* weather? You're crazy if you think I'm going to put that on."

Shrugging, he zinged the satiny material away from them. "Maybe next time, then. Perhaps our wedding night?"

His shirt came off, and he heard a muffled "Uh-huh." Her mouth was otherwise occupied doing crazy things to his chest, her tongue swirling down the central line of his abdomen as he massaged his fingers through her damp hair. He shifted down on the leather cushion, and his hands groped for her turtleneck sweater, trying to figure out how the heck to remove it.

She must've sensed his confusion because she suddenly giggled. Her hands flew to her collarbone and unclasped the hooks along the side of her neck.

"Complicated clothes," he grumbled. "No fair."

The turtleneck soared over her head and landed on the limo floor, revealing creamy skin with a dusting of freckles. She grazed one hand across her collarbone and tugged at her bra strap. "I think you've undone this bra before, Magic Fingers. You should have no problem there."

He thanked God for easy front clasps and had her bra off in seconds. Her swift shove, which plastered his back to the seat, surprised him. Looking up at her with wonder, the twinkling lights from Navy Pier showcased a hard curve on her left arm.

"What's this?" His hand brushed from her shoulder to her elbow.

She squirmed away. "The scar is fine, Grant. It's not your fault."

"No, Dr. Taylor," he said with a chuckle. "I'm not talking about your scar. I'm talking about this cut triceps muscle."

"Oh." She peered down her nose at her exposed skin as she straightened her arm. "I guess the swim practices are taking effect. Do you mind if I get a little muscular? That's what happens when I swim."

"Do *I* mind? It's your body, Sophie."

"I know *that*. I'm not asking for your permission. What I meant was, do you find a muscular woman…sexy?"

He exhaled. "Incredibly." He grasped her hand and drew her on top of him, feeling her smooth skin collide with his, the graze of her nipples on his chest shooting sparks of tingles through his body. Then her mouth was on his, and she kissed him with an intensity he hadn't felt in quite some time. How could he have gone so long without this? Without *her*?

His fingertips glided up her spine then pressed in sweeping arcs along the fine muscles of her shoulders. She responded with deepening kisses and by unbuckling his belt. A tight heat built inside him, and her fingers curled over his boxers, then ripped them down. He felt his erection spring free, pressing into her belly. With a sense of urgency, he clawed at her suede skirt and growled when it didn't budge.

Continuing to ply him with kisses, she guided his hands to the small of her back where he located the skirt's zipper. He shoved the skirt down only to find her wearing tights. "Damn it! Freaking Fort Knox up in here."

Her mouth lifted from his with a bright grin. "It's *your* fault you've got blue balls, Mick." But she took mercy on him by rocking back and sliding her tights and panties down to her crumpled skirt, which rested at the top of her boots. Her thighs were the color of freshly poured cream, and he thought he'd lose it the second she lowered herself back down, her slick heat coming into contact with his hardness.

"Sophie," he breathed, pressing her to him and holding so tight. He shifted an inch, found his way inside her taut fire, and ohhh… he'd missed her welcoming desire for far too long.

He heard her gasp as his hips bucked, but her blissful smile told him she was just fine. They rocked together, and all he could hear was his quickening breaths and her soft moans. God, she was beautiful. Her resounding shudders moments later jolted them both, knocking a wine glass to the limo floor. Thankfully the wine dribbled away from her sweater.

"Whoops," she squeaked, finally opening her eyes. "Sorry, Alex."

He took in the disheveled backseat. "Tommy might need to clean up back here before he picks up the governor."

She giggled. She reached up to caress his sweaty forehead, and he closed his eyes, reveling in her soft touch. Sophie massaged his buzzed hair as he stroked the length of her naked back, and her lips brushed against his, smooth and sweet.

"Are you feeling rewarded, McSailor?"

"You just reinforced my good behavior, Bonnie." Despite the looming drug deal, he knew he'd sleep very well tonight.

12. Conquest

Ricker Mullens was a free man, and *damn*, freedom felt good. He sauntered down State Street with his hands in his pockets and a cigarette dangling from his lips, thrilled by the looks of fear he elicited in passersby. Every time some bitch yanked her child to the other side of the sidewalk, a frisson of domination electrified his dick.

The Chicago Loop. He'd missed the energy, the depravity. What a travesty for a man of his stature to be stuck in that Gurnee hellhole for so long, with only his minions to entertain him. Steven had cried pussy tears at his release, of course. That boy would probably get shanked without his protection. His other boy would be fine, though. Bunky's fine mouth would certainly get him places in life.

But another lanky boy now caught his attention: coming toward him about forty meters away, with a baseball cap slung low over scruffy brown hair. That teen slouch turned him on every time, and he wished the boy would show his face, but his eyes stayed on the concrete as he shuffled forward. Just as the boy passed him, Ricker shifted to the left and knocked into his shoulder.

"What the fu…?" The boy blinked up at him.

Sweet Jesus. Big blue-green eyes, only a few zits, a sorry little scruff of facial hair, and the cutest pair of dimples.

"Watch where you're going," the boy said.

He laughed. His tongue swept across his lower lip. "Where you headed, sweetie? I'll *cum* with you."

The boy's eyes got huge. "Stay away from me!" He took off at a run, his red Chuck Taylors slapping on the sidewalk.

He sighed as he stared after him. Normally he'd give chase—perhaps teach the boy a thing or two—but he had more important prey to catch. Older, hotter prey. Prey with the prettiest blue eyes… soulful, vulnerable eyes…

He shook his head with disgust. Where *was* that fucking Grant Madsen? Ricker'd been out of the clink for two days already, with shit to show for it. No Madsen found on apartment or employee records anywhere in the city. That piece of ass was still on parole, but he hadn't shown to meet with his officer as far as he knew.

Tank had told him it would be easy to track down Madsen, but apparently he was going to have to shift to Plan B. And drumming up sexual interest in an adult woman—an essential element of that plan—was always a challenge.

"Fuck Plan B," he muttered, tossing his cigarette to the concrete and grinding it under his shoe. He'd much rather grind Madsen.

Nevertheless, forty-five minutes later, he strolled into an Asian fusion restaurant. He paused to check his reflection in the mirrored wall as he entered. His mother had always said he cleaned up well—when she was sober enough to notice her surroundings, anyway.

"Fuck me…" he muttered to his reflection. He *rocked* this black suit. It molded around his muscular torso, adding an inch or two of height, and no one would know he'd bought it off a thrift store rack minutes before—one of his first purchases with Mafia money, and it wouldn't be his last. He'd toss the constricting black tie the second he ditched this place, though.

"Do you have a reservation, sir?" the hostess asked.

He'd spent his time checking out the restaurant as he waited for the crowd in front of him to clear, and he had a pretty good idea where Plan B needed to take place.

He gave her what he hoped was a sweet smile. "No *wonder* you're the hostess. They put all the pretty girls up front."

A blush spread across her ample cheeks. *Score*. The fat chicks always ate up his compliments.

"No reservation, no," he continued. "But it is only one for tonight. No one to share my meal with. You must have a table for a bachelor who just left a funeral, right?"

Her face fell. "A funeral? I'm so sorry."

"Thank you. My wife and I used to sit by the windows, and I would like to honor her by dining there tonight."

She drew a hand to her mouth. "Your wife just died?"

He let out a heavy breath and looked down, giving a slight nod.

"I'll find you our best seat, sir," she promised as she scanned the seating chart.

When she marked off his table and grabbed a menu, he grasped her wrist and looked deeply into her eyes. "Thank you. You do not know what this means to me."

"It's the least I can do."

After Lardass left him with the menu, he unrolled his utensils, marveling at the heavy cloth napkin. Gurnee hadn't even bothered with *paper* napkins. He glanced around to see if he could spot the blonde who would be his waitress, and his fingers curled around the knife. It felt so satisfying to hold real silverware, instead of a motherfucking plastic spork. The handle of the knife fit so easily in his palm too. He remembered watching Enzo stick that shank into Tank, the oozing sluice of blood—

"What can I get you to drink?"

With a flinch, he looked up into blue eyes framed by wavy blond hair. Her eyes held the hint of shadows, but she seemed to possess a sense of optimism and perk he hadn't expected.

"Um…" He searched for words.

"I'm sorry. I didn't mean to startle you."

He waved her off. "Not your fault at all. I am…distracted. I will try to get with the program."

"Take your time." She smiled.

After he scanned the menu, he said, "Wine. Red wine. And lots of it."

"Seems like you've had a rough day?"

"You could say that."

The blonde's fidgeting puzzled him until she leaned in. "Listen, maybe you wanted to keep this private, but Wendy told me about your wife. I'm so sorry." She straightened again. "I understand why you need some wine."

"Wow." He shook his head. "Such unexpected kindness from strangers." His lips trembled as he drew one hand to his heart. "I am overwhelmed, truly."

"We treat our guests more like friends than strangers." Kindness filled her voice. "Now, which wine would you like?"

He peered at the list. "Would you choose one for me?"

"Of course." She pointed to a moderately priced selection. "I like this Australian Shiraz, but my more sophisticated diners prefer this Bordeaux."

Naturally she'd chosen the most expensive bottle on the menu. *Goddamn greedy servers, working me for a hefty tip.* "Only the best for tonight. Please bring a bottle of the Bordeaux."

"Right away, sir."

As she headed toward the bar, he zeroed in on her ass. *Whoa.* Tank hadn't told him she had such fine melons hiding under that black skirt. Quite squeezable and smackable—much tastier than the scrawny backsides of his boys. Maybe Plan B wasn't so fucked after all.

They performed the little wine-tasting ritual—he hoped he was doing it right—and he let out a sated moan when the wine slid down his throat. "You have excellent taste," he told her and watched her light up.

Having no clue what to order from a menu without a hint of sauerkraut or *spätzle*, he let her select his entrée as well. And knowing the Thai were dirty pigs, it surprised him how much he enjoyed the noodle dish. Of course, anything would be better than that Gurnee glop he'd forced down for several years.

"Your hair is *schyn*…beautiful," he told the waitress after sipping from his third glass. It had been months since he'd ingested anything other than a bit of smuggled alcohol in his cell, and he knew he'd better hit the brakes on the booze if he wanted to pull this off. "It looks so soft, so smooth."

"Thank you." A pleasing blush spread across her face. "I have to admit I was admiring your hair too."

"You *were?*"

She blinked several times, seeming embarrassed. "I like blond men." She shrugged. "Just something about them. They seem…more honest or something." When her blush deepened, he was shocked to feel his zipper tent with the beginnings of an erection. "And I like how your hair spikes up," she added. "It suits your face."

"Such kindness from…*friends*." They shared a conspiratorial smile, and he noticed with a sigh that the sickening sweetness of it all had made his cock go limp. "I will pass along your compliment to the barber. He just cut my hair yesterday."

"For the funeral?" she asked.

He tightened his mouth. "Yes."

"You know…" She leaned her hip against the table, almost sitting that perfect ass right next to his knife. "Wendy said you often sat here with your wife, but I've worked this section for a few years now, and I've never met you."

She was playing right into his fucking hands. Plan B was glorious! He leaned in an inch. "You've been so nice to me…you deserve the truth. My wife and I *did* come in here together, years ago. But then…" He tried to suck down a sob. "I found out she was cheating on me, and we got a divorce."

The waitress stared at him, seeming to judge every word, so he rushed ahead, "I attended her funeral today. My *ex*-wife's funeral."

She nodded slowly.

"And I try to make people understand how *devastating* it was to say goodbye to her, but nobody understands. She was my ex, but she was my everything. I never fell out of love with her." *Please, please, cry. Let a tear fall right now.* "And now she's gone. I will never have another chance with her."

The waitress nodded more vigorously.

He felt a burning in his nose, no doubt aided by the wine flowing through him, and he managed to squelch a victory dance when his eyes filled with tears. "But how do I explain this to others? My friends do not understand why I am so heartbroken…so bereft. '*She cheated on you,*' they tell me. '*She does not deserve your grief.*' But I lost the love of my life, and I will never find another. Nobody understands."

"*I* understand," she said softly.

He looked up at her through his tears, and she slid into the chair across from him. She took a deep breath, seeming to steel herself. "My ex was murdered eight months ago."

He flinched with feigned horror and seized the opportunity to capture one of her hands in his. Her skin was so soft, so delicate.

"And we'd never married, so nobody understood what that was like for me. But my son lost his father…" She abruptly sat up, yanking her hand away. "I'm sorry. Here you are having an awful day, and I'm blabbing on about *my* problems."

"No, please. Your pain is so much worse, dealing with a, a *murder*." He spat the word like it disgusted him. "And left all alone as a single mother. You seem so devoted to your son."

"He's a teenager—he can drive me crazy sometimes."

"Ah, teenagers. Too bad my wife and I did not have children before we divorced. I'll never have that chance now." His head shook. "Your son…Is that why you work such long hours?"

She nodded.

"I just realized…I do not know your name. I am Hans. Hans Fuchs."

She took his proffered hand and shook it. "Ashley. Ashley Frederickson."

"It is an *honor* to meet you, Ashley."

From her perch in the stands, Sophie surveyed the quiet swimming pool. There was a break in the meet for diving, and two lifeguards dragged the lane markers away from the boards to make room.

"Do you think you'll swim next year, Ben?" she asked as she dug around her handbag for an elastic band. *Damn, it's hot in here.* "Ah!" She worked her hair up into a ponytail and fanned the back of her neck, wishing she hadn't frittered away her swimming career over a battle of wills with her father at age twelve.

Then she noticed he hadn't answered her question. She turned and found his gaze glued to the other side of the pool deck where some of the girls' team had gathered. He had his eyes on Lindsay again. "Ben?"

He shook out of his trance. "I'm sorry, what'd you say?"

"I asked if you plan to swim next year."

"Hmm." He played with the zipper of his warm-up jacket. "Maybe not. It *is* kind of tempting never to swim the hundred 'fly again."

"Oh, c'mon, you love it."

He snorted. "I definitely don't love the practices from hell." His eyes drifted back to Lindsay. "But I guess this sport's not all that bad."

"Particularly since Lindsay will be a senior on the team next year too."

He gaped at her, and her only reply was a knowing smile. "Jeez," he groaned, massaging his temples. "Am I that obvious?"

"She's a great girl," she said. "She's a good student, a fantastic swimmer—a really sweet girl. You'd make a lovely couple."

He looked down. "'Cept she doesn't want anything to do with me."

"That can't be true."

"It *is*," he said. "Dylan went behind my back and asked her if she liked me. Apparently she said I'm a *pothead*." He held up curled fingers to perform air quotes.

"That's ancient history. Just because you smoked weed doesn't make you a pothead."

"That's what Dr. Hunter said."

"No wonder I like him so much." She smirked. "What did he suggest? Did he encourage you to ask her out?"

"Don't remember. I think we got sidetracked."

"Talking about what?"

When he hesitated, she said, "I'm sorry. I'm being nosy."

"Yeah, you are."

The sounds of divers bouncing on the board to warm up filled the air. She forced herself to be quiet.

He spoke after a few moments. "Then I found out Lindsay's dad is a police officer."

"He *is?*" She scanned the stands as her heartbeat accelerated. "Is he here?" The *po-po*, as Roger had referred to them, still made her uncomfortable.

"Nope. Dylan said her dad hasn't made it to any meets this year, 'cause he has to work."

"How does Dylan know so much about Lindsay?" She looked over and saw Dylan whispering in a girl's ear. "Oh. Dylan's dating Olivia, and Olivia's Lindsay's best friend."

"You catch on pretty good." He studied her. "So what's it like to swim with a bunch of high schoolers? Are you sick of the drama yet?"

Once she'd set Coach Bob straight on the fact that she was very much in love with Grant and very much off the market, she'd really enjoyed the practices. "It's actually a lot of fun," she said. "Especially spending time with you—getting to see your world. I love getting to know you better."

He ducked his head.

"Ben? What's the big deal if Lindsay's dad is a police officer?"

"She *definitely* won't want to be with me now."

"Why not?"

He widened his eyes and cocked one eyebrow. "Uh, helloooo… my last name? There's no way she'd date a Barberi."

"Oh." She'd had the same conversation—several times—with Grant. Vicenzo Barberi had surely infected the lives of several generations of descendants. "You know, Grant has tried to convince me over and over that he's tainted and unworthy because of his family."

Ben looked straight ahead, feigning disinterest.

"And I wouldn't believe him," she continued. "Not for one second. Because I *know* him. I know the good in him." She waited for him to meet her eyes. "Just like I know you."

"But he's a *Madsen*. He doesn't have to use this stupid name."

"So change your name. You could do that, you know. Take your mother's name…Frederickson, is it? Benjamin Fredrickson."

He scowled. "That sounds like shit."

She laughed. "*Ben* Frederickson?"

"But I kind of like Ben Barberi."

She nudged his shoulder. "I do too." She thought she saw a hint of blush on his cheek.

As the first round of diving began, a hush fell over the meager crowd.

His knee jangled. Then his fingers tapped a beat on his thigh. Finally, he whispered, "Sophie? Dr. Hunter wanted me to tell Grant something. But I don't know if I should."

"Okay?"

They watched another dive, which elicited polite applause despite the girl's resounding splash.

"Sophie?"

"Yeah?"

He chewed on his lip. "Lindsay's right. She shouldn't get involved with me."

She sighed. Hadn't he heard anything she'd said?

"I sold drugs." The words flew out of his mouth and his eyes bore into hers, daring her to show a hint of judgment. "I was a dealer."

"I see," she said, maintaining a neutral façade. "That must have been, um, frightening for you. When was that?"

He swallowed. "Last year."

"Are you still selling drugs?"

He shook his head.

She kept her voice low. "What made you stop?"

"Um…my dad dying, I guess. And my mom's stupid drug tests."

The request he'd made the night before ran through her mind. "So you're grounded now, after you told your mom about selling drugs?"

"Yeah." His cheeks flushed. "Can you *believe* she'd do that?"

She'd never been so proud of Ashley's parenting. "Sucks."

"Yeah." He watched another horrible dive and snickered. "That was a *fail*." Then his expression sobered. "So, um, how do you think Uncle Grant would react if I told him?"

"Well, I think he'd be upset and worried about you."

"Would he…hate me?"

"Absolutely not. He committed a crime too. I bet he'd want to make sure it didn't happen again, though. Is it possible you'll get pressured into using or selling in the future?"

"No."

She watched Dylan and Olivia playfully shoving each other. "Dylan wasn't involved in this, was he?"

"He chickened out."

Thank God. "He seems like a good guy."

"Nick and I made fun of him for wimping out." He cringed. "I was kind of a jerk last year."

"We all make mistakes." *Particularly me.* "You haven't talked about Nick much. Why didn't he join the swim team too?"

He blew out a breath. "He just got out of rehab a month ago. His dad found drugs in his backpack and went ballistic. His parents, like, kidnapped him and forced him into treatment right away."

"Wow." She tapped her chin. "I'm not sure about the legal definition of kidnapping, but I don't think parents can be charged with kidnapping their own son."

He elbowed her. "You know what I mean. Lucky for me my mom's got shitty insurance, or that'd be me too."

"Why isn't Nick here watching your meet?"

His grin faded. "His dad won't let him speak to me anymore."

"Oh. That must be rough, losing your friend over this."

He shrugged.

"I've seen that happen sometimes," she said. "Parents get scared when their child has a problem, and they blame their kid's friends. But it's not like you made Nick join you, did you?"

"No. He was into it all on his own. He thought it made him cool."

"Is that why you did it? To make you look cool?"

After a moment, he shook his head. "Nah. I'm *already* cool."

She laughed a little too loudly, and when a parent glared at her, she shrunk down. After the last diver executed a twisting nightmare, she straightened her spine. It wasn't like the crowd's silence helped the divers anyway. Normal crowd chatter resumed as the lifeguards dragged the lane markers back into place for last few races.

"I wasn't trying to be cool," he said, continuing their conversation. "I was mad at my dad, and I was trying to get his attention."

"I see." She marveled at his insight. "Seems like you're getting a lot out of your sessions with Dr. Hayes. So, uh, did it work then? Did it get Logan's attention?"

"Yeah." His teeth trapped his lower lip. "Sometimes I wish...I still had it."

A lump lodged in her throat. "Me too. You deserved a lot more of his attention than you got."

"Hey, Benji boy!"

They looked up to see Dylan climbing the stands. The boy's build was more like a football player than a swimmer.

"Coach said you're in the free relay," Dylan said.

"*What?* Why?"

He grinned and gestured to the locker room. "Yoshi's in there puking his guts out. You gotta take his place."

"Gross." Ben made a face. "I told him not to eat in the school cafeteria."

"I know, right?" Dylan smirked. "Thanks for scoring some pizza for me."

"No probs." Ben turned to Sophie. "You can tell Grant pizza's *always* welcome at my house."

"Yeah, tell him, Sophie," Dylan urged as he patted his belly. "We's growin' boys."

"You got nothin' to worry about, Dyl. Olivia brings you lunch every day anyway."

He turned around to find his girlfriend across the pool. "Isn't she awesome? I better go check on my woman. Later, guys."

Ben scooped up his goggles and towel.

"You know, Grant used to try to push me away because he didn't think he was good enough for me. But I didn't let him. It's *my* decision who I want to be with."

"Why are you telling me this?"

"Maybe Lindsay doesn't know what she's missing."

"I don't have a chance with her."

"Then it's her loss."

He made a sound of disgust as he stood. "Are you staying for the relay?"

"Of course. And I'll tell Grant about the pizza."

He paused. "Maybe…maybe you could tell him about the other thing too?"

She gave him a questioning look.

"The selling drugs thing." He tossed his towel over his shoulder and played with his goggles. "I might not get to talk to him for a while, and I don't want it hanging over my head. Would you tell him?"

"I think it'd be better if you told him yourself, but I get how hard it can be to talk with him these days. I'll think about it, okay?"

"Okay."

The announcer called the breaststrokers to the block.

"Sophie?"

"Yes?"

"Thanks for being here."

"You bet, Ben Barberi."

13. Conduct Unbecoming

Why did it have to be the *same* bar?

From the passenger seat of Vladimir's black Mercedes, Grant eyed the faded brown siding and neon sign of the bar located a block from the naval base: the scene of his crimes, past and present. The seedy ambience and uniformed patrons entering the bar were the same as the night he and Logan had sat in this very parking lot. But so many other things had changed.

This time it was Andrei seated next to him instead of his brother.

This time he pocketed the offered gun with cool professionalism instead of shaking hands.

This time the authorities *pushed* him to commit the crime instead of waiting to arrest him afterward.

"Has dark face and two chins," Andrei said as he gestured to the bar entrance.

"The man I'm meeting has a double chin?"

He nodded.

"Will he be in uniform?"

"Do not know. No uniform first meeting." He shrugged. "He will take you out to back for exchange."

"He will?" Grant frowned. "Was the first meeting here? At this bar?"

Andrei's eyes tapered into slits. "Why you ask?"

"Because there's a private room in the basement—I'm guessing that's where we'll go for the exchange."

"Ah. Then first meeting was in different place." He grinned. "You know bar from Navy days, *da? That* is why we use you for this." He tapped his temple with his forefinger. "Smart." His grin vanished. "You return with money missing, you not so smart." He patted his heart, where Grant knew he kept his weapon under his jacket. "You dead."

Grant nodded, ignoring the flip of his stomach. "Understood." He looked at the messenger bag Andrei held in his lap. "And if this goes down smoothly, Mr. Federov will forgive my debt?"

"Not *if*, when. *When* this goes down smooth, Vladimir knock down your debt." He winked. "There is never forgive in our world."

It was a world Grant knew well. He waited in silence until Andrei finally handed over the bag.

"Stay off the ice," he warned.

Grant glanced out the window—the unexpected warm-up earlier that day had melted the snow. Then he realized Andrei was talking about the drugs inside the bag.

"Is possible we have man inside watch you," he added.

"I'll remember that," he said as he exited the car into a blast of cold air.

He entered the crowded building and maneuvered his way to the bar. As he waited behind a pair of women also trying to snag the bartender's attention, he unwrapped the blue/gray striped scarf Sophie had given him for Christmas. His eyes floated over the men seated around the square bar, but failed to locate his target (*or* the Russians' hired baby-sitter, if Andrei was telling the truth). Fortunately Agent Bounter had shown him FBI photos of the officers suspected in the drug ring, which gave him more to go on than Andrei's vague physical description.

"See anything you like?" the woman in front of him asked her friend.

As she shook her head, her black hair swayed. "Nope. We need some fresh blood in this place." A second later, she looked behind her. Then her head whipped back around so fast her friend couldn't help but notice. She too turned to look, her eyes first scanning his face then zooming in on his crotch and resting there for several moments. He squirmed, wondering if his fly was unzipped.

She turned back to face the bar and leaned in to whisper to her friend. *Fantastic.* The last thing he needed was more attention tonight. Just as Long Black Hair seemed about to ask him a question, he stepped to his left and weaved his way to the other side of the bar. He lucked out by reaching a barstool just as a seaman slid off, and sighed as he took a seat. He unbuttoned his coat but left the messenger bag strapped across his chest. He now had a view of the pool table over in the corner. Right away he made eye contact with a man taking a swig from his beer bottle. When the man set down the bottle, Grant noticed his full face and buzzed brown hair. *Bingo.* Lt. Mitchell Jernigan's stocky build wouldn't last long if he kept using meth.

He sensed someone's presence and found the harried bartender giving him an expectant look. His heart thundered, as he had no idea what to order. "Tequila, on the rocks," somehow slid out of his mouth. Sophie had joined him tonight whether she knew it or not.

"Double?" the bartender asked.

"Uh, sure."

Nodding, the bartender seized the tequila bottle by its neck and had it flipped over a glass of ice in no time. The pour kept going, and Grant gulped as the double shot glass slid in front of him. The bartender gave him another expectant look, and he realized the man had already told him the exorbitant price of the drink. Money exchanged hands, and the entire process had taken less than thirty seconds.

It seemed the game of pool had also been swift, as the lieutenant now handed over some cash to one of his buddies—his frown an easy indication of who'd lost the game. He chugged the rest of his beer and slammed the bottle down on the pool table. Then he glared at Grant for a second before heading down the stairs.

Grant stared at the golden liquid in the tumbler. No time to nurse this drink—duty called. He pictured the flecks of gold in Sophie's eyes and downed the double shot in two long sips. Before the bartender could return to refill his glass, he slunk over to the old-fashioned jukebox. Still no sign of any Russian thugs monitoring him. He flipped through the selections for what seemed like a reasonable amount of time, then ducked down the staircase.

When he reached the bottom step, his spine tingled with the memory of Captain Lockhart staring him down, seeming to know something was wrong, blocking the staircase…

He reached into his coat pocket and brushed the cool metal of the gun.

"*It'll be okay*," Logan had promised. "*You're a Barberi. You're Dad's son. This stuff runs in our blood.*"

He would give anything to be another man's son.

"*Vwe poteryalees?*" came a voice from the dark hallway, jolting him back to the present. Impressive Russian from an American lieutenant.

Silently translating the Russian words, Grant took a second to ponder the question. *Was* he lost? No, unfortunately not. He wished he was and could turn around to go home. Wherever home was these days. "No. I know exactly where I am," he told the darkness. "I'm here to meet a friend."

Lt. Jernigan emerged from the hallway, dressed in black. "I was waiting for someone too." He glanced at Grant's bag. "But it's not clear if he's a friend."

"The Russian told you I used to be a lieutenant, right?"

Jernigan gave the slightest of nods but continued to glare.

How could he prove his Navy background? He looked over his shoulder — the stairwell was still empty. "You better watch out for article one-twelve-A, Louie."

After a moment, Jernigan nodded. "You're probably right. Come with me."

He matched his stride. As they headed down the hallway, a raucous cheer from the bar descended through the floor. The lieutenant stopped, and Grant did too. A second later they heard the opening notes of "You've Lost that Lovin' Feeling." Someone had cranked the jukebox to an epic volume.

"Fucking Tom Cruise," Jernigan muttered as he resumed his way down the hall. "As if that tool could ever be a flyboy."

"True that. About being an aviator — do you speak from experience?" Grant asked.

He hesitated. "No." He gave Grant the onceover. "So what'd *you* do?"

"Ops on bird farms."

"*Which* ops?"

Grant stroked the gun in his pocket and surprised himself by grinning. "I could tell you, but then I'd have to kill you."

"A fucking spook…*and* you're quoting that horrible movie." Jernigan groaned. He entered a code into the lighted security pad next to a door at the end of the hall, and Grant made a big show of looking away. He wondered if they'd changed the code since he'd broken into the room to recover Logan's lost money.

Once inside, Jernigan sized him up. "I'm surprised they discharged you with all the dirt you had on them."

"I gathered intelligence on the enemy, not the US."

"Right." Jernigan grinned.

"Andrei told you about my discharge, huh?"

"I told *him* I didn't trust him. Something ain't right with that Pinko."

Seemed like Jernigan was a good judge of character. Grant was surprised at how much he liked him. But first impressions weren't everything.

"I told him the only way this deal goes down is with someone I trust," Jernigan said. "Someone who fights on the same side as me—not some Commie bastard."

"You said that to *Andrei?* You're lucky you're still alive."

"It worked, didn't it?" He smirked. "So…let's see it."

Grant kept his eyes on the lieutenant as he opened the bag and extracted a baggie filled with crystal meth. He shook the baggie to let a couple of rocks spill out onto the table.

Jernigan's dark eyes gleamed as he reached for one. He held the rock up to the light and rubbed it.

"It'll light you up like a surface to air missile," Grant offered.

Jernigan shook his head. "I don't use. This shit will put holes in your brain."

"Oh."

"This…" Jernigan held up the rock. "That's what they got you on? The one-twelve-A?"

"No. That shit will put holes in your brain. My discharge was article one thirty-three."

"One thirty-three…" He scratched his head. "And which conduct of yours wasn't so becoming?"

Grant stayed quiet.

"The Navy kicked you out…but the Russkies got you now, don't they? You're still working the same crimes that got you discharged?"

His eyes narrowed. "Why do *you* fucking care?" He hoped he'd drummed up appropriate anger. Apparently his attempt at looking murderous was successful. Jernigan took a step back.

"Hey, man, you don't have to tell me. I just wondered what I'm looking at if things go FUBAR…if I get caught or something." He looked down. "If I live that long."

Grant studied him. "You're in deep."

Jernigan said nothing.

"You owe someone a lot of money."

"How'd you know that?"

He cleared his throat. "From experience. The conduct unbecoming charge…it was for gambling. I was a gambling addict."

"*Was?*"

He snorted. "Yeah, guess past tense isn't so accurate. You got me pegged, dude."

"Takes one to know one," Jernigan admitted.

Jesus Christ. He'd figured his easy rapport with the lieutenant had been about their military service, but now he realized Mitch Jernigan, gambling addict, was his brother all over again. He couldn't get away from Logan.

"Let's get this over with," Grant said. "They're waiting for me."

Jernigan nodded. "Me too. I'm supposed to make sure you have the right amount."

"Thirty eight-balls," he replied, scooping up the sample and stuffing it back in the bag. He opened the bag so Jernigan could see inside. "And I need to make sure you have the right amount too."

"I have it ready for you." Jernigan crossed the room and paused in front of a black safe on the floor. "Move over here, where I can see you."

Grant shrugged and moved into to Jernigan's line of vision before the man kneeled down to spin the safe's combination. The hideous dogs-playing-poker painting still hung on the wall, but apparently the safe was no longer tucked behind it. Or perhaps this was Jernigan's private stash.

From the safe, Jernigan pulled his own messenger bag and set it on the table. He removed a bundle of twenties and slid off the rubber band. Each bill stacked on top of another as he counted them off.

Then he gathered them back into the rubber band and stuffed the bundle in the bag. "There're twenty bundles in here."

Grant lifted the strap of his bag over his head, and they made an even exchange. "These bills better not be marked," he warned.

Jernigan glared back. "And this better be quality rock."

They stared at each other for a few tense moments, then burst out laughing.

"We make horrible criminals," Jernigan said, shaking his head.

Grant's smile faded. "Maybe we should stop trying so hard."

Jernigan leaned down to stuff the methamphetamine into the safe. "It's too late for me. But maybe you can get out?"

"I don't think the Russians will just let me go. Once the Mafia gets you, you never get out." Logan's words mocked him from the grave. *"You're a Barberi. This stuff runs in our blood."*

"You're probably right. C'mon, I'll show you the back way out."

"The *back* way out?" Why the hell hadn't he known about that three years ago? He would've never gotten arrested!

"Yeah, right here," Jernigan said as he led them out the door, yanked it closed, then stopped in the darkened hallway.

Grant pulled the bag's strap over his head and across his chest, and in the dark he made out the faint outline of a door. Damn it—he wished he'd seen that when the captain had thwarted his exit on the stairwell. He'd have never gone to Gurnee.

Oh. But then he'd never have met Sophie.

If he had to do it all over again, would he have left Captain Lockhart on the stairwell and hustled to this exit instead?

No. He would've served a *ten*-year sentence if it meant bringing Sophie into his life. If only he could make it up to the captain somehow, though. Hopefully this operation would stem the flow of bad blood between them…but there was still a lot that could go wrong.

Jernigan pressed the emergency exit door handle, and Grant almost reached out to stop him. But there was no alarm when it clicked open. Grant peeked out the door and saw a patch of night sky at the top of the shadowed stairwell—the perfect place for one of Jernigan's buddies to hide and attack him.

He patted the strap of the messenger bag as he studied Jernigan for one long moment. "There's nobody waiting up there to ambush me, is there?"

Jernigan tried to hide his look of surprise with a grin. "Nope. Wish I'd planned that, though."

"I think you *did* plan that," he shot back.

Jernigan's grin vanished. "Look, my guy's waiting at the top of the *other* stairwell, in case you pull anything funny. Since the drugs look legit, I'm letting you out the back way."

Grant's eyes traveled from the crumbling concrete steps back to Jernigan's face.

"You think I'd try to screw over the *Russians?*" the man asked, exasperated. "That'd be suicide."

Grant's heart thumped. Suicide wasn't on his agenda when *he* planned to screw over the Russians. "Okay." He reached out to shake his hand. "Good luck."

Jernigan's scowl softened. "You too, man. Don't get dead."

In another life, he sensed they could've been friends. But in this life, depending on how quickly Captain Lockhart ordered the search and interrogation, Article 112a of the Uniform Code of Military Justice — *Wrongful Use, Possession, Etc., of Controlled Substances* — was about to rain down on Jernigan.

Grant took the stairs two at a time, and just like Jernigan had promised, no one waited to ambush him. He rounded the side of the bar, his palm squeezing the butt of the handgun in his pocket. After a scan of the parking lot revealed no threats, he slid into the Mercedes.

"Give," Andrei demanded, and Grant passed the bag. He held his breath while Andrei counted the cash.

Suddenly Andrei was all smiles. "Very good." He patted the crown of Grant's head, and his rough hand was cold. "We report back to Vladimir. He is happy."

Anything to make Vladimir happy.

"The weapon," Andrei said, holding out his hand.

He handed over the Glock, and Andrei stuffed it into his jacket and peeled out of the lot.

Relief washed over Grant once they were back on the highway. This time his trip to the bar had a happier ending.

He hoped.

Andrei was quiet as he drove, leaving Grant to his thoughts. He mused about the past couple of hours. They'd driven from Great Lakes to West Town, this time stopping at another ancient, drafty house. He wondered how many of these Vladimir owned.

Andrei had handed the bag of cash to Vladimir, who seemed unimpressed. Just a drop in the *vedro*, Grant surmised. He'd waved them off and returned to making out with Katya on the leather sofa. Grant wanted to get the hell out of there before he hurt somebody. The bruise on Katya's skinny arm made him want to steal back the gun and shoot the don's freaking head off. His homicidal impulses abated somewhat when Andrei took them to a local bar to give his boss some privacy.

Now that they were done with another long evening, he couldn't wait to get away from the Russians. "You didn't have to drive me home," he said. The three vodka drinks hadn't seemed to affect Andrei at all, but Grant's head buzzed from the alcohol and adrenaline. He sensed the Russians were preparing him for bigger deals in the future, now that tonight's deal had built some trust.

Grant's eyes grew big as the car sailed past the lobby entrance of his apartment building. "Where are we going?"

"Home, like you ask." Andrei winked. "I come see where you live."

He gripped the armrest. Apparently the trust tests were ongoing. *Please don't make a surprise visit tonight, Sophie.*

It took some circling for Andrei to find a parking space. Once they did, Grant started down the sidewalk, only to realize Andrei wasn't following him. He remained standing near the hood of the car. He tilted his head toward the parking meter.

He expects me *to pay for parking? Unbelievable.* He shook his head as he swiped his Mick Saylor credit card on the meter. The power dynamics were clear in this relationship. *Just wait till I take you down. Get Innochka and Katya out of there, and get you and your boss behind bars.* Then the power would definitely shift.

"Chicago make you pay all day and night for park," Andrei mused as they began to walk. "Is bullshit. Corrupt government."

He suppressed a chuckle. *Mafia* complaining about corruption? *Pot, meet kettle.*

He rubbed his hands together as they entered the lobby and nodded at the doorman. He extracted the fob on his keychain and buzzed them through the door leading to the elevators. He was about to press the button when Andrei blocked him with his arm and pressed the number for his floor himself.

A chill bloomed up his spine. When had Andrei been in the building? Had he seen Sophie? Kirsten?

Andrei looked at the shining chrome handrail lining the elevator car. "Nice building. You hold back money from us?"

"I pay you everything I have," he countered. "Just wait till you see inside the apartment—it's not that nice. But the rent kills me all the same."

"Is not rent killing you," Andrei said. "Is way you lose at cards."

"Thanks," he muttered as he stepped out of the elevator. He mentally checked off the items in his apartment as he'd left them. The FBI's secure phone was hidden away in his dresser drawer. Sophie's clothes were all upstairs at Kirsten's. The props were in place. The button mic on his shirt was still recording as far as he knew.

What was he missing?

His heart fluttered as he unlocked the door. Andrei followed him into the dark one-bedroom apartment. He tossed the keys on the counter between the kitchen and living room. "Want a drink?"

One of Andrei's eyebrows approached his hairline.

He felt like an imbecile. He went to the kitchen and filled a couple of glass tumblers with ice. As he reached into the cabinet above the refrigerator for a bottle of whiskey, he caught a glance of the Russian thumbing through some books on a shelf.

With the two glasses, he approached the bookshelf. Andrei turned to him with a wicked grin. "Books not work for you."

He looked at the gambling instructional manuals then back at the mobster. "So you come here to insult me, then?" He pulled the drinks to his chest. "The door's right over there, bud."

Andrei chuckled. "Sorry to offend host."

"Hmph." He paused before extending a glass.

"No," Andrei said, pointing to the drink Grant held in his other hand. "That one."

He gave him the drink he wanted. "Did anyone ever tell you you have trust issues?"

"Not if he want to live." Andrei took a sip. "Poker like sex, *da?* If you not have good partner, you better have good hand."

Grant laughed.

The uninvited guest stepped over to the record collection. "You have old record player. Why?"

"It was my mother's." When they'd stocked his apartment with Mick Saylor props, he'd asked for a collection of records from the Frank Sinatra era. He couldn't believe it when the FBI found that record player at a second-hand shop—almost exactly like the one his mother had owned. They'd lost just about everything when she'd taken him and Logan to Joe's after his father's arrest, and it calmed him to have a piece of family history back.

"Your mother dead?" Andrei asked.

He swallowed. "Yes."

"Your father beat her."

He blanched, wondering if his cover was blown, then remembered telling Andrei about the abuse when he refused to whip Innochka. He looked down at his whiskey, then raised the glass to his lips.

Andrei asked, "He kill her?"

"No." He sighed. "She died from cancer when I was twelve."

"Make you tough," Andrei said as he patted his cheek. He gestured around him to the plain walls. "No photos. Why?"

"Would *you* put up photos of the man who beat your mother?"

"I would not." Andrei replied. He took a long sip. "I do not."

He nodded. He'd *thought* Andrei gave him a strange look that night at the house. "Your dad beat your mom?"

He looked away. "Is okay he beat me and brothers. Is way we learn." His jaw clenched. "Is not okay he beat *Mama*." He swirled his drink, and the ice cubes clinked against the glass. "Is not okay he kill her."

Grant drew in a sharp breath. "He killed your mother?"

"Is okay now." Andrei smiled. "We take care of it."

"*We?*"

Andrei strode toward the back of the apartment, all business. "Toilet here, yes?"

"Uh, yeah."

When the Russian closed the bathroom door, Grant poured most of his whiskey down the drain. He blew out a breath as he leaned over the sink, his elbows resting on the countertop.

"What is this?"

He straightened. To his horror, Andrei held Sophie's makeup. How had he missed that bottle of foundation? "You've been scrounging around in my medicine cabinet? That's not cool, Andrei."

"You have lover here?"

He blinked. "No. The truth is…I sometimes wear makeup on nights I sing." He manufactured a blush. "Frank Sinatra did it too." He thought that juicy tidbit would make Andrei laugh, but the Russian kept scowling.

Andrei then held up a tube of lipstick. "You wear lipstick too?"

He tensed. "Uh…"

"You have girlfriend. Just say it."

His mind raced as he searched for a plausible explanation. Damn Sophie for leaving her makeup all over the place!

"I will meet her." Andrei nodded. "Bring her to show tomorrow. We have drinks."

"But—"

He'd already tossed the makeup on the sofa and returned to the front door. "This place a dump, Saylor. Hope your lady look better than this."

When the door closed, Grant realized his mouth was hanging open. What the hell just happened? There was no *way* he'd bring Sophie near those thugs.

He marched into the bedroom and yanked open the drawer. He snatched the hidden cell phone and had Agent Bounter on the line in seconds.

"Bob's Bar and Grill," he answered.

"What the fuck are we gonna do? I can't bring So—"

"Shut up and calm down," Bounter said, lowering his voice. "He could've wired the place when he was there."

"Oh."

"We'll get some people in there to check for bugs tomorrow. For now, you sleep."

"But—"

"Listen to me," he ordered. "We won't let Sophie near them, okay? We'll figure something out. Give us some time."

"Okay."

"You were excellent tonight. Keep it up…not much longer now. I know how stressful this is, but you're handling it like a pro. You did good, Mick."

"Thank you."

"We'll be in touch. Be good."

The phone clicked. He stared at it for a long minute. Then he typed out a text:

Are your buns warm?

He paced for a few minutes and finally Sophie responded:

Sorry, was asleep. Come find out for yourself.

Oh sorry to wake u. Talk tomorrow?

U can't come up?

He sighed. He could almost feel the warm silk of her skin beneath his hands.

Too risky. ☹

Did it go OK?

Yes. Went great.

He wasn't about to share Andrei's invitation. As soon as he sent the message, he typed another:

I love you, Bonnie.

I love you so much, McSailor. Please be careful.

I will.

Ms. Broccoli loves you too. ☺

She better love me more than she loves Rog. Goodnight.

I'll dream about you, Jack Dawson.

He chuckled. She always had to have the last word. Once he lay in bed, her face floated in his mind, bringing a smile to his lips.

14. Connections

Ben flung himself on to his bed. This being grounded thing sucked balls. He'd already listened to music, studied for his physics test, and whacked off (Dr. Hunter had told him masturbation was completely normal). Now he was bored.

Discordant music emanated from his phone, signaling a text from Dylan:

Wazzup?

He smiled. Finally. Someone to talk to. His fingers flew over the phone's touchpad.

Uber bored. Want to go out but in prison.

Still grounded, huh? Nick is too. U guys r no fun.

He typed:

U talk to Nick?

Yeah, don't u?

Apparently Nick's dad had only put him on the no-associate list. *Thanks, Grandpa Barberi.* He sighed as he typed:

Nope. His dad thinks I'm a criminal or sumpin.

U r a badass, fo shizzle. Ur mom's at work?
Why don't u sneak out?

Have to be here if she calls home phone.

Dude, she's got the cell bars locked tight!

No shit.

And she used to be so cool.

He was about to respond when Dylan's next text popped up:

Momster's bitchin at me to go to bed. Hasta la vista.

Sweet dreams, Momma's boy.

Five seconds later, he was bored again. Then he heard a key in the front door. "Mom, can we get a Wii?" he called once he heard the door swing open.

"No, Benji." Her voice sounded tight.

"How 'bout a pet, then? A dog?" He rolled off his bed and headed to the family room. "I'm *so* bored—" *Holy shit*…there was a man standing next to his mother in the middle of their apartment.

She must've noticed him freeze in place because she pasted on a fake smile and dipped her open palm to the side, gesturing to the blond man. "Ben, this is Hans."

The man stepped over and offered his hand. "Hallo, Ben."

His accent was strange—German, maybe—and Ben hesitated. When he slipped his hand into the guy's rough grasp, a tendril of dread inched up his spine. He looked up to meet the man's eyes, trying to make sense of his physical reaction. When he caught a flash of something sinister, he yanked his hand back.

"Ben? What's wrong?" his mother asked.

"Uh…" He gulped. The man still stared at him with an eye-fucking gleam. "Nothing…"

She gave him another strange look as she headed into the kitchen. "We've talked about this before. This apartment's too small for dogs." She took down a couple of wine glasses. "Besides, *I* don't want to walk a dog in the winter. March in Chicago is bad enough."

Hans nodded. "Colder than a witch's tit out there."

His mother's giggle shocked him. When was the last time he'd heard her laugh? And why was she giggling at that stupid thing?

His mother had just started to reply when he blurted, "Where'd you guys meet?"

She extracted a wine bottle from a paper bag. "I served him at the restaurant tonight."

"It seems you're still serving me," Hans said, nodding at the bottle of red.

"Well, *you* bought the wine, handsome," his mother replied.

Ben made a gagging noise, which drew his mother's glare. "Isn't it a school night? It's past your bedtime."

He felt his jaw unhinge. *Bedtime?* "I don't have a fucking bedtime, *Mom*."

"Watch your language," Hans warned in a sharp tone.

He whirled to face the stranger in his apartment. "Who the fuck are *you* to tell me what to do?"

Glints of rage in his eyes, Hans took a step toward him.

"*Ben*," his mother said as she rounded the corner of the kitchen. She planted herself between the two men. "Hans has had a tough day, and I…I'm sorry I didn't warn you I was bringing home a guest."

Ben relaxed just a bit.

"Would you please hang out in your room?" she asked. "I'd really love some privacy with Hans. He'll only be here a few minutes."

"Is that all?" Hans crooned. "I hoped to spend more time with the beautiful lady."

Now Ben definitely was going to barf. "Don't worry — I'm outta here."

He almost fell over when his mother leaned in to kiss him on the cheek. What was her *deal* tonight? "G'night, Benji." She cradled his face in her hand.

Hans gave him a leering smile, and Ben swiveled and hightailed it to his bedroom. Once his door was closed, he leaned back against it, letting out a long sigh. There was something creepy about the German dude, for sure, but he'd never seen his mom so chill — so happy. Her trilling laughter floated through the flimsy wooden door, unnerving him further.

He grabbed his earphones from his pillow. The music couldn't come fast enough. Once the blasting grind of his favorite band filled his ears, he flopped back on his bed. After the pulsing drumbeat calmed him down, he reached for his phone to set an alarm. Morning swim practices were over now that the end of the season approached—thank *God* he didn't have to wake at the butt-crack of dawn. But now he wouldn't get to see Lindsay till afternoon practice.

He scrolled through photos on his phone, stopping at the same one he always did. He could stare at this photo for hours. Lindsay sat next to Olivia on a bench on the pool deck, and she had no idea he'd snapped her picture. Her long brown hair fell in waves over her shoulder, and she turned toward Olivia with a laugh parting her sweet mouth. He loved the squint of her eyes, the little dimple in her cheek, the flash of her slightly crooked teeth—her whole face lit up with happiness.

His thumb rubbed over the image, then he cradled the phone to his chest. *Do you ever think about me, Lindsay?* His eyes fluttered shut as he blew out a frustrated breath. Of course she didn't. She wouldn't. She thought he was a bad influence, which was probably true.

He lifted the phone and cracked open one eye, gazing at her beauty. *But I think about you, Linds. A lot.* She sat, frozen in a state of happiness. He was frozen too. But his state was far from happy.

You're pathetic, Barberi. His heart thudded with a dull ache.

Grant sat up with a jerk, the covers falling away from his chest, which pounded with a ragged heartbeat. What the heck had woken him? As he glanced around the apartment, his breath began to slow. Daylight fought through the corners of the blinds, illuminating the silent bedroom. *Damn.* How late was it?

He groaned as he found the alarm clock—already ten in the morning with nothing to show for it. In the Navy, his day would've been almost half done by now. This late-night gig just wasn't for him.

Swinging his legs over the side of the mattress, he flinched at a ding from his cell phone. *Ah.* That was probably the sound that woke him.

He padded over to the phone, still attached to its charger. He read the message from Agent Bounter:

Call me. Got plan for tonight

His throat tightened, and last night rushed back. His fingers flew over the numbers.

"Hey." Bounter sounded tired.

"What's the plan, sir?"

"Cut the sir business—your place might be tapped, remember?"

He winced. "Sorry."

"Go take a shower while our guys scan the place. Then we'll talk."

"Okay." He yawned, tossed the phone on the bed, peeled off his boxers, and tossed them in the laundry basket. He was just about to turn on the shower when he heard the faint click of his front door opening. *Damn, they're fast.* He peeked out from the bathroom and saw two men dressed in plain clothes. They stopped when they saw him, then one gave him a thumbs up. He nodded in return.

The warm water soothed his nerves, and soon he found himself singing "Pretend You Don't See Her." If those Russian bastards had bugged his place, he hoped they were getting an earful.

Feeling much more alive after he toweled himself off, he reached for his razor. The bathroom door creaked open. He whirled around to face an agent with some sort of electronic scanner, which he used to gesture around the bathroom. Grant got the hint and stepped into his bedroom. He'd just slipped on a pair of dark jeans when the agent beckoned him. The other agent had joined him in the bathroom, and he drew his index finger to his lips then pointed to the medicine cabinet.

Grant's eyes bugged when he crouched down to see the bug—a tiny little sphere attached to the underside of the cabinet. How dare Andrei sneak in to *his* apartment and plant a listening device right under his nose!

Oh. Then he remembered he wore a wire every time he neared the Russians. *Touché, Andrei.*

He waited for one of the agents to remove the bug, but the two men just stood there, staring at him in the cramped bathroom. Perhaps they wanted him to do the job? He reached toward the medicine cabinet, but an agent blocked his arm, then pointed out of the bathroom. Grant shrugged and led them out to the living room.

One agent crossed the room to turn on the TV.

Yanking a pad of paper out of his pocket, the agent who'd blocked him from removing the bug started scribbling. Grant approached and read:

Leave it. They can't know we found it.

He closed his eyes. *Duh.*

Give us your phones to check.

Rather than protest that Bounter had recently checked the phone he carried, and Andrei had been nowhere near the secure phone, he shut his mouth and retrieved them. Obviously he was new to this world of espionage.

The agent smiled after he examined the phones—apparently they were clear. More written directions were forthcoming.

Bounter needs to talk. Leave the apt and call on secure phone.

Grant nodded. He signaled for the agent's pen and stooped to write:

Thank you.

The agent nodded, then wrote one last message:

Let's get these fuckers.

Grinning, he reached out to shake his hand. The other agent offered a hearty handshake as well before they left the apartment.

With only the TV as his companion—some political news show berating Governor Grogan for his plan to reduce pension payouts for state employees—he scanned the empty apartment and shivered. He looked down to find his torso bare.

In his closet, he tugged the first shirt he saw off the hanger. It was a pale-blue button-down from Nordstrom's Sophie had given him for Christmas, thanks to her father's largesse. The shirt probably cost more than most of his wardrobe, and the crisp collar hid his button mic well. He stuffed his feet into black leather shoes, grabbed both phones, and snatched his coat from the front closet. *Crap*—he couldn't go far because he had to return the secure phone to his apartment, and he still had to shave. Rubbing his hand on his chest, he smiled as he decided the location for his call to Agent Bounter.

A quick glance out his front door revealed an empty hallway. He slipped into the stairwell and leaped two steps at a time to reach Kirsten's apartment.

Pressing his ear to the door, he heard nothing. As soon as he'd unlocked it and entered, though, he could hear the patter of the shower. He hoped it wasn't Kirsten.

Then he heard singing. He stepped closer to the bathroom, trying to figure out what song was being butchered. Was that Madonna? It was definitely Sophie. When she punctuated the lyrics with a high-pitched "Oooh!" he had to cover his mouth to prevent bursting out in laughter. Lord, her singing was awful. She was almost as bad as Rog.

But when the shower shut off, he found himself sad she'd also stopped channeling Madonna. There was something so endearing about her singing. "Soph? It's Grant. Gotta make a call up here."

She yanked open the bathroom door. "You didn't hear me sing, did you?"

"*What?*" He tilted his head, striving to keep a straight face.

Her cheeks flushed scarlet as she scowled. "Peeping Mick. I'm taking away your key. I thought I was alone!"

Droplets of water sliding down one shoulder distracted him. "Um, sorry 'bout that, Madonna."

"So you *did* hear me sing!"

"Singing isn't quite what I'd call it." A grin broke out, appearing to enrage her further. "I'd advise you not to quit your day job."

"Ooooh! Why the hell can't you call from your apartment?"

His smile vanished. "The Russians planted a bug in the bathroom. Sophie, you have to promise me you won't go down there."

"They were *here?* In the building?" She clutched her towel more tightly to her chest.

"It's okay now. But I gotta call Bounter to check in. Everything's copacetic — just need to touch base. All right?"

She blinked at him for a long moment. "I *guess.*" A few more trickles of water cascaded down her chest, and she turned toward the mirror. She opened her towel and tilted forward to wrap her hair in white terrycloth. Catching a glimpse of her milky skin, he leaned over to peer around the partly open door.

"I thought you had to make a phone call, Mr. Professional Singer," she said when she noticed him ogling. With that she closed the door in his face.

"Wow." He pulled out his secure phone and sat on the couch.

Bounter answered with a laugh. "I'm not thrilled you went up to Sophie's, but *damn* that was funny."

"So you overheard Sophie murder that song?"

"With an ax. Girlfriend's tone deaf."

"Hey!" Sophie huffed as she flew out of the bathroom. "He heard me sing too?"

She was naked except for the towel-turban wrapped around her head like a vanilla soft-serve cone. Grant eyed her perky breasts before his gaze flew south. "Unfortunately, yes."

Her eyes narrowed. "Better get a good look, pal, 'cause this—" her hands sashayed down her body, then rested on her hips "—you won't see for a loooong time."

He could see from the glint in her eyes she was joking—*thank God.* "Don't you own a robe?"

Her head tilted an inch. "Do you *want* me to wear one?"

"Definitely not."

"I'm still hot from working out," she said. "I don't need a robe."

"You *are* hot. You worked out?"

"At the gym downstairs."

"That's awesome. I haven't run in a week."

Her gaze floated down his body. "You still look quite fit, McSailor."

"*Do I need to be here for this?*" Bounter barked. "Eavesdropping on phone sex is plain wrong. Very wrong. And I want out."

"Oh, sorry." He winced, looking at Sophie. "Right, sir. She's just a bit distracting."

She laughed as she glided back to the bathroom.

"So what's the plan for tonight?" he asked, lowering his voice.

"The good news is we don't need Sophie."

Grant let out a breath. "Good." He paused. "And the bad news?"

"We have to make another woman credible as your girlfriend. So you need to get to the hotel to start rehearsing."

"Who *is* this girl? Do I know her?"

"I briefed Mr. Remington about what's going down tonight, and he gave me a perfect idea. But I don't want to say more over the phone."

"Sir! You can't leave me hanging. I have to know who she is—"

Naked Sophie strutted in the room, stopping him midstream. She'd jettisoned the towel, and her wet hair curled across her shoulders. When she shook out her hair, thick strands fell to her chest, barely skimming her nipples.

He became aware of Bounter's voice on the phone. "Mick? You still there?"

"Uhh…"

She smiled at him as she crawled over the arm of the sofa, approaching him with a flash of hunger in her eyes. Her hands darted up to his collar, and he felt the shirt tighten against the back of his neck as she drew him closer.

"Hey, we're getting static on the mic," Bounter said.

Grant couldn't care less. For once Sophie didn't seem stressed out by his work with the FBI, and he was going to go with it! She'd applied body lotion in the bathroom, and its intoxicating floral scent made his jeans bulge.

She purred, "I *knew* this shirt would look good on you."

"Oh *Christ*," Bounter muttered. "Is she about to do you?"

"I sure hope so." He smiled as she pushed him backward. Now he stared at the ceiling, his back resting on the sofa. He tried to remember he was still on the phone.

Her flushed face came into view, hovering over him as she unbuttoned his shirt. Still holding the phone to his ear, his free hand reached up to fondle her breast, marveling at the juxtaposition of soft tissue and hard nipple cupped in his palm.

Bounter gave a disgusted sigh. "Mick, get your ass to the hotel."

"You know, this is kind of your fault for keeping us apart so long," he fired back.

Sophie seized the phone. "Agent Bounter, unless you enjoy participating in *ménage a trois*, I suggest you hang up now." She giggled and tossed the phone to the floor.

"Good job getting rid of him," he said, enjoying her new attitude and the freedom to massage her breasts with both hands.

Her deep moan vibrated against his abdomen as she planted wet kisses along his sternum.

"So my singing's not so great." She gazed down at him. "But there're *many* things I'm good at."

"Amen, Bonnie." Her roving lips found his for a sensuous kiss, and his hand skated down to cradle her fine backside.

Thoughts about tonight still preoccupied him, but when she reached into his pants, all worries about a fake girlfriend vanished. He was with his *real* girlfriend—his *fiancée*—right now, and he savored every second.

"Hey, Kir." Handing her friend a latte, Sophie sank into a chair in Kirsten's office a few hours later. "Jeez…" She wiggled in the plastic chair. "These aren't comfortable at all."

"Try sitting in one for nine hours straight." Kirsten leaned back in her desk chair and stretched her arms over her head.

"Not fun." Sophie scrunched her nose. "At least you have a no-show."

"And good coffee." Kirsten held up her cup, then took a sip. "Thanks, roomie."

Sophie sipped her own coffee. "Sorry they don't have your fave flavor anymore."

"Don't remind me," Kirsten groaned. "Hazelnut will do, but I still miss Valencia. I guess I'm the only one who likes orange in her coffee."

"Hey, I liked it too." Sophie took another drink. "Starbucks lacks your excellent taste."

Kirsten snorted. "That's okay, I'm used to it by now—happens all the time. My favorite scent of body lotion? Production halted because it wasn't selling. The restaurant with the best Thai chicken eggplant in the city? Closed. Even the dating web site I joined told me my personality matched only one percent of men!"

Sophie laughed.

"Thanks for the sympathy."

"Sorry, but are you *honestly* taking stock in that bogus personality test? Isn't that the site that matched you with a pig farmer in Kankakee?"

Kirsten almost spewed her coffee down her shirt. She lunged for a tissue and dabbed the brown dribble on her chin. Her voice trembled with laughter. "Thanks for cheering me up."

"I mean, what do you have in common with a *pig farmer?*"

"Well, I do like me some bacon. Maybe I should've gone out with the guy," Kirsten said. "He could've stocked me up with bacon for a year."

"You obviously missed a big opportunity."

Kirsten sighed. "Too bad for me. But how's our dear McSailor?"

"That's actually the reason for the coffee." Sophie held up her cup. "I need to vent about McNavyboy, so I'm bribing you to listen."

"Are you kidding me? No bribe needed, I assure you."

"But you have to listen to your clients bloviate all day long."

"If my clients all had boyfriends as cute as Grant, I'd pay *them* to hear their stories."

"He's not that cute, believe me."

"*What?*" Kirsten skirted around her desk to the plastic chair across from Sophie. "Maybe you do need my services, 'cause, girl, you are certifiable. What happened?"

Sophie rubbed her thumb over the edge of cup. "He snuck into your apartment when I was in the shower…"

Kirsten leaned forward, elbows resting on knees. "Still waiting to hear the part about him not being cute. Or hot."

"He had to call the FBI from your place since his place is apparently bugged."

"Whoa." Kirsten sat back.

"Anyway, I overheard his conversation, and…" She shifted in her chair. "I don't know, but I don't have a good feeling about it. His voice got quiet, and he was being sneaky—"

"That does tend to happen when you're working undercover."

"Smartass." Her grin faded. "No, not about his assignment. He was making plans for tonight, and he kept referring to some girl…I think he might be seeing another woman."

Kirsten let out a high-pitched cackle. "You *are* crazy! Have you seen the way that man looks at you?"

"*Looked* at me. Since he's been working with the FBI, he seems distant. He made some crack about my arm muscles, and he bought me this teddy, as if he needs me to dress up like some whore to get turned on."

"Oh, my God. I thought you were getting back to your old self after prison—back to your old confidence—but I was obviously wrong. You sound so insecure." She reached for a worn, thick book on her shelf. "I'll find a diagnosis for this bizarre behavior of yours. PTSD? Depression?"

Sophie winced. "Okay, you've made your point, Dr. Holland—"

The ringing phone interrupted her, and Kirsten rolled her eyes. "Here." She thrust the manual onto Sophie's lap. "Have some fun with the big book of mental illness. That's probably the front desk telling me my client just arrived, forty-five minutes late."

She took the call, and Sophie looked down at the heavy book. With a sigh, she set down her coffee cup and flipped through the pages. As a therapist, she'd used this manual often, but it had been a while since she'd seen it. Toward the back of the book her hand landed on the page for paranoid personality disorder. *Repeated suspicions about partner's fidelity…*

"I know you miss being a therapist, but quit fondling my book."

She flinched as she met Kirsten's eyes. Evidently her phone call was over. "Is your client here?"

"Nope. And my next client had the decency to call ahead to cancel, unlike all my other college alcoholic no-shows." She returned to her chair. "So, did you find your diagnosis?"

She shrugged. "I'm too much of a whack-job to fit one of their categories. I'm sorry to bother you with all of this. I'm probably freaking out about nothing. I'm just so worried about Grant, and we never get to talk any more—no counseling sessions, no nothing—and when I don't know what's going on…"

"It's okay." Kirsten's voice softened. "Did you ask him about his phone call when it ended? Did he seem suspicious?"

"Well, not really. I, um, I sort of…seduced him. And then he left for the hotel."

Her mouth widened into a huge grin.

"Exactly what are you smiling about?" Sophie demanded.

"I just read this article about how women behave when they suspect their men of cheating on them."

"And?"

"Women flirt and make sexual advances much more frequently when they fear infidelity. It's kind of a way to mark their territory."

"Oh." She smirked, thinking of the bite marks she might have left in more than a few locations. "I guess he knows he's mine then."

Kirsten giggled. "You little slut." She lifted her hands, palms up. "Looks like my next hour's free. What're you up to?"

"I'm supposed to write my section of Anita's manuscript."

"Wow, you sound so excited."

"Oh, yes. Can't *wait* to get back to the office."

Kirsten winked. "I have a better idea. Did I tell you about Cécile, the theater professor I met during new staff orientation?"

"Maybe? Is she French?"

"*Oui.* She's totally adorable. Anyway, her office is right next to the storage space for all the costumes. We had a blast in there the other day, trying on hats."

Sophie frowned. "What does this have to do with McSailor?"

"You said you can't go to Capone's because he doesn't want the bad guys to see you, right?"

"Yes."

Kirsten smiled as she raised her hands in front of her face, pinched her forefingers together, then ran them over her lips and down the sides of her mouth, stroking an imaginary handlebar mustache. "My dear Sophia, Dr. Holland has a therapeutic intervention just for you. We will examine your fear that your fiancé is cheating on you, and I'm sure you will find him to be faithful as always. We will face your anxiety head on. A little *exposure* therapy, you could say." She rose from her chair, seeming inspired by her little speech, and pointed her forefinger in the air. "The only thing you have to fear is fear itself!"

"So are you supposed to be Sigmund Freud or FDR?"

"Neither." Kirsten yanked her up from her chair. "Let's go find some costumes for tonight," she said, hooking her arm around Sophie's elbow. "I'll be a pig farmer, and you'll be my date."

15. Conflate

Life was good on the outside. If Ricker had more cash in his pocket, then it would be *perfekt*. His payday from Enzo was still a ways off because that Fredrickson bitch had refused to talk about her brother-in-law last night. He'd peppered Ashley with questions about her dead husband's family, under the guise of mourning their common losses, but she'd given him zilch. And she'd only allowed one prudish kiss before she shoved him out the door.

But then he'd found a way to release his frustration. A most satisfying way. While writhing on the dance floor at a club in Boys Town, he'd met a bottom to his top—a skinny little Cuban piece of ass… and what a *nice* little piece of ass. The boy even had an apartment nearby, which Ricker had promptly commandeered and called his own. After a night of delicious debauchery, he'd left the boy to his chores, including laundering the sheets and scrubbing the kitchen floor. Little Daisy Fuentes's naked body sported a smoking red butt as a reminder to keep busy while his boss was gone.

Now he sauntered down the sidewalk, whistling Petula Clark's golden oldie "Downtown" and perverting the lyrics in his head:

> *Boys Town, can go down on sweet-cheeks in*
> *Boys Town, you'll never be lonely in*
> *Boys Town, all fucks will be free for you…*

He stopped short when he noticed a tiny white furball shivering on the sidewalk, its leash tied around a street sign. Was that speck of fur a *dog?* If so, it was the smallest he'd ever seen.

Scanning the surrounding area, he saw only a few pedestrians scurrying down the sidewalk. Bells jangled to his left, and a boutique door opened. *Ah, here's the owner.* But the woman who stepped out simply turned and walked away without a look in his direction.

He kneeled to inspect the little fella. The dog wore a white fluffy sweater, meaning its body was even scrawnier than he'd thought, under that layer. The owner must've given a damn about the creature. When he reached out to souse the dog's ears, a growl rumbled in its throat.

He laughed. "You're a big beast, yah? You want a piece of my hand?"

The little white shit's lips curled back to bare its teeth.

His smile vanished. At right was some frou-frou vegetarian restaurant, and two men were just getting up from the table near the window — maybe to pay their bill? Were they the tiny white fuck's owners? Resuming his whistle, he casually untied the leash and scooped the dog into his jacket. He kept his hand clamped around the dog's muzzle to prevent the little asshole from barking or biting. The dog mustered a soft whine, and he whistled louder to mask the sound as he strolled back the direction he'd come.

A smile tugged at his mouth as he turned the corner, his theft undetected. He now felt one step closer to Grant Madsen.

❧

Grant glowered at Agent Bounter as he sat across from him in Mr. Remington's office. His faux-girlfriend had just gone to the ladies' room to collect herself for the evening's show, and he already relished her absence. "I still don't understand why you couldn't get an agent on this," he said.

Bounter sighed. "I already told you, we don't have the manpower available for something like this. Government cutbacks, you know. The only agent we *could* get to pose as your girlfriend won't be appropriate."

"And why's that?"

"She's kind of…" Lucas looked away. "Butch."

"As in gay?"

"Well, yeah, but that's not the problem. She's pulled off straight before. I respect her abilities."

If Sophie ever found out about this, he'd much rather the woman bat for the other team. "So what *is* the problem?"

"She's just not pretty enough for you," Bounter said. Grant couldn't hide the blush that heated his face, and the agent grinned. "You're doing great with the Russians, and we don't want a plain-looking girlfriend to tip them off."

Grant groaned as he covered his face with his hands. "When will this be over?"

"Hang in there. Tonight could be a lot of fun, if you let it."

"Yay. So you think this is going well so far?"

"Very. Andrei planting that bug's a sign they're planning something big for you, I think. And he's really opening up to you. What he told you about his father—it helped us put some pieces together."

Grant leaned forward.

"We always wondered how Andrei's loyalty to Vladimir developed. We knew they'd been part of the same boxing club in Solntsevo when they were younger—not a great neighborhood, and Vladimir was Andrei's coach. But Andrei telling you his father killed his mother piqued the interest of our research guys. They looked closer and discovered something about Andrei's father's death."

"Andrei's father's dead too?"

"Murdered five days after Andrei's mother. Svetlana Kebin died in the local hospital from blunt head trauma on March twentieth, almost twenty-five years ago. Igor Kebin somehow escaped prosecution for his wife's murder—we think he had friends in high places. But apparently his skating free didn't sit well with his oldest son, Andrei, who was eighteen at the time."

"Andrei murdered his father when he was only eighteen?"

"No, we think Vladimir killed him."

"Why's that, sir?"

"Vladimir had moved to Moscow by this time—he was a contender for the Soviet Olympic boxing team. Guess where a national boxing tournament was held March twenty-fourth of that year, one day before Igor Kebin was murdered?"

Grant felt his throat tighten. "Solntsevo."

"Bingo. Apparently Andrei's father was so beat up they had to use dental records to identify the body."

"But if Kebin had friends in high places, how'd Vladimir and Andrei avoid prosecution?"

"The research guys speculate that's how these two ended up in the States. They both went off the grid for about ten years before they resurfaced in Chicago. Maybe they went into hiding after the murder."

Grant nodded. "Makes sense. You'd told me Vladimir was a boxing champ in the Soviet Navy. Did he serve in the Navy before he moved to Moscow?"

"Yep."

"But I didn't know he was an *Olympic*-caliber boxer." He remembered the chokehold the don had gotten him in that night with Innochka. "You think he gave that all up when he killed Mr. Kebin?"

Bounter shrugged.

"That'd be enough to make a man bitter—losing out on a dream to help a friend."

With a nod, Bounter added, "And that'd be enough to make that friend loyal to Vladimir for life."

The door to Mr. Remington's office swung open, and in walked Grant's date for the evening. His eyebrows lifted at her hot pink mini-dress, which clashed with her fiery red hair. So much for Bounter's advice to keep a low profile.

"You changed your clothes," Grant said.

"You keep a dress like *that* in your employee locker?" Bounter asked.

Miranda grinned as she wiggled down next to Grant. "You never know when a hotel guest will ask you up to his room after your shift. Working at the front desk does have its perks."

Grant stifled a groan. How on earth had he arrived in a situation where he had to pretend Miranda was his girlfriend?

"The Russians have landed," Bounter said, touching his earpiece.

Grant straightened on the sofa.

Bounter looked at Miranda. "Let Mick answer their questions, okay? The less you speak, the better. We'll debrief you when you go up to the room after the show."

Grant glanced at his watch. "I have to be on stage in ten minutes. We should head out."

"I wonder…" Miranda said.

"Yes?" Bounter asked.

She tossed her hair. "I think we should practice kissing before we meet the Russians. We gotta make it look real, you know?"

A knot tightened in his stomach.

"What do you think, Mick?" Bounter asked him.

"I think, with all your experience with hotel guests, Miranda, that we'll do fine making it look real."

She frowned.

"Just follow my lead, and Mr. Remington will make sure you get a plum job in his Miami hotel."

Her frown turned upside down. "At least I get to live somewhere nice. Miami weather's much better than the crapola Chicago winter."

A minute later he latched on to Miranda's elbow and led her into Capone's. Tony Bennett streamed through the speakers, and a healthy crowd had already gathered.

Vladimir, Andrei, and their dates sat at their usual table, double vodkas half-full in front of the men. As Grant led Miranda toward them, she snuggled closer, tucking herself into his shoulder. He'd have to get rid of her heavy perfume smell before he got anywhere near Sophie.

He noticed the stares of a few women in the bar's seating area. When Miranda nestled even tighter into him, those stares became glares. Maybe the waiters wouldn't deliver so many drinks bought for him tonight.

At last they reached the table, which brought Vladimir and Andrei out of their seats. "We finally meet your lady," Vladimir boomed, reaching over and planting a loud kiss on the back of Miranda's hand. Grant glanced at Katya, but she only looked bored. Bored and vacant. She'd probably shot up on something before they left West Town.

"Vladimir Federov and Andrei Kebin," Grant said, extending his arm toward them, palm up, "may I present to you Ms. Samantha Smith."

Miranda giggled when Andrei kissed her hand as well. "Charmed, I'm sure."

Andrei spoke Russian into Vladimir's ear, something about wondering if Samantha was a *true* redhead. Grant pretended not to understand. No need to defend Miranda-Samantha's honor so soon into the evening, with plentiful dangers ahead.

"What did he say?" Miranda asked.

Innochka gave Miranda a look of sympathy. "You don't want to know."

A slight narrowing of Andrei's eyes, and Innochka clamped her mouth shut.

"Sit," Vladimir ordered. Once Grant had guided Miranda to her seat, he took his own. "Samantha, tell me," Vladimir dove in, "what time have you been with Mick?"

When Miranda gave him a quizzical look, he answered, "We've been together a month or so."

"Time short," Vladimir said, a glint of mischief in his black eyes. "Will last?"

Miranda leaned forward. "Oh, yes." She laced her hand into his and beamed.

Andrei laughed. "Mick not look so sure."

"Of course I'm sure it'll last," Grant said. He drew Miranda's hand to his mouth and kissed her tanned skin. From the corner of his eye he could see that Andrei still appeared suspicious. Grant rotated her hand and kissed the inside of her wrist as well, trying not to gag at the cloying taste of her perfume.

He looked up to find her eyes darkened with lust. "You look beautiful tonight, Sam," he told her.

A smile spread along her lips. "Thank you. You're scorching hot, Mickey."

He winced. *Mickey?* What was he—a freaking mouse?

"How did you and Mickey meet?" Innochka asked.

He stalled for time. "Why do you want to know?"

Rosy pink crept up Innochka's cheeks. "I…I picture somebody different for you, I think." Her blush deepened when Miranda leaned back, appearing offended. "I am sorry," Innochka rushed ahead. "You are very pretty."

"Samantha works at the hotel," he said. Hearing tension in his voice, he took a subtle breath.

"*Da?*" Andrei tilted his head. "Where?"

Miranda smiled. "I work at the front desk. The best part of my job's always been Mick coming to work every day. I kept trying to catch his eye, but he's so shy. I called Mr. Remington to ask if Mick was single, and lucky for me, he was!"

He wished he could plug her diarrhea of the mouth.

"You close with Mr. Remington?" Andrei asked.

She shrugged. "He's my boss, so he can be kind of a jerk sometimes, but he's pretty cool overall, I guess."

"He rich man," Vladimir said.

"Oh, yes," she agreed. "He should pay me a lot more per hour!"

"Well, I see the piano player summoning me," Grant cut in. "Time for our first set."

Miranda turned to him and clutched his shoulder. "Go out there and kill it, Mickey honey."

"You bet, Sammie dear." As he leaned in, she closed her eyes and her lips twitched with anticipation. At the last second his mouth darted to her cheek, kissing her on skin layered with makeup.

He brushed off his mouth on the way to the stage. He felt the remnants of Miranda all over him—his lips, his skin, his clothes. He winked at Andy as he took hold of the microphone.

Before introducing himself, he glanced at the table he'd just departed. To his dismay, Miranda made sweeping gestures as she talked, seeming to monopolize the conversation. All focused on her except for Vladimir, who stared at him with a small smirk.

He swallowed. *Please don't blow it, Samantha.*

Sophie tucked a wayward strand of strawberry-blond hair under her black wig. Then she adjusted her red-framed glasses so they sat straight on her nose and stepped back from the bathroom mirror to view her plain black dress and sensible shoes. "I look like Janeane Garofalo."

Kirsten laughed as she finished applying lip gloss. "Except she's about a foot shorter than you."

She looked at her friend's long blond wig, black camisole, and tight red leather pants. "And you look like Britney Spears."

"Yes!" Kirsten raised her fist in the air and shimmied her breasts. "Just the look I'm going for. I'm testing out the blondes-have-more-fun theory tonight."

"No need for the test," Sophie replied. "We *do* have more fun."

Kirsten tossed the lip gloss into her purse. "Got news for ya, Janeane…*I'm* the blonde tonight."

Sophie frowned at her reflection. "Maybe we should switch wigs?"

"Not a chance, my little liberal activist." She grabbed her purse. "C'mon. I hear McCrooner's already started. Don't want to miss the show."

As Sophie followed her out of the hotel lobby ladies' room, she felt her stomach zing with butterflies. But when Kirsten opened the door to Capone's Spirits, Grant's sexy voice was quick to calm her. He sang one of her favorites — "I Get a Kick Out of You" — and she smiled and loosened her grip on her handbag. She wondered if he'd identify her, even in her disguise, but his attention seemed glued to the right of the stage.

Kirsten led them to one of the only remaining empty tables, in the far corner. As they sat, Sophie scanned the semi-circle of tables around the bar and stage, but failed to identify any party looking particularly thuggish. Maybe she'd need to clean her fake glasses.

"That guy's staring at me," Kirsten whispered as she tilted her head to the right.

Sophie took her time looking in that direction and saw a heavyset man ogling Kirsten's pants. "Apparently the red leather's a hit, Britney."

Movement drew her attention back toward the stage. Grant and Andy had choreographed the ending to the song. Grant leaned down to croon to one of the women in the front row, leaving his backside stuck out for Andy's boot to pretend to kick him off the stage. Grant wobbled before swiveling to glare at the piano player, then turned back to the audience to sing the final line. Laughter sprinkled in with the clapping.

"Andy Beecham on the piano!" Grant announced, extending his arm. More laughter came when his hand curled into a fist, which he shook in Andy's face.

His expression sobered. "I dedicate the next song to a very special lady in the audience tonight."

Sophie gasped as the opening notes of another Cole Porter song came from the piano. Did he know she was there?

But when he sang the beginning of "I've Got You Under My Skin," he wasn't looking at her. He gazed directly to his left. Sophie followed his line of vision to a table with two men and three women. When she noticed the hardness in the older man's face and the menacing stare of the man seated close to him, she bristled. *Russians?* But when the woman with long red hair sat up and cradled her cheeks in her hands, gazing up at Grant with rapture, Sophie's skin crawled. Who the *hell* was she?

She heard Kirsten say something, but it wasn't until she tapped her arm that Sophie peeled her eyes from the redhead. Kirsten pointed at the cocktail waitress perched next to the table. "What do you want to drink? I'm getting a cosmopolitan."

"Uh…" Sophie blinked up at the waitress, forgetting how to speak.

"Just get her a cosmo too," Kirsten said.

"No. Just water for me."

"What's your deal?" Kirsten asked as the waitress departed. "You're no fun tonight."

"Didn't you hear him dedicate this song to a special *lady?*"

Kirsten gave a dismissive wave of her hand. "At first I was worried, but then I figured he says that every night. That Remington guy probably puts him up to it. Better for business to single out a lucky lady and pretend he's into her."

"No," Sophie hissed, leaning in. "I found the *special* lady. She's real. She's sitting with the Russians."

Kirsten's face fell and her eyes darted around the other tables.

"I thought you said there's *no way* he's seeing another woman!"

Kirsten kept searching. "Where *is* the little ho-bag?"

"Center-right of the stage." Sophie felt her voice waver. "She's a redhead, sitting with two men and two women."

"I'll kill her," Kirsten promised as she scanned the audience. "Then I'll kill *him*." Her mouth dropped open. "*Her?* Ewww." She stared for a few moments with her nose scrunched up. "No way. No way he chooses her instead of you."

The song came to an abrupt end, and Grant hopped off the stage amidst the applause. Sophie's stomach dropped when he headed straight to the red-haired tramp and pressed a kiss to her cheek. She froze when the redhead popped off her chair, grabbed the lapels of his black jacket, and yanked his lips down to hers.

"Oh my God," Kirsten murmured. "This is a train wreck. I'm so sorry. I can't believe it…it seems so unlike him."

Suddenly aware she'd left her mouth hanging open, Sophie pressed her lips together. Her heart thumped. She looked down to her lap to find her fingers in a death grip on the cocktail napkin. *This can't be happening. This can't be…*

She looked up to find Grant and Slutty Pink Dress pulling away from their kiss.

"He's holding her chair out for her, like he's some *gentleman?*" Kirsten seethed. "That bastard. I'll kill him."

Despite her nausea, Sophie noticed something was off with Grant. His knuckles whitened where he clutched the redhead's chair. His typically cool blue eyes flared with heat, but it didn't look like passion he was feeling…no…he seemed *angry*. Yes, that was it — the ripple of muscle in his jaw, the narrowing of his eyes. It reminded her of the look he'd given Carlo when he'd burst into Kirsten's apartment to find him holding a gun on them. But why would he give that murderous look to Slutty Pink Dress?

She noticed she wasn't breathing, and forced out some air. The napkin ripped in her hands, and without something to grip, her hands trembled in her lap.

"This is my fault for bringing you here. Do you want to leave?"

"No." She swallowed. "This isn't your fault." She closed her eyes for a second, trying to comprehend the incomprehensible. "I don't want to go." She clenched her teeth and forced herself to look back at Grant's table. "I want answers."

The older man — the don? — chuckled at something, and his guests all laughed in turn. All but Grant. His full lips slid into a tight smile, but fury kept his eyes shrouded in darkness. Then it seemed everyone at his table stared at him. Had the black-haired man — the *consigliore?* — asked him a question? A blush bloomed up Grant's neck and spread to his cheeks. He started to say something, then paused. The redhead leaned in and spoke in his ear. He gave a slight nod, seeming to steel himself.

Sophie felt her stomach drop when he scooped the redhead into his lap, let her head fall back in the crook of his elbow, and lunged down to cover her in kisses. Now everyone at the table was definitely staring. As abruptly as he'd stolen her from her seat, he plopped

Slutty Pink Dress back into her chair. The color of her cheeks was somewhere between that of her hair and her dress, her eyes huge.

Kirsten's chair stirred next to her as she shot out of it. "I. Will. Kill. Him."

Sophie's hand darted out to stop her. "No! You'll break his cover!" Kirsten slowly returned to her seat. Sophie gripped her head with both hands. Surprised to touch coarse black hair, she remembered her damn wig. She never should've come here.

"Here we are," the waitress said, approaching their table with her tray. As she set Sophie's glass of water in front of her, she asked, "You sure I can't bring you a stronger drink, sweetie? Looks like you need it."

She tried not to glare. "No thanks. I need to think clearly right now." She took a sip of water as the waitress gave Kirsten her martini. Then inspiration hit. "I *would* like to order a drink for someone else, though."

Kirsten gave her a quizzical look.

"Sure." The waitress shrugged.

"The singer?" Sophie said as she gestured to the stage. "Do you know him?"

"Mick Saylor?"

"Yes." Sophie smiled. "I'd like to buy him a shot of tequila."

"Uh, I'm not sure that's a good idea —" Kirsten began.

"And please deliver it with this napkin." Sophie lifted her water glass to yank the napkin out from under it. She scrabbled for her purse to dig around for a pen. She scribbled on the napkin, then shoved it at the waitress. "Just add it to my tab, okay? And please, don't tell him who bought the shot."

"Of course," the waitress said.

After she'd left, Kirsten leaned in. "What exactly are you doing, Dr. Taylor?"

"Don't worry, Britney…everything will be fine."

"*Fine?* You just saw your fiancé cheat on you, and you think everything will be fine?"

She nodded, watching Grant tap his long fingers on his thigh.

❧

Grant wished he'd thought of attacking Miranda with a kiss like that earlier. Anything to shut her up. She now sported a glazed stupor sitting next to him, and for that he was grateful.

"Guess you *not* in such bad mood, *da?*" Andrei said.

He drew back in his chair. "How could I be in a bad mood with such great company?" His fake smile dropped when Shauna set a shot of tequila in front of him.

"From a secret admirer," she said. Her tapping finger lingered on the napkin, and he noticed writing on one corner.

Miranda sat up like a fire burned her butt. "*Who's* the secret admirer, Shauna?"

The waitress stepped back. "I'm not allowed to say."

"Can't she tell he's with *me* tonight?"

He capitalized on their argument to scoop up the napkin and shot glass. When he got a better view of the message, his heart stopped. That was Sophie's handwriting.

Meet me in Alex's office, McSailor.

He could feel Vladimir's gaze on him as Miranda and Shauna continued their bickering, and he crushed the napkin in his hand while knocking back the shot. Ignoring the don's stare, he scanned the bar, then the tables for Sophie. What the hell was she doing here?

"You *drank* it?" Miranda hissed.

Grant ignored her too. Where was Sophie?

"Don't you think you're egging on this secret admirer?" she railed. "Giving her false hopes? You should've sent that drink straight back to the bar!"

Damn it, where the hell was she?

A low chuckle emanated from Vladimir. "You let Samantha talk that way to you?" He shook his head.

Grant gulped. The sick bastards probably wanted him to backhand her for being insolent. "She knows her place." He gave her a pointed stare.

When her mouth closed, he resumed his scan. *No, not that table, not that one either…*An Amazon with long blond hair, sitting over in the corner, caught his eye. But she wasn't as lean as Sophie. His eyes flitted over another tall woman with straight black hair and glasses, a sense of elegance in how she held herself. His chest tightened with frustration. *Wait…* He doubled back to the brunette to find her eyes ablaze with such intensity that her glare almost plastered him to the back of his chair. Even with red-framed glasses, he'd know those eyes anywhere. He cringed inwardly to find them filled with hostility…or maybe hurt—he didn't know which feeling was stronger.

His heart galloped, and he felt the burn of tequila threatening to rush back up his throat. It seemed the air around him had disappeared. *I'll lose her. She thinks I'm cheating.*

"Are you okay, Mick?" Innochka asked somewhere in the distance.

She hates me. I'll lose her.

Miranda grabbed his wrist. "Mick?"

He stared at her for several seconds, then yanked his wrist free. "I…I have to use the bathroom. Before my next set." His chair scraped the hardwood floor as he stood. "Please excuse me."

Shoving open the doors at the entrance, he veered into the men's room, telling himself he needed to go there first in case he was followed. But really, he needed a toilet for when that tequila pressing at the back of his throat reappeared.

She's the only good thing in my life. I can't lose her.

He made it to a stall just in time to retch. The tequila burned even worse coming back up, and he splayed his palms against the stall, trying to quell the shaking of his insides. There was no food—he'd been too nervous about Miranda to eat.

Where had his stomach of steel gone? His tough gut was a thing of the past—a relic of his sad life before Sophie. Now he had something to lose—something his family hadn't stolen away from him, despite their efforts. Anytime he thought he might lose her, it appeared he had to vomit his fears out before they killed him.

Damn it, I can't lose her. I won't. I won't let those thugs take her from me again.

He pulled himself up and wiped the back of his hand across his mouth. He splashed water on his face, then swirled water around his mouth and spit out. He zoomed out of the empty bathroom and was grateful there were no Russians in the hallway. He turned toward the hotel lobby and froze when he saw Sophie standing outside Mr. Remington's door.

"It's locked," she said.

Her gaze seemed softer, not as angry, and he wasn't sure what that meant. His shaky stomach flipped. Had she already decided to leave him? There'd been far too much between them to let it end like that…right?

Gulping, he whipped out his keys and unlocked the door, glancing over his shoulder before he whisked her inside.

As his eyes adjusted to the darkness, he wanted to reach for her hand, but thought it too risky. "Sophie…"

"Shh." She stepped forward and placed a finger on his lips. "Take some deep breaths. If you keep acting so nervous, you'll blow your cover."

His brow furrowed. Why was she being so nice to him? "I can explain—"

"I know that redhead's part of the act," she cut in. "You don't care for her."

"You…" Relief washed down his chest. He could finally breathe again. "How'd you know?"

Her smile dazzled him. "Because I know you." She stepped closer to tuck her cheek into his shoulder. "I know you, Grant. I know you love me."

He wrapped his arms around her, one hand curling over the top of her head and the other resting on her shoulder, pressing her close. "Oh, Sophie. Oh, God, I'm so sorry. When I read what your wrote on that napkin…"

She pulled back. "I would've waited to talk to you later, but I was worried about how you were acting. You can't let that ho-bag throw you off your game."

"I know…they were asking me what was wrong, and I had to kiss her to keep up the act…" His eyebrows scrunched. *"Ho-bag?"* He grinned and reached up to twist a strand of long black hair between his fingers. "She works at the front desk."

She smacked his hand away as she gave him a playful grin. "Don't touch my wig." She slid her handbag off her shoulder and rifled through it.

"Where'd you get that awful wig? And the glasses?"

Still absorbed in her handbag, she murmured, "The theater director at DePaul…Kirsten knows her."

"Kirsten?" He leaned forward, alarmed. *"She's* here?"

"Yep. And she's ready to kick your ass for cheating on me."

"Ohh…"

"But *I* knew the truth. I know my McSailor. Listen, I'm sure you have to get back out there…aha!" She came up victorious with a roll of breath mints. "You need one of these."

His hand darted to his mouth. "Sorry." He popped a mint in his mouth. "I forgot about that once I found out you weren't mad at me."

"I *am* mad. You were planning this with Bounter on the phone this morning, right? Why didn't you tell me?"

He frowned. "I can't. I'm not supposed to disclose any of this."

"You're coming perilously close to losing your sexual privileges again, mister."

He couldn't match her teasing grin. He sighed as he rubbed the back of his neck. "It's supposed to be you in there."

"*What?*" Her eyes widened.

"When one of them found your makeup and lipstick in our medicine cabinet, he demanded you join us for drinks tonight. I couldn't let them see you."

She drew in a sharp breath. "Grant! I'm sorry." Her finger rubbed her bottom lip, intoxicating him. "I was looking for that lipstick." She tapped her finger on her lip. "But what about your coworker? The redhead? She's in danger now, isn't she?"

"Mr. Remington's shipping her off to his Miami hotel in a couple of days. She's thrilled to relocate."

"Oh, good." She adjusted her glasses. "You know, you didn't need her. I could've been your girlfriend tonight. Great disguise, right?"

"No!" She jumped at his loud response, and he lowered his voice. "You can't be anywhere *near* them, Bonnie." He clasped her hands in his. "In fact, what *are* you doing here? This is incredibly dangerous."

"You're right—it was stupid. I thought I had to make sure you weren't cheating on me, but there's no need for that. I trust you." She squeezed his hands. "I'm leaving, once I tear Kirsten away from her drink. Just one thing before I go."

"What?"

She darted into his arms, her hands wrapping around his back. He squeezed her tight, and their bodies molded together. This contact might have to last for a while, depending on what the Russians had in store for him next. Her warm lips feathered on his neck, his jaw, his cheek. Then she nibbled his ear, giving him a shiver.

"Be careful with them," she whispered. "Don't go in so deep you lose yourself. Don't lose *us* in this, okay?"

His eyes closed, he nodded. He could never lose what he valued most in the world.

She pressed another kiss to his cheek before stepping back and reaching for the door handle. "And get rid of that horrid perfume on your shirt before you see me again."

As he watched her go, her long black hair swaying over her shoulders, he truly smiled for the first time that night.

16. Contours

Following the contours of Lindsay's profile, Ben traced his finger down the screen of his phone. *You're so pretty.* Lindsay laughed at Olivia, and her delight made him smile every time.

"You look happy."

He looked up to see Dr. Hunter in the waiting room. Ben stuffed his phone into his jeans pocket and stood. "Not really," he mumbled. He glanced over and saw a woman with a blond ponytail watching them from her chair—yet another chick who thought he was a loser, no doubt.

"No?" Dr. Hunter cocked his head to one side. "But that was a rare smile from you."

"I smile all the time." Ben plastered a big shit-eating grin on his face and held it for two seconds. "Look, can we just get this thing started so I can get outta here? It's Saturday."

Dr. Hunter gave a terse nod. "Of course. Sorry." He extended his arm. "After you."

Ben's head bowed as he loped down the hallway. *Great.* Now he was being rude, and Dr. Hunter would be too pissed off to help him. And did he ever need help. *Good job, asswipe.*

Ben collapsed in the big chair, and Dr. Hunter sat on the sofa.

"I apologize for starting our session in the waiting room."

"It's cool." He squirmed in the chair, which seemed to swallow him up. Not only was he a loser, he was a *short* loser. Why couldn't he be as tall as Uncle Grant?

"Didn't mean to compromise your privacy," Dr. Hunter added.

He sighed. Why was *he* the one apologizing? "I didn't mean to be such a jackass. Sorry…sir." He ducked his head.

"*Sir?*" When he looked up, Dr. Hunter smirked at him. "Never heard you use that word, either. Does your uncle encourage you to address elders that way?"

"Nope. He said I should use 'sir' and 'ma'am' for people I respect." Feeling his face on fire from that cheesy admission, he stared at his shoes.

Dr. Hunter was quiet for a second. "I'm honored you respect me. I respect you too. You're really working hard to turn your life around."

Ben peeked up at him.

"For example, you showed your respect by arriving on time for our session. Good job."

"Well, I had an escort."

"Did Sophie walk you here?"

"No." He closed his eyes. "*Hans* did."

Dr. Hunter sat forward. "Who's Hans?"

"This guy my mom's dating. He's uber creepy."

His psychologist frowned. "Creepy? How?"

He shuddered. "Dunno…uh, it's hard to explain—he's kinda pushy, asking me all these questions…like, listen to this—he wanted to come to my therapy session. I told him no way, and he got all pissy."

"Did he say why he wanted to attend?"

"He said he wants to get to know me better, or something. But, like, he only met my mom a few days ago, and now he wants to pretend we're this tight, happy family. It's bullshit."

"As I recall, your mom hasn't dated anyone since your dad. Is that right?"

"Yeah." He folded his arms across his chest.

"It must be strange for you then—your mom with a man who's not your dad. It sounds uncomfortable, like it'd be hard to accept a new partner in your parent's life?"

"But my dad used to have chicks over all the time."

"Really." Dr. Hunter sat back, his eyes curious. "You've never told me that before. When you'd visit him on the weekends?"

"Yeah, when he would forget to pick me up." He unfolded his arms and began chewing his fingernails.

"Logan sometimes forgot to pick you up?"…

"Do you know how much this hurts your son?" his mother had yelled into the phone. Ben had been seven, sitting in that creaky wicker chair with his backpack on his lap, his mother pacing the cracked tile kitchen floor. *"He worships you! Then you don't even show up?"* As she listened to his father's response, her mouth pressed tighter. *"Well, what am* I *supposed to do with him this weekend? I'm working a double shift!"*

He'd squeezed his backpack to his chest, wishing he didn't exist…

"Ben?" Dr. Hunter stared at him, his eyes full of kindness. "That sounds very hurtful for your dad to neglect you like that."

Ben shrugged as he chewed on a hangnail. "It's okay. He had more important stuff to do. He was working for the family—he couldn't control his schedule."

"It's *not* okay." Anger clouded his psychologist's eyes. "*You're* his family. It's sad he wasn't there when you needed him."

A lump formed in Ben's throat, and he tried to swallow it down.

"I don't think anyone was more important to Logan than you were, according to Sophie. She said Logan's biggest regret was not being part of your life."

"Well whoop-de-do, he regrets it. Let's give him a medal."

"You're angry at your father."

"Wouldn't *you* be?"

"Damn straight. I'd be furious with him."

Ben felt his upper lip tremble as familiar words echoed in his head. *Dad doesn't care about me. I hate him.* Once he heard those words, he felt sick. Who talks that way about their dead dad?

"I believe anger's a sign you're working through your grief," Dr. Hunter told him. "It's perfectly normal to be angry. It's also normal to blame yourself for your father not being there for you."

"What do you mean?"

"Why do you think your dad failed to pick you up some weekends?"

"I already told you." He looked over at the aquarium. A clownfish swished his tail. "He had to do stuff for Uncle Angelo. He didn't have a choice."

"Really?" Dr. Hunter waited until he looked at him. "Are you sure you don't worry you're too bad, too unlovable, for your father to care about you?"

He gasped. How did Dr. Hunter know what went on inside his head?

"You're quite lovable, Ben. Your mother, Grant, Sophie, Uncle Joe — they all love you. And I believe your father loved you too. Sadly, he didn't tell you that."

Ben would've given anything to hear that from his dad.

Dr. Hunter studied him. "Did your dad ever hit you?"

"Nope." He let out a breath. "I probably deserved it a couple of times."

Silence floated between them. "I think that's the way he showed his love to you, Ben."

He scrunched his eyebrows together.

"Sounds like your dad didn't know much about being a good parent, but he made sure he didn't repeat his father's abuse. That must've taken much restraint on his part."

"Seems like he *wanted* to hit me sometimes," Ben admitted.

"I bet violence was his initial instinct. It's all he knew for how dads are supposed to act. But he tried to protect Grant, and I think he tried to protect you too."

Ben wanted to cry. He balled his hands into fists. "Sometimes he let me sit on his lap."

"He did? Tell me about that," Dr. Hunter said.

He couldn't believe the man wanted to hear the whole damn story, but he took a deep breath and launched into it — how one of his dad's girlfriends had yelled at him, and his father came to his defense. He made it through the whole thing with no pussy tears.

"That felt really good, for your father to hold you in his arms?" Dr. Hunter asked as he finished.

"Yeah," he choked out. So much for avoiding the tears. He cleared his throat.

"Do you ever get that feeling now? That feeling of being soothed and comforted?"

Holding a little white fluff-ball popped into his mind. Just that morning the tiny dog had lifted her head as her butt wiggled into his chest, her black eyes gleaming. She'd pressed her cool nose onto the tip of his then swiped his mouth with a sloppy kiss.

"You're smiling," Dr. Hunter said.

Despite himself, Ben chuckled. "We got a dog."

"Really? I thought your mom said your apartment was too small."

"Not for *this* dog—she's tiny. We already lost her underneath the sofa once. But my mom didn't get her for me. Hans did."

Dr. Hunter tilted his head. "Creepy Hans?"

"An obvious ploy to win my approval," Ben grumbled.

"Seems like it worked."

"Not really—I still think Hans is creepy. And why'd he have to get such a *girly* dog? I wanted a guy's dog, like a big German shepherd or something. Now we have this itty-bitty Maltese."

"It can be manly to care for small dogs too. So what's her name?"

Ben's eyes rolled up to the ceiling. "Dot."

"Dot…because she's so small?"

"No. Mom said she got to name her since she never wanted the dog in the first place. She named her after her Great Aunt Dorothy."

"It's a really cute name." Dr. Hunter smiled.

He folded his arms across his chest. "Awesome. I have a cute dog."

After a beat, Dr. Hunter said, "I wonder how you'll feel about Hans once you get to know him better."

"I'll *never* like him."

"Could be true." Dr. Hunter shrugged. "If your gut's getting a bad vibe, maybe he's not right for your mother. But you might want to give him a chance. Sounds like he went out of his way to buy you a dog, to get on your good side."

"I guess."

"It would also be nice to have some adult male attention, especially since Grant hasn't been around."

"Yeah. But Sophie said Uncle Grant's doing okay. Did I tell you he got me another pizza?"

"Wow, that must've scored major points with you."

"Lucky I was home when the delivery guy came." His smile faded. "I'm still grounded."

"Oh." Dr. Hunter's eyes turned down at the corners. "How much longer is your prison sentence?"

"Six whole days."

"So, our time's about up. Is Hans taking you home?"

"No way. I told him I had no idea when the session would end."

Dr. Hunter laughed. "Poor Hans. It'll take more than a dog to win *you* over."

"He better learn not to mess with me."

"If he's smart. So, what goal do you want to work on this week?"

"Um…" He thought for a second. "Maybe to study for my physics test instead of play with Dot too much?"

"Sounds good. See you next week."

As he walked toward the el stop a few minutes later, he replayed the session in his mind. He remembered feeling small against his father's big chest, cradled by strong arms. What if his dad had hit him? It would've hurt…a *lot*. He shuddered as he stepped onto the train. It was hard to imagine his dad being that small. He and Uncle Grant must've been so scared when Grandpa Barberi beat them.

Lost in thought, he almost fell when the train lurched forward, and he grabbed a metal pole to steady himself.

Darkness had fallen by the time he reached the apartment door. He'd barely made it inside when the fur-ball attacked him, her tail wagging double-time and her paws on his shins as she stood on two legs, gazing up at him. Her happy barks punctuated the air.

"Dot!" He laughed, scooping her up as he locked the door behind him. "Did you have a good day, punkin?"

Her frantic wiggle in his arms must have been her answer. After he set her down, she weaved between his legs as he took off his backpack and jacket.

He stopped short before entering the kitchen. Waiting for him on the linoleum was a puddle of pee. "Dot," he chastised. She lowered her head and peeked up at him with beady black eyes. He waggled his index finger at her. "Bad dog!" She whimpered and scampered away.

"Great," he mumbled, unrolling about a hundred paper towels and tossing them on the puddle. He stretched for his cell phone and texted his mom about the mishap. A few minutes later she replied:

Wonderful. Take her for a walk.

He scowled.

But it's dark out and I'm starved!

His text tone blared.

YOU'RE the one who wanted a dog! Walk her.

Ben exhaled. *Damn four-legged marshmallow.* "Dottie?" She'd made herself scarce. He checked out his mom's room, her bathroom, and under the sofa — no flash of white in sight. "Dot? Wanna go for a walk?" Grabbing the leash off the kitchen table, he wandered into his bedroom. No luck either, but wait…he kneeled down to peek under his bed and, sure enough, two little black eyes gleamed back at him.

"C'mon, girl, we're going for a walk!" He shook the leash, but she didn't budge. Five minutes of cajoling had no effect, and he finally figured he needed to lure her out with a treat. But of course there weren't any dog treats in the kitchen — his mom had already bitched enough about the cost of Dot's food and leash.

What the hell would the fluff-ball like to eat? The refrigerator revealed nothing of interest, but the third cabinet had some peanut butter. With a shrug, he shoveled a dollop into his mouth, then dug out some more to entice the little mop-on-legs.

Hoping he wouldn't lose a finger, Ben stuck his arm under his bed. A second later he giggled as she slurped some peanut butter with her rough tongue. He drew his hand out inch by inch until he had her cradled in his arms. "Sorry I yelled at you, Polka Dot." He kissed her fur.

Fifteen minutes later, Ben thought it'd be okay to go back inside: Dot had done her business in the grass near their building. He'd totally forgotten to grab a plastic poop bag and hoped no one had seen his civil disobedience in the dark. She now sniffed around a fire hydrant — what a cliché — and he yanked her leash. "C'mon, Dot!"

"Ben?" A pretty female voice that sounded just like…no, it couldn't be…

He spun around and grinned. *Score!* "Hey, Lindsay!" Then he cleared his throat and adopted a more manly affect.

"Is that your *dog?*" She leaned down to offer Dot her hand to sniff and squealed, "She's soooo cute! Oh my God, what's her name?"

Ben blushed. "Dot."

She took in a breath as her hand fluttered to her chest. "That's *adorable!* Can I hold her? Can I?"

"Sure." Ben gave a nonchalant shrug, trying to hide his trembling. Lindsay was actually talking to him! "Uh, what're you doing here?"

Lindsay let out the sweetest giggle as Dot licked her neck and jaw. "I met my dad for dinner." She tossed her head over her shoulder. "He's back there, on a call."

Ben's gaze followed to where she'd gestured, and he could see a tall man in a police uniform talking on his cell phone. *Holy shit*—her dad was a policeman. It was one thing to know her dad worked for CPD but another thing entirely to see him standing there in uniform. Ben's typical discomfort at spotting a cop now multiplied times ten. And, oh no, the cop had just finished his call and now came toward them.

"Linds, we have to go," he called.

She pouted. "Aw. Isn't this the cutest dog, Dad?"

As the man gave him the onceover, Ben straightened his spine.

"Do you *know* this boy, Linds, or are you bothering strangers again?"

"Daaad." She rolled her eyes. "This is Ben from swim team!"

When her dad held out his hand, Ben supposed he should shake it. He hoped there wasn't any peanut butter residue on his index finger.

"Nice to meet you, Ben from swim team."

"You too, sir." He blushed. He sounded like a total tool.

But her dad gave a faint smile, like he approved of the suck-up attempt. "It's *not* nice my daughter met your dog, though. She's been haranguing her mother and me for another dog since ours died a few months ago."

"It's time to move on, Dad." Lindsay had both of Dot's paws in her hands, performing a little canine dance with her. "Doobie-doobie-doo," she sang.

Her dad sighed. "Maybe. Well, Ben, I've got to get Lindsay home before my shift starts. Honey, let go of the dog."

Lindsay continued holding Dot hostage to her furry cabaret show. "Sha-sha-sha…shake it, girl, shake it!"

"Let. The. Dog. Go. You can do it, Lindsay," her dad ordered.

With an exaggerated pout, Lindsay sighed. "Fine." She handed Dot back to Ben, and he held her close to his chest. "But we *are* getting a dog soon, Dad. Just like Dot."

"No way, sweetheart," he said as he strolled away. "We're getting another Lab."

"But, Dad…" Lindsay trailed after him, turning around from ten feet away to wave. "Bye, Ben! See ya at swim practice tomorrow!"

He waved back, unsure of what had just happened. Their father-daughter interaction was so breezy and playful, so different from anything he'd known with his parents. Dot yelped as she watched them leave.

"Do you like Lindsay, Dot?" he asked. He snuggled his nose into her fur. "I do too."

Maybe a little girly dog wasn't *all* bad.

17. Congress

Anita's door stood partially open, and Sophie wondered if she should knock. As Anita's colleague, it would be fine to pop her head in the office. But part of her still thought of herself as Anita's former grad student, who would need to show respect.

When she finally knocked, there was no answer, and she was just about to walk away when she heard Anita say, "Wow."

"Anita?" No response. She knocked again, still getting no answer, and finally pressed on the door until it opened wide. Anita sat facing her computer with her back to the door. When Sophie saw black wires running from the hard drive to Anita's ears, it all made sense.

She spoke louder this time. "Anita!"

With a flinch, the redhead swiveled in her chair. "Hey!" She yanked the earbuds out. "Speak of the devil."

"Am I in trouble?"

"Of course not!" Anita laughed as she gestured to the chair across from her. "I was just listening to your interview of prisoner number six. You did a fantastic job."

"Oh! Um, thank you." Sophie closed the door and took a seat.

"Nora transcribed the interviews for us," Anita said, holding up some papers.

"I'm glad she joined our project."

Anita nodded. "You can never get too many pubs when you'll be on the job market soon. Anyway, I was reading the transcript for prisoner number six, and I was impressed at the depth of her responses. You got some good stuff, here. I wanted to know your secrets, so I decided to listen to the interview myself."

She felt a blush. "Aw, Anita, you should listen to *your* interviews if you want the good stuff."

"Are you kidding? I can write a cogent story with the data, but *you're* the one eliciting such rich data from the prisoners. I don't know how you connect with them so well."

A fire now raged in Sophie's cheeks. "It might help that I also spent time at Downer's Grove."

Anita shook her head. "That's not what I meant at all. You need to put that behind you and realize what a talent you have." She grabbed the transcript. "Listen to this." She read aloud:

"Prisoner: Then I found out I got a better chance of getting back my kids, once I get out, if I go to counseling. That's why I keep going, even though it was stupid at first.

Sophie: What parts seemed stupid to you?

Prisoner: Uh…(sighs). Thinking about the past again. Telling Dr. Ashby about it, too. I didn't want her to know what he did to me and my kids. What I let Tyrone do.

Sophie: Tyrone—is he the father of your children?

Prisoner: No—he long gone. Their dad's a loser, but he'd never hurt him like Tyrone did. And I just sat back…didn't do nothin' when Tyrone punched them…backhanded my babies…

Sophie: How awful for you to have to witness that. You feel tremendous guilt about Tyrone beating your children, when you were unable to stop it?

Prisoner: Dr. Ashby keep telling me it's not my fault, what Tyrone did to us…Tyrone told me he'd kill me if I fought him. I shoulda stopped him, though. I shoulda stopped him."

Sophie took a slow breath as she remembered Dominique's self-blame—exactly what Logan had experienced. She shook her head and tried to focus on Anita's voice as she continued reading the transcript.

"Sophie: He threatened your life, but you feel ashamed you couldn't stop the abuse. It still haunts you. The traumatic memories give you nightmares.

Prisoner: Well, I don't get nightmares as much since I started with Dr. Ashby.

Sophie: I'm glad to hear that. I wonder, what makes it hard to believe Tyrone's actions aren't your fault?

Prisoner: They…they're my babies. He beat them. He…he raped my little girl. (cries) I'm the one who brought Ty into their lives. I'm the one.

Sophie: (pauses as the prisoner cries) I'm so sad you and your children had to go through that. Simply horrifying. (pauses) Where is Tyrone now?

Prisoner: (sniffs) Six feet under.

Sophie: I see. That's why you're here at Downer's Grove?

Prisoner: He can't hurt my babies anymore."

Anita lowered the paper and stared. "That's an *appalling* story. She trusted you in such a short time to tell you what happened. How'd you manage to track her so closely without reacting in shock? How'd you keep going with the empathy? I mean, this woman killed the man who'd raped her daughter!"

"I…" Sophie swallowed. "I've heard a version of this story before, I guess."

"And *that's* why I never wanted to become a therapist." Anita shuddered. "But why did number six go to prison? Wasn't it self-defense?"

"I asked the CO the same question after the interview. He told me she'd stabbed her ex in his sleep…forty-three times."

"Oh." Anita cringed. "I guess that's not self-defense."

"No, I guess not." Sophie looked down at her hands in her lap. "I can see why she did it, though. After hearing her story, *I* wanted to kill Tyrone."

"Hmm. It sounds like counseling has really helped this prisoner."

Sophie nodded. "It's dangerous to show any vulnerability on the inside—those nightmares could've gotten her in trouble. The fact that her nightmares decreased is a big help in itself. Dr. Ashby did a good job."

"*You* did a good job with this prisoner, Sophie. You helped her."

"I…I was only with her for an hour."

"And in only one hour, she wanted *you* to be her psychologist instead of Dr. Ashby!"

She squirmed. "Um, so I came here to see if you'd like to get lunch?"

"Don't change the subject." Anita sat back in her chair and sighed. "You know, I was sad when you didn't follow my footsteps into academia, but I always understood why. You have a gift for therapy. And as much as I love having you here at DePaul, have you thought about going in front of the board to get your license back?"

Sophie pressed her palm to her forehead, feeling the beginning of a hunger headache. Or maybe it was a career headache. A regret headache.

"Sorry for badgering you," Anita said softly. When Sophie looked up, she was smiling. "I promise I won't say anything about therapy *or* research at lunch. C'mon."

•

"Warm night," Andrei said as he stomped out his cigarette on the pavement.

Grant nodded. They stood outside a bar in West Town. Agent Bounter had told him this was one of the Russians' favorite hangouts, but they'd never taken him here before. He wondered what that meant.

Andrei inhaled the night air. "Would not be so warm in home country in March."

In Solntsevo, you mean? "Just wait—it'll get cold again. Where did you grow up?"

Andrei glared at him, then headed into the bar.

Apparently personal questions weren't allowed. With a deep breath, he followed.

He heard some welcoming shouts as Andrei stepped inside, but once he came through the door, the reception cooled. Dark eyes studied him.

"Is my friend Mick," Andrei said to his buddies at the bar.

Though a few men nodded, the hard set of their jaws and coldness of their eyes revealed ongoing suspicion.

Andrei beckoned him to a booth. "Come."

Grant swallowed and slid onto the cracked plastic cushion on the bench, wishing his back wasn't facing the door. A stooped, gray-haired man arrived a second later with shots of vodka.

Andrei raised his shot glass. "*Budem.*"

"*Budem*." When Grant felt fire slide down his throat, he finally exhaled. *You can do this.* "You've never taken me here before."

"Is good place for talk."

Grant nodded as he listened to the faint sounds of a Cubs spring training game on a TV hanging over the corner of the bar. Likely it wasn't the atypical quiet of this place that made it good for a chat. Instead, the Russians had probably swept it for bugs that very day.

When another round of shots arrived, Grant tensed. If they kept up this pace, he'd soon be on the floor.

"Leave us now," Andrei told the man. "To your success," he added, lifting his glass. Grant clinked his glass to Andrei's and knocked back the second shot. Andrei wiped his mouth with the back of his hand and leaned in. "Vladimir like you." He paused for dramatic effect. "I not say that to many men."

Grant wasn't sure how to respond.

"But you still in debt."

"When I get my next paycheck—"

"Shut," Andrei ordered. "We all know once you pay, you lose again. You pathetic."

Grant found himself strangely wounded by the insult, as if he cared whether he won or lost at cards. Perhaps he was playing the role of gambling addict a bit too well. "C'mon, you know I'll pay up. And one day I'll win big…I can feel it."

Andrei blew out through his nose. "One day might never come, but today…is *here*. Now." Black eyes stared him down. "You do jobs for us, pay debt."

Here it comes. "What kind of jobs?"

"The kind we tell you to do."

Now Grant leaned in. "Listen, if you expect me to break the law—"

"Who say break law?" Andrei's eyes gleamed.

Grant suppressed a snort. "All I'm saying is if you expect me to…take *risks*, you better pay me a percentage of what we take in."

Mischief vanished from Andrei's eyes. "You in no position to bargain." His hand darted under the table and seized Grant's junk, squeezing his balls like a vise.

Following the sharp slam of pain came a flash of nausea. Grant couldn't breathe, and he definitely couldn't speak. *The pain.* His hands itched to break Andrei's damn wrists, but he didn't want to reveal the moves he'd learned at Quantico. His vision started to cloud, and he squeaked, "Okay."

Andrei held on for a few sickening seconds more, then finally released him. Grant sank back in the booth, sucking in air. Warmth flooded his injured groin.

"We have understanding now," Andrei said, his voice low.

He opened his eyes, the spots fading from his vision. "Yes, sir."

A small grin spread on Andrei's face. "You work submarines in Navy, *da?*"

"Uh…" Grant cleared his throat. "They trained me on subs, but I mostly worked on aircraft carriers."

"You know how to drive subs."

"I…" He shrugged.

Two black slits stared back at him.

"Yeah, sure," he said, feeling his heart flutter. "I can figure it out."

"Good. Go south, drive sub here. Leave in one week."

South? He remembered learning the Russians were probably using defunct submarines to transport drugs to the U.S. from several South American locations. *Columbia? Ecuador?* "South? Where are we going?"

Andrei ignored the question. "But first, we need cash — pay for product. That where you come in."

I thought I was already in.

"Break into safe at hotel."

His mouth dropped open. "I couldn't do that to Mr. Remington, after all he's done for me…and I don't even know how to get to the safe!"

"Find out." Andrei smiled. "If want to live."

Grant forced a swallow, finding his throat dry.

"You look upset."

He looked back, tilting his head. That was something Hunter would say, not Andrei.

"We help you feel better." Andrei nodded, then beckoned for the waiter.

His stomach clenched. More vodka?

After Sophie checked in at the storage office, she picked her way through the looming watercraft in the yacht yard to the familiar Eaton Tours ship. She patted the underbelly of the bow as she remembered pleading for a job last June—the day she'd first met Roger. The day she'd first immersed herself with Grant.

She also recalled hustling on deck, filling drink orders, and looking up to the bridge to find his sparkling blue eyes gazing down at her with warmth and intrigue.

She jumped when a hand rested on her shoulder. Those same loving eyes now stood before her. "You're early," Grant said, drawing her into his arms.

She closed her eyes and inhaled his fresh bergamot scent. She hadn't seen him for three days. "I knew McSailor would be on military time…"

"And you didn't want to miss one minute together," he answered. His hands roved down her back and sparked tingles of pleasure. She felt the warmth of his breath near her ear a second before he pressed a kiss to her cheek. He feathered a kiss to the tip of her nose then nudged her nose with his. But he kept her waiting, his lips hovering over hers for a frustrating few moments as he stared at her. "It's so good to be with my fiancée. Hello, the soon-to-be Mrs. Saylor—I mean Dr. Saylor."

She giggled. "Not too far off what students call me now."

"Roger pointed out our similar last names. He thought my alias was crap."

"*I* think it's perfect." Tired of waiting, she dived in for a hello kiss. He responded hungrily, and she cradled his head as she drew him closer. She nipped at his lower lip, and he growled deep in his throat. His hard body pressed into her like a blustery Chicago wind, almost knocking her off her feet. His fingers curled around her to scoop her even tighter—she wasn't going *anywhere*.

"How much time do we have?" Grant asked between kisses.

"Before the wedding planner arrives?" Sophie somehow peeked at her watch as his tongue danced with hers. "Twenty minutes."

"More than enough." When he hooked his hands under her arms and hoisted her up, at first she laughed with surprise, but then wrapped her legs around his waist, crossing her ankles underneath his taut Navy butt.

"Where're we headed, McSailor?"

He grinned. "See if she's sea-worthy."

"*What?*" Grant had carried her to starboard and with a grunt he stepped up a metal staircase one of the facility's employees must've scooted in place for the wedding planner's inspection. Sophie's eyes darted around the yard. "Shouldn't we wait for Cheri?"

"What I plan to do to you…" His eyes darkened. "Cheri wouldn't want to see."

Sophie gasped. "I'm not sure Cheri approves of premarital sex."

At the top step, Grant unclasped the small starboard-side door. "She'll have to get over it."

He set her down on the deck, then led her up another set of stairs to the bridge. When they reached the top, he stooped over to enter the security code. From this vantage point, she scanned the yacht yard and failed to detect any movement around surrounding ships. Still, her cheeks grew warm as he drew her into the ship's control area.

She squealed when he yanked her flush to his body. One hand pressed to the small of her back and his other hand curled around hers as he began rocking them together, humming "I Get a Kick Out of You."

"A sober dance this time," she murmured.

His gaze slid down her body then back up to her face. "I feel *anything* but sober."

She had to agree. When he lowered her for a dip, dizziness buzzed in her brain like she'd just downed champagne.

One of his hands supported her back and the other cradled her head, holding her body parallel to the floor. She returned the beaming smile he gave her — he was teasing her again — then let her eyes flutter shut as he lowered to kiss her, softly at first, then with more insistence, more fervor. She felt the contraction of his quad muscle against her thigh — his muscles alone kept them upright, hovering over the bridge floor. It surprised her how completely she'd relaxed into his hold. But he'd earned her trust. Again and again.

Unmolding his mouth from hers, he gently pulled her back to her feet. She swayed with him, dancing to his imaginary Sinatra beat, until he backed her into a wall. His hands found her waist to unbutton her pants. She cocked one eyebrow. "I see where this is headed, McSailor."

His impish grin vanished when she reached up to unbutton his shirt. "They told me not to mess with the mic."

"The FBI's *not* coming with us on this voyage," she said.

"But Agent Bounter told me not to turn off the mic again." He blushed. "At least not to get it on with you."

She laughed.

"Seriously," he said. "Remember that one time they turned off the mic? My family kidnapped you!"

"That's not going to happen again." She resumed her unbuttoning.

"What makes you so sure?"

She stared into his eyes. "Because if they even try to interrupt us, I'll *kill* them." Finally getting the last button undone, she split open his shirt and ripped it off. Once she held it in her hand, she wondered what to do with it. Then inspiration struck. She held up her index finger, crossed to the bridge doorway, and flung his shirt down the stairs to the deck. "Now those pervs won't get to listen in."

Turning back, she found her man bare-skinned with his mouth hanging open. "Jesus, Bonnie." He cleared his throat. "You are *hot*." He reached her in two long strides and practically slammed her up onto the counter, clawing at her clothing. She grasped his shoulders to steady herself as she lifted her thighs so he could peel down her pants, and soon she felt cool fiberglass beneath her naked bottom. Her gaze drifted to the plaque on the opposite wall. Roger must've added it after she'd resigned. *Beatings would continue until morale improved.*

"Morale's definitely up," she sighed, admiring the symmetrical grooves of lean muscle tapering down to Grant's groin.

He'd just shucked his jeans and boxers to his knees, and a wicked grin broadened his face. "*I'd* say."

Pride swelled within her, knowing she could turn him on so fully—knowing just the sight of him had fired *her* up, readied her for the glory about to come. And come they did, mere moments after he cupped her bottom and slid her forward onto him, filling her immediately. With a sharp inhale, she dug into the corded muscles of his upper back as they pulsed together. One of her hands reached up to smooth his black buzz-cut, and he groaned from the pleasure. He leaned into her for kisses, his tongue penetrating her mouth, and the rest of his body doing amazing things to her down below.

She heard a grunt of frustration as his lips skated down her neck—her turtleneck sweater. In a flash he'd yanked it off, and her hair sparked with electricity as it settled back on her shoulders. His lips and hands now attended to her breasts, massaging her through her silky bra. As waves of pleasure rocked through her, she tossed her head back, promptly thumping her skull on the glass window of the bridge.

"*Ouch.*" She rubbed the crown of her head.

His head popped up from her breasts. "Are you all right?"

She pouted. "Sex injury."

He laughed and batted her hand aside, taking over rubbing duty. "I don't think the bridge was quite designed for this." He drew her forehead to his chest and planted soft kisses on her smarting head as she snuggled into his chest. Combined with his smell of aftershave and sweat, his caresses soothed her, and heaviness weighed her though it was the middle of the day.

"I've missed you, Grant."

He tilted up her chin. "I've missed you so much, Bonnie." He pressed a kiss to the tip of her nose. She was glad he was still inside her—she could never get too close to him. "But our forced separation will be over soon."

"Really? How do you know?"

"The Russians let me in—they finally trust me, I guess. They want me to help them transport drugs from South America. They told me we leave within a week."

She let go of him. "*What?* How can the FBI keep track of you there?"

"They can't, but don't worry. They'll arrest the Russians before we get that far." He smiled. "When we rob Mr. Remington's hotel, Agent Bounter's men will be waiting for us."

"Grant." Her heart seized with fear. "I don't like this. Too many things could go wrong. What if they figure out you're FBI?"

He frowned for a moment, then eased out of her. He squatted to help her pull her pants back on. "It'll be fine. We're doing it the same way we did with Jovanovich—they'll arrest me too, and Vladimir won't be any wiser. It worked great before."

"Are you *sure* it went great?" Enthralled by the grace of his hands, she let him button her pants.

"I don't see any Serbs coming after me, do you?" His smile faded. "Or my father's men, either."

She cradled the side of his face. "Don't underestimate your father. He ruined your grand plan once before."

His mouth set in a grim line. "Then with Dr. Hayes's help, we went to Plan B. And that turned out even better."

Speaking of Hunter, she certainly wasn't using any of his communication skills. *Validate*, she reminded herself. *Validation is acknowledgement, not agreement or acceptance.* "Things *did* turn out well with Jovanovich," she admitted, placing her hands on his shoulders. "And it sounds like you're well prepared for the Russians." She mustered a faint smile. "Just like last time, I hope it goes even better than expected."

"Thank you." He closed his eyes and exhaled. He pulled his boxers back on. "I'll be back to you and Ben soon, I promise. I know what a strain this has put on us all."

"Speaking of Ben…He wanted me to tell you something." She felt his shoulders tense.

"Is everything okay?"

"It is now. He's been working through some things with Hunter…"

He hung his head. "I should be there for him."

"You *are* there, as much as you can be. He said keep the pizzas coming, by the way." He snorted. "Anyway, Ben told Hunter something he'd done in the past—it's been eating him up inside. Hunter recommended he tell his mother and you about it. When Ben told Ashley, she grounded him—"

"She *grounded* him?"

"I know, I was surprised too when I heard—and proud of her. She's actually trying to be his parent. Anyway, Ben felt the need to tell you too but wasn't sure when he'd see you next."

"What'd he do?"

"He…" She paused. "He sold drugs."

For a second Grant showed no reaction, but then his eyes clouded over with a coming storm.

"Breathe, Grant. He just sold ecstasy pills to his friends—"

"To other *kids?*" he roared. "How could he? Does he have a death wish?" He raised his fists then threw his arms down. "*God!*" Radiating energy, he looked like he needed to move, to pace, to smash something. But with his jeans pooled at his feet, he didn't make it one step before he tumbled to the floor, landing on his butt.

Sophie scrambled off the counter and kneeled by his side. "Are you okay?"

He rubbed his backside, which had to be bruised. One corner of his mouth twitched. "Sex injury."

She giggled. "We make some pair." She sat down facing him, resting her back on his bent leg while smoothing her hand over his taut abdominal muscles. "How're you feeling?"

He let out a long exhale. "I shouldn't judge him for selling drugs. I'm a big, fat hypocrite."

"Why?"

"I've killed a man, Sophie."

"Are you talking about Carlo Barberi?"

He nodded.

"That was self-defense, you idiot! He *shot* me. He would've killed us both if you hadn't stopped him."

He touched the mottled, pink scar near her elbow. "I know." He sighed. "But sometimes I wonder if I'm all that different from the Mafia guys. Vladimir's not far off from my dad. And Andrei? Sometimes he reminds me of Logan…"

She leaned in to kiss his collarbone. "You know, Ben craved Logan's attention. That's the only reason he sold the drugs. He promised he wouldn't do it again."

Grant nodded. "And now he'll never get Lo's attention."

"But he has ours," she said. "And his mom's, and Hunter's…and Lindsay—this girl he likes. He'll get her attention too once she comes around."

"Lindsay, huh? I bet she isn't near as cute as you are." He scooped her into his lap and ran his fingers through her hair. She sighed with pleasure as he plied her with deep kisses.

"My *eyes!*"

Sophie scuttled off Grant and looked over to find a short, dark-haired man peeking at them through his fingers.

"Oh, *shit*," Grant said, then hopped to his feet. "What're you doing here, Roger?"

Sophie's eyes almost popped out of their sockets. *Rog?* Where had all that hair come from?

"Helping you with your goddamn *wedding!*" Roger hollered. "I thought I'd show the wedding planner around. But it appears you've skipped ahead to baby-making in the fucking yacht yard!" When he lowered his hands, Sophie realized she was shirtless. One arm crossed her chest as the other lunged for her sweater, and Grant shimmied into his jeans.

"Where's my shirt?" he whispered.

"It's on the fucking deck below, numbnuts!" Roger answered. "That was my first clue some kinky shit was going on up here."

Grant brushed past him to the stairs. "Did you consider knocking, sir?"

"On my *own* fucking ship? Yeah, like I'd knock."

Now that she'd restored her clothing, Sophie regained the ability to speak. "You look fantastic, Rog! I hear you have a woman in your life?" She twisted her hair up into a messy bun.

The distraction seemed to work — Roger turned away from where Grant had gone and looked at her. His nose lifted a bit as he adopted an air of superiority. "Ana's her name. I'm bringing her to the wedding. That is, if you're not too ballooned up preggers to walk down the aisle by June."

"It's called birth control, Rog."

His hand shot up in front of his chest. "Spare me the gory details, Taylor."

A fully dressed McSailor returned to the bridge. "Sorry about that, sir." He stuffed his hands in his jean pockets. "It was my fault. It's just we don't get to see each other much right now."

"Why the hell not?"

"It's too dangerous," he explained. "I don't want to blow my cover or lead the Russian Mafia anywhere near her."

Roger's expression softened. "Oh. Yeah, that *would* be tough. I know I don't like to go too long without seeing Ana." He circled the bridge, appearing to check if everything was in place. "So, Madsen… got a *monster* case of blue balls, eh?"

She laughed. The old Rog had returned.

"Helloooo?" A lilting female voice drifted up from below.

She peered down. "That's Cheri, the wedding planner. Rog, will you help show her around your ship?"

"That's why I'm here." He glared at Grant. "Just make sure to keep it in your pants this time, sex addict."

"That'll be up to Sophie, sir." He draped his arm across her shoulders. "You think you can keep your hands off me for the duration of the tour?"

"Absolutely not!"

He grinned. "I was hoping you'd say that."

18. Converge

"Dot!" Ben snickered when the white fluff-ball attacked him, furiously licking chlorine off his face as he held her aloft. When her tongue swooped in his ear, he recoiled. "That's gross." He sat back on the sofa and settled her into his lap as he blocked her attempts to deliver another wet willy. Her little paws pressed against his thighs while she hopped and wriggled in his arms. "Chill, Dotbot!"

Finally she seemed to tire, and he loosened his hold on her tiny ribcage. She sniffed a couple of times, nose up in the air, then circled his lap twice and collapsed. "About *time* you let me do my homework," he grumbled as he scratched her ears. He wasn't sure, but when her mouth curled up, it looked like she was smiling at him.

He extracted his psychology textbook from his backpack and arranged it so he could read without disturbing Princess Dot, whose even breaths sounded like she'd already entered dreamland. *I wish I could fall asleep so easily.* He began reading about behavior modification. His eyes drifted to the *Psychology and You* sidebar question:

```
What's been your experience with positive
reinforcement, negative reinforcement, and
punishment today?
```

He knew all about punishment — he was still grounded for two more days. At least he wasn't alone anymore, though. Dot's black eyes blinked sleepily as he petted her. Then her head popped up, and she growled at the front door.

"What is it, Dot?"

She leaped off his lap just as there was a knock at the door. He pushed himself to his feet. "Coming!" Pausing at the door, he asked, "Who is it?"

"Chicagoland Pizza."

A smile stretched on his face. Uncle Grant rewarding him with a pizza: the very definition of positive reinforcement. He opened the door to see a tall dude maybe a little older than him with acne pockmarks covering his face. The tantalizing aroma of pizza wafted into the apartment. But his smile faded when he noticed a blond man behind the pizza guy, off to his left.

"Hallo, Ben," Hans said with a sneer.

Dot went wild with high-pitched barks as she rushed out to Hans's feet and seized the hem of his jeans. Hans laughed as her head veered right and left, tugging.

"Dot!" Ben admonished.

When Hans reached down to try to scoop her up, Dot high-tailed it back into the apartment, and Ben watched her disappear around the corner. He turned back with a questioning look, but Hans just shrugged.

"What're *you* doing here?"

"Is that a way to talk to a man who just ordered you pizza?" Hans asked.

"*You* didn't order it," Ben said. *How'd this tool think he could get by with a lie like that?* "My uncle did."

"Ah." Hans smiled as he stepped closer. "Then I will pay for it."

"My uncle already paid." Ben looked at the pizza guy. "Right?"

The dude took a moment to respond. "Uh, yeah." He gave Hans a lazy smile. "You could pay me too, though."

Ben smirked. "Nice try." He didn't want to be in *any* sort of debt to Hans. "Can I just have my pizza?"

The raspy scratch of Velcro pulling open unleashed the large pizza box, and Ben accepted the warm cardboard with a grin. "My uncle already tipped you, right?"

Pizza boy gave a reluctant nod.

"After I have a word with the pizza delivery man," Hans told Ben, "I'll be right in."

Ben backed into the apartment and kicked the door shut. *Like hell you will, Himmler.* The deadbolt slid in place with a satisfying click. He slid the pizza box onto the kitchen counter and felt a wave of relief. There must be some way to keep that creep out of his apartment. He'd have to make up an excuse like his mom didn't allow visitors when she wasn't home or some sort of bullshit.

He hunted for his dog. "Polka Dot?" She was hiding under his bed — her favorite spot. She'd tucked herself into the far corner, just beyond his reach, and he sighed as he picked himself up off the floor. "I know just what'll lure you out, baby girl."

He returned to the kitchen, opened the pizza box, and grabbed a scalding hot slice of pepperoni. "Shit!" He flung the meat down before it burned off his fingerprints. After he blew on it for a few seconds, he picked it up again and went back into his bedroom. "Yummy pepperoni, Dottie." Dropping to his belly, he held it out for her to sniff. It only took a second before she zoomed out from under the bed to chow down the greasy goodness.

Sitting cross-legged on his bedroom floor, Ben cradled her in his arms and felt her little body tremble. "Smart girl." He kissed the crown of her head. "*I* think Hans is creepy too. C'mon, let's get some more pepperoni."

⧫

"*Who* ordered the pizza?" Ricker demanded as he crowded Zitboy's personal space in the dim hallway of the apartment building.

"Dude, I don't know."

Ricker's hands itched to slap the little shit. "You have no idea?"

Zitboy shrugged. "They never tell us nothing. Just where to deliver."

Ricker reached into his pocket and waved a twenty-dollar bill in front of the boy's face, Zitboy suddenly seemed more attentive. "You don't remember *anything* about who ordered pizza to this address?"

"Um…oh…yeah. When Stan sent me out, first he gave me this other address. Then he was all, 'Wait, that's, like, where the order came from, not where it's, like, going.'"

Zitboy lunged for the twenty, but Ricker yanked it away. "Not good enough. I need the first address."

"Dude, I don't know!" Zitboy pouted. "It was on Michigan Avenue or something."

"I need an address."

"Why do you care so much, German dude?"

Ricker began to pocket his money when Zitboy said, "Wait! It was, um, like, nine-twenty North Michigan?"

"You sure?" Ricker asked.

"Yeah." Zitboy nodded. He held his palm up. "I'll take my twenty."

The bill did not reappear, but Ricker leaned in and hissed, "Get the fuck out of here, *now*." His eyes must have communicated his I-Will-Fuck-You-Up intent because the boy swiveled and took off in seconds. Ricker closed his eyes as he breathed in his success. His first break.

He knocked on the apartment door. "Ben?" When there was no answer, he said, "I cannot stay. Something came up."

"Okay!" came his reply through the door. He sounded thrilled.

Ricker scowled as he hustled down the stairs. "I got you the fucking dog, ungrateful little Mafia prince."

Twenty minutes later, Ricker weaved through shoppers and sight-seers on Michigan Avenue to arrive at the address Pimpleboy had told him. A hotel? A fucking hotel? That little shit had scammed him with the wrong address—good thing he hadn't given him the twenty. He stood with hands on hips, staring up at the high rise, when something hit his foot. He looked down to see a black Tumi suitcase almost roll over his foot before he stepped back quickly.

"So sorry," a man said in a crisp English accent. The taxi he'd just exited pulled away. Ricker took one look at the slight man's blushing cheeks and fell in love.

"No problem," he said. "It is my fault, truly." He gestured above. "I was admiring the hotel's architecture."

The man gave a polite smile. "Oh, yes. Don't you love the neo-classical style of the White City?"

Ricker had no idea what the fuck the man was talking about, but with that pretty accent he would go along with anything. "Yes. It is…nice." He knew most Germans hated the English, but how could he hate *this* fine specimen of flesh?

"Have you tried an architectural tour, then?"

Ricker found himself staring at those fine pink lips, and he forced himself to look into the man's eyes. "I have been…away. But I hear good things about the tours."

The man checked his watch. "Well, I best check in or I shall miss tea." His arm pointed toward the revolving door. "Are you going in?"

"After you." Ricker grinned. He followed the man to the front desk with his eyes glued on his small, tight derriere.

"May I help you, sir?" A voice jarred him out of his lustful reverie. Ricker glanced up to find a brunette smiling in his direction as Jude Law checked in with another front desk staff member.

He stepped forward and kept his voice low. "Yah. I seek a place to stay for my mother when she is in town for a visit." Which would be never, considering the alcoholic bitch had disowned him after his first stint in prison. "What can your hotel offer?"

"We're a four-star hotel," she said as she unfolded a brochure on the counter. "Our soundproofed rooms feature pillow-soft mattresses, and the *Tribune* named our spa the best in Chicago. Does your mother enjoy live music?"

How the hell do I know? Ricker nodded.

"Our cocktail lounge, Capone's Spirits, features live old-Chicago music six nights a week. Ladies love the singer, Mick Saylor." She pointed to a cardboard poster sitting on an easel. "There he is."

Crystal blue eyes stopped his heart. Madsen? *Singing? Here?* And why the fuck was he calling himself Saylor?

"Sir? Are you all right?"

Ricker coughed and hoped his woody wasn't too obvious. "Is he singing tonight?"

The woman glanced at her watch. "He starts in twenty-five minutes."

His second break. Madsen must have ordered the boy's pizza from a hotel phone. "Thank you." He smiled, showing all his teeth.

"You're welcome, sir. Would you like to make a reservation for your mother?"

"I will call. Later. The lounge—is this way?" He pointed to the right, beyond the poster with Mr. Fuck-Me Eyes.

"Yes, sir."

Ricker thought for a moment. "And the gift store?"

"Our gift shop is in the same direction, on your left."

The blood pooling in his crotch was almost painful at this point. "Excellent." He was about to head to victory when he heard the Englishman speak.

"A pleasure to meet you."

Ricker turned to his left and shook the man's extended hand. "You too, my good chap." The lad's smile intrigued Ricker. "I will be at Capone's Spirits if you would like to join me later."

"Sounds brilliant."

As Ricker watched that perky ass head to the elevators with his bag in tow, his heart pounded with excitement. This was turning into a good evening. A *very* good evening.

❧

The black Chicago Bulls cap shadowed his face and hopefully hid his blond hair. Ricker found a table far enough from the stage to avoid detection by Madsen. Oh, sorry — *Saylor*. What the fuck? Too bad the stage was empty, but there was an excited buzz throughout the growing crowd. Bobby Darin sang "Mack the Knife" on the speakers, and Ricker wondered if anyone in the lounge knew the German origins of the song. Probably not.

A cocktail waitress came to his table, and he barked out his drink order. His cash advance from Enzo had dwindled with alarming speed, and the price of drinks at a nice joint like this wasn't helping. But he felt like celebrating now that Enzo's son was in his grasp. And soon he'd have too much cash to count. He hoped Enzo would call him from prison tomorrow so he could share the good news.

Easing back in his chair, he noted couples at most of the nearby tables. *Dummkopfs.* When would they learn that monogamy never worked? His American father — at least he'd been smart enough not to hang around after he'd stuck his dick in his mother and knocked her up.

Every fucking night his mother had whined about his father leaving her, and her bitching had been even worse when she was drunk. But the dumbest thing she'd done was keep searching for a man to marry her. She'd been a looker once, before the booze turned her skin saggy and tired, and she'd always been able to hook some loser for a few months at a time. Though when the john would start feeling trapped—or realize Ricker would fight off his attempts to beat or rape him—he'd always leave. Every time. And Ricker would be left to deal with his mother's endless complaining, hollering in her scratchy smoker voice about men being the scum of the earth.

He shook his head. That's why he'd come to America…land of opportunity. Land of fresh starts. Land of the free. Too bad he'd spent most of his stay behind bars.

When two more couples walked in, Ricker watched the host guide them to a primo table near the stage. One of the chicks looked like a brunette Kate Moss—yeah, he'd do her—but why was she with that older, barrel-chested guy? What could *he* possibly offer? The other couple was a black-haired guy with a blond woman in a red dress—at least Black Hair was slightly younger and more attractive. As Black Hair held out a chair for Blondie, he scanned the bar with a shrewd and steady gaze. His eyes met Ricker's, and Ricker immediately looked down. *Fuck!* He needed to be more careful.

Patting his left coat pocket, he took out his phone and pretended to respond to a text. By the time he looked back at Black Hair, all four were seated at the table. The older man spoke to the waitress in a way that made him take notice. Her tray visibly shook in the crook of her arm. He sat up. Who *was* this gray-haired man, and why was his buddy scanning the room like a fucking SS agent?

"Sorry this took so long," Ricker's waitress said as she set an amaretto sour on his table. She also set down the leather wallet containing the check.

"I want to start a tab," Ricker said. It would be easy to drink and dash in a swanky place like this.

"Sorry, sir, we only run tabs for patrons we know."

He grunted and opened the wallet to reveal the exorbitant bill. As he fished out some money from his pocket, he glanced at the table of interest and watched the waitress set down four shot glasses and a bottle of vodka. No leather wallet.

"I guess *they* are well-known patrons?" He cocked his head toward the group without looking their direction.

"Yes. They're big fans of Mr. Saylor."

Ricker felt vibrations in his cock. "Really. Who are they…do you know?"

"All I know is they're Russian and very rude. One of them *screamed* at poor Alice for messing up an order once. Yet our manager keeps making her serve them." She shook her head. "I'm just glad I don't have to." She scooped up the bill. "Would you like change?"

"You keep it."

"Thank you. We're busy tonight, but I'll be back to check on you later."

And I will be gone. Once he'd tailed Madsen home, he'd pursue other locales, where the beer, sex, and domination were free. Time to drop in on his little Cuban amigo. But then he remembered Jude Lawless he'd met in the lobby. So many men, so little time.

As soon as Madsen stepped on stage, though, all thoughts of other men vanished. *God, he's beautiful.* Madsen still possessed shining blue eyes, smooth olive skin, and buzzed black hair. But he'd filled out a bit since prison, making him more man than boy, and he swaggered up to the microphone with poise and confidence Ricker had never seen.

Madsen seized the mic as a nondescript brown-haired man joined him on stage and slid onto the piano bench. A woman seated two tables away from Ricker whooped, drawing Madsen's eyes to the upper tier of the seating area. Ricker slumped in his chair and tugged the bill of his ball cap down to his nose as his cock strained in the opposite direction. Other chicks echoed her catcalls and elicited a shy grin from the man on stage. Ricker closed his eyes and swallowed, trying to wrestle back control of himself.

"Hello, Chicago!" Madsen boomed, and now everyone in the audience cheered and clapped. He pointed to the guy on the piano bench. "The talented stylings of Andy Beecham on piano…" He paused as the cheers continued. "And I'm Mick Saylor, your cruise director. We're taking you on a McRockin' and McJazzin' ride to*night!*"

When the crowd erupted in applause, Ricker's forehead creased. Was McDonald's a hotel corporate sponsor or something?

The piano player banged out the first notes of a melody, and apparently Ricker was the only one *not* to recognize the tune. Whistles and shouts rose up around him. Madsen started off slow, his voice surprisingly deep. When he sang something about throwing a kiss, those full lips mesmerized Ricker.

"Woo!" called a woman from the table next to him, and her friend giggled.

Mine, Ricker wanted to hiss back.

Ah, *now* he recognized the song, as soon as Madsen got to the lyrics about Chicago…"My Kind of Town." No wonder the Windy City crowd was close to orgasm.

A couple of upbeat songs followed, and Madsen tossed in a few dance moves. Ricker's eyebrows arched at the man's grace. This sexy performance made him want this fine piece of meat more than ever. Was that even possible? Given his nonstop fantasies about Madsen since he'd left Gurnee, he hadn't thought so.

Madsen walked to the back of the stage and returned carrying a wooden stool. *I'd like to push up* his *stool*, Ricker thought with a wicked grin.

Madsen looked around the crowd then focused on the table of Russians. "Since starting this show at Capone's Spirits, I've searched for songs to represent what's going on in my life—to capture a particular mood, a turn of a phrase. When I came across this song by Frank Sinatra, I knew I wanted to sing it to you tonight. You see, my girl just broke up with me."

A collective "Awww" emanated from the ladies, interrupted by one woman shouting "Date *me!*" which drew laughter from the audience and a precious blush from the performer.

Madsen had dated a chick? *Interesting.* Not that it mattered—he'd have Madsen either way.

"Here's Frank Sinatra's 'A Man Alone.'" Madsen closed his eyes during the piano introduction. He had such pretty eyelashes…Ricker couldn't wait to deflower that tight, puckering rosebud hole. He'd stick a stem in there and let it grow, and Madsen wouldn't be alone for long.

All too soon the song was over, and when Madsen announced he was taking a little break, Ricker groaned along with the rest of the crowd. He could sit and listen to that voice for hours. Ricker fought the urge to sprint up to the stage and take Madsen right there—"They Can't Take That Away From Me" style.

But like a good boy, he pressed his muscular buns into the chair and waited it out. What he saw intrigued him: Madsen made a beeline for the Russians. How did he know them? Ricker watched him shake the older man's hand with a sense of deference, and…was that *fear?* Madsen's shoulders tensed like he thought Gray Hair would hit him or something, and his body language didn't relax any when he shook Black Hair's hand. What the fuck did an Italian Mafiosi have to do with a group of Russians?

Ricker's head hurt from thinking too hard—he'd let Enzo figure it all out tomorrow. He stroked his cheek, feeling his two-day-old stubble. He bet Madsen's angelic face was freshly shaved, and he couldn't wait to nuzzle that smooth, beautiful skin once he'd subdued him.

19. Convinced

Lindsay sidled up to Ben as they walked out of physics class. "Can you believe the season's almost over?"

"It's *my* last practice today," he replied, managing to keep his voice from shaking. Ever since she'd met Dot, Lindsay had started talking to him. There really was a God. "But you'll qualify for the state meet for sure—you've still got a couple weeks left."

She tilted her head in that cute way of hers, and Ben realized he was now slightly taller than her. *Score!*

"You'd be going to state too if you'd started swimming as young as I did. It takes years to learn good technique." Her smile revealed her slightly uneven teeth.

"I don't think I'll ever be as good as you." Once the words were out of his mouth, he wanted to snatch them back. *Way to sound like you freaking* worship *her!*

The little dimple in her cheek appeared. "That's so sweet, Ben."

"Do you…" He swallowed. "Do you want to walk to practice, um…together?"

"Oh! Well, I told Liv I'd meet her at her locker." She twirled a strand of hair before tucking it behind her ear. "See ya on deck?"

"Oh, yeah, sure. See ya." *Now she thinks you're a psycho stalker.* He watched her walk away, zeroing in on her long legs and remembered her giggling as Dot squirmed in her arms. Would it be okay to bring a dog to the pool?

After tossing some books in his locker, he bounced out of the school and headed to practice. Wow — it was even sunny outside! He turned the corner on the sidewalk and heard someone call his name. When he looked to the street, he saw an open passenger window on a black car that crept down the road. He leaned forward to see who called for him.

"Hallo, Ben." Hans waved him toward the car.

Oh, no. What did he *want?* "I'm late for swim practice!" He pointed ahead of him and kept walking.

"Your mother needs you!"

That stopped him in his tracks. "She does?" He stepped over and heard an SUV honk behind Hans's now-stopped car. He leaned in the open window.

"Your mother asked me to pick you up. She had an accident."

"What happened?"

"I'll tell you on the way." He glared. "Get in." The SUV honked again.

Ben's heart galloped. "What happened to my mom? *Tell* me!"

"She…uh…she had hot water…she ran into another waitress and got hit with boiling water." *Honk!* "We have been at the hospital for hours. Come! We must go!"

His eyebrows knitted together. "She told me her shift didn't start till three today."

When Hans's glare deepened, Ben took a step back.

"Get in, Ben." Suddenly a gun materialized in Hans's steady hand. "Get in or I will kill your mother."

As he stared down the barrel of the gun, fear sliced through his heart. *Honk, honk!* His heart was in his throat, his stomach at his feet. The city street grew silent around him, and his vision narrowed. All he could see was the circle of the muzzle aimed at his forehead.

"Get the fuck in the car, *now*."

His mind whirled. Could he make it far enough away from the car to avoid getting shot? But then how could he protect his mom?

An extra-long honk made him jump and look over at the SUV. All the street noise returned, rushing his ears, and he knew he had to decide. Him or his mom. He flung open the car door and scrambled inside.

Hans stared at him a second before he put the car in drive. "You came this close to me blowing off your head, kid." He kept the gun trained on him as he steered. The auto-lock for the doors clicked as the car moved forward.

Breathe, he told himself. His hands shook and tears burned his nostrils. He squeezed his eyes shut, forcing down the remnants of his lunch. "Is…my mom…okay?"

Hans snorted. "For now. As long as you do what I tell you."

"Where are you taking me?"

"No questions."

Ben swallowed and sank back in the seat. Were they headed to the interstate? The silence in the car pressed down on him. "Who are you?" he finally asked.

"I am Hans. You know that."

"What's your *real* name?"

Hans looked over and his eyes traveled up and down his body. *Oh, shit*—was he going to take him somewhere and rape him? Rape him, then kill him?

"Too smart." Hans shook his head, his eyes back on the road. "You are a Barberi for certain."

No, I'm not! "They'll know something happened to me when I'm not at swim practice." The smirk on Hans's face rankled him. "They'll send the police out looking for me."

Hans chuckled. "Yah, like they care about you. Your mother hates you, don't you know that? You disappear, and she is one happy woman."

Ben's stomach clenched. His mom didn't think that, did she? He wasn't just a burden, was he?

"But you will live if you do what I tell you." Hans turned right, going north on the Dan Ryan. "Ashley will have to take you back—too bad for her."

"Please." Ben heard the quiver in his voice. "Please tell me where you're taking me."

Hans cuffed him on the ear and sent his head right into the passenger window. His vision clouded and his brain buzzed with pain.

"Shut the fuck *up*," Hans said with a sneer.

Trembling and fighting nausea, he didn't say another word for the next fifty minutes north.

❧

They'd passed the outlet malls when they finally exited 1-94, but Ben remained clueless about their destination. It wasn't until he passed a green road sign that he knew.

Gurnee State Penitentiary—2 miles

His head still throbbed, but he was sick of the silence. "Why are we going to Gurnee?" When Hans didn't answer, he added, "Is my uncle back in there?"

"*What?*" Hans stared at him, eyes flaring. "Of course not. Don't scare me like that."

Why would Uncle Grant being locked up scare him? And if he wasn't going to visit Uncle Grant, why were they going to the state pen? Wait—did his mom tell Hans about him dealing drugs? Would he be handcuffed? Would he just leave him there, in prison? His mind raced with possible scenarios—getting arrested, thrown in a cell, making license plates in a hot, dark room with a corrections officer standing over him yielding a whip...

Grandpa Barberi. He closed his eyes. *You're a fucking moron to forget about him.* But he'd never met his grandpa, so it had been easy to forget he existed. Not that Uncle Grant ever forgot about his dad. Dr. Hunter's words came back: "*Your grandfather was out of control when he drank, and he beat his sons. Grant's had a long road to recover from the abuse.*"

Seemed like his grandpa had lived on in his father's thoughts too. "*I think that's the way Logan showed his love to you, Ben...He made sure he didn't repeat his father's abuse.*"

"Why does Grandpa want to talk to me?" he asked, wondering if his grandpa wanted to *hit* him too.

"I am not supposed to say—that is for you two to sort out. My job is to get you there."

"He's paying you to drive me here?"

He didn't answer.

Ben remembered something from a few years ago. "Wait a minute. I'm a minor—I need my mom's permission to visit a prisoner."

Hans gave him an incredulous look. "How the fuck you know that?"

"I wanted to visit Uncle Grant when he was in prison. But my mom wouldn't let me."

"She *will* let you visit your grandfather, though." He patted his jacket. "I have the letter right here, with her name on it."

"She *will?*" Why would Hans threaten his mom's life if she'd allowed this? "You're lying."

Hans lunged for him, but this time he was ready. He ducked and tucked his body against the passenger door.

Hans didn't try again. "I do not want blood on you for the visit—the COs might get suspicious." Ben slowly sat back up, and Hans smiled. "The ride home is another matter."

"So you're taking me home after this?"

"Safe and sound, as long as you do not fuck up." The car slowed as they neared the Gurnee entrance, and Hans turned to him. "Listen to me, boy. Visiting hours end at five. You will go in there, talk to Barberi, and come right back to the car."

"You're not going with me?"

"No. You mention me or my gun, my people kill your mother. *Anything* goes wrong, your mother dies. Got it?"

Ben gulped. "Yeah." The life of his one remaining parent was in his hands. *Sweet.*

Hans rolled down his window as he pulled up to the guard station, and a rotund CO stepped out. "State your business."

"I'm driving the boy to see his grandfather, sir."

Hans's relaxed posture amazed Ben, who felt sweat bead at the back of his collar. He realized Hans had put away the gun without him noticing. *Pay better attention!*

"Let's see some ID, gentlemen," the guard said.

Hans dug into the inner pocket of his jacket to extract an envelope and what looked to be laminated ID cards.

"I don't have a driver's—" Ben began.

"I brought the boy's social security card," Hans interrupted, keeping his face turned to the guard. Behind his back his right hand made the shape of a gun.

The CO looked up from the folded paper. "Why isn't his mother with him?"

"It is in the letter, sir," Hans said smoothly. "She works during visiting hours. She just wants the boy to see his grandfather."

Ben tensed when the CO stuck his head in the car. "You okay with this, Benjamin Barberi? You want to see your grandfather in here? You sure?"

Hans didn't turn around, but he could feel his intensity all the same. He wished he could somehow communicate he'd been kidnapped, but it felt too risky. He met the guard's stern gaze. "Yes, sir. I'm here to see my grandpa."

The guard remained stooped forward for a long moment, then stood and handed the papers back to Hans. "Proceed to the visitor lot, on your right."

"Thank you."

As the car moved forward, Ben wondered how the guard up in the tower ahead kept warm all winter long.

"You waited too long to answer him," Hans hissed.

Ben's heart thumped louder, and he braced for Hans to hit him again. How could he get away?

"Do I need to take out my gun again, hmm?"

"No." His teeth clamped together. "I just wanna get out of here."

"You and me both, kid. Gurnee does *not* bring back happy memories."

"You were a prisoner here?"

Hans's silence answered his question about how he knew his grandpa. But why did Grandpa Barberi want to see Ben? How had he screwed up *this* time?

Hans backed the car into a space at the far end of the lot. "Take this." He shoved Ben's social security card and the letter into his hands. "Leave the backpack. Once Barberi's done with you, you come right back here, got it?"

Ben nodded.

"Remember, anything goes wrong in there, anything happens to me before we get back to Chicago…your mother dies."

"You already told me that!" His breath hitched as he watched the man's hand curl into a fist. He cringed and waited to get slammed.

But Hans only closed his eyes and growled, "Go."

Ben scuttled out of the car. He scanned the grimy limestone exterior of the prison until he found a door marked *Visitors* at the end of a sidewalk. As he moved, his skin tingled with the sensation of eyes watching him from above. *Man up, Barberi.*

There was a woman with a little girl in front of him, apparently in line to enter for visiting hours. Dangling from the mother's hand, the tiny girl had white-blond hair in pigtails and a smudge of something on her cheek. She squirmed. "You gonna visit your daddy too?"

Ben looked to her mother, but she seemed preoccupied with her phone. He kneeled down to be eye-level with the girl. Little children shouldn't have to endure this—their fathers gone, locked up, missing out on soccer games and birthday parties. "I'm visiting my grandpa," he said.

"My gwampa's died."

Her huge eyes blinked at him, and he suppressed the urge to respond *And* my *dad's dead.* "I'm sorry," he said instead.

"C'mon, Cora," the mother's voice broke in. Ben looked up at her eyes, full of suspicion. As he stood, she yanked the girl inside.

He was next. Nausea swirled through him.

"You," the guard said, and Ben looked up. "Step inside." Ben swallowed and followed directions. "ID," the guard said, and Ben handed him his social security card. "How old are you, kid?"

"Sixteen."

"Minors have to be accompanied by their guardian. No visitation for you."

When the guard grasped his elbow to escort him out, he blurted, "Wait! I have a letter from my mom." The guard paused. "She's working now but she really wants me to see my grandpa. I-I-I want to see him too. Please, sir."

The guard looked down at his ID card. "You're Barberi's grandson?"

"Yes, sir."

"You're sure you want to see *him?*"

"I've…I've never met him before."

The guard stared for a moment then led him toward the line for the metal detector. He handed the social security card to another guard behind the desk and nodded at the envelope in Ben's hands.

"Let's see it."

Ben held his breath as the guard read the letter. He bet Hans (or whoever the hell he was) had forged his mom's signature somehow.

From behind the desk, the other guard held up the social security card. "Looks legit, Marty."

"Thanks, Jim. This letter does too." Marty handed the letter to Jim then turned back to Ben. "Okay, Benjamin, anything in your pockets before you go through?"

"Do I get my ID back?"

"Not until after the visit, kid."

He nodded and walked through the metal detector. He'd heard of these in airports, but he'd never taken a flight before. And maybe Hans would kill him before he ever had that chance. Or maybe Grandpa Barberi would beat him to it.

All too soon he sat in front of an empty metal cage, listening to murmured conversations around him. Why did other visitors get to sit in open booths? When two guards led a chained older man through a steel door at the back of the room — his deep black eyes trained on Ben the entire shuffling trip — he understood. His bladder shriveled from the mere approach of his grandfather: the man who'd terrorized his dad and uncle. The man who'd killed a seven-year-old boy.

The guards plopped that man down on a chair in the cage. "You got ten minutes, Barberi," one said. "And any outbursts like before, you lose visiting privileges for a year."

Outbursts?

"Thank you, officer," his grandfather said in a flat voice, looking straight at Ben. His hair was gray, his skin tan, his body almost as tall as Uncle Grant's. His grandpa waited for the officers to back out of the cage and lock it before he spoke another word.

Ben's mouth popped open with a sudden need to inhale, and he realized he'd forgotten to breathe.

The man studied him. "You have Karita's eyes."

Karita? Who was that? Oh, right — his grandma. His grandpa had beaten *her* too.

"Mullens treated you okay?"

Ben hesitated. "Who's Mullens?"

"The German who brought you here."

"Hans?"

"That's what he's calling himself on the outside?" His grandfather smirked.

"What's his *real* name?"

"None of your business." The smirk was gone, and the man leaned forward, speaking in a low, menacing tone. "All you need to know is to follow his directions, or your mother dies."

"So *you're* behind the threat to my mom's life."

"But nothing will happen to you, Grandson. You're family."

"Cool." Ben shrugged, attempting to look relaxed. "We're BFFs now."

"You little shit."

Ben watched a bead of spit hit the metal of the cage between them. The man leaned forward more, and he leaned back in return.

"You *are* Logan's son, aren't you? Testing my every move…" His grandfather shook his head. "You want to end up like him, in a box buried under six feet of earth?"

A weight pressed on Ben's chest, and he wasn't sure if it was fear or grief. He couldn't unlock his eyes from his grandpa's. "No."

"Then you fucking answer my questions and do what you're told."

Trembling started in his shoulders and seeped down to his hands, which he squeezed together in his lap. *Please don't kill my mom.*

His grandfather seemed pleased he didn't talk back. "Are you close with Grant?"

Ben hesitated. Why did *that* matter?

"It's okay. You can tell me."

He nodded.

"Good. That's good you're with family," the man said.

He exhaled.

"So what do you do with Grant?"

He chewed the inside of his cheek. What were these questions about? "He buys me pizza."

His grandfather actually smiled upon hearing that. "He does… He's not in prison, then."

"Um, no?" Why would Uncle Grant be in prison?

"But he's on parole?"

Ben searched his mind…yes, he remembered his uncle was supposed to be on parole still, even though he'd been granted a pardon. "Yeah."

"Did Grant tell you what happened back in November when he went for a ride with Anthony and Mario?"

"No." He realized he'd answered the question way too fast.

His grandfather smiled, but he looked far from happy. It was a cruel smile. "You're a bad liar, Benjamin. You'll have to work on that if you want to get anywhere in life."

He tried to swallow, but his throat felt parched.

"Let's try that again, and tell the truth if you value your mother's life. Did Grant tell you what happened in November?"

The trembling returned. "All I know…is he didn't go to back to prison."

"And why is that, Benjamin?"

"My name is Ben."

The man leaned forward and snarled, "It'll be Little Orphan Benny if you don't start talking, fuckhead. Why didn't Grant return to prison?" When Ben didn't answer, he added, "Was he working with the feds?"

Ben felt his eyes double in size. *Shit!* He blinked like crazy to try to hide his reaction, but the damage was already done.

"Thank you," his grandfather said. "Thank you for confirming what I already knew."

"No, he wasn't working with the FBI—it just…they just decided he didn't violate parole!"

"Save it, Grandson. Save your lies for someone who doesn't live with liars every fucking day. Were you in on it, too, Benjamin? Were you working with the feds?"

He gasped. "No!"

The man nodded, allowing Ben to breathe again. Technically he *had* been in on it by helping to rescue Sophie, but his grandpa hadn't asked about Sophie.

"Is Grant still working with the feds?"

Oh God, how do I answer? Ben looked away, teeth clenched. A lump of terror pulsated in his gut. When he turned back, coal-black hatred seeped from his grandpa's eyes.

"That motherfucking traitor." His grandfather's face reddened as he muttered in Italian. His quiet tone scared him more than if he'd screamed the words. "How dare he interfere with my life. This is *my life!*"

He's going to kill Uncle Grant, he realized. *And it's all my fault.* To his horror, tears pooled in his eyes. His breath came in quick pants. *I've just signed Uncle Grant's death sentence.*

A noise of disgust drew his attention back to the prisoner. "Unbelievable. You're just like Grant, aren't you? My family needs me out there, Benjamin. They need my toughness, my leadership, or they turn into little crying babies, like you. Yet Grant thwarted me from getting out. And now he'll pay for that mistake."

"Please don't hurt him," he cried. His hand swiped at his nose. "Please, Grandpa. He's s-s-sorry for what he did."

"He'll *be* sorry. And you don't breathe a word of this to anyone, got it? If I find out you tell the cops or your mother or Grant or that whore girlfriend of his — if I discover you tell *anyone* about this visit — Ashley dies."

Now sobbing, Ben brought a hand to cover his mouth. Dread washed over him in crashing waves, and as the waves receded, guilt clung to him like foam on the sand.

A jangle of keys rang from behind the cage. The COs barged in. "Visit's over. You're upsetting the kid."

"Well, boo-fucking-hoo," his grandfather said. He looked at Ben as the officers yanked him to his feet. "We have an understanding, Grandson?"

"Yes," he whispered.

As the COs wrestled his grandpa out of the cage, he closed his eyes. *Stop crying. Don't barf. You've gotta get out of here — Hans is waiting. Don't barf.*

He flinched when a hand rested on his shoulder. Looking up, he saw a CO with a kind face. "You okay?"

"Um…" He swallowed. "Yeah. Can I leave?"

"Sure. Come with me."

He stood on wobbly legs and followed the officer, who guided him back through the metal detector. Another CO handed him his ID, and then he was outside, squinting in the late afternoon sun. He wiped his nose on the sleeve of his jacket. Then he covered his mouth as a vision of his father's funeral swam before his eyes. The mournful music, the bullshit Bible verses — he'd have to relive it all once they killed Grant. Taking away his father wasn't good enough for them. They wanted to take away the only man who ever loved him too.

Realizing he was almost to the parking lot, he paused. He could turn around and tell the officers about the extortion. He could run and hide inside while they called the cops — maybe they could call that cop Jerry, maybe that detective with the red hair…

His teeth chattered. But what if Hans had a man on his mom? What if the cops couldn't get to her fast enough? What if they couldn't get to Uncle Grant fast enough, either? Then he'd have even more blood on his hands, just because he wimped out on protecting his mother.

Ben straightened his back. He had no choice. Everyone would hate him for keeping this quiet — his mom, Dr. Hunter, Gruncle Joe, and most of all Sophie — but he had to go through with it. *Forgive me.*

When he forced himself back in the car, Hans finished sending a text and chuckled. "Aww. The boy looks upset. Need me to kiss away your tears, yah?"

"Fuck you, Mullens."

He hesitated. "You tell anyone my real name and your mother is —"

"Dead," he finished. "Yeah, yeah, I know — you told me already."

The smack upside his head didn't come as a surprise, nor did the resulting ringing in his ear and throbbing in his temple. But for the entire drive back to the city, the physical pain was nothing compared to the horror oozing up his throat. He would be responsible for the death of Uncle Grant. And there wasn't a damn thing he could do about it.

It was dark by the time Hans pulled up to his apartment building. Before he scrambled the hell out of the car, Hans grabbed his elbow. "Keep your trap shut, boy. Not a word to anyone."

"Okay!"

"If you say anything, I'll shred your mother to pieces. Right before I filet that piece of shit dog."

Dot! He leaned away from him, desperate. After a few seconds of his fingers digging into his elbow, Hans let him go.

He shuddered. As the black car eased back into traffic, he memorized its license plate. Not that the information would do him any good.

He wondered if Uncle Grant would live through the night.

He unlocked his front door and walked in to the warm, lit apartment. He wriggled out of his backpack, confused.

"Oh my God, is that you?" his mother called from her bedroom as she zoomed out to the living room, her cell phone in hand. Dot galloped behind her and barked when she saw him. "Where the hell have you been?"

He took a step back. "Why aren't you at work?" Dot circled his feet, begging to be picked up.

"Because your swim coach called me!" she shrieked. "He said you weren't at practice, and they were worried!" She shook her phone. "I was just about to call the cops."

"I'm fine."

"Where *were* you?" *Yip, yip!* Dot danced at his feet.

"Uh…"

"I was so scared something happened to you. I called Sophie—I even called Grant." She extended her arm, offering him the phone. Dot wouldn't shut up. "I want you to call Grant and Sophie and tell them you're okay."

Shit. He couldn't risk calling either. Ignoring Dot, Ben picked up his backpack and headed to his bedroom, but his mother blocked him. "Hey—where're you going? Call them right now."

"No! I'm perfectly fine, okay? *You* call them."

He tried to get around her, but she stepped over to block him again. "Wait a minute. Where'd you get that bruise?" Her hand touched his left cheek, but he shied away from her.

"Nowhere. Just get off my back."

"Ben, what's *wrong* with you?" She threw her hands in the air. "You've been such a good boy the past couple of months, then you disobey me right before your grounding is over? Are you taking drugs again?"

"No!"

"I want you to call Grant and Sophie. They're so worried about you."

"I'll see Sophie tomorrow at the meet."

"No you won't. Your coach said you're suspended from the meet for missing practice."

"*What?* He can't do that!"

"But he still wants you there to cheer for your teammates."

"Then fuck *him!*" he roared. He felt his whole body shake.

"Benjamin!" She leaned back, her face a mask of disgust, and he took the opportunity to dart around her and race to his room. He made it inside and locked himself in before she got to the door, where she now pounded. "Are you using drugs again?"

"No!" The tears had started for real, and he couldn't breathe.

"I want a urine sample from you right now, mister."

Ben huddled up in a ball on his bed, tears streaming down his face. "Go away," he cried. "Just…go away."

Dot whined and scratched at his door, and Ben did his best to ignore her.

"Way to throw it all away," his mother said in a familiar sarcastic tone. "Way to turn into your father."

He closed his eyes and wept. His father sure couldn't save him now.

20. Confiscate

In twenty-three years of imprisonment, he'd never experienced such silence in the cellblock. He'd never had insomnia this bad either.

Enzo grunted as he scrubbed his eyes and flopped over to his other side on the thin, worn mattress. His hand twitched with the desire to suffocate Jewels, who offered a steady, snoring stream of breaths from above, with his own damn pillow. Why could everyone else in this hellhole sleep? Goddammit. He'd heard insomnia increased with age, but he hadn't expected to grow old in Gurnee.

Just like he hadn't expected his own fucking son to betray him.

This is my life! he'd screamed at Benjamin, who'd shrunk away from the cage with the force of his words. The boy had tried to protect Grant, and the boy had failed. *Fucking informant.* Enzo clutched his scalp as he willed the image of the boy's frightened eyes out of his mind. *Just let me sleep.* But the thoughts kept coming—the conversation about Grant's betrayal playing in an endless loop. *Get out of my head, Grant.*

But tonight there was no peace. Actually, there'd been a lot of nights without peace…

"This is my *life!*" Enzo had stared down his brother. "How could you let this happen? How could you let that son of a bitch slip through our fingers?"

Angelo had swallowed. "Fanocelli beat us, Enz." He clutched his glass tighter. "He made it to the feds before we could get to him."

"Fucking informant." Bile rose in his throat, and he knocked back a swig of whiskey to push it down. The whiskey didn't even burn at this point, and it still didn't make him feel any better. The FBI had Fanocelli, witness to bad things he'd done. No *way* that fat fuck would take him down.

A noise by the stairs drew his attention.

Angelo stood and flipped the hallway light. "Carlo! You should be in bed."

"But I'm not *tired*." The nine-year-old's whine grated on Enzo's last nerve. His hand moved to his belt buckle.

"Anna Maria!" Angelo boomed. His wife materialized in seconds. "Take him to bed."

Without a word, she ushered the boy upstairs.

As Angelo slumped back down on the sofa, Enzo's jaw clenched, listening to his nephew's fading complaints from above. He would never tolerate that bullshit. "You know what Dad would've done if he'd found us out of bed in the middle of the night?"

Angelo's eyes held a hint of sadness before he looked away.

They both knew Angelo had raised a sniveling pansy, but for some reason he refused to hit Carlo. His brother's weakness disgusted him.

Thirty minutes later, Enzo entered his own home, the very home Fanocelli's eventual testimony threatened to take away. He cursed as he stumbled in the hallway and looked down to find a fucking toy on the floor. He scooped up the red action figure and continued into the family room, where Karita had fallen asleep on the sofa. The bitch hadn't even waited up for him.

Soft, blond waves framed her face, and her steady breaths made him aware of his own fatigue. *Tired. So tired of running the damn family.* He swayed a bit on his feet before he shook his head to snap out of it. "Thanks for waiting up for me."

Her eyes flew open, and she sat up, searching his face for a moment before noticing the toy in his hand.

"I almost broke my fucking neck on this!" He shook the action figure for emphasis.

Karita shrank back into the cushion. "Sorry, baby."

She's so pathetic.

"Did you, um, have a nice time at Angelo's?" Her voice wavered.

"A *nice* time? I don't think that's what you'd call it. I try to keep the family alive, and you try to kill me when I walk in the door." He waved the toy in front of her face. "Is that what you're doing with this? Trying to kill me?"

Her eyes widened. "No! I didn't see it—"

The toy whipping across her face shut her up. She lurched to the side as she cradled her cheek and wailed.

"You'll wake up the boys. *Silenzio.*"

She quieted immediately.

He stormed off to the stairs and ignored her whimpered plea to leave the boys alone. Once he yanked open their bedroom door, he saw Logan splayed out on his bed, mouth open, drooling in his sleep. He swore the boy had grown an inch since he last saw him. As he watched his son's even breaths, he felt his anger fade into fatigue. Logan would be a strong leader one day.

He was about to leave the bedroom when he heard a small gasp. He turned to see his younger son huddled against his headboard, eyes shining in the darkness. Grant had always been a light sleeper.

As he stepped closer, he noticed a red action figure clutched in Grant's hand: a companion to the one he'd found downstairs. "Clean up your fucking toys!" he hissed.

Grant blinked like crazy, and the sound of his rapid breathing filled the room.

"It's *your* fault I had to hit your mother with this."

Tears fell from those big eyes as the boy retreated farther from him.

When Enzo raised his hand, Grant's arms covered his head, and he curled into a ball on his pillow. He shook with fear.

"I'm sorry. I'm sorry," he whispered. "Don't hurt me, Daddy."…

Don't hurt me, Daddy. Enzo shifted in the prison bed and covered his ears. Mullens was out there somewhere, ready to exact revenge… ready to hurt his son.

What had he done?

❧

Grant clutched his cell phone as he paced Kirsten's apartment. "So everything's in place for tonight, then?"

"Looks like it," Agent Bounter replied. "The only unknown is how many men Vladimir will bring on his team and how many will be left to track down after we arrest the bastards."

Grant mentally rehearsed the planned robbery of the hotel's safe, a robbery in which he'd be the point man, sneaking Vladimir and his men into security strongholds—where Bounter and *his* men would be waiting.

"There're still a thousand things that could go wrong with this op," Bounter added, "which is what makes it so fun."

Garnt shook his head but found himself smiling. "You're a sick man, sir."

"Aw, c'mon, that's why you like me. I'm still invited to the wedding, right?"

"If I'm alive by then."

"*Grant.*" Bounter's sharp tone straightened his shoulders. "Man up. Look what happened last time: you were on your way back to prison—straight into the lion's den—when your family screwed it all up. But instead of buckling under the pressure, you came up with a new strategy on the fly. Your improvisation worked even better than the initial plan."

He sighed. It wasn't just his improvisation that had made that night work. There'd been a lot of luck involved too. And he wasn't sure if luck was his lady tonight.

"But this time everything will go according to schedule," Bounter promised. "We've been investigating the Russians for months, and I'm sick of them weaseling out of consequences. I'm sick of them dealing drugs to kids."

"That's why I need to get more details about the submarine tonight."

"That'd help," Bounter agreed. "But even if they're tight-lipped, once we separate Andrei from his boss, we'll get him talking."

Grant frowned. *I'm not so sure about that.* He heard a key in the front door. "I better go, sir."

"It'll be fine. Cool and steady, Frank Sinatra."

"*Cool and steady*," he sang in a jazzy beat. As he ended the call, he looked up to see Sophie coming in. "Hey, babe."

Her face lit up. "What a nice surprise!" She let him take her briefcase and handbag before he peeled her knee-length khaki raincoat off her shoulders.

"It's a good surprise for me too," he said, draping the coat over his arm and leaning in to kiss the nape of her neck. "I had to call Agent Bounter, but I didn't know I'd run into you."

"I need to change clothes before Ben's meet."

His face fell. "Oh…I wish I could go with you."

She headed toward Kirsten's bedroom and spoke over her shoulder. "Me too. I'm late, as usual—a student needed to chat. Come talk to me while I change?"

"As if you have to ask." He trotted after her and stood in the doorway as she plopped down on the bed. When she leaned down to unzip her high-heeled boot, he zoomed over. "Please allow me."

Sophie arched one eyebrow but leaned back and rested her weight on her elbows.

He took his time unzipping the boot, inhaling the scent of earthy leather mixing with her soft perfume and admiring the length of her calf. Once both boots were off, he kneeled to cup one narrow foot in his hands. He took his time massaging the fine bones.

"Ohhh," she murmured. Grant looked up to see her eyes closed and a faint smile on her face. "I can't wait till we live together again… then you can do this every night."

He chuckled.

"Remember when you dressed me at the hospital?" He noticed a glint of copper in her eyes as she shimmied out of her stockings. "That was *so* erotic."

He pressed his lips to the inside of her knee. "*Undressing* can be erotic too." His mouth crept under her chocolate-brown skirt to deliver another kiss, and he heard her inhale as his lips swept upward toward the Promised Land.

"Grant," she moaned. "I can't." She laughed at his pout. "Ben, remember? I have to get to his meet."

"Oh, right. Sorry…those legs are kind of distracting." He stood and pulled her off the bed. She unzipped her skirt and let it slide off. "I'm worried about Ben. Will you talk to him? Find out what got into him yesterday?"

"Of course." Her head disappeared as she lifted her silk blouse over her head, and he took in the soft curves of her lace bra. She turned to a rolling clothes rack and sorted through some shirts.

"Sorry you have to make do with this makeshift closet."

"Maybe it'd help if I had less clothes." She slipped a royal blue polo off the hanger, and when she turned he read Ben's school name embroidered over her left breast. "Now I need some pants…or maybe shorts." She leaned over to slide open the bottom drawer.

"Won't you be cold?" he asked her butt, which waved in the air not too far away.

She stood again to pull on some black yoga pants. "Natatoriums are always hot," she explained. "That's why I came home to change." Once she'd completed her ensemble with socks and running shoes, she asked, "What kind of tone should I take with Ben? Stern? Concerned?"

"I have no idea." He followed her to the kitchen, where he'd draped her raincoat. He held it out again and helped her slide into it as a knot of worry tightened in his stomach. "I still haven't talked to him since you told me about him selling drugs." He brushed a stray blond hair off her shoulder. "And now he's suspended for the meet? I thought he was really starting to turn his life around."

"He *is* turning his life around. But we all make mistakes."

"*What?*" He spun her around to face him and clasped her hands in his. "*We* never make mistakes."

She gave him a jaunty smile. "Said the man who was handcuffed multiple times last year."

Grant groaned. "How could you get me all riled up mentioning handcuffs, then walk out on me? That's just cruel."

She freed her hands and snaked a finger up to his chin. "Your hot-and-bothered status is your fault. *I'm* not the one who's constantly unavailable, McFederalAgent."

"That will change soon."

"Really?"

"If all goes well…tonight it will end."

She stared at him for a second, then started to unbuckle the belt she'd just buckled on her coat. "You'll be in danger. I'm staying."

"Sophie…" He stilled her hands. "Go. Ben needs you. I have the entire Chicago FBI division watching me tonight, but Ben only has you."

She seemed to hover in a moment of indecision.

"Please," he urged. "It'll help me focus tonight if I know you're taking care of Ben." Her eyes glistened with tears. "Oh, Bonnie." He wrapped her in a hug. "I'm sorry to do this to you. I shouldn't have told you anything."

"No. I want to know." She sniffed. "Text me when you get in tonight. I don't care how late it is."

He wasn't sure how long it would take to get out of handcuffs following his faux arrest at the hotel, but he nodded anyway. "As soon as I can." Cradling her head, he leaned down to kiss her. Her lips were soft as always, but he could feel tension in her mouth. When she started to pull away, he shook his head and nudged them back together. He continued kissing her until she relaxed in his arms. "It'll be okay, Bonnie."

"I just want you done with those Russians. They give me the creeps." She paused. "But…is it weird your family scares me even more than the Russians do?"

"Let's hope the Russians end up like my family—all in prison." *Or dead*, he silently finished. "Go ahead. I'll wait a couple of minutes after you've gone."

"Okay. I'll hug Ben for you." She gave him a peck on the cheek as she left.

He glanced around the empty apartment. As he moved Sophie's briefcase to the corner, out of the way, his phone buzzed in his pocket.

Head to West Town in 30 minutes. Mic is operational.

Grant nodded and said, "Yes, sir." His button microphone negated the need for a reply text. The smell of Sophie lingered on him, and her look of fear flashed through his mind. He glanced down when his phone buzzed again.

Stop worrying about Sophie. Grow a pair.

Smirking, he said, "Yes, sir, Agent Bounter."

After checking that the hallway was clear, he stole to the stairwell, hustled down a flight, then let himself into his apartment. The TV program he'd left on droned in the background, failing to interest him in his state of nervous jitters. How could he entertain himself until he left? He wished he had time to stop by Ben's meet, but he knew it would be a bad idea. There was a good chance the Russians were watching him every minute now, with so much on the line.

Deciding to visualize the evening ahead of him, he eased onto the duvet without rumpling the military corners of the sheets underneath. His mind drifted to Mr. Remington's office—the scene of the crime later tonight. The hidden safe in the coffee table, the combination scrawled on a note taped to the back of a desk drawer…it was all a ruse to make it look like he would lead them to the jackpot. Then he remembered another time the feds swooped in to arrest everyone… the scratch of thick carpet on his cheek after an FBI agent shoved him to the floor in Marina City…the strain of his shoulders as the agent cuffed his hands behind his back. It was time to get cuffed again. It was time for more mobsters to go to prison. He couldn't freaking wait.

There was a thump on his front door, and he bolted upright on the bed. *Who the hell was that?* Grant shoved the secure phone in its hiding place. He crept down the hallway and before he reached the door, there was another thump followed by a man's voice calling, "Pizza!"

Grant squinted out the peephole to find a tall, muscled man in a green, long-sleeved shirt and baseball cap with the Chicagoland Pizza logo. The man's left arm was in a sling, and he held the pizza box with one hand. He stared at his feet, obscuring Grant's view of his face.

When the man kicked the door—ah, that was the source of the thumping noise—Grant jumped back.

"Come on, man," the pizza delivery guy said. "I do not got time to wait all day."

The man's accent sounded strange, like he had a hearing impairment or something. "Wrong address," Grant called through the door. "I didn't order a pizza."

The bill of the man's cap lifted an inch, allowing Grant to see his mouth and a shag of blond hair near his temples. "Yah, you did. My boss gave me this address for a…" He looked at the bill taped to the box. "Benjamin. Pre-paid and everything."

"Benjamin doesn't live here." If the Russians could overhear this conversation through the bug in the bathroom, Grant hoped they wouldn't remember that name.

Pizza Guy's head sagged, and Grant heard muttering through the door. He looked pitiful in his arm sling, and Grant felt bad that the pizza place had screwed up.

"Look, man, my phone is broke," Pizza Guy continued. "I will get fired if I show up back at work without completing the job. Can I use your phone?"

The request took Grant off guard. He swallowed and tapped a staccato beat on his leg. He only had about ten minutes before he had to leave to strategize with the Russians. "Sorry, can't help you."

"Please?" The delivery guy's head tilted, but Grant still couldn't see his eyes. "I got a kid at home. I need this job, man. Please?"

"Why didn't I get a call from the doorman before you came up?"

Pizza Guy paused for just a second. "He knows me—I deliver to this building all the time. He tried to help speed things up for me with my shoulder sling and all, but I guess you are not as nice as him." His head drooped again. "Thanks for getting me fired."

Guilt settled in Grant's stomach. But something didn't seem quite right, and he couldn't let anything stand in the way of taking down the Russians. He'd worked too hard to become a man worthy of Sophie. And he owed it to his mother.

The man finally turned toward the elevator, and Grant caught a glimpse of his profile. For some reason he looked a little familiar. A twinge of unease tightened his throat, and he waited by the door until he heard the elevator's soft ding. *Good riddance.*

Too keyed up to do anything else, he paced his apartment until it was time to leave for West Town. Precisely thirty minutes after his text from Bounter, he grabbed his jacket and keys and opened the door. As he stepped out, a shadow to his left shifted. A flash of green flew across his vision as something sharp sliced into his collarbone.

He shoved against the man pressing into him, and looked down in horror at a syringe jabbed near his left shoulder. His heart racing, he threw Pizza Guy off him as he felt heat spread down his chest from the injection. *"What did you put in me?"*

The man gathered himself and straightened. He grinned as he gestured lewdly. "I will put much more in you before the night is over." His voice had changed, now sounding European. He yanked off his baseball cap, and Grant's eyes widened. That white-blond hair and pale blue eyes…he'd seen those before.

"He's from Gurnee," he whispered into his collar. "It's…Rick—"

Mullens slammed into him, taking his breath away. "You are wired?" he hissed as he shoved him backward into his apartment.

Grant tried to resist, but his muscles felt like rubber. *No!* He was helpless to prevent Mullens from ripping off his button-down shirt as he muscled him farther into the apartment. His eyelids began to droop, and he felt strangely grateful when he was pushed to the floor. He watched the man ball up the shirt and head to the bathroom. *Get the hell outta here!* he screamed inside his head, but his tremendous effort resulted only in sitting up a bit, propping his back against the sofa. His vision thickened. He heard a splash and realized Mullens must have stuffed the shirt into the toilet. *Bounter.* Agent Bounter and his men would rescue him, right?

"How you like *that*, Barberi?" Mullens said as he shot out of the bathroom.

Grant gasped. The Russians could definitely hear that through the bug. Mullens was screwing with the entire sting operation!

Mullens was on him again, dragging him to his feet. "Get off me!" Grant tried to shout, but it came out more like a whisper. His shoves against the German's body were ineffective taps. Mullens punched him in the lower back, and he staggered. Sharp pains radiated up his spine.

"That's payback now that Daddy B's not here to protect you. Get moving, Justin Bieber," he growled as he hustled him toward the door. "The fucking feds will be here soon."

Stumbling forward, Grant could no longer support the weight of his head, which bobbed like a pendulum. All he could see was the geometric design of the hallway carpet as they pushed ahead to the elevator. *Bounter. Where's Bounter?* Mullens's dirty hands were all over his bare torso, manhandling him. He remembered him and his boys circling him his first day at Gurnee, after he'd refused his father's protection.

"*Fresh meat, boys,*" Mullens had crowed. When he'd backed up, he'd added, "*Don't be scared, sweetheart—we just want to get to know you.*"

The elevator opened, and Mullens pushed him forward, one arm pressed across his chest and the other cupping his ass. He shuddered, realizing what the German wanted from him. And there wasn't a damn thing he could do about it. His heart thumped a sickened cadence.

Once the elevator doors closed, Mullens drew him to the back of the car. "You are sweating," he said, hugging Grant's back to his chest. The German's fingertips skated up his shivering abs. "Slick. Wet. Just as I like it." Rough lips pressed to the back of his neck. He did his best to squirm away, but he was too weak. What had he been injected with…some kind of sedative? The German's breath smelled like rotting garlic, and he groaned as he fought to break free.

"Moan for me, baby," he whispered, pressing more kisses on his shoulder. "We will have a good time before I hand you over to the Russians."

"*What?*" Grant breathed.

"Oh yah. Papa Barberi found out you work with the feds. He pays me to give you to the Russkies, right after I tell them you are a snitch."

Grant slumped further and let his eyes close, fighting nausea. After Mullens raped him, Vladimir was going to skin him alive, and Andrei would surely help. *Sophie.* He wouldn't get to say goodbye.

"Stay with me, Pretty Boy Bieber," Mullens urged, propping him up in his arms. "Nobody gives *me* orders. Papa B did not know we will have some fun together before I hand you over. I will take good care of you."

The elevator arrived at the first floor. No neighbors to save him in the empty lobby. No FBI agents to the rescue. Mullens tried to drag him toward the rear exit, but he had trouble putting one foot in front of the other. His cheek stung from a sharp slap. "Move it!" Mullens barked.

His tongue felt fuzzy. He wanted sleep—he just wanted to sleep. A warm sensation flowed down his leg onto his shoe.

"Son of a bitch!" Mullens cried. "You just pissed on me!"

It took a second for the words to register. They sounded like they were spoken underwater. He'd peed in his pants? Was that a bad thing? He couldn't even feel his feet.

"Goddamn it, I gave you too much, you skinny piece of shit." Mullens grunted, and Grant was suddenly airborne, slung across the German's back like a long sack of flour. They blew through the rear exit, and a cool afternoon wind whipped across his naked skin.

There was a screech of tires. A spark of reprieve ignited as Grant prayed Bounter had finally arrived, and he managed to pry open his eyes. His body bobbed up and down across Mullens's shoulders—oh no, they were running away—would Bounter catch up? As a car door slammed behind them, Grant used any remaining strength he could muster to claw at Mullens's waist, attempting to get a hold from which to lever himself off. "Trying to get in my pants, yah?" he panted.

That comment and the jostling made him want to barf, but when he heard a man's voice from behind them, vomiting seemed inevitable.

"Stop!"

That was Andrei, not Bounter.

"Fuck," Mullens breathed, huffing from running with Grant's dead weight. "The fucking feds."

Grant wasn't about to correct him. *Faster*, he silently urged. The Russians couldn't get him now — not when Mullens would tell them everything. His vision faded in and out…flashes of the sidewalk, a blur of stores and businesses in his neighborhood. He could feel them slowing as Mullens extracted a key from his pants pocket.

The German leaned over and flung open a car door. Just as Grant felt himself get stuffed inside, Andrei's shout filled his fuzzy head.

"Stop!"

"Fuck." Mullens glared at Grant, sprawled helplessly on the reclined passenger seat. "Maybe our love will have to wait." His face vanished from Grant's field of vision. "Oh, hallo," he called, still breathing hard. "I did not know it was you…" Grant forced his eyes open and strained to listen to the exchange. "Vladimir, I presume?"

"Who the fuck are you?" Andrei yelled. "Mick, are you okay?"

No. I'm definitely not okay.

"Barberi is fine," Mullens answered.

I'm Grant Madsen! he wanted to scream. The wet sensation on his pant leg had grown cold.

Andrei paused. "Barberi his name?" He didn't sound entirely surprised, and Grant pieced together the reason the Russians had arrived so quickly — they'd overheard Mullens through the planted listening device.

"Barberi," Mullens confirmed.

He closed his eyes, wishing he would lose consciousness before Andrei killed him. Another vehicle screeched to a stop and footsteps pounded the pavement. *Bounter. Where's Bounter?*

Instead Andrei spoke in quick Russian to his boss. Grant could make out the words *prick*, *dead*, and, of course, *Barberi*.

"Look, gentlemen," Mullens interrupted, "I need him for a few minutes, then he is yours. I…I need to take him to visit his father… in prison."

"Fuck that. Get out here, Mick," Vladimir demanded.

When he didn't move, Vladimir's voice deepened. "Move your ass, Barberi."

If he could move, that would've had him on his feet. As it was, all he could do was wait to be killed. He thought he heard the distant wail of a police siren.

"He is sick," Mullens said, his voice now tinged with desperation. "I need to get him to hospital."

Andrei's voice was closer now. "*Nyet*. You say you take him to father in prison."

"After hospital." Mullens's German accent had thickened. Now his voice went up an octave — something had changed. "Hey, guy, I am on your side. Put away your gun. I get him back to you, I promise…"

Andrei sounded right on top of the car now, and Grant could hear him even over the increasing volume of the police siren. "Who the fuck *are* you?"

Pulsing blackness crowded Grant's vision, and he knew it would be seconds before he succumbed. Maybe Mullens had injected him with poison? He was too tired to care.

"I am your friend," Mullens gasped. "I…I have a message from Enzo Barberi."

Gunshots rang out and something slammed into Grant right before he slipped away into darkness.

21. Condemn

Sophie knew something was wrong.

She'd known the second she saw Ben. He hadn't looked at her when she'd joined him on the bleachers, and tension radiated from his stony profile. When she'd tried to hug him, he'd shied away.

"Ben," she said after a few minutes. "I love you."

He faced her then, his watery blue eyes huge. "You shouldn't," he whispered.

"What? Of course I should. You're very lovable. Both Grant and I —" She paused when he flinched. "What's wrong?"

"Nothing."

"Grant and I are confused…and upset about your behavior last night, but we love you. Nothing could change that."

A scoff rumbled from his throat.

"You've done something to make us stop loving you?"

He froze, which made her even more curious. The announcer called the girls' medley relay to the blocks. "You know that's impossible," she continued. "We'll always love you."

"You're so full of shit!" he hissed at his feet.

She leaned away from him. "Are…are you angry with me?"

"No." He sniffed. "Sorry."

"Would you look at me?" His head shook. "C'mon, honey." She placed her hand on his shoulder. "You'll get through this, whatever it is. Please tell me what's going on."

"No." His voice trembled. "I can't." His arms hugged his torso, a huddled ball of misery.

"Why can't you?" She touched his chin and tried to tilt his face toward hers.

"No!" As he struggled away from her, she saw tears.

Oh. He didn't want her to see him crying. She dug around in her handbag for tissues and sighed when she couldn't find any. She'd always had tissues when she'd been a therapist. "It's okay to cry. I worry more about the people who never cry than the ones who do. It takes a strong person to feel the feelings."

He made the scoffing noise again and mumbled something—the only word she caught was *kill.* "What did you say?"

He looked up at her with defiance in his eyes and trails of tears etched down his cheeks. He had dark circles under his eyes and… was that a bruise on the side of his face? "Does it take a strong person to kill someone?"

"*Kill?* Why would you say that? Are you thinking about what happened to your father?"

"He's *already* dead," Ben sneered.

"If this is about Carlo, you know Grant had to kill him in self-defense."

"This isn't about *Carlo!* Screw him. Screw the whole family."

What the hell was he so upset about? The starter instructed the girls' backstrokers to enter the water for the first leg of the medley relay. Lindsay popped into the pool, but Ben didn't even look in her direction—he just kept staring down. Sophie tried again. "You're mad at the family?"

His hands stilled.

"The family…" She felt her throat tighten. "The family's going to kill someone?"

He looked at her with alarm. "No," he whispered, shaking his head. She'd never seen him look so scared.

Truth dawned on her like water flooding her lungs. "Grant," she gasped.

He collapsed forward, elbows on knees, palms squeezing his ears, his body shaking from sobs. Cheers and whistles pierced the air as the race began, but she barely registered them. She circled her arm around his shoulders and tucked her head down next to his so he could hear her over the din. "What's going to happen to Grant?"

"I'm sorry," he moaned as he rocked next to her. "Sorry, sorry…"

She looked up to find all the spectators absorbed in the race. It was so loud she couldn't think. She leaned down again and shouted, "C'mon, let's get out of here." When he didn't respond, she grabbed his elbows and yanked him to his feet, surprised at his lack of resistance. Seizing his hand, she wove them through the crowd and out into the hallway. She dragged him around the corner then plastered his back against the wall. His eyes widened.

Her voice was strangled. "Talk to me, Ben. Tell me what's happening."

"They'll k-k-kill my mom."

"They threatened her if you tell me about Grant?" When he nodded, she demanded, "Who?"

"Please. They'll murder her."

"*Who?*" she cried, her voice sounding shrill.

Ben's upper lip trembled. "Grandpa," he finally managed. "Grandpa Barberi."

She stepped back, her hand covering her mouth. The Barberis. She should've known. She should've known her life had been going too well. She should've known they would try to take away everything again. Her nose burned with imminent tears, and she fought the urge to crumple to the floor. The image of Grant huddled on Hunter's sofa, stuttering about the time his father had beat him till he bled…

No! She wouldn't let it happen again. Not again, damn it!

"Tell me everything." She clasped Ben's shoulders and stared into his eyes. She held him tight against the wall. "I'll do whatever I can to keep your mom safe. Tell me right now!"

She wanted to hug him, but she knew time was ticking. She knew the Barberis moved fast. "My m-m-mom…" he finally said. "My mom started dating this guy, Hans, uh, um, Mullens. He works for Grandpa."

Sophie ground her teeth together. *Ashley! How could you be so stupid?*

"He made me go with him to Gurnee yesterday to see Grandpa."

Yesterday…pieces clicked together, explaining his absence. "That's why you missed swim practice?"

Ben nodded.

"You trusted him? That's how he got you in the car?"

"No." He exhaled. "He held a gun on me. He said he'd kill Mom if I didn't go with him."

"Oh God." When she let go of his shoulders, he swiped his hand across his face. "Is that where you got that bruise?"

"Grandpa made me tell him about Grant."

She stopped breathing.

"About why Uncle Grant didn't go to prison after the Jovanovich thing. He asked me if Grant was working with the feds, and I swear I said no, but he knew I was lying. He knew…" Ben's face flushed, and he started to cry again. "I'm sorry, I'm so sorry…"

Enzo knew. He knew Grant had thwarted his plan to get out of prison. Her stomach twisted into a knot.

Watching the poor boy cry, she gathered him up in a hug. "It's not your fault. It's *their* fault." He quivered in her arms, and a steely fury rose in her. "So Enzo said he'd kill Grant?"

Ben shrugged out of their hug and sniffed. "Not exactly. But he was really mad at him. He called him a fucking traitor."

With a shaking hand, Sophie reached into her handbag. When she pulled out her phone, he lunged for her wrist. "Grandpa said he'd kill Mom if I told anyone!"

"Ben, I *have* to tell the FBI. Maybe Enzo hasn't gotten to Grant yet — maybe they can pull him out." When he didn't let go of her, she added, "Agent Bounter can send men to pick up your mom."

"But Grandpa said — "

"Are you *really* going to trust the word of Enzo Barberi?" she snapped. "Maybe he's bluffing. Bounter told me the family was finished…though I have no idea who this Hans person is."

Ben paused. "He was in Gurnee too at some point."

"You see?" She shook her phone for emphasis. "He's probably the only man Enzo has left to do his bidding. I'm calling."

He stared at her for a long moment, then shrugged, looking utterly spent. "Your funeral." He laced his arms across his chest.

Waiting for the call to connect, she at first wanted to smack him for his snarky attitude. Then she realized he was back to his old self, and she felt a rush of gratitude. He'd been carrying around that awful secret for a whole day.

When an unfamiliar voice answered, she said, "I need to speak to Lucas Bounter! There's an emergency with Grant." She heard a rustling and then Bounter was on the line.

"Sophie!" He sounded frantic. "I didn't have your number, damn it. I've got two agents coming to the pool to pick up you and Ben. That's where you are, right?"

"Why are you coming to get us?"

Bounter was silent for a moment. "Grant's off the grid."

"No!" She squeezed the phone.

Ben pulled on her sleeve. "What happened?"

She ignored him and tried to focus on Bounter's voice.

"A man forced himself into Grant's apartment and made him take off the wire — now we don't know Grant's location." When Sophie gasped, he added, "We think this man was another prisoner at Gurnee —"

"Mullens," Sophie whispered, then watched Ben's mouth drop open. "His name is Hans Mullens."

"Hans is a fake name!" Ben hollered. "Oh my God, Sophie, what happened?"

Bounter said something she couldn't hear, and she glared at Ben. "Shut up a second — I can't hear!"

Instead of obeying, he ripped the phone from her grasp. When she tried to recover possession, he angled his body away and stiff-armed her. "This is Ben Barberi," he yelled into the phone. "You gotta listen to me. They're gonna kill Grant."

Sophie could no longer contain her tears. *They're gonna kill Grant.* She stopped groping for her phone and sank back into the wall, fighting to stay upright. *They're gonna kill Grant.* Ben related yesterday's events in rapid-fire, and cheers leaked from the natatorium, but all she heard was one sentence — a death sentence. *They're gonna kill Grant.*

Ben snapped her from her trance when he grabbed her arm with one hand and stuffed her phone back in her handbag with the other. "C'mon, they'll be here soon. They want us to wait for them by the back door." When she didn't budge, he shook her. "C'mon, Sophie! Grandpa might try to kidnap you again!"

She nodded, and now Ben was the one dragging *her* toward the exit. With her fuzzy brain, she wondered why Enzo would try to kidnap her. He was already getting what he wanted. The evil bastard was already getting his precious revenge on the man she loved—taking him away from her when they hadn't even known each other a year. She choked on a sob.

"It'll be okay," Ben told her. He looked out the window, bouncing on the balls of his feet. "The agent guy said they would find Grant. They've got the entire division searching for him, and knowing Mullens's name will help them. I even remembered his license plate number!"

She stared at him, wondering the source for his sudden optimism. His mouth formed barely audible words as he kept vigil on the parking lot, and she strained to hear him.

"Please, God, let Uncle Grant be okay. Please, God. I can't take it if he dies. It'll be my fault. Please, God."

She closed her eyes and mumbled a prayer herself. Then she looped her arm around Ben's shoulder and touched the side of her head to his. "This isn't your fault, Ben—it's Enzo's. This is all about Enzo's sick sense of revenge. *He's* the bastard, not you."

He shuddered, and she knew he didn't believe her words. Then he wiggled out of her hold. "They're here! Let's go."

Following him at a jog, she watched him scan the parking lot. She didn't even bother. If they'd already killed Grant, her self-preservation was meaningless. Ben scrambled into the back seat of a government sedan, and she scooted in next to him.

After the agent showed them his badge, they sped away from the natatorium.

"Where are you taking us, Agent Thompson?" she asked.

His eyes remained on the road. "Somewhere safe."

She closed her eyes in silent disagreement. Nowhere was safe unless Grant was there with her.

❧

Sophie sat in a conference room in what she assumed to be the Chicago FBI office. The décor was so stark that she thought maybe it was an interrogation room. She bent over to peek at the underside of her chair.

"What are you doing?" Ben asked, halting mid-step behind her.

"Trying to see where they handcuff the prisoners to the chair." A long breath left her lungs. "I can't believe they took my phone!"

"At least you got a few calls off in the car." He resumed his pacing.

"This is ridiculous. Why won't they tell us anything?" She stood and stalked over to the door. Yanking it open, she narrowed her eyes at the man standing outside. "Agent Thompson, I demand to know what's going on. Why do you have us in here? Why'd you take away my phone?"

"Just following Agent Bounter's orders, ma'am. We don't want anyone tracking your location with it."

"Oh." *That sort of made sense.*

"And we don't want you announcing your location to the whole world, either."

"I only called people I trusted!"

"Yeah," Ben echoed behind her, apparently joining the conversation. She stepped into the hallway, and he followed her.

"Despite me telling you not to make those calls," Agent Thompson growled.

A flash of red caught Sophie's eye, and she turned to see a short, auburn-haired woman rounding the corner. She broke out in a relieved smile. "Marilyn!"

Detective Marilyn Fox rushed forward. Before she reached them, Agent Thompson stuck his arm out to block her. "Who're you?"

Marilyn flashed her badge. "You guys already gave me enough crap downstairs. I'm with CPD."

"You're with the Chicago police now?" asked Sophie.

"Just transferred last month."

When the agent appeared satisfied, she tucked her badge back into the pocket of her suit jacket.

"You're the detective who found my dad's body, huh?" Ben asked.

Sophie gasped.

"And you're Benjamin Barberi," Marilyn countered as she shook his hand. "I remember you from the police station last year." She turned back to Sophie. "Jerry and your father are downstairs—the agents won't let them up."

"And how'd *you* make the cut?" Agent Thompson asked.

"Lucas Bounter is a friend of mine. You know, Agent Bounter… your *boss?*"

Thompson appeared ready to retort when his cell phone buzzed. As he turned away to take the call, Marilyn turned to Sophie. "How're you holding up?"

"Not so good," she rasped.

"Oh, dear." Marilyn wrapped her arms around her and squeezed her tight. The top of the detective's head came up to her chin, which made her smile through her tears.

"I think I'm taking all my anger out on poor Agent Thompson too," Sophie added.

"Said by the psychologist—always analyzing behavior. Thank you for having the wherewithal to call us." Marilyn let go of her. "Have you heard anything?"

"No! I keep asking them to call Bounter—"

"No need," Thompson butted in, holding the phone out. "He wants to speak to you."

Sophie snatched the phone. "What's happening?"

"Put it on speaker!" Ben urged, but she ignored him.

"We have news." She closed her eyes and braced herself as Bounter spoke. "It looks like the Russians have Grant."

Oh, God. "Is he alive?"

"We don't know." He cleared his throat. "We haven't honed in on his location yet."

"How do you know it's the Russians, not Mullens?"

"We have an eyewitness at the scene, a block from your apartment. She says she saw a man in a baseball cap carry a shirtless man, slung over his back, to a car and shove him inside. Then some more men—we think four—approached in another car, and they shouted at each other. Shots went off—"

"*Gunshots?*" Sophie looked up to find Ben with a look of horror and Marilyn's mouth set in a firm line.

"Yes," Bounter replied. "Unfortunately Grant and Mullens are gone, and so are the Russians, but Mullens's car is still there…"

Sophie clutched the phone. "Do the Russians know Grant's working undercover?"

"We're not sure what Mullens has told them. Uh, there's some blood…the car's rented to a…" He paused, and she heard the rustle of paper. "Hans Koch Fucher…oh Lord, I just realized what that sounds like when you say his name out loud…"

"Bounter!" she barked. "You said there's blood?"

"Sorry. We're testing the blood for a match, but it might take a while."

To her embarrassment, a sob erupted from her throat. *They're gonna kill Grant.*

"I'm so sorry," he continued. "We were setting up the hotel job for tonight and couldn't get to him fast enough…"

She swallowed, unable to find any words of forgiveness.

"We'll find him," he promised. "We're getting warrants for all the Russians' properties. We'll do everything we can, okay?"

She looked at Ben as she asked, "Have you talked to Enzo Barberi?"

"No." Bounter paused. "Why would we?"

How stupid was the FBI? "Because *he's* the one who set this all up!"

"Wait a minute. Based on what Ben told us, we believe Enzo is behind Mullens kidnapping Grant. But Mullens didn't count on Grant's apartment being bugged by the Russians, or the Russians scooping him up. For all we know, Mullens is dead, and Grant will make up some story about him. Hell, Grant could still show up tonight ready to rob the hotel with the Russians."

"Or maybe Enzo's working with the Russians," Sophie said. Ben fidgeted next to her.

"Do you have any evidence of that?"

"Do I have any evidence of Enzo trying to ruin Grant's life? I have *plenty!*"

"Calm down, Sophie," Bounter admonished. "We have to stay cool-headed here."

"Like *hell* we do!" she roared. "Spare me your sexist rhetoric, Agent Bounter. Emotions are just as important as reason. Nobody knows Grant better than I do, and nobody knows what hell Enzo has put Grant through better than me."

"What're you talking about? I am *not* sexist—"

"I want agents interrogating Enzo Barberi. Now. He's still involved…I can feel it." When he didn't respond, she asked, "Did your mother ever sniff out your misbehavior when you were a kid? Even when you hid it well?"

After a moment, he admitted, "Every time."

"Call it female intuition then. I know you're worried about wasting manpower, but *please* find out how Grant's father is involved. Please."

She held her breath until finally he said, "Okay. I'll send two of my best to Gurnee. Meanwhile, you stay put, got it? I don't have anyone to spare to go out looking for you too."

"Got it." She exhaled. "Thank you."

She handed the phone to Agent Thompson, but Marilyn intercepted it.

"Hey!" he protested.

"Bounter," she said. "I want to go to Gurnee."

Ben studied Sophie with tired eyes as Marilyn walked down the hallway, phone in hand, with Thompson trailing her. "Is Uncle Grant gonna die?"

Sophie tossed her hair back and squared her shoulders, attempting a sense of optimism she certainly didn't feel. "No, Ben. Grant's going to make it." She forced a faint smile. Grant *had* to make it.

22. Confess

Blinding brightness.

Icy cold.

Grant returned to consciousness gasping for air, with pricks of freezing water dripping down his face. His eyes couldn't blink fast enough to adjust to the light shining down on him. But after a moment he could see that beyond the circle of light was darkness. He heard the scuff of a shoe on the floor but could see nothing beyond the brilliant glow. He smelled earthy mildew and urine.

His thundering heart told him he was alive. So Mullens hadn't given him poison—just some sort of sedative. A sound drew his attention, and Andrei stepped into the light. He set down an empty metal bucket. Any hint of warmth that had once shown in his eyes was gone, replaced by ironclad resolve.

"Take three buckets of water to wake you," he said, his voice flat and low.

Grant peered down at the rivulets of said water on his naked chest. When he moved to wipe them he found his arms trapped behind him. Andrei had bound his wrists together. The burning sensation seemed to indicate rope, and his wrists were secured to the wooden chair beneath him. He looked back up to find Andrei prowling around the circle, pinning him with a hostile stare. Was this what it felt like to be in the ring with the former boxing champ?

"He give you strong drug, yes?"

Now that his eyes had adjusted, he could see the shadowy outline of another man off to the right, also tied to a chair. Andrei scooted the man's chair toward him—a scrape of wood against concrete. This man slumped forward, revealing a crown of short blond hair. His green shirt hugged his muscles, and Grant knew who he was before Andrei seized a clump of the man's hair and yanked his head back.

When Ricker Mullens moaned, Grant's airway constricted. Perhaps he would've been better off if Mullens *had* poisoned him.

"Who is he?" Andrei asked.

Another moan from the German and now Grant could see two oozing stains on his shirt, shiny black against the green. *Gunshot wounds*. No wonder he was groaning, looking half-dead. He prayed Mullens would be all-dead before revealing he worked for the FBI.

Andrei let Mullens's head bob back down and took a step toward Grant. "Who is this man?" he repeated, more menace underlining his words this time.

Grant knew he'd better answer soon, but he had no idea what to say, and his fuzzy brain wasn't helping. Did Andrei already know he worked for the FBI? If so, he'd have killed him already, right? Was he testing his honesty? He tensed at the sounds of a scuffle behind him. He felt something brush by as the bodyguard came around his chair and scowled down at him. He clasped the chair's back and he leaned in with a leer. Grant braced himself to get hit.

"Vasily!" Andrei barked.

Grant had never heard the bodyguard's name before. At Andrei's harsh Russian words, Vasily straightened, muttered something in retort, and skulked off the direction he'd come from. Grant wondered if Vladimir was back there too.

In a flash, Andrei delivered a searing uppercut to Grant's chest. With his breath whooshed out of him, he slumped over, straining his shoulders. His body position likely mirrored Mullens's as he fought for air.

Apparently Andrei wanted to conduct the interrogation himself.

His shoes stopped right under his line of vision. Suddenly he looked into Andrei's blazing eyes, his head ripped back by the Russian's forceful grip. "Provide answer, Mick."

Grant attempted to swallow, but his throat was too dry. "Yes, sir," he rasped.

"Good." The pressure on his forehead abated as Andrei stepped back, gestured toward Mullens, and nodded. "This idiot say you work for Barberi."

Grant liked how his family name sounded with a Russian accent. He wondered if the name's origin had any connection to Russia.

Andrei snapped him out of his reverie. "Is true?"

Grant tried to remember the question. Something about Barberi? His eyelids drooped. "Is *what* true?"

Andrei's fist slammed into his jaw, sending him reeling to his right, nearly toppling him. The crunch of contact and blast of pain made him wonder if his jaw had broken. As the rope chafed at his wrists, he realized blood pooled in his mouth. Something hard floated in the blood coating his tongue…Oh, God, it was a tooth. His gag reflex kicked in, and he spit a spray of blood onto the dirty concrete floor. The tooth rattled as it skipped into the darkness.

Once he righted himself, Andrei got in his face. "Is true you work for Barberi?"

Christ. Should he confess his lineage? That had to be better than admitting he worked for the feds, right? Sorting through his thoughts, he watched Andrei's fist cock back and braced himself for more blood.

"The drug make him slow," said a deep voice in the darkness.

Andrei dropped his arm and looked to where his boss emerged from the shadows. Vladimir glared at Grant. "He not, as you say, fire on all cylinders."

He bent down and gripped the armrests of Grant's chair. Grant pressed back against the wooden slats but couldn't escape the stink of stale cigars as the don's unshaven face filled his world. "Focus, Mick," he ordered, adding to the olfactory onslaught.

Grant blinked several times in an attempt to follow the order. Apparently he didn't look coherent enough because Vladimir walloped a stinging slap across his cheek. He barely had time to catch his breath before the Russian backhanded his other cheek. His face on fire and his vision blurred, he panted for air. *Interesting refocusing strategy.*

As his head lolled, he noticed blood on the back of Vladimir's hand. He couldn't see a cut anywhere, and he realized the blood had come from his face. He felt a bead of wetness sliding down his chin. The tip of his tongue found the hole in his lower jaw left by his wayward tooth. Another warm puddle of blood in his mouth made him cringe.

"Look at me, Mick," Vladimir growled.

With effort, he lifted his head.

"Why this man call you Barberi?"

"I…I don't know, sir."

A fist seared into his side with a thud and a crack. "Ooogh," he grunted. Waves of pain pulsed through him.

Wrong answer.

"I want truth," Vladimir said. "No lies. Talk."

Every breath felt like shards of glass. He fought the urge to beg for mercy, and wondered what would happen if he refused to speak. Whatever the Russians planned, it would certainly escalate the situation. FBI training had taught him the Russians meant business. His upbringing had taught him that mobsters never gave up.

When Vladimir kicked his shin with a steel-plated boot, Grant screamed. The intense sting radiated up his leg to his gut, where his stomach threatened to heave. Vladimir's attack had gone straight to the bone.

"Talk!" Vladimir seethed.

Afraid to open his mouth lest the pooling blood and potential vomit make an appearance, Grant stayed silent.

Andrei approached and nudged Vladimir, who stood back. Grant's eyes widened when he handed his don a rusted pistol. "Is time to play roulette, no?"

Spinning the pistol's chamber, Vladimir grinned.

Grant didn't like that grin at all. Russians plus roulette equaled death. Aware of his dwindling time on this earth, he slumped in the chair and tried to keep his breaths shallow. *Sophie…I'm sorry.*

Vladimir lifted the gun and pressed the muzzle against Grant's temple. "Talk, Mick."

His heartbeat exploded. "I…I won't. You'll kill me anyway." He felt blood dribble down his chin.

"Not true," said Vladimir. "Tell him, Andrei."

"We need Navy man for sub, like I say before. But we need trust you first."

What about my *trust in* you? he wondered. He knew they'd kill him in the end, no matter what he said. And if he admitted his lineage, the Russians might tie him back to Sophie. He couldn't let that happen.

Vladimir shoved the muzzle into his mouth, and Grant closed his eyes. *I love you, Sophie.*

He wasn't sure how much time passed before Vladimir cursed, withdrew the gun, and turned to mutter a few Russian words to Andrei. Grant tasted rust mixed with the metallic flavor of his own blood. Vladimir spun back around and studied him for a long moment as he caressed the bloody gun. Then he looked at Andrei. "Get her."

Grant's stomach dropped. His breaths accelerated, bringing spots before his eyes. If he was again responsible for harm coming to Sophie...

Andrei's brief hesitation was too long for Vladimir, who gestured emphatically and shouted for him to get moving. Andrei crossed behind him and hollow footsteps ensued — it sounded like he ascended stairs.

Vladimir smiled. "She make you talk," he said, nodding.

Grant closed his eyes. *Please, don't have Sophie. Please.*

When the click of heels accompanied Andrei's footfalls down the stairs, his eyes flew open. *Please not Sophie.* He heard a feminine yelp and saw a flash of blond hair as Andrei shoved a thin woman into Vladimir's arms...

He exhaled as he saw Innochka before him. His relief was short-lived, though, when Vladimir seized her arm and held her tight against his chest. He raised the bloody gun to her temple. Grant wasn't sure whose eyes were wider — hers or his own.

"We play roulette now, *da?*" Vladimir said.

Grant looked to Andrei, who seemed about as pleased by this turn of events as he was. Had Andrei developed real feelings for this girl?

"One bullet in chamber?" Vladimir asked Andrei, who nodded.

Innochka squirmed in his arms, her face a mask of terror. "Please, Mr. Federov." Vladimir clenched her tighter to him.

"Please," Grant echoed. "Don't hurt her."

"Up to you, Mick," he said calmly.

Damn! He had to say something…*what?* Innochka struggled, and tears spilled onto her cheeks.

"Talk!" Vladimir demanded.

Grant opened his mouth, but nothing came out. He heard a soft click as Vladimir fired the pistol against Innochka's head. A soft click but no loud boom: *empty chamber.* Grant's shoulders collapsed, and he heard a huge sigh. Andrei had breathed out with relief.

Vladimir's eyebrow arched. "Play again, Mick?" He shook the gun for emphasis, and Innochka whimpered. "Or talk?"

"Okay!" he said. His shout rattled and echoed in his aching head — everything hurt. Now three pairs of eyes locked on him, and he knew Vasily the bodyguard was nearby as well. "I am a Barberi." Disgust settled in his belly, admitting that. "Vicenzo Barberi is my father."

Innochka gasped, and Vladimir lowered the gun and let go of her. In Russian, he ordered her to stand by the wall, saying something about needing her again. Then he took a step toward Grant, with Andrei joining him.

Time to spin a credible story. He spit out more blood and took a slow breath, shallower than he needed to avoid searing pain. If there was ever a time one of Hunter's deep breaths would help, this was it. "My father ordered me to join you, to work with you."

"Why to work with us?" Vladimir asked.

"I'm not supposed to tell you this…but my family isn't as strong as it used to be. We need more manpower to keep the business running. My father wants to explore a takeover."

Andrei blanched. "We far too strong for takeover."

"No, no," Grant countered, making shit up on the fly. "Not taking over you. He wants you to take over *us.* He wants to sell our business to *you.*"

Vladimir stared at him, eyes narrowed. "Why you not say this before?"

"Because it takes time to build trust, both ways." He swallowed saliva mixed with blood and ignored his throbbing jaw. "If I approached you with this sale right off the bat, you'd never go for it. You'd smell a trap. If I told my father you were trustworthy and then you screwed us over, he'd have me killed. I had to check you out first."

"You do not like your father," Andrei said. "Why you do job for him?"

As Grant hung his head, he noticed deep, purple bruises blooming on his torso. No wonder every breath hurt. "I had no choice. He said he'd pay off my debts if I came to you and forged an alliance. If I didn't, he'd let the men I owed money to kill me."

Andrei's laugh rumbled in his throat. "You suck at gambling, Mick."

"Wait," Vladimir said, holding up his beefy hand. "We come to you — to Capone's Spirits. You no come to us."

Crap. Grant nodded, his mind whirring. He felt the fog begin to lift from his brain, replaced by a pounding ache. "My father had people watching me at Capone's. I tried to hide by using a fake name, but they still found me. When they saw us talking, I got my orders to get to know you."

"You not Navy then?" Andrei asked.

"I am. I was." Grant's voice filled with genuine emotion. "I wanted to get away from my family. I joined the Navy, but…" He looked down. "I got kicked out for gambling."

Mullens moaned, drawing their attention.

"Who *is* he?" Vladimir demanded.

Grant's fingers twitched behind him. *Don't you dare wake up, Mullens.* "He works for my father." *True.* "I hadn't obeyed my father, so he showed up to teach me a lesson." *Also true.* "I fought him, and he drugged me." *True again.*

Vladimir stroked his chin. "Your father in prison."

"Yes, sir." Grant nodded. He watched Vladimir look at Andrei then tilt his head to the area behind Grant.

"We talk." They trudged up the stairs.

Now what? His headache wasn't so dull anymore, and he felt a shiver crawl up his spine from the cold. His spike of adrenaline had flattened. He looked over at Mullens, who still appeared unconscious.

"Mick," Innochka whispered. He jumped in his chair. He swallowed a moan and looked up at her scowl. "You let him shoot me."

"I'm so sorry," he whispered back. "You could've died — please believe me I didn't want that. I just couldn't get the words out."

Her knowing smile unnerved him. She traced his stinging jaw with one finger. "Because your story is bullsheet," she purred. His attempt at a poker face must've failed because she laughed and said,

"Don't worry, Mick. Your secret is safe with me—whoever you are, whoever you work for. I hate Vladimir more than you do."

"Then untie me from this chair." The words were out of his mouth before he had time to think.

Her smile was sad as she shook her head. "How stupid do you think I am? They would kill me in an instant. I like you, but not enough to die for you."

"You're right," he rasped. "I'm sorry I asked that."

A door opened somewhere behind him, and Innochka flitted back to the darkness. Boots clamored down the stairs, and Andrei rounded in front of Grant.

"You talk to him, 'Nochka?"

"*Nyet.*" She scoffed. "Barberi scum."

"He *is* scum."

Grant bristled. Something had changed—a rising tension in the air sparked against his skin. Andrei disappeared into the darkness and returned with a cushioned chair, which he placed between Grant and Mullens. At first he thought Andrei had gotten the chair for himself, but then Vladimir lumbered over.

"Mr. Barberi," Vladimir began as he sank into the chair. Andrei stood off to the side, his eyes cold and hard. "Do not look good for you."

"What?" He willed his body to stop shaking.

"Tell him," Vladimir commanded.

Andrei glared at him. "Everyone know Barberi empire dead. We no *buy* Barberi business—you pay *us* to take business off hands."

"That's not true!" Grant protested. "My father still has contracts in place…money's still coming in."

"Good," Vladimir said. "He will need money. He will pay to get you back."

Grant's mouth already hung open—it had become difficult to close as the night wore on. "No, he won't!" He winced from the pain of speaking. "My father hates me, and I hate him. It's *his* fault I have this gambling problem." He paused, realizing he was channeling Logan. Logan had blamed their father for all of his faults, and that lack of self-reliance had gotten him killed.

"You offer business proposal," said Andrei. "We negotiate. No money in buy business. But good money in sell you. We sell you back to your father."

"No!" His heart seized with fear. His father would jump at the chance to tell the Russians he worked for the FBI—a perfect revenge for keeping him stuck in prison. "He'll deny he sent me here! It would make him look weak."

Vladimir shook his head. "We see." He nudged the empty bucket with his boot and looked up at Andrei. "Try wake him up," he ordered, pointing at Mullens. "We check his story with what Mick say."

Grant swallowed, tasting blood.

23. Concessions

Sophie's hands shook so badly she had to sit on them to hide her fear. It had taken every psychological ploy she possessed to convince Jerry and Marilyn to agree to this, and she didn't want to provide a reason to back out now.

Parole Officer Jerry Stone gripped the steering wheel. "It's starting to snow."

Ahead in the darkness, wisps of white shone in the headlights.

"Be careful, Jer," Marilyn said from the passenger seat.

Jiggling her leg against the backseat, she clenched her jaw. Traffic out of the city had already slowed their progress north, and every minute lost was another opportunity for the Russians to kill Grant. "Hurry, Jerry."

"Pipe down, Taylor," he growled. "Your dad would *kill* me if I got us into an accident. He already busted my balls for agreeing to drive you on this harebrained stunt."

She groaned. "Don't remind me." She could still hear her father's shouts roaring in the FBI office.

"That's the dumbest idea I've heard yet!" he'd thundered. "You're putting yourself right in the path of a murderer!"

"He'll be in a cage, Dad," she'd said.

"Haven't he and his—his *ilk*—hurt you enough?"

"Grant's not ilk…he's my fiancé!"

Mesmerized by the flakes of snow that disappeared once they hit the highway, she sighed. How could she stand by and do nothing? If Enzo had something to do with the Russians holding Grant—*anything*—she had to try to get it out of him. Sure, Enzo had stonewalled Marilyn and the FBI agent when they'd interrogated him earlier. But she refused to give up.

When the headlights illuminated a road sign, her heartbeat galloped. Gurnee was only two short miles away.

"If Enzo *is* involved," Marilyn mused, staring out the passenger window, "this might work."

Sophie scooted forward. "Really?"

"I thought he didn't tell you anything," Jerry said.

Marilyn rubbed her cheek. "He didn't. But when we showed him those photos…"

"*What* photos?" Sophie demanded.

"Crime scene photos." Marilyn hesitated. "Of other men likely killed by the Russians. Well, mutilated might be the better word for it, really."

Sophie collapsed back in her seat.

"Nice job, Mar," Jerry said.

"Sorry, Sophie. But when we showed those photos…I swear Barberi flinched. Agent Powers didn't see it, but *I* did. I think Barberi may have experienced a millisecond of emotion there…maybe remorse."

A millisecond was better than nothing, Sophie thought. Perhaps she could build on that.

Five minutes later, a corrections officer let them through a back entrance to Gurnee State Penitentiary. The first thing she noticed was the assaulting stench. She'd thought Downers Grove had smelled bad, but female prisoners could never compete with this. Her nose burned with imminent tears when she thought of Grant spending more than two years in this wretched place. *Keep it together*. She forced a swallow as her eyes took in the grimy dark stone.

"Let's see some ID," the CO ordered. Marilyn and Jerry flipped open their badges, and she offered her Illinois driver's license. Thank God the words *Registered Offender* no longer appeared on it.

The CO's eyebrow went to the ceiling as he returned the license. "*You're* the one talking to Barberi, Ms. Taylor?"

"Yes, sir."

"It's Dr. Taylor," Marilyn corrected.

Sophie jumped when a loud buzz accompanied the barred door sliding open. Once they were through, the CO pointed and said, "This way to visitation."

"Oh," Marilyn said. "We're not heading to an attorney conference room?"

"That was for you guys," he explained. "Warden wants Barberi in the cage to talk to the civilian."

Marilyn nodded.

"The cage is in the visitor's area," the CO said. "Let's go."

Sophie watched the group walk away from her. "Wait!"

They turned, and Jerry gave her an exasperated look. She cleared her throat. "I want to be in a conference room. I want to speak to Mr. Barberi face to face."

"Taylor," Jerry said. "This is a child-killer we're talking about."

"Agent Powers and I are trained law-enforcement officers," added Marilyn. "You're not. Even though he'll be chained, it's too risky to have you in the same room with him."

She shook her head. "He won't tell me *anything* from inside a cage. I need to build rapport with him. I need to show him some respect."

"No can do," the CO said. "Warden's orders."

"Grant's *life* is on the line!" she shouted. "I cannot meet him as Prisoner Barberi, child-killer. I have to meet him as Mr. Barberi, father to Grant and Logan. Please."

The CO exchanged glances with Marilyn and Jerry, but nobody said anything.

"I'm a psychologist!" Her cheeks flushed with warmth. "I mean, I was. I know what I'm talking about here. I know Grant's father. *Please*, Marilyn."

The detective stared at her then turned to the CO. "Get your warden on the phone, officer."

"He's at home. We're not to disturb him unless it's an emergency."

"Then *I'll* talk to him," Marilyn said. "Just call him."

The CO exhaled and pulled out his cell phone.

Jerry came to stand next to Sophie against the wall. "I see you're still pushing boundaries, Taylor."

She shrugged wearily. "Sorry. It's what I do, I guess." She watched Marilyn accept the cell phone from the CO.

Jerry's shoulder nudged hers. "Nothing wrong with fighting for the one you love."

"Thank you" was her soft response. She felt tears well up again and took a long breath to fight them.

"Listen to *me*, Warden Arthur—" Marilyn's voice cut through the hallway quiet. "I wouldn't be asking unless it was completely necessary. I know Dr. Taylor—"

"Damn, she's hot," Jerry said, smirking as he watched Marilyn pace the linoleum floor.

Sophie actually smiled.

"She's the feistiest damn gal I've ever met. I love watching her in action."

"Okay," Marilyn announced, returning the phone to the CO. "We're good to go for the attorney conference room."

The CO's eyes bugged. "What'd you say to him? Could you stay on as our staff representative?"

Marilyn laughed. "Oh, I might've mentioned something about exposing prisoner abuse at Gurnee."

"There's no abuse *here*," the CO retorted.

"Really?" Marilyn glanced at Sophie then back at the CO. "Open your eyes, officer. Don't accept bribes, and don't trigger your inmates' trauma reactions by throwing them in the hole for months."

The CO's eyes narrowed. "What exactly are you insinuating?"

"Hey, bud," Jerry broke in as he pushed himself off the wall. "I think she made herself clear. Let's get to that conference room now."

The CO looked at the three of them and seemed to realize he was outnumbered. "Fine." He led them in a different direction as he radioed for the prisoner to meet them at a revised location.

Sophie hustled to match her step with Marilyn's. She hoped the squeeze she gave the detective's hand communicated her gratitude for going to bat for her. Marilyn smiled back and returned the squeeze.

They had to pause every forty yards or so for the CO to unlock another door. While waiting at one stop, Marilyn said, "Don't mention Ricker Mullens when you're with Barberi. He seemed to get pissed off when we mentioned Mullens. Focus on the Russians."

"All right." Her thoughts raced as they moved ahead. "Marilyn, let me ask you something. How'd you feel when you couldn't get anything out of Enzo earlier tonight?"

"How'd I *feel?*" Her eyes narrowed. "You're still a psychologist, asking a question like that—you can't deny it." She sighed. "Well, I guess frustration was what I'd call it."

"Helplessness?" Sophie asked.

Marilyn nodded.

"Disappointment?"

Another nod.

"Hopelessness?"

"Yes, all that. What's your point?"

"That would be quite a downer to go home tonight feeling the same way."

She stopped. "Yes, it would. And I'm still waiting to hear your point."

She hoped Marilyn couldn't hear her thundering heartbeat. "In order for Enzo to feel comfortable enough with me—to tell me what he knows about the Russians and Grant…I need him to be… unchained."

Marilyn placed her hands on her hips and appeared about to unleash holy hell when Jerry popped his head around the corner.

"Hey, you guys coming?"

"Jerry!" Marilyn called. "Sophie wants Barberi unchained when she meets with him!"

"*What?*"

Sophie ignored their glares and glided past them to catch up with the CO. Soon the detective and PO sandwiched her, matching her brisk strides. "You're just like Madsen," Jerry fumed. "Do you have a death wish?"

"No, I don't!" she cried. "I'm trying to prevent a death—*Grant's*. His father won't hurt me. I know it. I just need to talk to him."

They arrived at a corridor lined with black metal doors. "Here we are."

"Officer," Sophie panted. *Get yourself under control.* "Do any of these rooms have one-way mirrors?"

"Of course." He gestured to a door. "We'll use this one."

She nodded. "And what's your response time if I need help? If you need to get in there?"

"Couple seconds." His chest puffed out, straining his black uniform.

"Good. I want Mr. Barberi's chains removed when he meets with me."

Jerry snorted. "This is *insane*."

"Warden will never go for that," the CO said.

"Marilyn." Sophie grabbed her elbow. "The warden agreed to us using the conference room. He never specified the prisoner was to be in chains, right?"

The detective shook her head. "Sophie, don't go there."

"Your father would never agree to this!" Jerry barked.

"I'm thirty years old." She stood tall. "This is *my* life, and Grant's life too. I'll sign whatever waiver I need to, but Enzo Barberi will *not* wear chains. I will meet my father-in-law without the shame of shackles between us!"

☙

"Mr. Barberi." She swallowed and reached out to shake his hand. "I'm Sophie Taylor."

Enzo stared at her for a moment, and a sense of wonder seemed to lighten his dark eyes. Then he grasped her palm, slowly curling his coarse fingers around the back of her hand. His touch was rougher than Grant's, but just as warm.

Sophie realized he probably hadn't held a woman's hand for more than twenty years. She also realized, so close to him that she could smell soap and washed denim, that he could easily hurt her: pull her into him, choke her, punch her, slap her — things he'd done to his wife. To Grant and Logan.

But he didn't do any of those things. Instead he looked down at their joined hands for a moment, then over to her left hand. "That's quite a rock you got there."

She glanced down at her engagement ring, sparkling even in the dull prison light.

A male voice boomed from the corner, and Sophie looked up to find a speaker mounted on the ceiling above the one-way mirror. *"Release her hand and sit* down, *Barberi."*

Enzo paused for a moment, staring into her eyes, then let her go. But he didn't circle around to the other side of the table like she'd expected. Instead, he held the back of a chair and gestured for her to sit. She took a deep breath as she folded herself into it. If it hadn't been bolted to the floor, she was relatively certain Enzo would have scooted her closer to the table. And here she'd thought Grant had inherited his exquisite manners from Uncle Joe. She wondered what other surprises were in store for her with this frightening man.

"My son Grant…he bought that for you?" Enzo asked after he sat himself across from her.

It took a second to remember he'd admired her ring. "Yes."

"He could afford that rock?"

She noticed a look of pride float over his face. "He has a good job."

His eyes narrowed. "The feds pay him well to ruin men's lives."

"No." Her response came out too harshly, and she took a deep breath. "He sings. He has a lovely voice." She watched him carefully. "I understand he got his singing talent from you."

His only response was a guarded stare.

"I suppose you don't get to sing anymore," she ventured. "It must be very…sad, living here. All your basic freedoms stripped away."

"If you were a little shorter, with blue eyes instead of brown, you'd look like Karita."

She hesitated, thrown off by his change of subject. No wonder he'd been staring. "Thank you," she finally replied. "I hear Grant's mother was beautiful."

"She was."

She gauged what to say next. "You and Mrs. Barberi did a wonderful job raising Grant."

That was clearly the last thing he expected to hear.

"I know some of what happened, of course," she said. "I know there were…*difficult* times when Grant was young. But sometimes adversity like that makes a person grow stronger. Grant has empathy for others like I've never seen. You fostered that in him. I know you did the best you could as his father."

"What makes you know *that?*" He leaned forward, his words full of hate.

Her heart raced as the small space seemed to close in on her. She focused on her breathing as she pictured Grant's loving eyes. "I know that…because of Grant. Because of the amazing person he is. He had to get some of that integrity from you, whether you realize it or not." She'd promised herself she wouldn't cry, but her eyes welled up.

"Why are you here?" Enzo asked bitterly.

"I'm here to try to save my fiancé. Your son." A tear slid down her cheek, and she swiped it away. "I haven't given up on you like the rest of them."

He shook his head. "This is bullshit. A waste of my time."

"So you don't care at all what happens to Grant."

He shrugged.

Sophie leaned in, her eyes flaring. "*That* is the bullshit, Mr. Barberi."

His tired eyes looked away from hers, and she knew she had an opening. *Stop crying.* "You haven't been able to sleep since you ordered the hit on Grant, have you?"

When he ignored her, she cursed under her breath. Of course he wouldn't admit that with the authorities watching.

"It's hard to sleep in prison — you're always on edge, worried someone will shank you." She skimmed her tongue across her front teeth. "I remember what it's like."

He remained quiet, but she knew she'd piqued his interest, so she pushed ahead. "Did you know I spent time in prison too?"

"I may have heard that."

"Do you know why?"

His expression reminded her of Logan: a smirk that said *You'll never know what I know*, a tension in the shoulders that belied the toughness he tried to portray. "I have a feeling you're fucking going to tell me."

She nodded. "I was very naïve before I met your family. I've wised up a lot since then, so thank you for that." His deep black eyes were so intense that she found herself trembling. "Logan…the court ordered him into counseling after Grant got arrested. I'd just gotten my psychologist license, and Logan started therapy with me. I knew nothing about the Barberi family at the time."

Enzo had leaned forward just a bit, and Sophie continued. "Your son Logan was troubled, Mr. Barberi. He had a gambling addiction, and as I learned later, he'd broken many laws, killed countless men. But that's not how *I* knew Logan." She had to look away from those piercing eyes. "I knew him as a good man. A man who wanted to be a better father to his son. A man who, as a boy —" she stared directly at Logan's father "— had tried to protect his little brother from getting hit."

Observing a flicker of anger in those obsidian eyes, she admitted, "I fell for that man." She hoped her past with his sons would forge some kind of connection with him. "When Logan told me what he and his brother had endured…" She sniffed. "It hurt me. I wanted to fight for those boys — I wanted to protect them, make it better." She sighed. "I understand you faced a similar situation once — wanting to protect a child, to save him. You could've left Carlo to die after he'd been shot."

Enzo's jaw tightened.

"But you didn't. You got him to a hospital, and they arrested you there."

"Thanks for the recap," he sneered.

She ignored his hostility. "My world collapsed when I discovered Logan had stored guns and money in my office. But I had to take responsibility for my mistakes, and I went to prison, just like you." She had his attention. "I never thought I'd recover from the shame. I never thought I'd live a good life again. But then I met Grant."

Tears welled in her eyes again. "You and Mrs. Barberi created two amazing sons — do you know that?"

"I do know that."

His response surprised her. *Then why did you hurt them so much?* she wanted to yell.

Enzo looked down at his hands, and she watched him massage his wrists. This was probably the first time he hadn't been cuffed or chained when he was out of his cell. "Those boys…they're the only thing I did right in my life." When he looked back up at her, his gaze was cold. "And now Logan's dead."

"That doesn't mean *Grant* has to die too!" His eyes widened, and she knew she'd hit a nerve. "You can still have one of your sons alive. You could work on your relationship with him."

He shook his head. "My son wants nothing to do with me."

"That's not true. What do you think that letter he read to you was for?"

"You know about that damn letter?"

Sophie nodded. "Our jerk PO made Grant and me attend couples counseling. I heard all about the letter. And I heard about how much Grant wants your approval — it would mean everything to him."

Enzo folded his arms across his chest. "Grant never visited me in here once in twenty years."

"And what have you done for *him?*" she challenged. "Have *you* ever written *him* a letter? Have you ever thanked your wife's brother for raising him? Did you ever try to take care of Grant when he came to Gurnee, scared out of his mind? Or did you feed him to the wolves when he wouldn't renounce the one father who'd showed him some kindness?"

Enzo popped out of his chair and drilled his index finger on the table to emphasize every shouted word. "*He. Betrayed. Me!*"

Keep breathing, she told herself. She prayed Jerry and the CO wouldn't crash the room. She bet Marilyn was holding them off. "You're fucking pissed off at Grant."

"Damn right I am!" His chest heaved.

"You're furious. You believe he took away your freedom."

"He *did!*" He began to pace.

For some reason she didn't feel scared. Maybe because she'd witnessed explosions like this from both his sons, and they'd never hurt her — once she'd talked them down, at least. "Mr. Barberi? It's fine to be angry, but I'm concerned they'll stop this meeting if you don't sit down. Would you please sit, sir?"

He blanched and looked at her as if she'd just told him she was an alien love child. But he did sit.

She exhaled. "You look like your anger has come down a notch."

"What do *you* care?"

She met his eyes. "You're my future father-in-law. You're important to Grant, and you're important to me."

His fingers drummed on the table, which reminded her of Grant tapping his thigh. He breathed out through his nose as he shook his head. "This always happens."

"What happens, Mr. Barberi?"

"I fly off the handle then I feel like a fucking idiot." He continued to tap a random rhythm on the table. "I'm not stupid. I know *I'm* the one who took my freedom away. I'm the one who fucked up that night. Grant had nothing to do with it."

She resisted the urge to stand up and cheer. They were getting somewhere! "But you did two things right that night at Richie Fanocelli's."

He looked at her, his face a question.

"You took Carlo to the hospital, and you didn't kill Fanocelli when you had the chance."

"Big mistake." He shook his head. Silence stretched between them. "Now that I know what it feels like to have a son murdered, I bet Fanocelli *wishes* I'd killed him."

"But you didn't. You know what that's called, Mr. Barberi? That's called empathy. You knew how awful Fanocelli felt after his son was shot. That's why I haven't given up on you."

He grunted. His fists clenched with the caged energy of a predator.

"Bet you'd love a drink right now, huh?"

His eyes blazed.

"Yes, I know about that too. It doesn't surprise me you had a drinking problem."

He laced his arms across his chest, the Logan-like smirk returning. "And why is that?"

"A lot of people develop an addiction when they're battling PTSD."

"What the fuck is that?"

"Post-traumatic stress disorder. When you're re-experiencing a trauma through flashbacks or nightmares, and feeling on edge all the time, sometimes you turn to alcohol to numb out."

A smug grin tugged at his mouth. "So you're diagnosing me now? What's this supposed *trauma* I had? My ice cream scoop dropping off the cone when I was a toddler?"

"I apologize, Mr. Barberi. I've never met you before, and it's not right of me to throw out diagnoses like that. It's even more inappropriate because I lost my license when I went to prison." She sighed.

"All I know is what Grant told our psychologist — about the time he made you a sandwich when he was seven. You were drunk, and you told Grant a story of when you were his age. Your father had you bring sandwiches to him and his associates in the basement."

Enzo showed no flash of recognition, and she wondered if he'd been blackout drunk when he'd told Grant the story. She also wondered if he'd buried the memory so deep he wasn't aware of it. "When you gave your dad the sandwiches, there was a man tied to a chair."

Enzo froze.

"Mr. Barberi, are you breathing? Mr. Barberi?"

He took a sharp breath.

"I want you to keep breathing as I tell you the rest of the story, okay?"

"Don't," he said in a strangled voice.

"Avoidance of anything associated with the trauma is another symptom of PTSD. It's okay — this happened in the past. This story will be over soon." She swallowed. *Trust it.* "The man tied to the chair looked really scared, and you wanted to get out of there, but your dad made you stay."

He stared straight ahead. "Stop," he choked out.

She ignored his plea. *I have to do this to save Grant.* "Your dad handed you a gun, and he told you to shoot the man." His glassy eyes looked far away. "You didn't want to, but your dad threatened to beat you with his belt. So you took the gun, you pointed it at the man…"

Enzo flinched, like he felt the gun go off in his hands. "No." His voice shook.

"Please breathe, Mr. Barberi. *Breathe.*"

He flinched again, then glowered at her.

"You're okay — we're here at eight twenty-three p.m. at Gurnee State Penitentiary, on Friday, March seventh. You're an adult. Can you look around you and see the stone walls? Hear the hum of the fluorescent lighting?"

"Fuck!" he roared, jumping out of his chair to pace the floor again. "What the fuck are you trying to do to me?" His breathing was so erratic that he had trouble getting the words out. "Stay *out* of my head!"

She sat quietly in her chair as he grabbed his head with both hands. An internal war played out before her. The battle had begun sixty years ago, and he was still fighting today. He gripped the chair with trembling hands and emitted a guttural cry. She looked at the one-way mirror and mouthed, *It's okay.*

"Why did you tell me that fucking story?" He glared at her.

She reminded herself to breathe. "You asked me what trauma you experienced as a child. Being forced to kill a man…that's the only trauma I know about, but I'm sure there were other incidents of abuse."

"Abuse?" he scoffed as he pressed his hands on the table and leaned forward. "My dad was teaching me the business."

Her mouth dropped open. "Of course it was abuse. It's *not* okay to force your child to shoot another human being!"

"No." He shook his head. "He *had* to be hard on me. I-I-I was weak—I was stupid. It took a long time to get anything through my thick skull. He had to drum it into me."

Her heart ached. "Those are excuses perpetrated by an abuser, Mr. Barberi…nothing more. Your father switched the blame from him to you, but that's not fair because it wasn't your fault—you were only a child. What your father did was wrong. *He* hurt you."

"No." His voice held less conviction this time. "He had to toughen me up."

"No!" She waited until he looked at her to continue. "It *wasn't* your fault! Of course you took the gun—you'd have been beaten if you hadn't. Any child would've done the same thing. He was your father, and you wanted to please him. Being forced to kill a man at the tender age of seven…it would've destroyed *any* child. The guilt that you've endured your whole life since that day? Your father hurt you deeply. It wasn't your fault."

He stared at her for what felt like five minutes. With the deep crease on his forehead and the confusion swirling in the thick oil of his eyes, she assumed he was replaying that childhood moment, perhaps integrating this new perspective…that Enzo Barberi wasn't such a horrible person, he wasn't unredeemable.

He finally slid into the seat across from her. "Did *that*…really happen? Did my dad force a gun in my hands?"

She stroked her chin. "I don't know for sure. From your reaction, and Grant's reaction, it seems likely, though."

"Did I…" His voice grew softer. "Did I kill that guy?"

"I don't know that either. I do know it wasn't your fault—you were just a child. But that's not the point now."

He threw his hands in the air. "Then what *is* the fucking point?"

"The point is that *you* are not an evil man!" she shouted. "Everything you've done—the alcoholism, the child abuse, the crime—it's all understandable. It's not excusable, but it's understandable. You parented like your father showed you. You didn't know there was a different choice."

"There *was* no choice! I had to take care of my family. They needed me. Look what's happened since I've been stuck in here. My *family!* Fucking destroyed!"

"There *is* a choice now," Sophie said. "There's a choice involving your family." She stared into those deep eyes. "Choose good…Choose *love*. Don't let your father's actions keep destroying you. Tell me how to help Grant."

He slouched in the chair, no longer possessing the gravitas of a mafia don. "I already told you I don't know where Grant is."

"Mr. Barberi." She leaned forward and grasped his hands. "I love Grant…so much. I want to marry him. Please. I know you can help us. You're the leader of this family, and you can do this. It's not too late."

He held her gaze for a moment before pulling his hands away. "Fuck." He stared at the mirror on the far wall. Her heartbeat thrummed—each passing second of silence like a thread of Grant's life unraveling, her connection to him more and more distant. Maybe it *was* too late for Grant's father. Maybe he'd been in prison too long to ever feel love or empathy again.

Finally he turned back to her. "Okay." He scrubbed a hand over his face. "I was approached tonight after chow. The Russians want money or they'll kill Grant."

Jesus. Chills bloomed up her spine, and she snuck a glance at the mirror. "I thought visiting hours ended a while ago."

He didn't respond. *Oh.* The Russians had contacts in the prison.

"But even if I wanted to buy his freedom, I couldn't."

"Why not?"

"Because I don't have that kind of money anymore."

Her shoulders slumped, but then she sat up. "Wait—my father will put up the money."

"Your old man's got two million dollars?"

"Um…"

There was the sound of a key in the lock, and Marilyn burst in the door, quickly shutting it behind her. "Hello, Mr. Barberi."

She grunted and gripped the doorknob. Sophie realized someone else was trying to get into the room. Frantic knocking ensued, and Marilyn rolled her eyes, then wrenched open the door. "Officers," she hissed at Jerry and the CO, "let the women handle it." She closed the door in their faces and sat next to Sophie.

"Mr. Barberi, thank you so much for meeting with us. You remember I'm Detective Marilyn Fox, Chicago PD?"

Sophie caught the suspicion in Enzo's eyes. "She's the detective who found Logan's body," she said. "She's helped Grant and me so much."

Marilyn leaned in. "Mr. Barberi, I understand there wasn't any love lost between your family and the Russians. Do you want to destroy their organization?"

He eyed her, his face pale and tired. "I don't care what happens to them." His eyes locked on Sophie's. "I just want to get my son back."

Thank you, she mouthed. She smiled at him as tears spilled down her cheeks.

24. Congest

"Why haven't they called?" Ben cried. He ran his fingers through his mess of scruffy brown hair.

Sophie opened her mouth to formulate a response, but Marilyn beat her to it, patting his shoulder. "Agent Bounter will call soon. It's hard to wait, I know."

The understatement of the year. Sophie glanced around the interrogation room. Everyone seemed as anxious as Ben. Next to him, at the head of the table, his mother, Ashley, stared down at her lap, guilt emanating off of her. Across the table, Marilyn fidgeted constantly, and Jerry sat still as a stone. Her father sat next to her, but he kept his back to her as he talked with about the tenth construction contractor he'd called, pumping each man for information about the Russians. He again seemed to be coming up empty. Agent Thompson stood by the wall with a helpless expression, frowning occasionally at his cell phone, which remained silent in his hand.

And she knew she wore her emotions on her face as well. She wasn't just anxious; she was terrified.

Ben turned to her, the circles under his eyes now darker and hollowed. "Grandpa said he'd talk to the guy at Gurnee tonight, right? Pretend he wanted to pay to get Uncle Grant back?"

"Yes, Ben." He'd asked that question several times, but she couldn't be irritated. She was barely holding it together. What must this wait be like for a teenager?

"Mr. Barberi did speak with another prisoner a couple of hours ago," Marilyn said. "As far as we know, the other prisoner set up an exchange between the Russians and someone they think is the Barberi representative — but will actually be thirty FBI agents."

"But how'd the prisoner get word to the Russians?" Ben wondered. "They're not allowed to make phone calls this late, right?"

"We're guessing the other prisoner paid off a CO to call the Russians for him. Like I said, the place is corrupt." Marilyn's eyes blazed.

"They better catch that dirty guard, whoever he is," Jerry grumbled.

"They will." She patted his hand absently.

Ben's fingertips drummed a dirge on the table.

"How 'bout you lay down in that corner?" Sophie suggested. "I'm guessing you didn't get any sleep last night. You look exhausted."

"As if I could sleep right now!"

Ashley looked up, mascara streaks down her face. "Ben, honey, Sophie's right. You should get some sleep. Or how about some food?" She pointed to the plate of untouched bagels on the table.

"Jesus, Mom! You look like a freaking raccoon. Stop crying!"

Ashley swiped at her cheeks.

"Agent Thompson, can you get some tissues?" Sophie asked. She worried he would find that task beneath him, but he actually looked relieved as he bolted out of the room.

"I'm sorry," Ashley murmured. She sniffed. "I'm so sorry for bringing that awful man into our lives, Benji."

He looked away. "I already told you it's not your fault."

"Yes it is!" She was about to say more when Agent Thompson returned and handed her a box of tissues. She plucked a few and scrubbed her cheeks. "I never should've trusted *Hans*." She looked down. "I should've known he wasn't interested in *me*." She dabbed under her eyes, which had filled with tears again.

"Ashley…" Sophie searched for the right words. "You're a beautiful woman with a beautiful heart. Don't give up."

She cried harder.

"I know how frightening it is to trust again." Sophie felt her father's stare and glanced over to find he was off his phone. She swallowed. "It's *so* uncomfortable. But you'll find love with a good man. You deserve more love in your life."

"How can you say that?" she asked. "After I risked Ben's life by being so stupid? What if Grant *dies?* It'll be my fault!"

Sophie's heart hammered. Grant wouldn't die…Grant *couldn't* die. She took a deep breath. "Grant was aware of the risks of going undercover. But he felt he had to do it, to honor his mother's memory. He loved his mother, and he didn't want the Mafia hurting anyone like her again." She gestured to Ashley's son. "Ben's like his uncle that way. Of course he didn't say anything about the threat to Grant's life, because he was scared they'd kill you. He loves you."

Ashley turned to Ben. "I love you so much. I'm gonna be a better mom to you, okay?" She reached out, and Sophie exhaled when Ben accepted her hug.

You're already a better mom, Ashley.

Her father patted her hand and smiled at her. "I'm glad you took the risk to trust again, Soph."

Her upper lip quivered. "Me too, Dad." She blinked away her tears. "Do you…do you think Grant will be okay?"

"I do." He held her hand. "Grant's a fighter. He certainly fought *me* hard." She managed to smile at his grumpy tone. "He fought for you."

She sniffed and nodded.

"And *you* fought for Grant." Her father's eyes squinted like they did when he was mad at her, and she held her breath. "I was so ticked at you for going to Gurnee, and you didn't listen to me…But you did it, Sophie. I don't know how you convinced that bastard to save Grant."

She shrugged. "Well, Enzo is Grant's father. I knew he couldn't be all bad if he produced a son like Grant."

"How'd my daughter get so damn smart?"

It certainly wasn't reading accounting textbooks, she wanted to retort. Instead, she said, "She takes after her parents."

"Thompson." The agent answering his phone brought all eyes to him. He listened for a few seconds, then broke out in a huge grin. "They have Grant!"

Sophie shot out of her chair and ran to Ben. He leaped up and hugged her, and they circled around as he laughed and she cried happy tears.

"Sophie."

The agent's voice halted her celebration. "Yes?"

"Bounter wants you to meet him at the hospital."

Her smile vanished. "Did he get hurt in the exchange?"

Agent Thompson shook his head. "It's Grant. They're rushing him to the hospital."

Her shaking hand covered her mouth.

❧

Northwestern Memorial Hospital. She hadn't walked these halls since she'd been a patient last August — a gunshot victim.

She shivered as she followed Agent Thompson's brisk steps. "Where did they take Grant?"

"The ER."

"What *happened* to him?" she asked through a tightening throat. "Tell me!"

He waited for her to catch up. "He has multiple injuries — that's all I know. Apparently the Russians roughed him up."

When they rounded the corner, she identified Bounter standing next to another agent. "Agent Bounter!"

He handed his coffee to the other agent and scooped her up in a surprise hug. She closed her eyes as he enveloped her in his arms.

"That was a tough one, Sophie, but we did it," he said. "I'm pretty sure we've got most of those bastards locked up now. When they realized we were feds, not Barberis, you should've seen their faces. It was like the return of the Cold War."

"Excuse me, ah, it's great you busted the Russians, but how is *Grant?*"

"Oh, sorry. They've taken him for tests. CT scans, I think?" He looked over her shoulder at Agent Thompson. "Ms. Fredrickson and her son are secure?"

"Yes, sir," Thompson said. "How's John?"

"In surgery," Bounter answered.

Sophie wasn't sure she wanted to know, but asked, "Who's John?"

"Another agent." Bounter's rubbed his hand over his face. "He got shot a few times in the exchange, but he'll be okay. Better than Mullens, anyway. He's in the morgue."

Sophie's eyes bugged. "Did *Grant* get shot?"

"We don't think so."

"You don't *think* so? Why does he need CT scans?" Her voice trembled. "What'd they do to him?"

"They knocked him around a bit," Bounter admitted. "He's, ah, he's a little bruised."

Two orderlies rolled a hospital bed around the corner and swung it toward her. The patient had a gauze bandage wrapped over the top of his head and under his jaw. He had buzzed, black hair, and his feet stretched to the very end of the bed beneath the sheet. As the bed wheeled closer, she felt stirrings of nausea and her lips parted in horror. "A *little* bruised?" She raced to the bed and clutched the metal rails, looking down at Grant's battered face. His beautiful, destroyed face.

His eyes opened as she whimpered. Thank goodness they hadn't hurt his crystal blue eyes. He croaked out a word that resembled her name.

"No talking, Mr. Santino," the male orderly said.

"Ma'am, we have to keep moving," the other orderly said. "We need to get some fluids in him."

She swallowed and began walking with the bed. "Of course."

When they reached the ER, one orderly caught her elbow. "You need to stay out here."

"No." She wrestled out of his hold.

"Sophie," Agent Bounter called. "Listen to them. Grant's going to be all right."

"This is *your* fault, Bounter!" she hissed. "You've lost the right to tell me what to do."

The glass doors to the ER slid open, and a nurse waited inside. "Who are you?" she asked.

"I'm his fiancée. And I'm not leaving."

The nurse exchanged a glance with the orderly, then nodded. "Okay. Just for a few minutes."

Sophie followed the bed through another sliding glass door into a cubicle. The nurse busied herself hooking Grant up to a heart monitor as Sophie stared into his eyes.

Thank you, he mouthed.

The bruising was deepest around his nose and along his jaw, but the purplish color bled out into his cheeks, darkening his whole face. As she reached down to hold his hand, she noticed his wrists were red and raw. "They…they tied you up before they beat you?"

His attempt to nod made him groan.

"Please don't ask him any more questions," the nurse said as she started an IV. "His jaw's broken."

"Dislocated, actually," a white-coated woman said as she breezed into the cubicle. "Mr. Santino, I'm Dr. Tucker." She turned to speak to the nurse about medication doses in rapid-fire abbreviations, then looked back at Grant. "You have a dislocated jaw, a broken nose, a bone bruise on your tibia, and three broken ribs. We're watching for a possible concussion as well. You're getting some pain meds and muscle relaxants, and soon I'll reduce your jaw dislocation. In a few days, after the swelling goes down, we'll schedule a rhinoplasty with plastics."

Sophie broke in, "Is he bleeding internally?"

"And you are?" the doctor asked.

"Sophie Taylor, his fiancée."

"There doesn't appear to be any internal bleeding, but we'll keep Mr. Santino for observation overnight."

The nurse was about to leave when Sophie asked, "When can Gr…when can he speak?"

"Not now." She swept out of the cubicle.

Grant's eyelids drooped, and she could tell he fought to stay awake. "Are you in pain?" She cringed. "Whoops, don't answer that. Of course you are." She leaned over to press a gentle kiss on his forehead as she cradled the bandage. "My brave McSailor." She smiled, her heart swelling with warmth. "I love you."

He blinked up at her with shining eyes. He didn't have to speak for her to know his reply.

All too soon the doctor returned. "Okay, let's fix up your jaw." She nodded at Sophie. "You probably don't want to be here for this. Even with the meds, this procedure will cause some pain."

She rubbed circles on his palm. "Is it okay if I stay? Squeeze my hand if yes." When pressure tightened on her hand, she looked at the doctor. "I'm staying."

"Try to stay out of the way, then." The nurse pressed a button to elevate the mattress and put Grant in a more upright position, then she pushed down the railing on the side of the bed.

The doctor slid on a pair of latex gloves as the nurse unwrapped the gauze from Grant's head. Once the bandage fell away, his mouth plopped open, and he shuddered.

His eyes opened wide as the doctor sat on the mattress and leaned forward. "Breathe as deeply as you can, Mr. Santino." She placed her thumbs far into the recesses of his mouth and seemed to press down. Grant moaned and gripped Sophie's hand. His other hand shot up to clutch the doctor's arm.

"Let go of my wrist," she said. "We're almost there."

When he cried out, Sophie had to look away.

Dr. Tucker sighed. "I'm having trouble getting good pressure. Oh, *hell*." She stood and grabbed some gauze, then wrapped it over her thumbs. She planted her left knee on the mattress and swung her right leg over to straddle Grant, staring down at him. "Let's try this again."

Grant let out a sidesplitting scream, but when the doctor dismounted, his eyes fluttered shut and his mouth relaxed and closed. Sophie immediately backtracked her silent threats to the doctor's life.

But forgiving Grant for getting himself into this mess was another matter entirely. "Hey," she said, forcing him to open his heavy eyelids. "This will never happen again." Her pointed finger emphasized every word. "You *will* quit the FBI, mister."

His eyes closed again, and she thought he'd already slipped into sleep when she felt his long fingers stroking her hand. Her eyes filled with tears. Her McSailor was back.

❧

Grant jarred himself awake with his own snore. Brightness sliced into his eyes, and he moaned in pain as he turned his head away from the lights. Where the hell was he?

A soft touch clasped his hand, and he rolled his head the other direction to find Sophie gazing down at him with a beatific smile.

"Nice snoring, Roger."

"Sorry." He winced.

"Does it hurt to talk?"

He opened his mouth and gingerly shifted his jaw. "I'm sore, but it's a lot better."

"Good. They told me blood's draining down your throat from your nose and mouth—yeah, you'll need some dental work too—and that's why you're snoring." She gave him some water, which he gulped greedily.

"Where are we?"

She sighed. "The ICU. They moved you here to monitor you overnight. Due to your rib fractures, apparently you're at risk for something called flail chest." She let go of his hand and waved her arms wildly overhead to demonstrate.

His chuckle reminded him how bruised he was. He swallowed another moan. "So flail chest is the uncontrollable urge to flail your arms?"

"It's a potentially fatal condition involving a piece of rib breaking off."

"Oh." This time he didn't laugh. "Sorry." He couldn't believe she was still with him after all he'd put her through. After all she'd done for him. "Is Ben okay?"

"He's here, in the waiting room, along with Ashley." She sighed. "And my dad."

"Your dad must hate me even more now."

She took his hand again. "He doesn't, Grant. He saw how destroyed I was when the Russians had you. He finally gets it."

"Even though you spoke to my father, unprotected and alone?"

"You know about that?"

Grant managed to swallow. "Bounter told me about it in the ambulance—how Mullens made Ben go to Gurnee, holding him at gunpoint, how my father forced Ben to tell him about me working with the FBI…"

"Are you mad at Ben?"

"Am I *mad?* At *Ben?* Hell, no! I'm furious with myself for putting a sixteen-year-old in that situation. God, that'll mess him up for life."

"Ben's going to be fine, Grant." She squeezed his hand. "Once he told me about it, he seemed much better. Keeping that secret was killing him, but now that *you're* okay, he'll be fine."

"Because of you." He gazed into her caring eyes. "You got Ben to tell you what happened. That alone was incredible, but then you demanded to see my father…you got him to confess to a plan to *murder* me…" He paused. "Why are you crying?"

"I…was so scared. So scared of losing you." Her eyes glittered.

He drew her hand to his lips, navigating the multiple wires extending to the machines surrounding him. "Oh, Bonnie." He kissed her soft skin. "I bet you were terrified of my father."

"I wasn't." She shook her head. "I knew he wouldn't hurt me. I knew there was good in him, deep down."

Grant looked at her with wonder. "How did you know?"

"He made *you*." She sniffed and smiled through her tears. "I thanked him for that."

"And I thank God for you, Sophie. You saved my life."

Her lips trembled. "Now we're even."

"*Even?*" He tried to discern how she could think that. "Oh, because of Carlo? You think we're even because I stopped *my* cousin from killing you? My family — my blood — we've hurt you so much. It was my brother who sent you to prison!"

"Logan sent you to prison too." She leaned down and gazed into his eyes for a long moment. "Thank you to Logan for bringing you in my life." When she pressed her lips against his, he felt her tears on his cheeks.

"I *wondered* why your heart rate spiked," a male voice said. Sophie popped up as a nurse entered the room with a smirk on his face. "This is why we don't usually allow spouses in the ICU." He winked at Sophie.

"I'm not his spouse," she said. "*Yet.*"

As the nursed checked the machines and took more blood, Grant clutched the promise of marrying the woman he loved.

The nurse nodded as he wrote on the vial of blood. "Everything looks good for now, Mr. Santino. How are you feeling?"

Grant met Sophie's eyes. "Excellent."

"Hmm, don't typically hear that response in the ICU." The nurse grinned as he departed.

"I get the fake name, with maybe some Russians still out and about, but why Mr. Santino?" Sophie asked.

"Agent Bounter has watched *The Godfather* one time too many."

She laughed. "He's one happy camper with so many bad guys under arrest." Her smiled faded. "He said you saved some women too…some women they were hurting."

"When we were in the ambulance, I told him about one of the Russian's girlfriends who'd been there — Innochka. She wasn't at the exchange, but luckily the FBI found a woman matching her description on the street. When they threatened to arrest her, she led them to the house where they'd held me. We got to the hospital before I heard about everything they found, but it looks like there was enough guns, money, and drugs in there to put them away for a long time."

"Thank God."

"Do you know if they found Katya? Vladimir's girlfriend?"

"I don't know—Bounter didn't say. Did they…beat the women like they beat you?"

"They whipped them with a belt."

She gasped. "No wonder you were so committed to following through." She shook her head. "Why did they beat you so badly? Did they discover you were undercover?"

"No. They would've killed me long ago if they'd known."

Her eyes widened.

"Luckily Mullens never regained consciousness, or he'd have told them. He *was* able to tell the Russians I was a Barberi…I think it was before they shot him, and I passed out from the drug he gave me."

She shook her head, disgust scrunching her nose. "He gave you Rohypnol, the doctor said."

"What's that?"

Based on her hesitation, he wasn't sure he wanted to know.

"Roofies," she eventually said. "The date-rape drug."

Thick nausea flowed over him. "Mullens is dead, right?" When she nodded, he shuddered. "He told me my father paid him to turn me over to the Russians. He was supposed to tell them I worked with the feds."

"Enzo, how *could* you?" She pressed her hand to her mouth.

"But he wanted to rape me first." He looked down. "He wanted to do that from my first day at Gurnee."

Sophie was quiet. She eventually asked, "Did he…get what he wanted?"

"No." He let out a breath. "I don't think so. He dragged me out of our building, but I was so out of it…he was furious I couldn't walk…" A flash of memory sparked his synapses, and his eyes scanned the length of his body. He was wearing a hospital gown—his pants were nowhere in sight.

"What is it?" Sophie asked.

He closed his eyes and cringed. "Nothing."

"*Did* Mullens rape you? Are you remembering—"

"No." He clenched his teeth, even though it amplified the ache in his jaw. "I think I might've peed my pants." Heat flushed his cheeks. "That's what slowed Mullens down."

She stared at him. "Then *that's* what saved your life."

"What?"

"Thank God you still pee in your pants now and then." She grinned. "Or you wouldn't be here with me today. It slowed Mullens down so the Russians could get you both. If you'd peed even more, maybe Bounter would've gotten there too, and you wouldn't have been beaten to a pulp."

"But then the FBI wouldn't have found all the evidence," he said with a slight smile.

"True." She seemed to brace herself. "Grant, I know you went undercover to honor your mother. To save women like your mother. But was it worth it?"

He considered. "They're bad men, Soph. I'm so relieved they can't hurt people anymore." He sighed. "But I was a fool to think I could take this on and not bring danger to you and Ben. You don't know how sorry I am." He remembered the feel of warm blood pooling in his mouth as he sat tied to the chair, stabs of pain with every breath…"I thought I would die, and all I could think about was you."

She blushed.

"*You're* what's most important in my life—not some stupid job. I promise I'm done with the FBI, okay?"

"Oh, thank you." She looked to the ceiling, seeming to battle more tears.

An image of Andrei's fist flying toward his nose assailed him, and he fought to breathe. But Dr. Hayes's advice for handling flashbacks helped calm him.

"It's interesting, facing your death," he said once his chest relaxed. "It makes you think." She met his eyes. "Sophie, life is short. We can't let anything stop us from reaching our dreams. We have to keep fighting for our dreams."

Her forehead creased as she listened.

"And my biggest dream is marrying you."

She smiled as she cradled his head in her hands. "That's my dream too. You've got three months for those bruises to heal, McSailor. And they *better* heal before the wedding photos, 'cause I'm only marrying you for your good looks."

Ignoring the pain in his face, he grinned.

25. Consummate

Sophie brushed her hand down her wedding gown, then tugged and straightened the delicate material. The lively notes of Pachelbel's Canon floated from the sanctuary into the narthex, sparking a pulse of excitement in her belly. *This is happening.* She tried to hold her head up high.

In her deep purple bridesmaid gown, Anita looked back and gave her a thumbs-up before she turned to walk down the aisle.

"You look amazing," her father whispered in her ear.

Clutching his elbow, she turned to him and smiled. "Thanks, Dad."

"*Almost* as pretty as your mother on our wedding day."

She elbowed him, and he laughed.

Tanya swiveled to wink at her before she began her slow walk down the aisle. Her tall colleague looked regal in her flowing gown. Then only Kirsten remained in the narthex with Sophie and her father.

"If Mom were here," said Sophie, "she'd be on the other side of me to walk me down the aisle."

"Huh?" Lines creased her father's forehead. "That's not how it's supposed to work. The *father* gives the daughter away."

"Do you know where that tradition comes from, Dad? It's from a time when women were men's *property*. The father literally gave his daughter away to the next man who owned her: her husband. I don't want to support that patriarchal misogyny."

"Oh, Lord." He shook his head. "I know you're seeing therapy clients again, but could you please stop the insufferable women's libber psychobabble for one day?"

A giggle escaped. She'd missed his cranky complaints.

"Your new husband will want to return his property right quick if you keep that up."

"I can't believe you just said that."

"Don't worry," he murmured as he nodded ahead. "You can tell *Grant* will never give you up. Check out the way he's looking at you."

She realized Kirsten had already started down, and the white aisle runner now extended before her. Her eyes drifted from the beaded straps on the back of Kirsten's gown to the front of the church. Standing to the right of the altar was a handsome hunk of sailor decked out in his dress whites. *I'm so glad he's back in the Navy.* His khaki uniform was sexy enough, but his whites? *Have mercy.* Sliding up the gold buttons on his chest, her gaze locked onto his. His eyes lit up with joy, filling her with their kindness and love. She suddenly wanted to cry. *How cliché.*

"He loves you — it's clear." Her father squeezed her elbow. "And I love you. Are you ready?"

The lighting dimmed as the church organist and violinist flowed into Thais' "Meditation Act II." Then the entire congregation was on its feet, staring at her with expectation. The enormity of it all made it hard to breathe. Her heart galloped, and her hands trembled, shaking her jasmine bouquet as everyone waited for her to take the first step. Then she found Grant's eyes…and she gulped a big breath. He smiled at her, and his slight nod released her from her anxiety. What was there to fear? They would face any challenge together now.

The aching beauty of the violin accompanied her first slow step. Her father stayed at her side, supporting her like he now knew how to do. She kept her eyes glued on McSailor as her father propelled them forward, one step at a time.

Uncle Joe smiled next to Grant in his more decorated uniform, and standing next to the best man were the groomsmen, Ben and Roger, both dressed in handsome tuxes. Ben grinned at her while Roger wore a stoic expression. He seemed to be trying to appear taller with his chin in the air.

Her eyes returned to Grant, who drew her toward him with the force of his love. She blinked as fast as she could to keep the tears at bay. The guests in the pews were a blur of faces until she made it to the front rows and heard, "Way to go, Taylor."

Sophie looked over to find Jerry wearing a faint smile. Marilyn leaned around him. "You're beautiful. We're proud of you."

A tear leaked down her cheek as she nodded. Thank God Kirsten had insisted on waterproof mascara. Suddenly she was mere feet from Grant, and she paused as Pastor Tom said, "Knowing that your love and your choice to be life-long partners stems from God's will and the blessings of your families, who gives this woman to be married to this man?"

"Her mother and I do," her father said in a clear voice. Then he pressed a kiss to her cheek and drew her hand into Grant's. More tears spilled over her cheeks as she watched him nod at Grant.

She'd have to find her father a partner of his own one day. If Roger could get a girlfriend, *anyone* could.

Grant's warm hand led her a few steps forward, and he wiped her cheek before he clasped her other hand. "Happy tears?" he whispered.

"*Delighted* tears," she whispered back. She felt her gown lift and peeked over her shoulder to see Kirsten fluffing the train of her dress, letting it swirl toward the pews in an elegant arc. *Good maid.* She smirked as she remembered Kirsten's laugh every time she'd referred to her as "maid" in the past month.

"Sophie and Grant," Pastor Tom began, "today you enter as individuals, but you will leave here as wife and husband. You will blend your lives, expand your family ties, and embark upon the grandest adventure of human relations. The story of your life together is still yours to write. All those present have come to witness and celebrate your love and commitment this day—eager to share the part of the story not yet told."

The pastor's words continued, but she focused on Grant. His warm, steady hold on her hands…his masculine scent of bergamot and sandalwood…his freshly shaved olive skin. The bones had mended, the bruises faded, and his shining eyes revealed his emotional healing too. He had a sense of confidence and peace she'd never seen before.

Oh, time for a reading. As Ashley skirted behind Roger and up a few stairs to a side pulpit, Sophie admired her lavender dress and her happy smile. How different her expression was from the time she'd done a reading at Logan's funeral. Sophie glanced at Ben and waited until his eyes met hers. He stared at her a moment before he looked down at his polished black shoes. He was thinking of Logan as well, she knew.

After Ashley returned to her seat, Hunter made his way to the pulpit. She hid a smile and looked at Grant, who smirked back. They'd first had to cajole Hunter to attend their wedding, overcoming his concerns about compromising their confidentiality. But that was nothing compared to his reluctance to do a reading. After much begging on her part, he'd thrown up his arms and told her he'd do it, *damn it*, but he'd choose his own reading. She felt a flash of curiosity as he began to read:

> *"Sophie and Grant, you stand here right now*
> *Aware of each breath, each tear, each laugh*
> *Seek within yourselves*
> *Courage to keep going*
> *Communication to speak truth*
> *And acceptance of what's real*
> *Live mindfully in each moment*
> *As you experience and share*
> *The journey to beauty and love."*

Grant squeezed her hands as Hunter's words reverberated. She silently vowed to communicate better on the journey ahead of them.

They turned to face Pastor Tom, who shared with them his own words of wisdom. It felt heady to be married in front of the altar, and she hoped she wouldn't let God down. "And now it's time for the exchange of vows," the pastor said.

She blinked. *Already?* The ceremony had flown by, and she'd wanted to be completely present for every moment—every second of her new life with Grant. They joined their hands together again, and she looked into his eyes as Pastor Tom asked:

"Do you, Sophie, choose Grant to be your partner in life, to support and respect him in his successes and failures, to care for him in sickness and in health, to envelop him in Godly grace and love, to nurture him, and to grow with him throughout the seasons of your life together?"

Yes, yes, yes, McSailor! she wanted to shout. Instead she got out a shaky "I do" before she started crying again.

Grant chuckled, low and deep.

She barely heard Pastor Tom ask him the same question, but she definitely honed in on his smooth, sexy voice as he answered, "I do." Right away he leaned toward her ear and whispered, "I love you, Bonnie."

They were married! When his warm breath left her cheek as he straightened, she smirked at him. "I love *you*, McHusband."

Roger was the first guest Grant noticed as he and Sophie boarded the Eaton Tours ship for the wedding reception. "'Bout time you two got here!" he boomed, unthreading the rope from the cleat.

"Let me help you with that, sir," Grant said, stepping forward.

"Nonsense." Roger stood, and the ship floated a few feet from the dock. "Wouldn't want to dirty your prissy whites, Lieutenant."

"Well, you're in a *tux*," Sophie observed.

Roger glanced down as he brushed off his lapel. "And looking damn fine, if I say so myself. So why were you two so late? All your guests arrived twenty minutes ago." He nodded to the limo parked near the dock. "Getting your honeymoon started early?"

Grant felt his cheeks grow warm and hoped his tunic was back in place.

"We had to finish up the photos," Sophie lied.

"How come the photographer got on board forever ago, then?" Roger asked.

"Um…" She licked her bottom lip, which mesmerized Grant.

Roger shook his head as he pointed at her wedding gown. "I thought the white was for virgins. So why're *you* wearing it, Taylor? You put the whore in horizontal."

Her mouth hung open for a few seconds, then she started laughing.

"Enough, Rog," Grant growled. "I gotta meet your girlfriend. I don't know *how* she puts up with you." As he took Sophie's hand and guided her toward the guests, Roger guffawed from behind them.

"You look fantastic in that dress," Grant told her, earning a smile from his bride. It was an off-the-shoulder gown that showcased her delicate collarbone and slim, muscular shoulders. The fitted bodice angled into a thin, dark purple belt. Beneath the belt, flowing curves swirled around the dress like waves, sounding a whispering bustle as they walked. He knew she'd debated with Cheri about whether to keep her hair up and down. He'd stayed out of it, but he was pleased by her decision: long strawberry-blond hair rested in soft curls down her back, held in place by an ornately beaded headband.

Guests mingled on deck, enjoying appetizers and drinks. When the light jazz music faded, everyone stared at them. From the bridge, the DJ Cheri had hired spoke into the microphone: "Ladies and gentlemen, please welcome Mr. Grant Madsen and Mrs. Sophie Taylor Madsen!"

The guests broke into applause a second before he wheeled to face her. "I thought you were keeping your name?"

"Professionally, yes." She squeezed his hand. "But I decided to take your name for the *rest* of my life…as a sign of my love for you."

Could he adore her more? The sound of a fork hitting a wine glass rang out, accompanied by Detective Fox's feisty cry, "Kiss!" He grinned at his Bonnie, released her hand, cradled her head, and met her soft, sweet lips. He felt her hands grasp his hips as she leaned into the kiss. The applause swelled, but his heart swelled more.

When he finally broke away, he smoothed his hand down her hair. "Thank you for your wedding gift, Mrs. Madsen." He pressed a kiss to the back of her hand. "My bonny wife."

She opened her mouth to answer, but Roger interrupted, speaking over the microphone. "Welcome to Eaton Tours, everyone. The cruise will now begin. As you take in the stunning Chicago architecture, please enjoy cocktails and appetizers on deck, and the buffet down below."

Classical music started up. Grant scanned the familiar environs of Ogden Slip and remembered the first day he'd worked on Roger's ship. He'd been so lonely then…until Sophie had joined him on board.

"Congratulations, you two," Mr. Taylor said as he approached. Grant felt his shoulders stiffen, and noticed his former hotel boss,

Mr. Remington, trailing Sophie's father. Mr. Taylor kissed Sophie on the cheek as he hugged her, then reached out to shake his hand. "What a handsome couple."

"Thank you, sir." He searched Mr. Taylor's eyes for signs of disapproval. "Thank you for the amazing reception on this ship."

"It's a bit informal, but that's how you two wanted it. My pleasure, Grant." He stepped aside so Mr. Remington could shake Grant's hand after hugging Sophie.

"I thought we might hear a song from you during the ceremony."

"Yes!" Sophie added. "I asked him to sing, but he didn't want to."

His throat tightened. "I…I just wanted to enjoy the experience." He squeezed her shoulder and kept his arm wrapped around her waist. "You know, keep the focus where it belongs: on this beautiful woman here."

She dipped her chin, and Mr. Taylor laughed. "You got it bad, Grant." He looked behind him to see more guests waiting to speak to the couple. "I'll let you go." Reaching out to stroke Sophie's cheek, he said, "My beautiful daughter, all grown up." Then he pumped Grant's hand again. "I'm glad to have a son now too."

As he walked away, Grant turned to Sophie for a wide-eyed exchange. "Wow," she breathed.

He straightened when he saw two men in uniform next in line. But first Kirsten zoomed in from the side to slip champagne flutes into their hands. "Nobody ever gives the bride and groom any time to eat or drink at these things," she murmured.

"Thanks, Kir," Sophie said as her friend darted away. She clinked her glass with his and knocked back a swig, but he didn't dare drink in the presence of the two decorated officers standing before them.

He held his glass to the side as Joe hugged him. When his uncle thumped him on the back, he heard the clang of gold buttons colliding on their uniforms. "Excellent job, Grant." Those Danish blue eyes beamed at him. "Your new wife is truly a treasure. You've chosen well, son." Grant closed his eyes, overwhelmed by emotion. His biological father would die one day in prison, but Joe would be there for him on the outside, as always. As Joe drew Sophie into a hug, Grant opened his eyes to face his current boss.

Captain Archie Lockhart also shook his hand. "Never seen you in your dress whites before, Lieutenant."

"No, sir. But I'll be wearing them at the charity benefit in a couple of weeks."

"Right." Captain Lockhart nodded. "I'll get to hear you sing for the first time."

"Yes, sir."

His boss smirked. "Your entertaining duties at Navy events *have* to be more fun than working as my assistant."

How am I supposed to answer that? "Well…"

"Grant just loves working for you, Captain," Sophie interjected. "And I'm thrilled you took him on at Great Lakes, because *I* love…" Her voice drifted off, and he thought he noticed her blush. "Well, I love a man in uniform." Her hand rested on his chest. "It's a dream come true."

His face flushed as well, recalling her pawing at his uniform in the limo.

Joe laughed. "How's it going with your practice up in Lake County, Sophie?"

"So great." Her proud smile made Grant happy he'd encouraged her to plead her license reinstatement to the state psychology board. "I saw my first client a couple of weeks ago. I'm also teaching a summer class at DePaul since it'll take a while to build my caseload."

"That's wonderful." Joe nodded. "I'm happy for you both. C'mon, Archie, let's go teach Rog how to drive this ship."

Archie shook his head as he followed him. "Good luck with that, Joe."

After snapping a few photos of Ben and his friends, the photographer got some shots of Grant and Sophie with her hair flowing behind them in the cool breeze. They couldn't have chosen a more beautiful backdrop. "Are you warm enough?" he asked after taking a sip of bubbly.

"I'm just glad it's not super humid today," she answered.

"Me too. Hungry?"

"Starved." She grinned.

"Quick, let's get you some food before more guests hound us." He led her to the appetizer table.

She giggled. "The guests are the point of having this wedding."

He fed her an olive. "I thought the whole point was the wedding *night*."

"You're incorrigible."

"Yes, ma'am."

He scooped some hummus onto a pita and wolfed it down. Delicious. He was reaching for a carrot stick when he heard a male voice say, "Your nose looks perfect." Grant straightened to find Dr. Bradley Washington studying him. Hunter came up behind Bradley.

"I told you not to bother them," Hunter scolded.

Sophie clapped her hands together. "You came to the reception!"

"Yes, we did," Hunter said with a sigh. "Bradley wanted to see the surgical results up close. I must say, I can't even tell you've had a rhinoplasty, Grant."

Bradley circled him like a predator. "I agree. I did a fantastic job."

Sophie smirked. "Grant's whole face is gorgeous now, but I liked his old nose too. It was a little crooked, but it fit his face."

Grant wished he could crawl under the deck.

"You must've been in some hell of a car accident," Bradley said. "There was a lot of old scar tissue in there — the surgery took me longer than expected."

"I've never been in a car accident," Grant said. He swallowed. "I, uh, I broke my nose when I was a kid."

"Really?" Bradley tilted his head. "How? Sports injury?"

Grant exchanged a knowing look with Sophie before his gaze flitted over to Dr. Hayes, who shifted his weight from one foot to another.

Sophie took the hint and changed the subject. "So, Bradley, how'd you decide to specialize in plastics?"

When the surgeon launched into an explanation, Grant reached out to shake Hunter's hand. "Your reading at the church was excellent, Dr. Hayes."

"Oh…thanks." Hunter nodded.

"We'll try to do our best, sir." He swallowed. "We'll try to communicate like you taught us, and to…accept the things we can't change."

"I know you will. I know how strong you both are."

Sophie broke in, "It's so great you and Bradley made it."

"I wasn't sure if it would be ethical to attend your wedding, but I figured, what the hell?" His eyes crinkled. "It's been one ethical challenge after another with you two anyway."

She tilted her head. "What do you mean?"

"Well…You know, uh, agreeing to take you on as a couple after I'd done individual work with you."

"*And?*" Bradley prompted, grinning like a fool.

Hunter's face turned a delightful shade of red. "Shut up, Bradley," he said through clenched teeth.

"Oh, come on, Dr. Hayes," Bradley cooed. "You're always touting the importance of being open and honest."

When Hunter remained tight-lipped, Grant just had to know what made his psychologist so uncomfortable. "Turnabout is fair play, Dr. Hayes. Answer the question."

A look of betrayal swam in Hunter's eyes, then his mouth turned down. "Fine." He cleared his throat. "I…I, um…used to have a crush on you, Grant."

He felt all eyes on him, gauging his reaction. Again he was flummoxed, without a clue of how to respond, and this time it looked like Sophie wouldn't swoop in and rescue him. Finally he smirked. "*Used* to have a crush on me? Why the hell don't you *still* have a crush on me?"

Relieved laughter flowed out of Hunter. "It's Sophie's fault," he said. "Every time I saw you two make out on the therapy sofa, it knocked the attraction down a notch."

"*Breeders*," Bradley added with disgust. They all laughed.

"I'll be heading downstairs now," Hunter sighed as he backed away. "I couldn't be *more* mortified."

After they left, Sophie tucked herself into Grant's chest, clasping his collar. "That was hilarious. Poor Hunter."

He plucked a carrot stick off the tray and held it up. "Sexy vegetable?"

"Ha! Where's Rog? We have to terrorize him."

He looked up to the bridge but saw only the DJ and one of Roger's new employees driving the ship. "Let's head downstairs — maybe he'll be there. I want to make sure Ben's okay too."

"But Ashley's here to keep an eye on him," Sophie said as she followed him down the metal steps.

"Thank goodness." He stopped by the table near the bottom of the stairs. Colorful gifts stacked on top of each other, and a donut-shaped life raft rested next to the gifts. He picked up a permanent maker and noticed some writing on the white raft. "What's this?"

"It's your guest book," Cheri explained as she appeared next to him. "Guests sign the raft, and you can hang it in your home after the wedding."

"Aw." Sophie leaned into read a few best wishes. "What a great idea for McSailor."

He chuckled. "Thanks, Cheri. Is everything going as planned?"

"Yes, as long as Roger stays out of my hair." Grant followed her scowl to a table where Roger sat with Jerry, Marilyn, and another woman. "If he threatens me one more time about a wedding guest causing damage to his ship…"

"He's harmless," Sophie said. "Just ignore him."

Cheri breathed out. "I'll try. How about you two grab a bite, and then we'll have you cut the cake?"

"Sure." Grant followed Sophie to the buffet, but she stopped short when Tanya reached up from her chair and tapped her on the elbow. Grant smiled at Kirsten, Anita, and Tanya sitting in their matching bridesmaid dresses. "Hello, ladies. Having a good time?"

Kirsten and Anita nodded, but Tanya whispered in Sophie's ear. Kirsten said, "Try the Thai noodles, Grant. They're yum!"

Sophie straightened and subtly gestured to a table near the bow where Agent Bounter sat with Agent Thompson. "Grant? Is Bounter single?"

He glanced down to find Tanya squirming in her chair. "Maybe." He gave Sophie an innocent look. "Who wants to know?"

"Grant!" Tanya cried. "Stop torturing me."

"Okay. I'm pretty sure he *is* single," he told her. "You know he works for the FBI, right? I don't think he has much time for a relationship."

"Who wants a relationship?" Tanya retorted. "I'm a college pro-fessor. *I* don't have time for one either."

Sophie and Kirsten cracked up.

"We'll leave you to it, then," Sophie said. She grabbed a plate off the buffet and beckoned for Grant. "What can I get for you, my husband?"

"A little of everything, please." He nudged her hair to the side and smooched the back of her neck. "You smell so good."

"Thank you."

Once she loaded the plate, he took it. "Want to meet Rog's girlfriend?"

"Absolutely. *And* save Jerry and Marilyn too."

Grant carried the plate over to their table, and the two couples stood when he and Sophie arrived. He studied the fit, older woman at Roger's side. Her black hair was up in a high ponytail, and her fuchsia dress dipped low at the bust. "You must be Ana," he said as he reached out his hand.

"*Ay yi yi*," she fussed as she shook his hand, then smacked Roger on the shoulder. "Why didn't you tell me how fucking cute this boy is?"

"Ew." Roger shuddered. "As if I'd look at him that way. So he's tall. Big fucking deal."

Grant could tell Sophie was trying not to laugh as they sat. Was it possible Roger's girlfriend had an even worse potty mouth than Roger himself?

Marilyn patted Sophie's hand. "Are you having a good night?"

"The best." Sophie bit into a shrimp.

"Listen to this joke I just told your PO, Madsen," Roger said.

Grant glanced at Jerry, who did not appear amused.

"Why do ex-wives make great parole officers?"

"I have no idea."

"Because they never let anyone finish a sentence!" Roger chortled, and Ana cackled.

Sophie smiled. "Good one, Rog."

"Tell 'em the other one," Ana urged.

Grant grimaced. *There's more?* He shoveled a bite of pasta into his mouth and discovered Kirsten had excellent taste.

"Why do divorces cost so much?" When nobody answered, he yelled, "'Cause they're worth it!"

Ana's laugh was high-pitched. And loud.

"What a great joke to tell at a wedding," Jerry growled. He stood and told Marilyn, "I'm getting us more wine."

Sophie giggled.

Grant nudged her. "Do you want more champagne?"

"I'm good for now."

"No, Roger!" Ana smacked his hand, and he set down the forkful of pasta that had headed toward his mouth. Ana offered him a carrot stick dipped in salsa instead.

"Just one bite?" Roger pleaded. "You know we'll be dancing all night."

"One bite, you little bastard."

Marilyn leaned closer to Grant. "I hear they found quite a stash in the Russian house. Including the location of the submarine in Baja."

"Yes, ma'am." He grinned. "And the FBI took care of the Russians' girlfriends. They're safe now."

"You did good." She smiled at them. "You too, Sophie."

Jerry set a glass of red wine in front of her and sat back down.

"Is that dance music I hear, *mamacita?*" Roger asked Ana.

"*Sí.*" She nodded. "Time for the samba, *papacito.*"

As Roger stood, his head tilted toward the table where Hunter and Bradley sat. "Those two are as gay as a three dollar bill."

"I thought it was a two dollar bill?" Grant said.

"Inflation." Roger slapped his shoulder and headed upstairs with his girlfriend.

Marilyn shook her head as a pleasing silence drifted over the table.

"Imagine working for him for a whole summer," Sophie said.

Jerry narrowed his eyes. "Surely that had to be worse than hawking hotdogs at the Cubs games, Taylor."

She stroked her chin. "It's a tough call. What do you think, Grant?"

"Your buns *are* pretty warm," he said with a straight face.

She smiled. "Don't you forget it."

Ben approached the table with two flutes of champagne. "What're you doing serving alcohol?" Grant demanded.

He shrugged as he handed a glass to him and set one down in front of Sophie. "Uncle Joe sent me over here—ask him. I didn't drink any, I promise."

"Thank you, Ben." She took a sip.

He swept down in a bow, and when he straightened again he was grinning. "May I get anything else for the lovely couple?"

"How gracious, Benjamin." Her hand fluttered to her chest. "No, thank you. I want you to enjoy your time with Lindsay and your friends. Are you having fun?"

He nodded. "This wedding *rocks!*"

Grant smiled. "Have you gotten a new dog yet?"

"Did your dog *die?*" Marilyn asked as her hand covered her mouth.

"Nope." Ben hung his head and kicked his foot on the deck. He explained how Mullens had stolen Dot, and when Ben had returned her to her owners, they'd paid him one hundred dollars as a reward. His mom had promised to get him a new dog.

Sophie chuckled as he dashed off to the table filled with teenagers.

"Why did he invite so many friends?" asked Jerry.

"We wanted to have a few people on *my* side of the church," Grant said.

"Hey—my side was mostly my father's business associates," Sophie countered. "You had a fair number of guests. If all the women from Capone's knew you were getting married, the church would've been packed."

Grant shook his head as he lifted his champagne glass. "Now I only have my nephew buying me drinks." He watched Ben laugh at something Lindsay said and could tell he was smitten. "Sophie, I thought you told me Lindsay wouldn't date Ben. Why'd she change her mind?"

"I don't know." She shrugged. "Ben wouldn't tell me."

Jerry cleared his throat, and Grant looked up to see him nudge Marilyn. "What is it?" he asked.

"Lindsay's father works for the CPD," Marilyn said. "I *may* have said something to him about Ben being a good guy."

Sophie smiled. "Thank you, Marilyn."

"Thank you for sticking up for Ben, ma'am." Grant kissed the detective's hand.

She fanned herself. "I think I'm going to swoon. Do you have the smelling salts, Jer?"

"Back off my woman, Madsen."

He grinned. "Yes, sir."

"So, we have a gift for you two," Marilyn said. She reached into the pocket of her black suit-jacket and placed a small wrapped box on the table.

The detective seemed strangely embarrassed. "Want to put that on the gift table?" Grant asked.

"Um…no."

"We want to make sure you have it…tonight," Jerry added.

"What is it?" Sophie wondered.

"Go ahead and open it," Jerry said.

"Wait!" Marilyn sprang to her feet, and Grant stood as well. "Not while we're here. C'mon, let's go for a spin on the dance floor."

"I *hate* dancing, Mar."

"Then let's check out the architecture."

Jerry rolled his eyes. "Fine." Before he followed, he lowered his voice and said, "We have a pair of these ourselves. We thought you'd enjoy them."

Grant sat down and felt as confused as Sophie looked.

"That was weird." She shrugged, then scooped up the present and tore off the paper. "Oh, my God."

"What is it?" He tried to see, but she'd hidden the box under the table. She passed the box to him, and when he looked inside, he laughed.

Handcuffs.

"Who knew how kinky law enforcement types could be," she marveled.

He waggled his eyebrows. "I like it."

After they cut the cake and fed each other a few bites, they headed up to the converted dance floor on the deck. A fast pop song played, and Sophie's stylish moves got Grant in the spirit. They joined Kirsten, Tanya, and Anita, and soon Bounter and Agent Thompson moved into their circle. Grant wondered if "YMCA" was next.

"And now it's time to slow it down," the DJ announced. "Couples, please come to the dance floor. We have a special song for Grant and Sophie."

Sophie's head cocked to one side, listening to the song, as she stepped into his waiting arms. He didn't recognize the opening piano melody, but she groaned. "Bless the Broken Road," she told him. "A required song for anyone getting married over the age of thirty."

His hand caressed the small of her back, and his other hand clasped her fingers. She swayed in his arms while he listened to the lyrics. "But this song is particularly true for us." He twirled her, and she came right back to him. "Our road's been destroyed, smashed to pieces…but still, it led to you. I'm blessed." He felt no pain as he nuzzled her nose before planting a kiss on her waiting mouth. She tasted of champagne and sweet icing—of dreams and possibilities.

The ship was now out on Lake Michigan, cruising past the majestic Chicago skyline. He drew his bride closer as he checked out the other couples on the dance floor. She kissed his neck. Her soft lips brushed his Adam's apple, and her warm breath lingered on his skin as he inhaled the soft notes of her perfume. He closed his eyes, hoping he'd remember this moment the rest of his life.

He felt Cheri by his side, and he snuck the microphone from her grasp. He looked up at the DJ who gave him the thumbs up before fading the volume of the current song.

"Thank you for being here, everyone," he said into the microphone.

Sophie stepped back and stared at him with surprise.

"You thought I wouldn't sing to you tonight?" he teased. "I was just waiting for the right time." He scanned the deck and found all eyes on him as the ship approached Navy Pier. He backed up to the railing for support and locked eyes with his bride. "So, Sophie and I met at our parole officer's door. Isn't that right, Officer Stone?"

From the stern, Jerry raised his bottle of beer above his head.

"He doesn't look like a matchmaker, does he?"

Laughter drifted through the night air.

Grant looked back at Sophie. "I was in a hopeless place…until I found you, Sophie Taylor. You've filled my world with hope."

She pressed her forearms against her chest, her folded hands under her chin. Her eyes glittered with tears.

"So I wrote you this song to thank you for that hope. It's titled 'Con Me.'" He closed his eyes to collect himself, worried he'd start crying too. After a deep breath he connected with her again. His wife. His Bonnie.

We both knew a man—dark, beaten, and blue
But I never imagined he'd lead me to you.

If I could conjure a woman so warm, smart, and kind,
God would grant me a Sophie, at Jerry's to find.

I held a conference between my heart and my mind.
I confess both chose you for the ties that bind.

Confirm me, convince me, conspire to own me.
Conceivably you're first to confront me and know me.
Can you con me all over again?

You said unconditional love was hard to find.
I hadn't known such connection until you were mine.

I concede that you knew me all of the time.
I concur that time spent with you is sublime.

Confirm me, convince me, conspire to own me.
Conceivably you're first to confront me and know me.
Can you con me all over again?

I'll write my prose and cons, concert of my heart.
You're conduction, you're confection, you're breathtaking art.

And so to conclude, but never to end,
This contract that we so eagerly begin…

Congratulations to my lovely and stunning new wife,
For the conjugals that start our beautiful life.

Confirm me, convince me, conspire to own me.
Conceivably you're first to confront me and know me.
Can you con me all over again?

As he finished, Sophie's tears ran tracks down her cheeks. Amidst applause, she skipped into his arms, and he breathed in her intoxicating scent as he held her tight. She snuggled into his chest. "I'll con you every day, McSailor."

"Good."

There was a loud pop seconds before the dark sky filled with brilliant white and purple fireworks. A cheer went up from guests all over the boat, but Grant and Sophie heard nothing, saw nothing, but each other.

Acknowledgments

I'm so grateful to the fine women of Omnific Publishing for making The *Con*duct Series a reality! Their best behavior supported, encouraged, and improved my writing. My thanks to:

Jessica Royer Ocken: You are an extraordinary editor! I've learned so much from you about writing, and you're a fun, kind person too.

Cindy Campbell and CJ Creel: What would I have done without your literary and legal knowledge? Sophie and Grant may have landed back in prison.

Elizabeth Harper: You're a "psycho publisher" who's got chutzpah for starting your own publishing company, featuring Romance Without Rules.

Coreen Montagna: You beautify my books and play a mean game of Words With Friends.

Micha Stone and Traci Olsen: Thank you for spreading the word about Bonnie and McSailor.

I'm also grateful to my pub sisters Nicki Elson, Lisa Sanchez, Carol Oates, Trisha Wolfe, Debra Anastasia, Cherie Colyer, and Jennifer DeLucy. Thanks for being such wonderful listeners on this journey!

And big smooches to supportive readers like Gwynn, Mitsy, Djeni, Roche (Uncle Joe lover), Cécile, Janine, Smash, Syrah, Darcia, Nora, Nancy, Amy, Lorne, Ina, Christy, Laurie, Victoria, Ana, Christina, Babs, Annette, and Sophia.

About the Author

People fascinate the psychologist/author (psycho author) known as Jennifer Lane. Her therapy clients talk to her all day long about their dreams, and her characters tell her their stories at night. Jen delights in peeling away the layers to scrutinize their psyches and emotions. But please rest assured, dear reader, she isn't psychoanalyzing you right now. She's already got too many voices in her head!

Stories of redemption interest Jen the most, especially the healing power of love. She is the author of The *Cond*uct Series—romantic suspense for adult readers—of which *On Best Behavior* is the third and final installment. *Streamline* is her first foray into writing for young and new adults, but she's found this sort of writing even more fun. A former college swimmer, Jen is able to put a lot of her own experiences into her books.

Whether writing or reading, Jen loves stories that make her laugh and cry. In her spare time she enjoys exercising, attending book club, and hanging out with her sisters and their families in Chicago and Hilton Head.

Erotic Romance

The Keyhole Series: Becoming sage (book one) by Kasi Alexander
The Keyhole Series: Saving sunni (book two) by Kasi & Reggie Alexander
The Winemaker's Dinner: Appetizers & Entrée by Dr. Ivan Rusilko &
Everly Drummond
The Winemaker's Dinner: Dessert by Dr. Ivan Rusilko

Paranormal Romance

The Light Series: Seers of Light, Whisper of Light, and Circle of Light
by Jennifer DeLucy
The Hanaford Park Series: Eve of Samhain & Pleasures Untold by Lisa Sanchez
Immortal Awakening by KC Randall
Crushed Seraphim and *Bittersweet Seraphim* by Debra Anastasia
The Guardian's Wild Child by Feather Stone
Grave Refrain by Sarah M. Glover
Divinity by Patricia Leever
Blood Vine and *Blood Entangled* by Amber Belldene
Divine Temptation by Nicki Elson

Historical Romance

Cat O' Nine Tails by Patricia Leever
Burning Embers by Hannah Fielding
Good Ground by Tracy Winegar

Romantic Suspense

Whirlwind by Robin DeJarnett
The CONduct Series: With Good Behavior & Bad Behavior & On Best Behavior
by Jennifer Lane
Indivisible by Jessica McQuinn
Between the Lies by Alison Oburia

Anthologies

A Valentine Anthology including short stories by Alice Clayton,
Jennifer DeLucy, Nicki Elson, Jessica McQuinn, Victoria Michaels,
and Alison Oburia

It's Only Kinky the First Time by Kasi Alexander
Learning the Ropes by Kasi & Reggie Alexander
The Winemaker's Dinner: RSVP by Dr. Ivan Rusilko
The Winemaker's Dinner: No Reservations by Everly Drummond
Big Guns by Jessica McQuinn
Concessions by Robin DeJarnett
Starstruck by Lisa Sanchez
New Flame by BJ Thornton
Shackled by Debra Anastasia
Swim Recruit by Jennifer Lane
Sway by Nicki Elson
Full Speed Ahead by Susan Kaye Quinn
The Second Sunrise by Hannah Downing
The Summer Prince by Carol Oates
Whatever it Takes by Sarah M. Glover
Clarity by Patricia Leever
A Christmas Wish by Autumn Markus

www.ingramcontent.com/pod-product-compliance
Lightning Source LLC
Chambersburg PA
CBHW020333120726
47904CB00002B/389